Twisted Ethics

Twisted Ethics

HOW THIN
THE LINE

Gerard Michael

Marilyn Keenan

Marimac Publishing

Like many other books out there today, this one is self-edited and self-published. I want to thank Marilyn Keenan for the countless hours she has spent going over this manuscript with me. We do our absolute best to minimize mistakes and polish the grammar.

We have most likely missed a few things and for that, I apologize. Consider it part of the human element that makes life so enjoyable. If I waited for perfection in all that I do, I would never write another story, sing another song, paint another picture or bake another cookie. It does make me very appreciative of professional editors and one day, I hope to be able to afford one.

In spite of all the possible imperfections, I find my stories meaningful and enjoyable, and I hope you do too.

Due to the length and character richness of this story, I have added a 'List of Characters' page to help you navigate. Thank you, Anne and Anna for that suggestion!

List of Characters/Locations

LIST OF CHARACTERS

Name	Location	Title
Judd Bentley	MCNY	Montgomery County Sheriff
Dean Madris	HHI	Retired Detective
Greg Webster	HFNY	CEO City Hospital
Sara Shand	HFNY	Mary Webster's Best Friend
Jocelyn Webster	HFNY	Greg and Mary's Youngest Daughter
Mary Webster	HFNY	Greg Webster's Wife
Dr. John Shand	HFNY	Greg Webster's Friend
Veronica Chalmers Daughter	HFNY	Charles Chalmers' Adopted
Destiny Chalmers	HFNY	Veronica's Daughter
Priscilla Chalmers	HFNY	Charles' Natural Daughter
Trey Lawrence	ANY	Detective, NYS Police
Charis Andrews	VA	Special Agent, FBI
Kenny Shaw	NYC	Detective NYPD
Ethan Baylor	HFNY	Physical Therapist at City Hospital
Jack Webster	HFNY	Greg's Son
Cliff Alvord	ANY	Lieutenant, NYS Police
Audra	??	Online Illustrator
Lilijac MacNamara	HFNY	Ethan's Girlfriend
Alfred MacNamara	HFNY	Lilijac's Father
Tilman Sweeney	QVA	Sheriff
Delilah	QVA	Waitress, Til's Friend
Alan Swart	QVA	Til's Deputy

Alpha Samuel	QVA	Church Leader
Alpha Isaac	JNY	Church Leader
Dr. Amelia Lanford	ANY	Medical Examiner
Doc Flanders	QVA	Medical Examiner
Joe Stern	MCNY	Donut Shop Owner
Kathy	HFNY	Greg's Secretary
Rennie Andrews	DCVA	Charis' Father
Lester Moran	CSD	Sheriff, Custer County, SD
Doreen Hillabrandt	CSD	Detective, Custer Police
Martin Ballard	MTN	Detective, McMinnville, TN
Myron Hawkins	VA	FBI Agent, Quantico, VA
Laroy Climm	CCMO	Detective, Festus, MO Police
Leland Hadwell	SLMO	Supreme Leader
Paul Jenner	VA	Director, FBI Quantico, VA
Lynette Slater	HFNY	Mease Funeral Home
Maury Slater	HFNY	Mease Funeral Home
Alpha Timothy	CCMO	Church Leader
Alpha Mark	MTN	Church Leader
Omega Owen	MTN	Church Assistant Leader
Bill Dillon	HFNY	Greg's Friend
Angela	DCVA	Rennie's Date
Agent Broderick	HFNY	Agent, FBI

LOCATION ABREVIATIONS

HF	High Falls, NY
HHI	Hilton Head Island, SC
ANY	Albany, NY
VA	Quantico, VA
NYC	New York City, NY
QVA	Quicksburg, VA
MCNY	Montgomery County, NY
CSD	Custer, SD
MTN	McMinnville, TN
CCMO	Crystal City, MO
JNY	Jordanville, NY

1

Prologue

I have always been amazed when the world shows me just how small it really is. Like when you run into someone you know in a place far from home. You both live in the same small town but never see each other in your day to day activities. Travel across the continent and you will cross paths in a faraway airport as you both await your connecting flights to divergent destinations. Is it coincidence or destiny?

Some say that if you look deeply enough, you can find a connection to most other people on the planet. That may be true if you look back over hundreds or perhaps thousands of generations but what about random connections that span just one generation? This is a story about just such a connection. About individuals brought together without any clear meaning or purpose.

The Fourth of July weekend is undoubtedly the busiest of the year for outdoor gatherings in the continental United States. It is no different in the Mohawk River Valley region of upstate New York. As the temperatures are typically in the low eighties to low nineties and with the shade provided by the canopies of the tall sugar maples and the cooling breeze off the Mohawk, most would say the weather in the Shands' yard was perfect.

Close to fifty people RSVP'd and all of them showed. After all, it's just once a year that we formally celebrate our nation's independence but it may be just once in a lifetime that we get to gather for a reason as special as this. Now, baby showers happen hundreds of times every day and perhaps, every hour of every day. Each one is extremely important and worthy of celebration but most will not rise to the unconventionality of this one.

This is not just a celebration of a baby's birth. No, this gathering is in honor of the rebirth of an entire family, one that is connected not solely by genetics but also by sacrifice, community and generosity that knows no bounds. It is that generosity that shines through the darkness of unimaginable misfortune and perniciousness, and a love that cannot be defined in any dictionary.

Greg Webster is kind, funny and one hundred percent absolutely human. He loves his family as deeply as any man ever has and he makes sure they know it. What sets Greg apart from most others is his empathy for every other person on the planet. Some people watch the news and think, "that's terrible" or "that's so sad." Greg's mind immediately goes to, "Is there something I can do about that? Is there some way I can help?"

<u>Greg will turn to his ever-growing band of friends and family for help. Some are professionals he has met along the way and others are everyday heroes, the kind that are mostly invisible but always present. I invite you to come along as we follow Greg while he searches for truth, fairness, and justice. "He has a habit of being in the wrong place at the right time." -Jack Webster- Buried Ethics: Digging Up Bones.</u>

Chapter 1

July 2, 2016 Montgomery County, NY

The small parking lot next to the Lock Twelve operator's house was filling up quickly. The first to respond to the 911 call was Montgomery County Sheriff's Deputy Lance Conover. He was talking to the lock operator on duty when Sheriff Judd Bentley arrived. Conover walked toward the door to meet him. Bentley motioned for them to move outside.

"What do you have?" Bentley asked.

"The operator said he saw something floating down the river, west of the lock. He thought it was a log at first. As it got closer to the spillway, he could see that it was a body. He called 911 and then went to look for where it came to rest."

"Did he find it?" Bentley continued.

"Yes sir, he said it stayed close to shore and was wedged between the gate and the concrete wall. The dive team got here a few minutes ago and they are trying to retrieve it."

"Let's go have a look, Lance." The two men walked down to the bank of the river. The operator house which is down river from the spillway didn't provide a view of the up-river lock gate so they walked on to the bridge that went across the top of the spillway and looked over the western rail. They could see the divers and the ambulance near the bank of the river but still couldn't see the outside of the gate.

"I guess we'll have to go down there, Sheriff," Conover said.

The Sheriff didn't respond but began walking in that direction. Once they cleared the end of the bridge, they descended down the grassy hill toward the lock. There were two divers in the water about eight feet below where they were standing at the top of the wall. They could see a portion of the body floating on the surface. The divers were being careful to not release the body from the corner where it was wedged until they had attached a harness to it. If they miscalculated and the body went over the spillway, they could be chasing it downstream for a long way. On top of that, critical evidence could be destroyed if the body was mangled by the fall.

Bentley and Conover watched for another twenty minutes as the divers secured the body and began the arduous task of getting the body up the wall to the awaiting ambulance. After the stretcher was hoisted and resting on level ground, Bentley and Conover approached the body. It appeared to be a young woman in her mid to late twenties. He didn't see any outward signs of trauma. She didn't have any tattoos that he could see although she was still partially clothed. He didn't see any rings or a watch but she did have a medical alert necklace on. He turned the medallion over and saw that it was for diabetes.

Bentley looked at his deputy and began walking away. "Let's talk to the operator once more," he said as he walked. They interviewed the guy once again. His official title was Canal Structure Operator. He had been working in the system for seventeen years and at Lock Twelve for the past ten. His story was believable and he was a local guy so they knew where to find him if they needed to question him again.

"We'll wait to see what the coroner has to offer." Bentley said, "I'll see you later."

2

Chapter 2

Hilton Head Island, SC
July 3, 2016

"Dean, I'm heading down to Coligny Circle with Anna for a while. I won't be gone long. Is there anything I can get for you while I'm out?" Shelly asked.

"Actually, there is. If you pass a dollar store, I could use a couple spiral bound notebooks."

Shelly knew exactly what he wanted them for. "Of course, dear. If you think of anything else, just call or text." She picked up her keys and headed toward the door. Shelly had made fast friends with a few of the neighbor ladies since they moved into the complex two months ago. She loved that Dean was finally retired and that she didn't have to lose any more sleep worrying about him at work. She wasn't convinced that he would handle retirement well but so far he had surprised her.

Dean had his feet propped up on the ottoman and looked out the fourth floor window at the horizon. His laptop computer was resting on his thighs as his brain thought of what to type next. The sliding door was open just enough to hear the waves gently rolling on the shore and the back and forth banter of a flock of gulls. The back edge of the beach was just twenty yards from where he sat, with the water's edge being an additional ten to thirty yards depending on the tide.

He and Shelly had never been to Hilton Head Island. When they decided to look for a place near the southeastern seaboard, they initially thought about Florida. They devoted a few weeks to exploring the southern coast but immediately knew that Florida was not going to be their home. Shelly didn't like the constant heat and Dean had been surrounded by enough cement and tall buildings to last a lifetime. Neither was looking for the Manhattan of the south.

Shelly had a cousin who lived in South Carolina and they decided to pay her a visit on their way back north. Lettie lived in Beaufort, not too far from the Marine Corps Air Station where her husband had served prior to his retirement. She loved the area and it was easy to see why. Port Royal Island is the largest of the sea islands and boasts a small but charming downtown and views that have served as the backdrop for many famous movies.

South Carolina was feeling more like home every day. They enjoyed Beaufort very much but Beaufort, while surrounded by water, didn't have the same feel as that of being right on an Atlantic beach. That's when they decided to explore closer to the coast. Hilton Head seemed to have it all. It was still far enough north to offer a change of seasons, adequate shopping, fabulous restaurants, and a little nightlife for those who so desired it. Peak summer months brought big crowds and too much traffic but nowhere near what Manhattan used to offer. The other ten months of the year promised to be quiet and peaceful.

Before making his final decision to retire, Dean thought about what he could do in place of work. He knew there would be hobbies he would enjoy but he needed something a little more structured. He thought he might enjoy writing but he couldn't adapt to an author's number one rule; write about what you know. His career had been in service to the public via the police department. Writing about crime would just feel like work again so he considered his other options. He decided to try writing stories for children.

"How hard could it be?" he asked Shelly. "Just a few verses surrounded by pretty pictures," he said, "just enough to keep the little crumb snatchers occupied for five minutes."

Shelly just said, "go for it, dear." She knew better than to question him. It was always better for her to let Dean try and fail than to be encouraged not to try.

So Dean began writing a few notes describing possible story lines. When he had completed his first story, he shared it with Shelly. She was very surprised and very impressed. For a man who had lived his entire life without children of his own, he seemed more attuned than she gave him credit for. He was excited and eagerly began looking for an illustrator. Not knowing anyone in the field, he relied on internet searches to teach himself the business of self-publishing.

There were many self-employed, contract artists offering their services. He was surprised to find that most were charging more than one hundred-fifty dollars per illustration. He was looking at three grand or more to have the twenty-four page book published. While he wasn't writing to make money, he wasn't doing it to lose money either. He decided to go a step further and looked into learning how to make digital drawings.

He had ordered a new tablet and digital pen and downloaded a digital art software program. In the short time that he experimented with it, he learned two things: the first was that it would take him a long time to master it and the second was that digital art was created using the same technique cartoonists used a hundred years ago. It was done in several layers.

He searched the internet one last time looking for a reasonably priced professional. He stumbled across an ad offering professional illustrations for as little as fifteen dollars. He went to the site and looked around. It seemed legitimate and there were several artists in the children's book genre to choose from. After looking at samples of their work, he made a selection and opened a job. He entered his credit card details and provided the information the artist needed to begin the sketch. Within twenty-four hours he received a black and white single line drawing. It reflected his vision well enough, so he approved it and waited for the colorized version. Two days later it arrived. He downloaded the file and opened it with his new software. He quickly realized he could look at every layer individually.

There were seven layers in all. When he came to the fourth layer, his heart skipped a beat. He wasn't looking at a drawing or a color overlay. All he saw were the words *Please Help Me!*

Chapter 3

July 4, 2016 High Falls, NY

As usual, the Shand's property looked amazing. Any one of the popular home and garden magazines would have welcomed this vista on the cover. The three thousand square foot house rested a good fifty yards back from the quiet street. Other than people who lived in this neighborhood or people visiting them, there was a noticeable absence of traffic. Except of course for an occasional delivery truck.

Sara was on the huge, wrap around front porch tending to her flowers when the Websters arrived. Greg parked the car at the far end of the driveway, closest to the road. "Dad, why are we parking way back here?" Jocelyn asked.

"Because, Honey, when everyone else is trying to get out of here after the party has ended, we will be the first ones out," Greg replied.

"You have watched too many of those National Lampoon movies, Dad!" she returned.

"It's such a beautiful day. Will walking the extra hundred feet kill you?" Greg said sarcastically.

"No, Clark!" Jocelyn replied, referring to the Clark Griswold character in the movies. She opened the back door and stepped out. Mary gave Greg the look.

"Why the look?" he asked.

"You know why," she answered. "Do you not see that your actions invoke those types of responses?"

"So, I should have parked on the porch?"

"No, parking here was fine, but the reason you gave for parking here set you up."

"I can't have a little fun with my family?"

"Sure you can, Clark," Mary said and got out of the car. "Could you please bring the bag from the back seat?"

Greg got out, opened the back door of the car, and hoisted the bag. "What's in here, bricks? This bag is heavy!"

"Maybe you should have parked closer to the house."

Greg closed the door with his knee and followed Mary toward the porch.

Sara and Mary were finishing their customary introductory hugs when Greg finally reached the porch steps. He rested at the bottom for a moment before beginning the five step ascent. "Greg, those will need to go in the freezer immediately." Mary instructed. Now Greg realized what was in the bag, ice cream. He bent his neck over the top of the bag and sure enough, printed on the side facing away from him he could see *Stewart's Shops.*

He walked in the front door, down the central hall to the kitchen and placed the bag on the counter. John was working at the sink. "Hi, Greg, good to see you! Welcome to our first annual 'You Can't Blow Up Greg Webster Fourth of July Extravaganza!'" John said. "By the way, why did you park all the way down by the street?"

"Good seeing you too John," Greg replied, ignoring the parking comment. "I thought this was a baby shower."

"It is that too, Greg. This is a celebration of all the gifts that have been bestowed upon us over the last year. The first of course is our independence, without which we would not be able to celebrate at all. Then there are the Chalmers', including baby Destiny, and our group of heroes. We have a lot of celebrating to do!" John said with genuine excitement.

"We have a lot of ice cream to eat as well," Greg replied as he place one container after the other in the freezer. "Do you realize we have ten half gallons of ice cream here? How many people are you expecting?"

"We expect around fifty and Sara thought we should have everyone's favorite flavor. She thought that ten flavors should please them all. Do you know that we had one hundred percent of the invited guests reply in the affirmative? I think that's not only unusual, but a testament to the people being honored here." John looked at his watch. It was approaching 11:30. "Greg, the guests will be arriving soon, would you mind managing the parking? You picked a perfect spot for your car. Start there and have them follow your example. If you run out of room on that side, you can begin a row across the driveway."

"I would be happy to, John. Where did the ladies go?" Greg asked.

"I'm pretty sure they went to the tree house with Maria and Jocelyn. They should be back any minute."

The tree house had been the favorite location for the kids to hang out from the time that John and Greg built it almost fifteen years ago. They selected a well-spaced group of sugar maples in the side yard near the back of the house and built a three room condominium ten feet off the ground. It had all the comforts of home with the exception of a bathroom. They even built a gradually sloping, multi-tiered ramp entrance so they didn't need to worry about the kids falling off a ladder.

Greg went out the back door to have a quick look before moving around to the front to take his parking attendant post. The image brought back so many memories. His kids were all little and when he was first reintroduced to the Shands, they didn't have any children. It was the ugliness of the City Hospital murders that brought them together with Maria. In fact, it was that incident that brought them all together and they have been inseparable ever since.

Once Greg moved his family to High Falls, just down the road from the Shands, John and Greg began working on the tree house. From the ashes of ugliness arose an unfathomable beauty. He could hear a car pulling into the driveway. He walked briskly around the house to the front where there were three cars attempting to pull in.

Greg went to meet the first car and gave them directions. Once the trend was set, the others followed naturally. Greg just took a few steps back each time allowing just enough room for the next car to turn in. As each car emptied, he greeted the guests. He knew them all by name of course so the greetings consisted of hugs and kisses which slowed the parking process down just a little. Everyone seemed very patient with the flow knowing that when it was their turn, the welcome would be just as personable. Some of those who gathered were nearly daily encounters for Greg, most of whom worked at the hospital. Others were old and new friends who he hadn't seen since the college bombing incident concluded nearly a year ago.

Over the next quarter hour the rest of the guests arrived including the guests of honor, Veronica Chalmers and her daughter, Destiny. Greg had grown quite close to the Chalmers family over the preceding ten months. Charles Chalmers owned and operated a dairy farm just a few miles from High Falls. His daughter, Priscilla, was the reason he knew them at all.

Greg was working with Special Agent Charis Andrews from the FBI. They were sharing information on the University bombings and had developed a close relationship. In many ways, she was the female version of himself. Greg offered to interview Miss Chalmers after it became known that she had met Korben Kovak. Ben had recently become a suspect in the bombings that took place in New York, Vermont, and Pennsylvania. Greg went to the farm to speak with her.

Priscilla had only met Ben once by that time but they seemed to hit it off and had a follow-up date planned for the next week. She had become the primary hired hand and caretaker for her father after her mother died a few years prior. She was a pleasant girl and easy to talk to. She was sad and reluctant to believe that the Ben she met could be involved in something so dark. She had also told Greg that her mother died brokenhearted due to the disappearance of her youngest child at the age of two. It was at that time that Greg had the foresight to ask if her mother had left any personal affects behind.

Priscilla shared her mother's hairbrush with Greg. He sent the hair from that brush to forensics at the FBI. In a convoluted investigation that followed, it was proven that Timmy Chalmers was kidnapped at age two by a couple who raised him as their own. It was in that dysfunctional home that Timmy morphed into the killer, Ben Kovak aka Ben Korben. In the meantime, a girl by the name of Veronica Sweet had a fifteen minute sexual tryst with a young man she met in a convenience store. She never even knew his name but she would end up pregnant with his child.

That child, named Destiny is being celebrated today with a baby shower given by the people that Veronica didn't know existed ten months ago. The father of her baby is not just a famous killer, he was also the kidnapped son of Charles Chalmers. In an unlikely but heartwarming outcome, Greg suggested, encouraged, and facilitated the adoption of Veronica and Destiny into the Chalmers' family. Charles would have a new daughter and grandchild, Priscilla would gain a sister and niece and Veronica and Destiny would be a part of a real family.

Greg knew that there were other dynamics at play here today and not all of them would be of the feel good type. But he knew all the players and he believed that they could all see the greater good. The one that worried him the most was the introduction of Charles Chalmers and New York State Police Detective Trey Lawrence. Trey was an undercover sergeant who made the kill shot that bought down the City Hospital killer. He was also the detective who Charis Andrews called upon to back her up at Ben's house. Trey Lawrence made the kill shot that took out Ben and saved Charis and Greg's daughter, Jillian. But it was also Charles Chalmers' son Timmy.

Chapter 4

July 4, 2016
Hilton Head Island, SC
The past came screaming back to Dean Madris. While he had never heard of a distress message being delivered this way, the situation had all the markings of someone being kept against their will. It's what he dealt with day in and day out for the last ten years of his career. He supposed he could play the retirement card and look the other way but once a cop, always a cop.

He decided he would call his old partner in the NYPD and pass it off to him. Once he relayed the issue, he could rest easy and continue to move on with his retired life. He knew the number by heart and dialed it. "NYPD Trafficking Taskforce, Detective Shaw speaking."

"Put the donut down, Kenny!"

"Hey, Dino, is that you?"

"It's me, Kenny. Do you miss me yet?"

"Like a toothache! How is retired life? Did Shelly throw you out yet?"

"Not yet, but she is out of the house a lot."

"Who can blame her, right?"

"Yeah, you're right, Kenny. Hey, I need to ask for a favor."

"You need a dozen of Mac's donuts? They will mail them out to you."

"No, believe it or not, they have donuts in South Carolina too. I think I received a distress signal today. It came to me in a digital drawing. Have you ever heard of anything like that?"

"I've received a lot of pictures with messages you know, usually from one of the guy's stag parties."

"This is different, Kenny, this was a message buried in a seven layer digital drawing that I purchased for my kid's book. I have a program that can separate the layers and hidden right in the middle was a message that said, 'please help me.'"

"I've never heard of anything like that, Dino. Can you tell who it came from?"

"That's the thing, I'm afraid to ask if the artist needs help because her email is probably being monitored. You know how it is in this business, if she is being held, reaching out like this could get her killed."

"You're right, Dino. Send me the details and I'll look into it for you. And if you have a dozen Mac's sent over, it might make me move a little faster."

"You've got it pal, drive by tomorrow and I'll make sure a dozen is waiting for you. I appreciate your help, Kenny."

"No trouble, Dino. I'll catch up with you in a couple days. If you receive any more messages, pass them along."

"I will. Talk to you soon." Dean ended the call then immediately dialed the number for Mac's Donuts in Manhattan.

Chapter 5

High Falls, NY
With all of the anticipated guests having arrived and parked safely and

orderly, Greg made his way to the party. Guests were both inside and out, which was precisely what this house was designed for. Even under the protection of myriad shade trees, the July humidity, and the food of course, would drive people inside periodically. Most guests grabbed a plate and a fresh beverage and made their way back to the large, welcoming porch, the rear patio, or for the more youthful, spirited folks, the tree house.

Greg made his entry via the front porch. He was looking for Ethan Baylor, his most recent hire at the hospital. Ethan was one of the most likeable young guys he had met in quite a while. He was just twenty-eight years old but possessed the maturity of most men twice his age. He had only been in the workforce roughly four years, so when his resume' crossed Greg's desk for consideration as the new Director of Physical Therapy, Greg was concerned.

The Director of Personnel had attached a note to his paperwork. "I know he seems young and underexperienced, but I think he deserves a look." Greg had great respect for the people working for him and had trained them to speak freely. He heeded the advice and took a deeper look. The young man was a local high school graduate which was always a positive. He received an academic scholarship to Siena College where he received dual diplomas in healthcare management and physical therapy. He did all of that in six years.

After graduating with honors, he entered the workforce as a staff physical therapist at St. Peter's Healthcare in Albany where he had done some of his clinical rotation as an undergraduate. He listed several references from both the hospital and the college. The summation sheet from the calls to references suggested that anyone would be a moron if they didn't hire this guy. His outside interests included hiking, music, and cooking.

His personal data revealed that he lived in Herkimer County and that he was single. Greg found himself wishing his daughters were a little older before he even met the guy. He was convinced enough to set up an interview. Ethan turned out to be an amazing young man to whom Greg had no reservations offering the job. Ethan gladly accepted and assumed his management role at the beginning of the year. This was the first time he was joining a family function. Greg wondered if it may be too soon but he was just that impressed with this man.

Ethan wasn't on the front porch. Greg's second guess was the tree house. He walked through the house just in case his hunch was wrong and while doing so, picked up a couple appetizers. He went out the back door and turned left toward the tree house. Maria, Jillian, Jocelyn, Priscilla, and Jack were all there. They were sitting in the living room talking with Ethan. Even with the younger adults, Ethan was able to lead the conversation with the ease of a public speaker. Greg approached slowly in order to catch some of the conversation. Ethan was discussing the importance of being organized but balanced when attending college. Jack was going to be a Junior at Syracuse University in the fall. He supported what Ethan was saying. Jillian would be entering her senior year of high school while Jocelyn and Maria would be sophomores. Greg was delighted with the way the conversation was flowing.

"I know it's been a few years since I was in college but do you mind if I join in?" Greg asked.

"Sure, Dad," Jack said.

"Of course, Mr. Webster," Ethan replied while the younger girls just looked at each other.

"No lecture though, okay, Dad?" Jocelyn tossed her two cents in.

"Me? Lecture?' Do I ever lecture?"

There was silence. "Alright, never mind. I was really just looking for Ethan anyway. I want to introduce you to my wife and to Mrs. Shand. Do you have a minute?"

Ethan wasted no time getting up. "Of course, it would be my pleasure," he responded.

"Come back soon, Ethan," Jillian said.

Greg just gave her the "forget about it, you're too young look" and he and Ethan walked out and down the ramp.

"They're a great bunch of kids!" Ethan exclaimed as they walked.

"Don't let *them* hear you say that," Greg joked.

"This is a really cool tree house!" Ethan exclaimed as they walk down the ramp. "Dr. Shand is a talented guy."

"Whoa!" Greg said and grabbed Ethan's arm so that both men stopped walking. "You do know that I built this too, right?"

"I just assumed, based on what your children were saying that Dr. Shand was the builder," Ethan retorted.

"Rule number one, "Greg began, "disregard everything my kids say about me or neglect to say about me. I was the architect and the brains and the primary builder of this fine elevated fun factory."

"I stand corrected. It won't happen again, sir," Ethan replied with a note of sarcastic cowering.

"With that resolved, let's go meet the ladies." Greg placed his hand on Ethan's shoulder and directed him down the remaining portion of the ramp and toward the house. From the bottom of the ramp, Greg could see Sara and Mary mingling on the front porch, eliminating the need to go back through the house. As the men rounded the corner of the porch, Mary noticed them and waived them up. She moved toward the top of the porch stairs to greet them.

"You must be Ethan, I've heard so much about you."

"Ethan, this is my wife Mary," Greg said. "You can't really believe anything she says about me either."

"It's a pleasure meeting you, Mrs. Webster. I've heard some great things about you as well. Actually, I have heard wonderful things about your entire family. It sounds like you have had a lot of exciting things happen over the last few years."

"it's been about fifteen years," Mary responded, "and I don't know if exciting is the word I would use to describe them. Let's just say that it has been more excitement than most families can expect in a lifetime."

"They say that what doesn't kill us makes us stronger, right honey?" Greg interjected.

"I think they were talking about viruses, Greg," Mary answered, "but let's hope it makes us smarter as well," she said rolling her eyes toward Greg. "Ethan, let me get a beverage for you and then we can sit and chat a while. I want to introduce you to Sara and some other folks as well. Greg, would you grab that table in the corner for us, please?"

"Of course, dear. Ethan, after you." Greg said while pointing toward the table. By the time the men were seated, Mary was on her way back with the drinks. At the other end of the large, wrap around veranda, Greg spotted Charis Andrews talking with Trey Lawrence.

"Here you go fellas, fresh lemonade with a little iced tea mixed in."

After thanking Mary for the drinks, Greg excused himself and made his way between guests in the direction of Charis and Trey. "Hey guys," Greg said as he approached, "are you enjoying the party?"

"I am," Charis answered. This is such a beautiful place."

"Me, too," replied Trey. "Did you see that tree house Dr. Shand built? That is amazing!"

"Yes, I've seen it once or twice," Greg said with more than a hint of disdain. "How was your drive up, Charis?"

"I actually flew this time. I have a ton of airmiles that need to be used up eventually."

"Albany or Syracuse?" Greg asked.

"I looked on the map and Albany seemed just a little closer," she replied.

"And you would be right, but not by much. It's only four miles shorter from Albany but you had a much prettier ride."

"It was beautiful, especially between Schenectady and here." Charis added.

"Trey, how have you been? Anything exciting happening in your life?"

"Not since the last time I got involved with you, Greg." They all had a good laugh. Charis seemed a little distracted to Greg. In the relatively short time he had known her, she always came across as having laser sharp focus.

"What's going on in your life these days, Charis?" Greg asked. She just stared off into the distance and didn't answer right away. "Charis?" he said again.

"Oh, I'm sorry, were you talking to me?"

"Hey, if you both will excuse me, I see someone I really need to talk with," Trey interrupted. Not waiting for a response he walked away.

"What's up, Charis?" Greg asked.

"Jet lag, maybe?" she responded.

"From DC to Albany? I don't think so. You don't seem like yourself. Do you want to talk?" Greg inquired.

"You have lots going on here, Greg. You should stay focused on that."

"The day is young and right now, I'm worried about you." he said and walked toward the front door. On the way in, they passed Sara. "Sara, would it be alright if we used John's office for a few minutes?"

"Of course, help yourself. I am going out to meet that handsome young man you just hired."

"You are going to love him! He is a special guy," Greg replied.

"I can't wait!

"Then wait no longer," Greg retorted, "they are on the porch, all the way to the left."

"Thank you," Sara said and walked between them to the front door.

Greg led the way to John's office toward the back of the first floor. He looked back to make sure Charis was following. When she entered behind him, he closed the door.

"What will people think, us in here with the door closed?"

"Anyone who knows us will think we have something important to discuss," Greg assured her. "Have a seat. Can I get you anything?"

"I'm fine, thank you," she said.

"Talk to me."

"This is going to sound silly and I apologize for even bringing this to you. I just don't know who else to trust right now."

Chapter 6

Montgomery County, NY

Sheriff Bentley's phone vibrated on his hip. He was hoping that just once, he could make it through a holiday without taking a business call. He also realized that would never be the case.

"Bentley," he answered gruffly.

"Are you having a nice Independence Day, Sheriff?"

"I was until ten seconds ago. Who is this?"

"Cliff Alvord, State Police. I have some news for you."

"Lieutenant Alvord, it has been a while. It looks like you don't have the holiday off either."

"I have been lucky at Thanksgiving once or twice in twenty years but never on the Fourth of July," he replied.

"I hear you Cliff, what's up?"

"It's about the floater you pulled out of the Mohawk a couple days ago. The state coroner has released the preliminary report."

"I guess he doesn't get holidays either," Judd replied. "Was it a drowning?"

"He didn't find any water in the lungs, Judd. She was dead when she hit the river. He also found ligature marks on the body."

"Cliff, I was sure I checked her wrists and ankles when they pulled her out. I didn't see any evidence of that."

"That's because the marks were on her thighs, Judd. Underneath her pants. The marks weren't all new either. He thinks some of the scarring may be several months or even years old."

"How about identification?" The sheriff asked.

"None yet. We're checking the missing persons database and dental records. She had been in the water too long to get a fingerprint."

"Cliff, were there other bruises on the body?" Bentley asked.

"Only a few small ones that were caused before death. Other than that, the body was pretty clean."

"If she was still completely intact, that means the body was dumped in the river between locks thirteen and twelve. If she had gone over the spillway, she would have been torn up." Judd suggested.

"That's what I'm thinking as well. Listen Judd, I'll give you a shout when the toxicology comes back. Maybe that will give us a clue. In the meantime, check your area for surveillance cameras that may have caught something. I don't imagine you will find many between thirteen and twelve but you might get lucky. I hope you get to enjoy the rest of your day!"

Chapter 7

High Falls, NY

"Whatever it is Charis, I'm glad I can be here for you." Greg said compassionately.

"There was never any doubt that I could come to you or trust you, Greg, I just find it hard to not be in control of a situation. I have prided myself on finishing my own fights. I have never felt vulnerable."

Charis was visibly frightened by something. In the time Greg had known her, she exuded confidence, even bordering on cocky sometimes, but never fear. He was not quite sure how to respond. "Is it someone in particular that you're afraid of? Someone from your past perhaps? You have put a lot of criminals away although you always seem to kill the ones I've dealt with," Greg said with a hint of humor.

Charis wasn't laughing or even smiling and that told Greg that this situation was much more serious than he realized. "I'm sorry, Charis, this is not the time for insensitivity. Tell me what you know."

"That's just it, Greg, I don't know as much as I should. I seem to be a target and I have no idea who is looking through the scope. The one thing I could always trust is my instinct of knowing who the criminals were and who the good guys were. I seem to have lost my compass."

"Okay, so let's start at the beginning. Where did this particular journey begin?" Greg suggested.

"About four weeks ago, I left my apartment to go to work. When I approached my car, I used the remote starter as always. It fired right up and I began my usual walk around the car. I looked in the windows and checked the tires to see if they looked like they were properly inflated. When I got to the front passenger side, I realized the tire was flat. I wasn't alarmed, flat tires happen. I texted the office to say I would be a little late and retrieved the spare and tire iron from the trunk."

"Wait," Greg interjected, "you change your own tires?"

"Of course, my dad taught me everything I needed to know about changing tires, checking, and changing the oil, replacing air filters, etc. Being a girl didn't buy any special exclusions at my house."

"Okay, I just want you to know that I'm very attracted to you right now," Greg stated.

"Knock it off Webster, I'm trying to be serious here."

Greg shut up and listened as Charis continued her story.

"I changed the flat and made it to work and I was only twenty minutes late. The day progressed as normal and I finished my shift. On the way home, I dropped the tire off at a repair shop to see if it could be patched. The next morning, I stopped at the garage on my way to the office. I was told that the tire had a gash in the sidewall, most likely from a knife. I shrugged it off as a teenage prank and bought a new tire. I live in a relatively safe neighborhood but teens will be teens anywhere, right?"

"Was your car in a parking garage?" Greg inquired.

"Yes. I have never had an issue nor have I heard of any from other tenants. There are a few closed circuit cameras in the garage but my parking space was not visible. I put the event behind me. A few days later, I went to retrieve my car from the garage at work and again, my right front tire was flat. This time, I had office security take some pictures and review footage from surveillance video. They could determine what time the event took place and had an image of what appeared to be a male, about six feet tall, slender build. He was wearing a non-distinct hoodie and a plain black cap. No one saw him enter or leave the garage. This time, I left the tire for forensics to examine."

"The results could only conclude that the knife used had a six inch, serrated blade. The widest cut was about 1.3 inches. I retrieved the other tire from the garage and had forensics do a comparison. It looked like the same knife was used on both tires."

"That was four weeks ago, I assume there is more to the story," Greg interjected.

"There is. The next five or six days were without incident. Then I received a call on my cell from an unknown caller. I just disconnected the call without answering. About 10 seconds later the same call came in. Again, I disconnected the call. When my phone rang a third time, I answered. A male voice said, "Leave it alone. If you don't, a slashed tire will be the least of your problems." Then the caller hung up.

"This was on your cell phone, inside FBI headquarters?"

"Yes," Charis replied.

"Okay, but you guys have all the fancy toys right, like decoder rings, shoe phones and x-ray glasses, tell me you have something that can trace a phone call!" Greg said with more than a hint of astonishment.

"Of course we do, but the call came from a burner phone. No way to trace it."

"So what have you been involved in that would raise someone's hackles?" Greg asked.

Charis just looked at Greg with obvious disappointment for a few seconds before speaking. "Really? Everything I do pisses off somebody. It comes with the territory. I have been asking myself that same question for weeks. I have gone over my current caseload as well as some of the old ones and I can't put my finger on anything meaningful."

"What about your supervisor, is he or she any help?"

"It's a he and he is trying to be helpful but there is not a lot to go on. They added a couple cameras to the parking garage at the office as well as at my apartment complex. We have gone over my cases together and we still come up blank."

"Has anything else happened recently? I mean this caller must know he needs to give more information if he expects you to understand his request."

"Yes, and this is the part that really freaks me out. About two weeks ago, I found a note on my desk. It was sealed in a small envelope addressed to "Agent Andrews." I found that a bit strange but I thought it was just an invite to a wedding or baby shower so I set my bag down, sat behind my desk, and opened it. There was a handwritten message in all capital letters. The letters were so large, it reminded me of a child's printing. It was written in black ink. The note said, "THE PEOPLE YOU ARE LOOKING FOR MAY NOT WANT TO BE FOUND SO STOP!"

Greg waited to make sure she was finished. "The obvious question is who are you looking for? We will come back to that, but first, what did the handwriting, paper, and ink analysis determine? And secondly, who has access to your office?"

"Very good questions, Greg. Are you sure you won't consider coming to work for the FBI?"

"And inherit your kind of trouble? No thanks," Greg responded.

"Hey," Charis snapped back, "there is only one person in this room that has been blown up and it's not me!"

"Touché," Greg said and then quieted down.

"The paper, pen and envelope are all government issue. The printing didn't prove anything and we don't lock individual offices at headquarters. All we can guess is that the note came from inside. That is what worries me the most. It could be almost anyone affiliated with the FBI."

"Have you asked your immediate co-workers if they have noticed people from other departments or areas of the building snooping around?"

"Yes, but as with any fraternal organization, people don't want to be involved. Besides, the very people I would ask may be the culprit. That's why I feel so isolated and why I don't know who to trust. When the bad people are on the outside, we trust each other fully."

"Do you have security cameras on your floor?" Greg inquired.

"No. Security cameras are limited to the outer perimeter and the entrances. Because of the sensitive nature of our business, no cameras are allowed in the work areas. Listen, I have taken you away from the party long enough. Let's get back out there."

"You're probably right. We will continue this conversation later though. Okay? In the meantime, try to enjoy yourself. I'm sure you are safe here and there is nothing you can do about it right now. Besides, you are one of the main people we are celebrating today."

Greg walked over to Charis and gave her a tight, fatherly hug. "We will get you through this. I am at your disposal anytime and anyplace."

"I know you will watch my back, Greg. It helps to talk to you. Thank you!"

"After all you have done for all of us, we all have your back."

Chapter 8

High Falls, NY

Detective Trey Lawrence walked across the front lawn slowly. He was heading toward a covered swing where Charles Chalmers was rocking his granddaughter, Destiny. Trey was extremely nervous. All of the action he experienced in police work never amounted to this level of nervousness. Cops received training to help them deal with issues in the field but there was no training for what he was about to do.

As he got closer, Trey could see the look of wonder and love the man held for this little girl. "That's a beautiful granddaughter you have there, Mr. Chalmers," Trey said when he was still ten feet away.

Charles looked up and replied, "Sure is, nothing short of a miracle really." Trey was now just a few steps from the swing.

"Do you mind if I join you for a moment?" Trey asked.

"Not at all, please do," Charles said as he placed the girl on his lap to make room for Trey. "I'm Charles Chalmers," he said holding out his hand. Trey reached slowly to meet his grip, his anxiety reaching the pinnacle. When their skin touched, Trey could feel the tears welling up in his eyes. He was having difficulty controlling his voice. Through broken vibrato, he managed to get something out. "My name is Trey Lawrence, Mr. Chalmers and I have been waiting for this moment for a long time."

Still holding the handshake, Charles said, "I am familiar with that name but I'm having trouble placing it." Then it hit him. Trey could see the connection on his face and in his eyes. Something was coming but he didn't know what. Charles stood holding Destiny in his left arm but never let go of Trey's hand. Their eyes met and locked onto each other, neither saying a word.

Chalmers' eyes began to tear as well as he let go of Trey's hand and put his free arm around his waist, pulling him into a tight hug. Trey reciprocated and the men remained like this for a full minute. They could feel each other's chests heaving and catching as they both cried silently. The energy that flowed between them began to patch the hole in each of their souls like magic medicine. Destiny didn't make a sound or movement the entire time as if she could sense the magnitude of the moment.

When both men were able to catch their breath, they released the embrace but remained close, Charles kept his arm around Trey's waist and Trey placed his hand on Charles' shoulder. Trey began an apology but Chalmers cut him off.

"No need Trey, you did what you had to do. This must have been very difficult for you. I really appreciate and admire you coming to me. Thank you. Trey, my Timmy died the day he was kidnapped and became a victim of that horrible couple. It took me a while to admit that but it is the truth. If not for you and the other angels gathered here today, my family would have never been made whole and a murderer would still be out there taking innocent lives."

"Charles, you have no idea how much your words and this moment mean to me. For a year now, my heart has ached with the grief of your loss. Of all the things I have done and seen in my career, nothing has come close to the pain I felt for you. Your generosity will allow me to begin the healing process, so it is I that should be thanking you."

"Look around here Trey, evil can only be smothered by the rising up of good. Look at all the good that has come from this. The difference between people who experience tragedy in their lives and move on and those that don't, can't see the good that has come about because of it. I didn't see it for a long time but with the help of family and strangers who are now friends, I can understand how blessed I truly am."

"Thank God for all these fine people, and for you, Charles. I will go through the rest of my life a better man for having met you."

"I'm just a simple dairy farmer, Trey, but I know good people when I see them and you're at the top of that list. You keep that in mind the next time you need to do something difficult."

"I surely will, Charles. Thank you again. Trey stood to return to the party and he realized he felt much lighter. "Can I bring you a beverage, Charles?"

"Thank you Trey, but I think I'll walk over there with you, if you don't mind."

"It would be an honor, Charles."

"Would you like to carry this little one? I could use a break."

"If she'll have me, I would be delighted," Trey replied.

"Children have a natural sense of who can be trusted. I think she will be fine with you, Trey."

Charles stood with Destiny and as if on cue, she held out her arms to Trey. The three of them walked happily toward the magnificent front porch.

Chapter 9

High Falls, NY

Mary, Sara, and Ethan were sitting at a small table at the back of the porch. It was beginning to warm up but the shade of the porch roof and the several ceiling fans made it quite comfortable. There were people milling about the house and the expansive yard. It was just about 12:30 pm and many folks were making their way in and out with plates of food. Sara and Mary planned the event to facilitate self-service so that they could mingle. So far, it seemed to be working beautifully.

"Ladies, I am so impressed by your event organizing skills," Ethan said, looking back and forth between the girls, being certain to make eye contact with each other. "And Sara, he continued, your home is fabulous! Do you do all the upkeep yourself?"

"Most of it," she replied, "John helps me when he can and Maria will pitch in now and again but you know teenagers, they don't seem to stay focused for very long unless of course, they are on their phone."

"Let's talk about you, Ethan." Mary abruptly entered the conversation. "Why aren't you married?"

"Gee, Mare," Sara said with disbelief, "how about a few warmup questions?"

"It's alright, Mrs. Shand, It's a fair question." Ethan paused briefly, organizing his thoughts and being careful to avoid the emotional flashbacks that this particular topic often brought to the surface. The ladies didn't make a sound. Sara, though quick to admonish Mary for asking, was just as anxious to hear his answer.

"The truth is just this simple." Ethan had a serious look and tone about him now. "You see, I have had an anatomical anomaly since birth that prevents me from having an intimate relationship. It is because of this that I..."

"Hey, are you kids having fun over here?" Greg had suddenly returned to the party and thrust himself smack in the middle of their conversation.

"Bad timing Greg, go grab me an empanada from the house, would you please?" Mary impatiently barked the order.

"I didn't see empanadas in there, are you sure we have them?" Greg asked naively.

"Then make some, Greg!" Mary said briskly.

"Oh, I get it now, I interrupted something juicy that you girls can't wait to hear. I'll just go find someone else to talk to."

"Okay honey, I will catch up with you shortly," Mary said.

Greg leaned in and Mary offered her cheek for a little kiss. "By the way," Greg added, I hope Ethan is sharing his eunuch story, I love that one!"

He walked away leaving Mary and Sara looking at Ethan's sheepish grin. "You were fabricating a story for us, weren't you?" Sara asked. "You see Mary, you had to ask the big question right up front."

"I should have known that Greg's wise ass demeanor would rub off on him," Mary said.

"I was in love once," Ethan offered, "but it ended and I just threw myself into my education and career. "Perhaps someday, it will find me again."

"I'm sorry, Ethan." Mary said. "Maybe you can share that story with us someday?"

"Not much to tell really, we were young and in love and then she was injured and her parents sent her away for treatment. Not for my lack of trying, but we never spoke again. Water over the falls as they say."

Ethan appeared saddened momentarily so the ladies let it lie. "We should be getting ready for the real party, Mare," Sara said, "It was a pleasure meeting you, Ethan. We will talk again later. Please help yourself to anything you desire.

"Thank you, Mrs. Shand and Mrs. Webster. Great party!"

Greg had wandered off but he was keeping an eye on Ethan, waiting for the girls to leave before he approached again.

Chapter 10

Somewhere

He stopped moving so that he could listen intently for a moment. Sure enough, the landline was ringing. He could count on one hand the number of times that phone had rung in the last five years. Very few people had access to that number. He hastened his pace, moving from the soft light of the study to the darkness of the office.

"Hello?" There was a few seconds of silence. He was ready to say it again when he heard a woman's voice.

"Please hold," she said. Another break before a male voice came on.

"Is there something you need to tell me?" The voice asked. He knew it was Alpha.

"Not that I'm aware of," he answered with an obvious nervousness to his voice.

"That's interesting because someone else tells me there is a story I need to hear. Would you like to try again?" Alpha asked.

The man thought about his response, frightened to tell the truth. "Yes, I am sorry master, I do have something to tell you. I was afraid to tell you and for that I am heartily sorry. Please forgive me."

Again, there was an intentional pause at the other end. "Tell the truth and all is forgiven."

Alpha's voice was deep and menacing, which added to the fear. "There was a situation that had to be dealt with. I thought about the options and potential ramifications of each and then I acted on what I believed to be the most prudent choice. I am sorry I didn't ask permission first but I thought it may be better if you didn't know, not because I don't value your position or your opinion but because I thought if you didn't know, you wouldn't need to lie someday if you are asked about it."

The silence was longer this time. He knew enough not to interrupt.

"While I appreciate your sensitivity, I would prefer to know," Alpha said.

"The girl posed a risk to the operation," he answered. "She wandered outside the perimeter and may have seen something she shouldn't have."

"I see," Alpha responded. "Did anyone witness this breach?"

"Just our people as far as we know."

"No chance of a delivery or service vehicle observing?" Alpha spoke again.

"No sir."

"Then why the concern? What did she possibly see that may have exposed the operation?"

"She managed to get beyond the fence, Sir."

After the anticipated pause, Alpha spoke again. "So you believe she may have noticed something that could disclose the location?"

"Yes, Sir."

"Is she traceable?" Alpha followed.

"Doubtful, Sir, she has been with us for a while and there is no known family."

"And what was her assignment there?" Alpha continued.

"She was a member of the morale services team, Sir." There was one last pause.

"I am going to be following this closely, my son. I may be following up with you again. If you have further information to share, be sure to do so timely."

"Yes, Sir. Thank you, Sir." The connection was already severed.

He returned to the study, to continue his work.

Chapter 11

High Falls, NY

Greg waited until Mary and Sara left the table and then made his way over to Ethan who was just getting up. "Leaving so soon?" Greg asked. "I was just about to join you and finish my drink. Keep me company for a moment?"

"Of course, Greg, I would be happy to." Ethan sat back down and Greg joined him. "I wasn't leaving the party, just a stretch break. You know, we should do that every fifteen minutes at an event that involves long periods of sitting."

"I did know that," Greg replied, "in fact, I learned that during my recent annual employee education training. Our new Director of Physical Medicine taught us that and he takes his job very seriously." Greg smiled.

"Sorry, I forgot you were there," Ethan replied.

"No worries, Ethan. I am the kind of boss that can forget about being forgotten. How did it go with the girls?"

"That was great! I really like them both," he said excitedly.

"That wife of mine can be very direct sometimes, I hope she didn't pry too much."

"Not at all, Greg, they were both very charming."

Greg could see Sara and John beginning to pull people together. "It looks like it's time for the official festivities to begin. Care to give me a hand, Ethan?" Both men rose and Ethan followed Greg to the porch steps. They walked briskly to the side of the porch where there were stacks of folding chairs waiting to be set up.

"We going to create a semi-circle facing the porch," Greg instructed. "This way, people who already have seats on the porch can remain where they are and the others can fill in the circle here. Everyone will be able to see and participate without adding an undue sense of formality."

Ethan didn't require any further direction. He effortlessly moved the chairs to Greg's position opening each one as he returned. It was all over in less than five minutes. "What's next chief?" He asked.

"We need to bring one of the big, high back wicker chairs off the porch for the guest of honor. We can place it right here between the folding chairs and the porch. Perhaps at an angle so that we don't obscure anyone's view with the back of the chair."

Ethan bounded up the steps two at a time and quickly returned with the chair. Greg put it in place. He then went back to the side of the porch and returned with a small folding table. Ethan grabbed one end from Greg and they each worked to unfold the legs and flip the table upright.

"Time to get the girls. Ethan, would you mind running to the tree-house to tell everyone there that it's time?"

"I'm on it, Greg." He spun off toward the side yard. Greg turned back toward the porch to see Mary and Sara carrying arms full of gifts toward the steps.

"Hey, let me help you with those!" he said as he darted up the steps. "I assume these are going on the table?"

"I'm afraid they won't all fit on the table, Greg. Feel free to set the others on the ground near the table. Thank you," Sara said. Greg placed the first load on the table and turned around to see the girls coming with their arms full again. "You see what I mean?" Sara asked.

"This is one popular little girl!" Greg exclaimed.

People were making their way toward the seats both on the porch and on the ground. Many had refreshed their drinks and all of them wore a smile. When everyone was seated, John appeared at the door with Veronica Chalmers and her daughter Destiny. John held the door and then escorted mom and daughter to their place in the new center of their universe.

The ambiance was nowhere near that of a bride being walked down the aisle. The were no bouquets of flowers, no candles and no wedding march emanating from a pipe organ. No flowing train gliding over rose petals dropped by angelic little hands, yet the effect this moment had on everyone's throat muscles and tear ducts was just as spontaneous and perhaps ever more spectacular.

Veronica was wearing a white knee length linen and lace dress with red and navy striping at the sleeves and hem. Destiny looked like a sparkler with a light silvery dress with hundreds of sequins that made the dress seem alive. It was hard to tell the true color because of the changing reflection of everything around her. Both ladies looked elegant and both were totally barefoot.

Veronica carried Destiny down the steps and then set her down. She had only been walking for a short time but when she saw the colorful, shiny packages on the table, she took off in that new toddler sprint. Mom allowed her the freedom knowing that it would probably end in a gentle fall. Nothing a farm girl can't handle.

When Veronica was seated with Destiny resting patiently on her lap, John Shand began the program. He was holding a folded paper in his hand as security. Even though this was planned as an informal event, nearly everyone in attendance had an active role in getting to this day and he didn't want to leave anyone out. He was quickly reminded once again that he would rather treat a cardiac arrest than give a speech. All he really needed to do was get the ball rolling. The invitations made it clear that anyone and everyone was welcome to speak as they saw fit.

"Dear friends, it is a privilege to not only stand before you but also beside you as friend and family. We have so many reasons to celebrate today that I feel a little sad for the rest of the nation who focus only on our independence. From dozens of divergent points on paths that some of us chose and others just found ourselves here, we have been united not by chance as it now appears but by destiny itself, and by Destiny herself." He smiled and raised his hand toward the young girl.

"When I try to comprehend what we have all been through or better yet, what drove us here, I find myself grabbing for labels like love, respect, decency, duty, honor, sacrifice, camaraderie, brotherhood, and sister-hood. Any one of these labels doesn't seem sufficient. In fact, all of them together still seem to pale in comparison to how it feels. I have found one word that works for me and that is heart. I believe that heart may be at the very root of any unselfish act. It is the very root of life both physically and emotionally.

All of us here today have heart. An immense measure of heart. I know that I feel as though my emotional heart has grown tremendously since our paths have crossed. I also know my physical heart has doubled in size since that delicious feast we just enjoyed. As a doctor, I'm telling all of us to knock it off. Right after cake and ice cream!

So, you will all have an opportunity to speak as the day progresses and we encourage you to do so. Right now, this young lady has been so patiently staring at these gifts. Veronica, I just want to welcome you again to this fabulous extended family and to thank you for all the joy that you have brought us."

The crowd rose in unison and with thunderous applause. Veronica stood with her little girl in her arms. She pulled Destiny's head to her chest and kissed her forehead as the tears poured from her eyes. After a few moments, she tried to speak but she couldn't ascend the noise from the cheering crowd. When the others realized Veronica was struggling to speak, they began to quiet down.

"I am so thankful for each and every one of you." She began, her eyes moving slowly, intently across the entire crowd. "When the skies are dark and threatening, do not be afraid. For it is at these times that indelible light will find you. All of you are the light that came for me. I was alone, vulnerable, and misguided and now, I am at the top of the world. I have a beautiful daughter, a family that loves me beyond belief and a bountiful group of friends. What more can one hope for? Destiny and I are blessed to be counted among you and I vow for both of us that we will always be there for you. That we will see others as you have seen us."

The crowd applauded once again. "If you approve, I would like Destiny to open her gifts in your presence. I know this will take a while and I don't want you to miss time with each other so please mill about and enjoy the day. If you would like to be present when she opens your gift, we will wait for you. Thank you all so much."

With that, some people remained seated where they were, some moved toward the gifts and others moved about the vast lawn and porch, conversing as before.

Chapter 12

Hilton Head Island, SC
Shelly Madris had returned from shopping with several ring bound notebooks as well as a variety of other writing and drawing items she thought Dean could use. "That was fast!" he said as she walked in the door.

"Really? I was gone for over three hours, I thought you may be getting worried about me." Shelly sounded disappointed.

Dean realized he was in a sticky situation. "I always worry about you dear. In a good way, of course. I just know how much fun you have shopping with Anna and it really didn't seem like you were gone that long. Is it busy out there?"

"You have no idea," she replied, "the island is wall to wall today. The shops are all running Fourth of July sales, the beaches are packed and there is a big festival happening at Shelter Cove. Traffic will be at a standstill once the fireworks are over. It's a good thing we can see them right from here!" she exclaimed.

"Best seats in the house!" Dean replied.

"Have you had a productive day so far dear?" Shelly inquired.

"I have. I've been learning a lot about this art software and I even had a chat with Kenny back home. He asked me to say hello for him."

"Oh, how nice! And how is Kenny? Does he miss you?"

"Like a toothache! Or so he says."

Shelly was on her way toward the door again. "Leaving so soon?" Dean asked.

"If you don't mind, dear. Anna and I want to check out the deals at the outlets in Bluffton."

"That's fine Hun, just remember how small this place is. We barely have room for our toothbrushes let alone our clothes."

"That's why God invented storage lockers, dear."

She gave him a kiss and was out the door. He opened his browser and continued searching for anything he could find about the company that hosts the artists. The website was called Art Job Depot. He typed in artjobdepot.net and hit the enter key. The landing page of the website gave an overview of the types of services offered and some sample listings of artists. He chose the category of Children's Books with the subheading of Illustrations.

There were several pages of results. Each included a sample illustration, estimated prices and a short bio of the artist. Most listed a photograph of the artist as well. Dean clicked on the one he was doing business with.

The picture was of a young woman, in her mid-twenties he guessed. She looked American but her location was listed as Jakarta, Indonesia.

He noticed a button below the image that said, *Contact the Artist.* Dean was reluctant to initiate a conversation just in case someone was monitoring her activity. He decided to ask her some very basic questions that wouldn't raise any alarms. He pressed the button. A dialogue page popped up. *Hi, I'm Audra. How can I help you today?* Dean ruminated for a moment.

Hello, Audra. My name is Dean. I have opened a job with you for some illustrations. I was wondering if you could tell me about yourself.

What would you like to know, Dean?

How long have you been an artist?

As long as I can remember. I think I was born with a crayon in my hand!

Dean was impressed with her use of English. He would try a more difficult question.

Audra, have you ever illustrated a book of prose?

I haven't had that request before but I would certainly like to try it!

I know your day is about 12 hours ahead of me. I'm sorry if I'm keeping you up.

Not to worry, Dean, I do not have a set schedule so I often work all hours of the day and night. Whenever I am not available, you will see a notice stating such.

Thank you, Audra. I will be back in touch soon!

It has been a pleasure chatting with you, Dean. Have a lovely day.

Dean closed that link and sat back in his chair. He was no longer just impressed with her English, he was confounded by it. He looked at some of the other artist, searching for another in the same region of the world. He came across one in Sri Lanka. He clicked on it.

This one's name was Sinu. He opened the chat.

Hello, my name is Sinu. I can answer question?

Hi Sinu. My name is Dean. Do have any experience illustrating prose?

Sir, I can do. Explain prose.

That's okay, Sinu. Thank you for your time.

Dean disconnected and tried a few more with similar results. There was something very different about Audra. He also confirmed his suspicion that Audra's conversations were being monitored. The desperation of her original cry for help was in stark contrast with the casualness of today's chat.

He browsed the bottom of the website where they list the contact information for the company. Artjobdepot.net was based in Jerusalem. He dialed Kenny's number in New York. He would be better suited to investigate the company.

Chapter 13

High Falls, NY

It was almost eight o'clock by the time the party officially ended. More than half of the guests had left and those who stayed helped with the after-party cleanup. John and Sara invited the helpers to hang around for drinks and watch the fireworks as they rose from the valley below. All of the adults had regathered on the front porch while the teenagers went to the treehouse. From there, music and laughter carried on the warm evening breeze.

John had started a fire in the stone and iron pit in the front yard not far from the porch. The night didn't call for additional heat but the smoke helped keep the mosquitos at bay and the flames and the scent of the burning wood added a true summer ambience. It would be at least another hour before the fireworks would begin.

Sara had reheated some of the finger foods from earlier in the day and placed them on a hot stone serving tray in the middle of the large table. There was a cooler with beer and wine resting near the front door. John, Mary, Ethan, Greg, Charis, Richard and Marilyn Ingraham, and Trey Lawrence were gathered around the table.

Ethan was praising John and Sara Shand for the wonderful event. "Thank you, Ethan," Sara said, "we could not have done it without all of you!"

"We make a good team." Greg added.

"Always have!" Richard said.

"You are so right about that, honey." Marilyn agreed with her husband.

"I know dear, I'm always right. It's a heavy load," Richard offered sarcastically.

"You are also an egotistical ass, Richard, but his time you are right. For almost two decades, this team has banded together to accomplish the unthinkable. I am so proud to know each and every one of you." Marilyn was obviously choked up. Sara reached out and held her hand.

"How long have you been married?" Ethan asked.

"How long have the dinosaurs been gone?" Richard quipped.

Ethan was afraid to laugh although he did find the comment funny.

"You talk a good game, Richard," John said. "You wouldn't give this woman up for love or money and you know it."

"Don't pay any attention to him, Ethan. I know how much he loves me. We have been married for fifty-two years."

"Is that all?" Richard responded.

"It is if you keep this up!" Marilyn joked.

"What about you, Ethan? Are you married?" Marilyn inquired.

Ethan paused a moment. He looked a little sad. "I am very much single at the moment."

"How can that be?" Charis asked. "A handsome young man like you. Heck, I would marry you in a heartbeat!"

"So would I," said Mary.

"Get right behind me," Sara said.

Ethan felt himself blushing.

"Easy girls," Greg said.

"We're just having a little fun."

"I know, Mary, I was saying that you girls are easy!"

There was a lot of laughter around the table.

"There is nothing wrong with being single," said Charis, "isn't that right, Trey?"

Trey looked surprised to be pulled into the conversation. "That's right Charis. I mean other than being lonely, returning to an empty house every night, shopping for one, walking into a theater alone and eating takeout six times a week."

"It can't be that bad," said Richard, "you can have sex with a different woman every night if you want!"

"That only seem appealing when you can't have it," Trey said, "I'm not into the dating scene and I haven't been for a long time. I didn't find it very rewarding at all."

"Same here," added Charis, "who needs that kind of aggravation? I would be very happy to settle down with the right partner but finding one who could understand my career and my schedule is a long shot at best. Besides, I'm already married and his initials are FBI."

"What about you, Ethan? You're young and eligible, what can you tell us about love from your perspective?" Mary asked.

"Gee Mar, didn't we go down this road once tonight?"

"Yes, Sara, we did but we didn't get very far down that road as I recall."

"Ladies," Greg chimed in, "let's allow Ethan some space."

"He doesn't have to answer, Greg, we would just like to get to know him a little more." Mary answered.

"Thanks for looking out for me Greg. I can handle it. What would you like to know?

"Earlier, you said you were in love once," Mary started, "can you tell us what happened?"

"Sure. As you know, I grew up around here. I was a quiet kid in a small town. This is not your typical small town though. Usually small means everyone knows everyone else. In High Falls, most folks live in the rural areas. We have a very small community nucleus, not much of a down-town and even the high school is outside of the village. When I was in school, more than ninety-five percent of the children were bussed. There was no such things as neighborhood friends, walking to school together or playing kick the can in the streets. Your best friend was usually the kid who lived next on the bus route.

Meeting girls at school was easy but getting to spend time with them was anything but. The closest friend, geographically, was a girl. She was also in my class. For eleven years, she and I sat next to each other on the bus. We really got along well. I can't say that we were romantically involved but I always knew there was something special about our friendship.

I worked hard the summer before my junior year so that I could buy a car when I turned sixteen. I thought having wheels would make it easier to spend more time with her and in some ways it did. Her parents were sort of old school, I guess you would say. When she was allowed to go out, she had to be home before dark even on weekends. Her folks were very active in a church somewhere south of here which meant that she was also an active participant. She never wanted to talk about it much.

We were able to spend more time together in the late spring to early fall when it remained light into the evening. We enjoyed being outdoors mostly. Long walks, hiking and walking through the gorge at Wintergreen Park. That was probably our favorite thing to do."

"What was her name, Ethan?" Charis asked gingerly.

Ethan smiled for a second before he began answering.

"She had a great name! One that sounded like she would be famous someday. Lillian Jacqueline MacNamara. I called her Lilijac Mac. She seemed fond of her pet name. It was as if it bestowed a new personality upon her, like a new name would take her away from the overly protective, near missionary life she was living. I'm sure this all sounds very juvenile and unimportant compared to the exciting lives you all have."

"Not at all!" Mary replied. "I think it's sweet. I know you don't describe the relationship as a romantic one but it sure sounds like a legitimate childhood crush. Who does not remember their first crush? By the way, Ethan, I'm not trying to minimize your situation at all. Love is love whether it's romantic or platonic."

"Thank you, Mary. I knew then just as I do now, that it was very special. I always longed to be around her. I felt complete when we were together. As we got older, we were both aware of other awakenings in our bodies but between the shyness, religious pressure and no time after dark, without even thinking, we both just chose to not poke the bear."

"It sounds like something needed poking to me!" Richard blurted out.

That brought a little laughter from the group until Marilyn gave

Richard *the look*. Everyone quieted down again anxious to hear Ethan continue.

"In retrospect, you may be right, Richard. Somehow we were content. We talked about the future, you know, who we would become once we were no longer under parental influence. Lilijac loved to draw and paint. She was a wiz with a pencil and a crayon. She didn't quite know what to do with her talent but somehow, she would be working in the visual arts arena. I, on the other hand, had no idea what I was going to do. That is until she showed me. It was our senior year, the Saturday before the Memorial Day weekend. It was unusually warm and the sky was cloudless. As we often did, Lilijac and I decided to go to Wintergreen Park. Most of the time we were content to walk along the path overlooking the gorge and the falls but with the warm temperature, we were inclined to walk the river through the gorge.

I'm sure most of you have been there and are familiar with setup. We made our way from the parking lot to the camping area. We were wearing our bathing suits and brough towels to sit on. You can enter the river from the camping area which is about halfway to the falls but if you first head upstream for about four hundred yards, you will find a series of smaller falls. The entry side of the river tapers from tall, wooded cliffs to the water. The other side of the river is sheer rock that goes straight up for fifty to one-hundred yards. It is quite breath-taking.

Depending on the time of year and the amount of precipitation, the depth of the water running over the solid rock bottom ranges from zero inches to more than a foot. The deeper it is, the faster it flows. This particular day, the depth averaged two-four inches. At this level, there is ample rock edging that remains dry and easy to navigate.

We made our way upstream toward the middle falls. This was our favorite spot of all. We stayed on the dry rock floor until we were level with the falls which was equal distance from both shores. The tricky part is getting from the dry side to the falls. There are spillways on each side of the falls that create a fast current. Stepping in the wrong place could mean your legs would be taken out from under you. It also made a great slide that emptied into small pools about fifty feet downstream.

We left our towels on the dry edge and held hands as we gingerly stepped toward the falls. We both had old sneakers on to improve our grip on the slippery floor of the river. The sound of the falls as we approached was awesome. We decided to make one run down the slide before going into the falls. I helped Lilijac get into a seated position in a pool of water about a foot deep. There was a medium sized boulder that you had to navigate your butt over before the water swept you away. There was just enough room for me to sit behind her.

I wrapped my arms around her waist and asked if she was ready. She placed her arms over mine and nodded her head. She raised her bottom a little and off we went. The force of the water immediately pushed her back against my front and we were racing through the s-turns toward the pool in a reclined position. There was only one thing to do now. Scream!

We laughed and screamed all the way into the pool holding on to each other as tightly as we could. When we spit out into the pool, we both went under the water. We continued to hold each other, neither of us in a hurry to surface. When I loosened my grip, she turned around under the water and kissed me on the lips. We held that embrace until we surfaced. We were both ecstatic, smiling from ear to ear. We rested our foreheads together and let the streaming water surround us like a whirlpool.

When she raised her head my gaze was straight at her chest. The rushing water had adjusted her swimsuit just enough for me to finally realize that Lilijac had grown up. I felt giddy and dizzy, but also elated. It was as if we were instantly transported from child to adult. Life from now on was going to be different. I didn't understand how, but I was changed and she was changed.

"Shall we try that again or go right to the falls?" I had asked.

"Take me to the falls, please."

It was my task to make her every wish come true for the rest of the day. For the rest of our lives! We worked our way out of the pool and back on to the dry riverbed. Hand in hand, we walked upstream to where we first entered the water. Our towels were right where we left them. We once again entered the water and stepped our way very carefully toward the falls.

The water slowed just before the falls itself because almost all the water flooded straight over the top. The canopy of water was nearly ten feet overhead, creating a cavern behind it. Once behind the water, we were sheltered from the outside world. Even the sound inside seemed much less than the thunder on the other side. It was beautiful. Magical.

I didn't remember it being this extraordinary before. I felt as though all of my human senses were elevated tenfold. We stood for a moment, holding hands, and facing the back of the wall of water. We then turned toward each other, my arms around her waist and hers around my neck. We gazed deeply into each other's eyes, both seeing things for the first time. I could feel my pulse throughout my entire body. We pulled ourselves closer than I believed possible and brought our lips together.

The wall of water filtered out enough of the sunlight that if looked like dusk inside the cavern. I tried to speak but the words I was familiar with no longer had meaning. I just stared at her and touched her skin as deeply as I could without fear of hurting her. She spoke first.

"Ethan, everything feels different now. Bigger somehow. I hope I didn't ruin anything by kissing you. I couldn't face losing our friendship. Does it have to be one or the other?"

"Lilijac, I promise that my love for you will never diminish our friendship. Don't be afraid."

"I believe you, Ethan. I love you too. I guess I always have."

We rested behind our live curtain until we felt the chill from the lack of sunlight. I held her hand and drew her out into the sun. It took our eyes a moment to adjust to the brightness so we stood still and allowed it. Once my eyes were fully adjusted, I looked at Lilijac and told her we should make a move toward shore. She was having difficulty keeping her eyes open. I pulled her gently toward me but her feet were frozen.

Lil, we need to move. Can you come toward me?

She was trying to speak but I couldn't understand her. She mumbled something, She was slurring her speech. She was wobbling and I was doing my best to hold her upright. Then she started to shake. Her knees buckled and she went down. I tried to catch her but I couldn't and I entered the water with her.

We were caught in the rapid flow just downstream of the falls. I called her name as I tried to keep her face out of the water. She wasn't responding. I tried to steer us toward shore while holding her as high out of the water as possible. We were traveling faster as we got nearer to the major falls. I was frightened. I kept kicking with my legs, reaching for some foothold to stop our movement. Looking ahead, I could see a small jetty of rocks extending into the water. I thought if I could position us behind that jetty, I could work our way to the shore.

As it came up on our right side, we were forcefully thrust down a slope to our left, further into the rushing river. I looked at Lil and called her name but she was still unconscious. I gazed along the passing shoreline looking for help but couldn't see anyone. I yelled for help anyway, my voice lost in the crashing waves.

I was tiring quickly and I knew we were getting close to the edge of the falls. It was at least a fifty foot drop to the boulder laden pool below. I remembered reading a news article several years ago about a young man who dove off the cliff. His girlfriend and dog paced anxiously along the wooded edge of the trail waiting for him to resurface. Several hours later, a rescue team pulled his lifeless body from the pool where his body was wedged between the rocks. His dog stayed for days after his body was taken away, refusing to leave without him.

The thought gave me renewed strength. I was not going to let this be the end. Not right after our lives truly began. I fluttered my legs, reaching for anything that I could get a hold of. I thought about letting go for just a second to get ashore and then find a way to pull Lilijac out but I knew that if I let go, she would surely go over the falls.

We were getting close. The roar of the water cascading over the rocks was now thunderous. I could feel the vibration in the rock beneath me. I grabbed a tighter hold of Lil and wrapped my legs around her so that I could cushion her fall. All at once, I could feel the downward pull of the water as if being sucked down a drainpipe. I closed my eyes and prayed to a God I didn't even know.

We went down a steep slope and made a sudden jerk to the right. Then, when I expected to feel the weightlessness of the giant fall, the water leveled out and slowed down. I looked over the top of Lil and realized we were cast into a shallow pool. I could feel rock beneath me. There was another sudden move forward and my leg hit a large rock. I don't know if I felt or heard the bone break first. It didn't matter, I knew my left lower leg was fractured. Still, I was able to get us closer to shore, away from the potential of re-entering the mainstream.

I made sure Lil was secure at the edge of the shallow pool. We were close to the dry edge of the bedrock. I could see some pieces of driftwood laying at the edge of the water. I shifted my body to my right side. I screamed when the left leg tried to follow. I thought if I could reach the driftwood I may be able to splint the leg enough to go get help. I checked Lil's pulse. Her heartbeat seemed steady and strong. I put my cheek to her mouth and I could feel the warm air when she exhaled. I yelled for help again.

I grabbed two shorter section of the wood and used them to hoist myself onto a rock. I took off my wet tee shirt and ripped several long strips of cloth. I tied one piece of cloth loosely around my ankle and another closer to my knee. I slid the first piece of wood down the outside of my lower leg, underneath the cloth. I then did the same thing on the interior side. The wet wood slid easily into the loose bands.

I found a five inch length of this wood and placed it between my upper and lower incisors, not knowing if it would help but it looked good on TV. I bit down on the wood and pulled the ends of the cloth tightly and quickly around my ankle. Biting the wood helped stifle the scream but it tasted terrible. I repeated the steps on the upper end of the splint, just below the knee. From my sitting position on the rock, I reached out for a long log that I could use to steady myself. I placed the distal end between some rocks so that it wouldn't slip. I grabbed ahold of the top and raised myself up. The splint was working, the bones no longer moving within my skin.

I called Lil's name over and over again. I could see some subtle movement in her extremities. I looked around me and saw no one. A beautiful, sunny Saturday and not a soul around. I hollered for help again. I yelled at Lil to wake up. There was no way I could get myself and Lil up the hill to the road. I was just about to sit back down on the rock when I heard voices. They were in the distance but I could tell it was at least one male and one female voice. Help! Help! Somebody help us! I yelled at the top of my lungs. A minute later, I could see the bodies running toward the river. I held myself with one arm and waved the other frantically. Over here! Hurry!"

"My God, tell me they heard you!" Mary said.

"Thankfully, they did. They were really helpful and very sweet. They carried Lil carefully to their car that was parked in the camping area. I followed behind for a short way but I couldn't make it up the incline on my own. The young man came back to assist. I sat in the back and held Lil in my lap. She was beginning to come around. Her eyes opened and looked at me but she couldn't speak. I kept my hand on her wrist, checking her pulse and let her drift off to sleep.

The couple took us to St. Luke's Hospital in Utica. They were from that area and felt comfortable driving there. When we arrived in the ER, I gave the staff Lil's contact information as well as my parents' number. They ordered an orthopedic consult for me and a neuro workup for Lilijac.

The police arrived a short time later followed by my parents and the MacNamaras. I retold the story of events to everyone albeit at three different times. The police were sympathetic, my parents were concerned and a little proud, and the McNamaras were pissed. They wanted to blame me of course and I can't say that I blame them.

My leg didn't need resetting. It was put in a fiberglass cast, I was given some meds to take home and sent on my way. Lil was admitted to ICU. I tried calling her parents over the next several days but they wouldn't return my call. About a week later, I drove to their house. Her mother Gloria was not home but her father Alfred was and he let me in. Maybe he felt sorry for me because I was on crutches.

We sat in the living room which was really old-fashioned and dark. The curtains were barely open but it wouldn't have made a difference. The walls were dark wood, the furniture dark and colorless and the lights were so yellow and dim that we both looked like we had jaundice.

I asked how Lilijac was and he replied that she was out of ICU but still in the hospital. The CT scan showed a rare brain disorder that caused her to pass out. There wasn't any evidence of traumatic brain injury. He couldn't repeat the name of the condition but he said it wasn't good and that Lil couldn't speak and she was very depressed. The doctors were recommending inpatient rehabilitation at a facility.

I asked if I could visit her at St. Luke's. He said she wouldn't be there long and that the doctors didn't encourage visitors. He strongly recommended that I stay away. I told him that I loved her and that I needed to see her again, that maybe she would feel less depressed if she saw me. I'll never forget what he said next. "Son, there's not much left to love. You should move on." I couldn't believe what I was hearing.

He stood up, letting me know that our conversation was over. He just pushed me toward the door, opened it and closed it behind me. I felt awful. I didn't know what to do. My lifelong friend and the recently discovered love of my life just vanished."

"Ethan, did you try to go to the hospital on your own?" John Shand asked.

"I did, Dr. Shand. I went the next morning. When I arrived at the information desk, I was told that she had been discharged. I asked where she was discharged to and they said they didn't have that information. When I asked when she was discharged, they told me it was two days earlier. The day before I met with her father."

I tried calling rehab centers in the area and most wouldn't give me any information. I wracked my brain for months trying to find out what happened to her. I read obituaries every day waiting to see her name pop up. I even visited local cemeteries looking for new graves and headstones. Before this happened, I was enrolled at Herkimer County Community College. In July, I withdrew my application from HCCC and applied to and was accepted at Siena College. I knew the only way to get over my loss was to find a way to help others. A career in Physical Therapy seemed like a good way to do it. I can't say I haven't looked back and I can't say that I have moved on. But I found a healthy way to deal with it."

"You sure have, son. That's an amazing story and I am profoundly sorry for your loss." Richard Ingraham volunteered.

"Thank you for sharing, Ethan. I am even more proud of you and more honored to have you working at High Falls Hospital. Welcome to the family!" Greg added.

"Hey, wait a minute," Charis interrupted, "look around this table. We have a hospital administrator by way of the state health department, the FBI, the state police, two physicians and two totally impowered women who are the glue that keeps us together. Do you really think that together, we can't find out what happened to Lilijac?"

Before anyone could answer, the sky exploded in red, white, and blue. Charis' phone was vibrating in her pocket.

Chapter 14

July 5, 2016
Quicksburg, VA

"My, ain't you lookin' pretty as a picture today, Delilah! 'Bout the only thing missing is the high heels." She stared at him from the other side of the counter.

"Now Til, they don't pay me nearly enough to prance around this diner in high heels. If that's what you want to see, you'll have to pay a little extra and throw in a fancy meal. And I don't mean here!" She set down a cup of black coffee in front of him and moved back down the counter to the pickup window. She grabbed two plates filled with eggs, sausages, hotcakes, and grits, whirled around, and set them down on the counter in front of two guys dressed as if they were going hunting. "Will that hold you boys for a while?" She didn't wait for an answer.

Working her way back to Til, she said, "the usual Sheriff?"

"I think I'm going to change things up a bit, just so y'all don't think you know me so well. I'm gonna have a country ham biscuit and some grits with sausage gravy if you don't mind."

"Won't bother me none, not my hips that biscuit is going to sit on!"

"Heck Dee, you move so fast that biscuit could never catch up to you."

"That's why I'm never slowing down, Til."

Til's phone started ringing.

"Sheriff Sweeney," he answered. "Uh huh...uh huh..alright. You just wait right there. Delilah, hold the grits and make that biscuit to go please!"

"If you say so, Sheriff but I was just about to change into those heels. You just think about that while you're out playing cops and robbers."

Til gave her a smile and dropped a ten on the counter. She handed him the bag and gave him a wink.

Fifteen minutes later, he caught up to Deputy Swart at the crime scene. He parked behind Alan's cruiser on the shoulder of I-81 south just as it crossed over the Shenandoah River.

"What do you have here, Alan?" he said over the toothpick stuck between his lower front teeth.

"It was called in about an hour ago. Some older guy kayaking down below spotted him on the edge of the river. Looks to be a male, maybe 30-35 years old. The coroner and photographer just arrived."

"State Police?"

"Not yet, but they've been notified, Sheriff."

"Is this the only way down there?" the sheriff asked looking down a pretty steep embankment.

"It's either this or by boat, Til."

"Oh shit. There goes my shoeshine." Til and his deputy worked their way down the side of the overpass through the tall grass. It was July 5th and there hadn't been much rain so the grass was pretty dry. The coroner was examining the body while the photographer did his thing. "What you thinkin,' Doc?"

"Hell if I know, ain't been here but five minutes. Male, around 30, didn't die here."

"That seems like a lot for five minutes!"

"That's because I'm so good at what I do, Sheriff. First off, he's been in the river for a while. Secondly, he was found face down but all the blood pooling was on the backside. He was most likely killed somewhere else and brought here. Judging by the condition of the flesh, I would say he's been in or near the water for close to a week. The water is not very deep here and with the July sun, he's not in very good shape."

"Any ID?"

"Any idea about what?" Alan replied.

"Not idea, you moron, ID. You know, identification?"

"Oh. Right, Sorry. No, no ID."

"Anything on him at all?"

"I checked all the pockets, Til. I didn't find anything. Once we clean him up, we'll look for tattoos, scars etc. We can move him now. I'll give you a call when I've got something."

"I appreciate it, Doc."

"Sorry about the moron thing, Alan."

"Don't give it another thought, Sheriff."

Chapter 15

High Falls, NY

"Good morning, Charis." Mary was standing at the counter, wearing her pajamas, and pouring coffee. She didn't ask, she just grabbed another mug and filled it with coffee. Handing it to Charis she said, "how did you sleep?"

"Better than I would have staying at the hotel. Thank you for having me here, Mary."

"There was no way Greg or I were going to take no for an answer after you received that creepy phone call. You are always welcome here, Charis. I hope you know that."

"I do know that and it is very sweet of you both."

"Hey, a pajama party!" Greg said as he entered the kitchen. He walked over to the coffee pot and filled a mug.

"Do you mind pouring another one, Greg" Trey Lawrence joined the group. Greg handed his mug to Trey and poured himself another. Everyone took turns saying good morning to Trey.

"Thanks for letting me borrow a set of your pajamas, Greg."

Mary responded, "You're welcome, Trey. They look better on you anyway!"

Trey looked at Greg like a dog that was about to be punished.

"It's all good, Trey, Mary is just kidding. Right dear?"

"If you say so, Greg." She winked at Trey.

"Everyone sleep okay?" Greg asked.

They all responded in the affirmative.

"What a day yesterday turned out to be. I was expecting fireworks but I didn't imagine the phone call. What a finale! Ethan's riveting story, fireworks and then, the call."

"Nobody was more surprised than me." Charis said. "By the way, thanks for staying last night, Trey. I felt much better being surrounded by all of you."

"We have each other's backs. Glad I could be here. So what is the next step?"

Charis had a contemplative, unsure look on her face. "I'm not sure. I mean ordinarily, I would reach out within my department, but I'm convinced someone in the bureau is involved. It's been a couple weeks since the last call. I thought that maybe it was over."

"Tell us again what the caller said, Charis."

"Ok, Greg. I answered as usual, *Special Agent Andrews*. There was a two second pause and I could hear a slight buzz in the phone. I think he was using voice distortion again. He said, *"I see you're still at it. You don't listen very well*. I said maybe if you were more specific. Tell me what I'm supposed to stop doing. *Some people go missing. Some are not meant to be found*. Tell me specifically who is not to be found. *You know. Maybe you need a reminder of my seriousness. Nice party today, it would be a shame if something happened to that little girl*. How do you know... Click. He hung up."

"Who knew you were coming upstate? Did you mention that to anyone in the office?" Trey asked.

"I told my boss I was headed out of town, but I didn't say where. The only other person who knew was my dad."

"Maybe your phone is tapped? Better yet, your dad's phone is tapped!" Greg offered.

"Or maybe," Trey said, "your apartment is bugged. Or even your car!"

"All possibilities, I guess," Charis replied. It would be difficult to tap a bureau phone unless of course the tapper is inside. I've been sweeping for bugs in my apartment since this began. My dad's phone seems to be the most likely."

"And your car?" Greg asked.

"It's possible," she answered.

"Isn't the bigger question, who?" Mary asked. "if you could figure out who then you would know why. Or why then who. Sorry, I should stay out of it. You're the experts."

"It doesn't hurt to have an eye on the outside," Trey said," can't see the forest for the trees and all that."

"Charis, we touched on this for a moment yesterday but I think it's worth revisiting. What are you working on that is getting under someone's collar? Particularly someone inside."

"Greg, I always have a list of open investigations, some that go back years."

"But this started a few weeks ago. Which case would coincide with that timeline?"

Charis thought for a moment. Then she said, "let me go upstairs and get my laptop. I'll be right back."

"I'll start some breakfast," Mary said, "are eggs and pancakes good for everybody?"

Mary began opening cupboards and Greg put another pot of coffee on. Charis returned and sat at the end of the counter near a power outlet. She plugged the unit in and pulled out a stool. She sat and opened her computer. "Is your internet connection secure, Greg?"

"As secure as I know how to make it." He responded. "There is a secure router connection and everyone's computer has its own unique password."

"Okay. What is the network and password?"

"The network is HFW1185G. The password is sPiDeR123456."

"That's a secure password?" Charis questioned.

"As secure as it can be while providing a slim chance that any of us can remember it! At least it has upper and lower case letters."

"Are you aware that sixty percent of all passwords last year contained the numbers 123456?" Charis quizzed.

"But how many started with sPiDeR?" He asked.

"I'm not sure but probably no more than forty percent." Charis added with sarcasm as she typed in the password. "Okay I am on the network. Now, my encryption software will select a one time, thirty six digit password to log me in to the bureau."

"Who's hungry?" Mary said as she set down a platter of scrambled eggs and blueberry pancakes. "I'll just leave them here and you can all help yourselves."

Greg and Trey went right for the food. Charis remained focused on her computer and Mary was kind of watching over her shoulder. "I think what you do is extremely fascinating, Charis."

"Most of the time, Mary, it is. I love my job! Even when I've been in danger, I've managed to keep the plus and minuses in perspective because I always knew who the enemy was. I feel very misplaced this time. However, I am convinced that you can all help me figure it out. Sometimes, just talking about it out loud can add clarity."

"Okay, here is what I have been working on for the last three months." Greg and Trey came closer." I'm only looking at cases that actually started in the last three months. There are plenty of older cases that are still active. I wouldn't want to give the impression that I'm a slacker."

"Not possible, Charis." Greg said.

"Alright then. I have eight active cases. I can read them for you and you can take notes."

"I have a better idea, Charis. Can you print the list? We don't need all the details, just a title for each."

"Good idea, Greg. What is the name of the printer?"

"Greg," said Greg.

Charis just smiled and shook her head. "The only more obvious answer would have been, PRINTER." She pressed a few keys and Greg walked to his office to retrieve the papers. He carried five copies back to the kitchen and handed a single sheet to everyone.

"You may all be more comfortable at the dining room table or out on the patio." Mary offered.

"May I help clean up first?" Trey said.

"No, but thank you, Trey. The kids will be coming down soon and they will finish everything up. No sense in cleaning twice. You folks go on out and I will catch up in a minute."

Thanks, hon." Greg added.

Greg led them out to the patio which was just off the back of the kitchen. The July sun was still low in the sky and was filtered by the tall maples at the back of the property. Even without direct sunlight, they were comfortable in their pajamas. They were all reading down their list.

1. Arlington Cemetery Defacement, Arlington, VA
2. Multiple State Robberies of Federal Credit Unions, Nashville, TN; Tucson, Az; Rockville, MD
3. Murder for Hire, Bethesda, MD
4. Interstate Transfer of Stolen Goods, NY, PA, VA
5. Child Abduction, Bowling Green, KY
6. Unidentified Teenage Body, Crystal City, Mo
7. Unidentified Adult Body, McMinnville, TN
8. Unidentified Young Adult Female Body, Custer, SD

"Wow! That is a fairly diverse list," Trey observed.

"No kidding," Greg added. "Which ones can we eliminate based on what we know?"

"So far, the only thing we know is the caller keeps mentioning that people may not need or want to be found. Based on that, I think we can remove numbers 1,2, and 4 for now." Charis responded. "Number 3 doesn't involve a missing person. The hitman missed his target so now it's just a victimless crime. It's more of a find the shooter and try to pin him to a group.

"Okay, that leaves us the bottom half of the list. It seems to me that in case 5, someone actually reported a child missing. Cases 6,7 and 8 are found victims who no one is looking for yet. Is that correct?" Greg asked.

"That's the way I see it," Charis replied.

"So Charis, no one else is assigned the same cases as you?" Greg asked.

"That's correct. Other agents are usually pulled in as needed. No one has been pulled in as far as I know. As I advance on my cases, I send a report to my supervisor. He views the information, makes suggestions, and sends the information to the bureau chief. My supervisor oversees seven agents in addition to me."

"So, if your numbers reflect an average caseload, you're supervisor can be involved in sixty or seventy cases concurrently."

"At least that many, Greg. Keep in mind that this list is just the new ones for me. I have at least twice that many that are ongoing, open cases."

"Do you trust your supervisor?"

"Completely. Or, at least I did. He hasn't given me any reason not to trust him but the fact that someone on the inside knows what I'm up to, I believe it is healthier for me to try to figure it out without the bureau's involvement."

"Alright, I suggest that we dig into the details of cases 5-8 on our list. Is that okay with you Charis?"

"Yes. For now, I will leave out any real names. We can refer to them as victim 1, 2, 3, or 4. Actually, victims 2, 3 and 4 don't have names as of yet. I think we should set up a grid so that we can compare the four cases. The case number will be on the left. The next column will be age and sex followed by location, date found and finally, special circumstances."

"Charis, I have a large whiteboard and stand around here somewhere. Why don't we all get showered, I'll find the board and we will reconvene in thirty minutes. We can use this house as home base for the weekend. Will that be okay for you Trey and Charis?"

They all agreed.

"Alright! Everyone off to the showers. Trey and Charis, you can use the bathroom between the guest rooms. Mary and I will use ours and the kids have their own. Mary and I like to share the water. Feel free to do the same. It's all in the name of conservation." Greg joked.

Charis looked at Trey who was staring back at her. "I'm not standing in the back," she said, "too cold back there."

"I'm not either!, Trey countered, the cold makes me shrink."

"Sorry, Greg, I guess we will be taking separate showers. In the name of conservation, we will make them short."

Chapter 16

Somewhere

"Hello?"

"Hello Alpha Sam, this is Alpha Isaac. Can you talk for a few minutes?"

There was a short pause.

"Of course. What can I do for you?"

"I have a bit of a problem, Sam. We found it necessary to retire one of our resources. I was hoping you could offer some guidance."

Sam wasn't sure he wanted to get involved but after thinking about it for a few seconds, he realized this may help deflect attention from his own situation.

"What happened, Isaac?"

"A long term male resource made contact with someone on the outside. He was part of our ground services crew. A good worker and a nice guy according to his omega."

"Were you directly involved in the incident, Isaac?"

"No, I was notified by the omega. It appears that our resource approached a delivery person who showed up off schedule."

"Did you review the surveillance?"

"Yes. It was a brief encounter. We weren't able to clearly capture the audio because they were standing next to the idling truck. We have a tail on the driver."

"How long was the breach?"

"Less than one minute, Sam."

"Who else knows about this, Isaac?"

"Just our supervisor who interceded and now you."

"You didn't go to headquarters?"

"Not yet, I wanted to get your advice about that."

"Do you expect any trouble from the authorities?"

"I don't see how. The body is unidentifiable and being in the water for several days in this heat isn't going to help them."

"I see. If I were you, I would just sit on this for the time being. I don't think there is any point in getting others involved. If the delivery driver looks suspicious, you may need to alter your plan. Keep an eye on things and contact me in a week with an update, would you?"

"Of course, Sam. Thank you for your advice and your discretion."

The call ended. Sam sat at his desk chair and gazed out the window. He wasn't sure if this new wrinkle would affect him in any way but he didn't think so as long as it didn't escalate. *Let sleeping dogs lie.*

Chapter 17

Hilton Head Island, SC

"Shaw."

"Hey, Kenny, It's Dean."

"Dino! I was just thinking about you."

"Are you out of donuts?"

"That's not why I was thinking about you but now that you mention it, Yes."

"Give me some good news and I'll see what I can do to remediate that problem, Kenny."

"We made a few calls and we talked to a few people. We called the company headquarters in Bethlehem. Their English isn't very good."

"In comparison to U.S English or Brooklyn English?"

"What's the difference, Dino?"

"Are you kidding me, Kenny? Have you ever been outside of New York City?"

"Of course, I go to New Jersey all the time!"

"Well then I guess you should know, Kenny. Every time I speak down here, people think I'm in the mafia. But then again, the English they speak is a little different too. I guess that's what makes the world go round, right?"

"If you say so, Dino. Anyway, The company sounds legit. They have been in business about ten years now. From what I can tell, they serve three purposes. They advertise artists services. They match clients to artists and they serve as a payment processor. Except for the staff they maintain for business purposes, they never lay eyes on any of the independent contractors."

"When I asked for information about your girl specifically, they said they are not allowed to provide any details. That needs to be done online with the artist directly."

"Kenny, can they verify where the artist is physically?"

"Not really. They can verify that you are connecting to a server located where the artists says they are but we all know that a router in Indonesia can be re-routed any number of times. So, your girl can be sitting in Jakarta or her ass could be in a chair in Peoria, Illinois."

"Or," Dean said, she could be standing."

"Gee, you're right. I didn't think about that. I guess that's why you were in charge here, Dino."

"Okay, Kenny. Hey, thanks for your help. I'll call a dozen in for you today, my friend."

"Thanks, Dino. I'm sorry I couldn't be more helpful."

"I appreciate all you do. Hey Kenny, the next time you're thinking about a road trip, instead of New Jersey, drive two hours north of the city and listen to the people talk. You will be amazed."

Dean disconnected the call and dialed the number for Mac's Donuts. He knew the number by heart. He no sooner hung up the phone when his tablet gave a tone signifying an incoming message. He had a new mail message from Audra.

He opened the message to find a new illustration and a note.

"I made a few changes. Please review and approve. Thank you! Audra."

Dean opened the file. The drawings were much more defined and colorized. He transferred the file to his new software program. Taking the digital pencil from the holder, Dean opened the file. He clicked through the pages and was delighted with the quality of the drawings. He pressed the layer key and a thumbprint of each of the seven layers loaded on the right edge of the screen. He tapped through each one. When he reached the fourth image, he enlarged it.

On the pastel background he found pale white lettering forming the words:

I'm being held captive. Please help. Order another illustration.

Dean put together a synopses of the next chapter with suggestions for character development and scene layout. He ordered the job and paid the fee. Less than ten minutes later he received a new sketch. It was just a single line drawing with a single color background. He opened the file and quickly leafed through the layers. As usual, page four spelled out the message in faint but definite thin, white letters.

"Verify that you're receiving my messages. Add a layer to the proofs that I send and make it layer five. Choose the same background color by copying my layer three. Do not send too much at one time. For now, just verify. TY."

Now Dean knew that he could ask some questions. At least he knew in his mind that it was Audra initiating the risk. He could only imagine her torment to be this desperate to risk getting caught. He began writing and laying out the next chapter, less concerned about the product than the hidden messages.

When he inserted layer five, he thought about what he would ask. He had been in similar situations before but the questions were asked in person after the victim was freed from their captor. Being limited in how much he could ask at one time, the order in which he asked became crucial.

He would typically assess the victims physical status using questions like: Are you hurt? Were they feeding you? Have you been physical or sexually assaulted? Those questions now were secondary. He needed to know where she was.

Using his e-pencil, he printed *Do You Know Where You Are?*

He sent the file back with the heading *Looks good. Can you forward the fully colorized version?*

He had to be very careful to avoid using words that would create a red flag. It was time to wait.

Chapter 18

Quicksburg, VA

"Sheriff's office, Deputy Swart speaking. Yes, he's right here Doc, I'll put him on." Alan Swart looked across the room at the Sheriff. "Til, it's Doc Flanders on the line."

"Which line, Alan?"

"The telephone line, Til!" Alan answered, innocently confused.

"One or Two, Alan?"

"Oh, sorry. Line one."

"We need to get these lights fixed, Deputy. Call Harry over at the county building again. Tell him we have been waiting long enough." Til picked up the receiver and pressed the unlit button for line one. *Thank God we only have two lines.* He mumbled to himself.

"Good afternoon, Charlie. Do you have something for me already?"

"I'm afraid I don't have much, Til. This boy is not talking to me."

"Funny thing about the dead, Charlie, they kind of keep to themselves."

"Well that's not really true at all, Til, I've had a good number of dead folks tell me all kinds of things. I just need to ask the right questions. Heck, I'll bet you I can get more answers from the dead than you can most live folks. Especially 'round here!"

"You may be right about that, Charlie," Til said as he looked over at his deputy. "You may be right. So now, what do we do now?"

"We keep looking. There were no scars or tattoos but he has had some unusual dental work done. It doesn't look like anything I've seen before."

"Different how, Charlie?"

"Do you remember that guy out on highway 16 that tried to fix his own roof a couple years back? It looked like a jigsaw puzzle when none of the pieces are in the right place?"

"Oh shit yeah! Funny as all get out! Didn't get a permit for it either! That cost him an extra fifty dollars."

"I guess that's twice what he spent on the entire roof judging from the looks of it," Doc replied. "Anyway, this guy's dental work likes a lot like that. There don't appear to be any rhyme nor reason to it. Sort of like he went to an auto repair shop to have his teeth fixed."

"So what do you make of that?" Til followed."

"I'm guessing it means we're not going to ID this guy by his dental records, but I'll run him through the system anyway. I'm also going to do some head to toe x-rays to see if he's had any broken bones or diseases he's been treated for. Can't find an exact cause of death either, no definitive trauma, except what he got postmortem rolling around in the river. No ligature marks. Hopefully, the lab can tell us something. I put a rush on the results but you know how that goes.

"That sounds like a plan, Doc. Oh! What about fingerprints?"

"I'm afraid the fish and turtles got them, Til."

"They can do that?"

"Sure, especially once the body's been marinating in that warm water. I'll keep plugging along. Sooner or later I'll ask the right question."

"Good luck, Doc. Keep me informed now."

"You know I will, Til. Hey, there's a funny little rhyme."

The call disconnected. "Really? The telephone line, Alan? Shit. Here's what we're gonna do Alan. I want you to get the boat and go upriver from where we found the body and try to find out where it entered. Look for footprints, tire tracks and whatever else you can think of. Check both shores now! Just because he was found on the north side he could still very well have entered from the south. You got all that?"

"Yes, Sheriff."

"Call me if you find anything and be sure to take the camera with you."

"Yes, Sheriff."

Chapter 19

High Falls, NY

They had just finished lunch at Webster's place and were getting ready to reconvene. The Sun was high overhead now with its aim directed fully toward the back patio. They decided to stay indoors with the AC on and the shades partially drawn.

They were set up in the living room now where the seating was more comfortable. Greg was standing to the side of the whiteboard with a marker in his hand. The graph in front of him was set up just as Charis had requested.

"I think there are two cases we should add to our list," he opened. "One and probably both won't correlate with the others but you never know. The first is the young girl found dead at lock 12 a few days ago. I know it's not on your list, Charis, and I'm sure there must be reasons for that. However, as far as I am aware, the body has not been identified which places it squarely in our wheelhouse."

"I'm not aware of it Greg which means the FBI may not be aware of it. Sometimes, it takes a while. Much of it relies on the local authorities' procedures. The FBI is often an unwanted presence so they wait until they reach a dead end. We also have a reputation for taking control of the situation and for not being fun to be around."

"I can vouch for that," Trey chimed in, sorry he couldn't reel his words back in. "What I mean is, I have heard stories to that effect."

"Nice try, Trey! Greg said through laughter. "Whatever the reasons are, I think we should get ourselves involved somehow. What about the State Police, Trey?"

"Let me see what I can find out."

The doorbell rang. "And this would be the second item. This is not linked in any way that I can see but we did say that we would help Ethan find out what happened to Lilijac so I asked him to join us. Greg walked to the front door and let Ethan in. "We were just talking about you, come on in."

Ethan greeted everyone and claimed a seat on the sofa between Mary and Charis.

"Brownnoser," Greg said, looking straight at Ethan.

"What? It was the only seat open!"

"Whatever," Greg said and moved on. "So, our list of four has grown to six. I suggest we look at one thru five as connected and number six as being isolated from the others."

"I appreciate all of you volunteering to make some sense of Lilijac's disappearance but it shouldn't hold the same importance as the other cases."

"Well if you help us with these other cases and we help you with yours, we should be able to solve them all in the same amount of time. Does that sound fair?" Charis asked.

"That does sound fair, although you all have more experience at this than I do. In fact, I don't have any." Ethan answered.

"Neither do I," said Mary. In fact, what we have found is that our combined effectiveness is far greater than the sum of our parts."

"That is very true," added Trey. "As professionals, we can often be blinded by our hyper focused approach. We should never assume to know everything about solving crime."

"Greg could be the poster boy for that statement," Charis said. "When I first met him, it was difficult for me to be open to the view of a non-law enforcement individual. But his intuitiveness and circular way of thinking not only impressed me, but also made me a better agent. Sure, he acts like a four year old at times but the man knows how to figure things out."

"Thanks, I think, Charis. Ethan I'm sure you know from working with me that I value everyone's opinion. I won't always agree with it but I never think it is unimportant. Every time we really listen to each other, we can find something of value, even if it just forces us to re-think what we believe to be true. The worst that can happen in we check ourselves and come back to the same conclusion. So what do you say? Are you onboard?"

"I am definitely onboard. Where do I begin?"

"The same place as the rest of us. Let's go through each case and find the next steps. We will assign the steps to one or more of ourselves and establish times to check back. We will not all be able to meet in person each time so we will need a way to coordinate and communicate our progress. I suggest that Ethan and I handle that part of it. We can set up a spreadsheet file and use our personal email accounts to connect. That way, there is no conflict of interest with the FBI, NY State Police, or the hospital. Sound Okay?"

"Yes," said Charis.

"Perfect," replied Trey.

"Good." Greg said. Keep in mind that we have others who can help. John and Sara, Richard and Marilyn, Bill Dillon, Lacey Meadows, Priscilla and Charles Chalmers, and my son Jack. They are capable thinkers and are no strangers to dangers. They have lived through something like this on a personal level. I have no wish to subject them to harm again but I value their input. They will be there if we need them. Hey Charis, is that safehouse down the road still available?"

"I'm sorry, what safehouse?" Charis asked.

"You know, the FBI safehouse?"

"I'm sorry, Greg, I don't know what you're talking about."

"What do you mean? You took us all there during the last adventure!" Greg exclaimed.

"I'm sorry, Greg I don't know what you're referring to. Come closer, Greg."

Greg moved closer to where Charis was sitting. "Come on, Charis, I know you remember."

"Come closer, Greg." He moved toward her. "Still closer," she said.

When he was right in front of her, she said, "now ask your question one more time, please."

"Is that safehouse..." she kicked him as hard as she could. Greg winced in pain and retreated quickly. The others were laughing hysterically.

"What was that for?" Greg cried.

"Are you kidding me, Greg? That is supposed to be secret!"
"But we were all there! It's not a secret to us!" He was still crying.

"And if you keep talking about it, it won't be a secret to anyone. You were supposed to forget about that the moment you left. Do you remember the little conversation we all had the first night there? Did you forget the part about never mentioning the place again?"

"I may have missed that." He was holding his shin.

"Well now, every time you think of mentioning that place, your leg is going to hurt and you will be reminded to keep quiet."

"Did you need to kick me so hard?"

"Apparently, I did. But you will get over it. You survived being blown up, you will survive this."

"I think it hurt less being blown up."

"That's because you were wrapped in a carpet. A brilliant move, I must say."

"You don't get to kick me and then complement me!"

"Sure I do. You're lucky I didn't flip you and knee you in the testicles. Now no more talking about the safehouse that doesn't exist." She waited a moment, "It was pretty damn nice though, right?"

"Lesson learned," Greg said, "where were we?"

"Let's dissect case one, shall we?"

Chapter 20

Montgomery County, NY

Sheriff Bentley was sitting in his office in Fultonville. It was situated in a rural area just off NY 5S. His office was near the back of the building with a nice view of not much. He was only a thousand feet from the Mohawk River but he couldn't see it. About a mile west is where Interstate 90 collapsed over the Schoharie Creek on April 5, 1987, A passenger car and a tractor trailer were passing over the bridge when it collapsed, falling about one hundred feet into the churning water below. Moments later, not realizing the bridge was gone, three more passenger vehicles drove into the abyss at sixty miles per hour or more.

The recent rain on top of the snow melt caused the flow of the Schoharie to increase more than thirteen fold in twenty-four hours. Ten people lost their lives that day and it took three weeks to find all of them. Judd Bentley had only been in the sheriff's office for two years at that time. Thirty years later, not a day went by that he didn't think about it. About how fragile life is. About how little control we have over some things.

The first thing on Judd's mind today was finding out why a young girl's body came ashore in his jurisdiction. It had been a few days since then and he hadn't received any news. He dialed the number for his contact at the state police, Lt. Cliff Alvord.

"State Police, Lieutenant Alvord."

"Cliff, Judd Bentley. Do you have a minute?"

"Of course, Judd. What can I do for you?"

"I know not much time has passed but I was wondering if you had any new information on our victim from lock twelve."

"We haven't received the results of the lab work yet, Judd, That could take several weeks."

"Yeah, I'm aware but I thought maybe the coroner had more to say since his preliminary report."

"I haven't seen anything come across my desk, Judd but feel free to give her a call."

"Who is her?"

"The new pathologist at the state lab. Her name is Amelia Lanford. They call her Al. Actually, they call her Doctor Al."

"Al for her initials?"

"You got it."

"She is a delight to speak with and not too hard to look at either. Give her a call."

"I will. Is she at the usual number?"

"That would be the one. Hey, Judd, have you found any surveillance footage yet?"

"Negative. We are still beating the bushes. Thanks for your help, Cliff."

Judd hung up and searched his directory for the state crime lab in Albany. He dialed the number and waited. It rang about six times before it went to an automated message telling him that all associates were busy at the moment and to please hold on. He held on. After what seemed like an hour, he was once again greeted by the auto attendant announcing that all associates were still busy helping other customers. He could either hold or leave a message by pressing the number three key. He decided to leave the message.

"This is Sheriff Judd Bentley in Montgomery County. Please have Doctor Lanford call me at her first convenience." He left the number and hung up. He didn't know if he was just getting older or if the world was really changing that much but he longed for the time when there was always someone available to answer the phone.

The signal from his radio jarred from his thoughts. "Montgomery base, Sheriff Bentley. Over."

"Judd, it's Lance. We're on the river behind the Dunkin Donuts on Riverside Drive. Something here you should see. Over"

"On my way. Out"

Judd grabbed his hat and was out the door. Less than five minutes later, he pulled into the parking lot of the Dunkin Donuts and drove around the back. He parked the cruiser out of the path of the drive thru, on the grass. The river was only about forty feet from where he sat. He could see Deputy Conover and officer Hastings on the shore near where they docked the boat. As he walked toward the water, Lance walked up to meet him.

"What do you have, Lance?"

"Tire tracks leading to the water, chief. They're deep enough to get a print for sure."

They both turned to walk to the water's edge.

"You picked this up from the boat?"

"Yes, sir. I'm not sure if it was our angle or the lighting was just right but the tracks just jumped out at us."

Bentley was staring at the tracks.

"I'm guessing that the fact the tracks were exactly perpendicular to the water helped. A few degrees left or right and you might have missed it."

"Have you notified anyone else, Lance?"

"Not yet, sir."

"Alright. There's a roll of DNC tape and some stakes in the truck of the cruiser. Why don't you and Hasting tape off the perimeter and I'll call the Trooper barracks. Careful not to step too close to the tracks. Give us a nice wide berth."

Conover called Hasting and they walked toward the cruiser. Sheriff Bentley called Cliff Alvord for the second time that morning.

Cliff wasn't in the office but they patched Judd through to his field phone. Cliff was only fifteen minutes out and on his way. Judd leaned against the hood of the cruiser and scanned the area for other clues. It looked like the tire tracks had to originate in the parking lot. Anywhere else would have left a much longer set of tracks. He looked at the exterior of the D.D. for any sign of security cameras. He left his perch on the hood of the car and began walking around the building. There was one camera on the front west corner under the eaves and another on the rear east corner that looked like it was pointed in the direction of the tracks.

He went through the front door and waited in a short line. There were only two employees that he could see. One was well behind the service counter in the food prep area and the other was taking orders and payment. When it was his turn, he ordered two coffees for his men and then asked to speak to the manager.

The young clerk by the name of Kaycee informed Bentley that the store manager was not on the premises. She did however have his contact information, which she kindly wrote down on the back of one of the Sheriff's cards. Judd asked her if she was aware of who may have made the tire tracks but she wasn't even aware that there were tire tracks.

Judd went back outside and delivered the coffees to his guys. The perimeter ribbon was properly in place. It was just moments later when Lt. Alvord pulled in.

"Good day, Sheriff."

"Hi, Cliff, thanks for coming right over. This way."

Cliff followed Judd around the side of the caution tape and toward the water's edge. Just before they reached the water, they ducked under the tape.

"So, you think is where they dropped the body, Judd?"

"It's anyone's guess right now, Cliff but it's more than we had an hour ago."

"True enough." Cliff removed a small digital camera from his pocket and began capturing photos of the tracks and the surrounding area. He took one shot of the tracks with the opposite edge of the river in the background so that he had a reference point. There weren't any houses directly across the way, just the county fairgrounds.

"Judd, have there been any evens happing at the fairgrounds in the last week or so?"

"I know they hosted some auto races and fireworks Saturday night but I'm not aware of anything earlier in the week. That doesn't mean there weren't people around. Maybe some grounds workers and such. I'll check it out."

"I'm going to give the state forensics team a shout if you don't mind Judd. They will make cement castings of the tracks and sweep the area for other evidence."

"I don't mind a bit, Cliff. We appreciate the assistance."

"You are welcome," Cliff said as he looked around. "Are those surveillance cameras on the building?"

"Yes. I already spoke with the staff inside. The manager's not here but I have his contact information and will give him a call. It looks like the camera in the rear faces the area of interest."

"Hopefully, it will show us something. Of course it could be just somebody dropping a boat in the water. It happens a lot around here."

"Anything is possible, Cliff, we work with what we have. What are the hours here?"

"They are open daily from 6:30am until 10:00pm, Judd replied, "so I'm guessing those tracks were left somewhere between 11:00pm and 5:30am."

"I would agree with you, Judd. I'm heading out to make that call. Do you mind having your boys hold down the fort until forensics shows up?"

"I think they can handle it. Thanks again, Cliff."

"Sure thing. Oh, did you get a chance to speak with Doctor Al?"

"No one answered the phone. I left a voicemail requesting a call back."

"Doesn't that piss you off!" Cliff said.

"You have no idea."

Chapter 21

Hilton Head Island, SC

It was almost three hours later that Dean heard the incoming mail signal on his tablet. It was from her. He quickly sent the file to his software and opened it. Following the same steps, he opened the layer feature and perused the thumbprint files. He clicked on layer four to enlarge it. It was a different colored background but the lettering was still pale white.

I do not know where I am. There are others. Many others.

Dean added a new layer five and formulated his next question.

Are the others Indonesian like you? Can you see outside?

Dean closed the file and sent it back with the heading: "I like it. Let's move forward. I will be ordering the next job soon."

Dean realized he was heading right back into the arena he had waited ten years to get out of. If there are indeed many other being kept against their will, he would need help from an anti-trafficking team. He could keep working with Kenny but he knew from experience that they had their hands full with just the metropolitan New York trafficking cases.

He had worked with other agencies over the years, usually at their request. Sometimes it was with U.S. Immigration and sometimes it was the FBI Task Force on Human Trafficking. He worked well with both. If this was truly emanating from another country, he would probably need to get an international agency involved.

He would need to wait for more information from Audra before he could determine which direction to take. The best he could do right now is keep ahead of her and be ready to submit new jobs when she was ready.

Referring to the text of his story, he laid out the next page complete with suggestions for the illustration.

Chapter 22

High Falls, NY

It was getting close to dinner time in High Falls. The group led by Greg had been brainstorming since early morning. Greg and Mary's son

Jack had joined the group just after the lunch break. Greg was at the whiteboard which was now full of headings, columns, and details in a variety of colors.

The six cases were listed in the first column. Greg was beginning to review what they had accomplished.

"Case number one is the child abduction in Bowling Green, Kentucky. The abduction took place at roughly 2:45 pm. on June 20th. It was reported at 3:10 pm when thirteen year old Samantha Wilson failed to get off the bus. Samantha's mother was waiting at the bus stop so the theory is that she either did not get on the bus after school or she got off at a previous stop. Charis, you decided to lead this case since you have the background. Trey will be your backup. Charis, review with us what we know right now."

"We have learned through interviews with school staff and kids on the bus that Samantha never got on the bus that afternoon. We also know that Samantha was not in line for the bus so she didn't exit the school at that time. Her teachers claim that she was recorded as present for her first three classes. That last class discharged at 11:10am. Our guess is that she disappeared between the 11:10 and 11:13 bells. There would have been a lot of traffic and commotion at that time and she could have left the building without being noticed. We have yet to prove whether she left on her own or was forcefully taken. I will be going back there tomorrow to continue the investigation."

"Thanks Charis. What date should we put down for follow up?"

"Put me down for July 9th, Greg."

"Will you also be checking your dad's phone?"

"Yes. Thanks for reminding me."

"Thank you Charis for kicking me."

"Time to move on, Greg," she replied.

"Alright," Greg continued, case number two. An unidentified teenage body found in Crystal City, Missouri on Friday, June 3. The victim is estimated to be a male between the ages of fourteen and eighteen. No official cause of death has been determined. The body was found in a river and is estimated to have been in the water for several days. They could not obtain a useful fingerprint. There are trying to compare dental records and they are awaiting DNA analysis.

"This one is assigned to Trey and Ethan. Trey will make any initial contact with authorities and Ethan will perform whatever legwork that Trey assigns. In addition, Ethan will try to find Lilijac's parents. See if they're still around and if so, what they are up to. We may try to approach them again. Perhaps time has softened them. Let's have a follow up by July 11th. Does that sound okay?"

Trey and Ethan both nodded their agreement.

"Moving on. Case three is an unidentified adult body, female found in a riverbed again this time in McMinnville, Tennessee on May 31st. Estimated to be between the ages of forty-five and fifty-five. No scars or tattoos and no reports of missing persons matching her description. Charis will notify local officials that she will be having assistants. Mary and I will take this one. We will also report back on July 11th."

"Case number four is also an unidentified body. This time it is a female estimated to be twenty to twenty-six years old. This young lady was found in Custer, South Dakota on June 3rd. Can anyone guess where? You got it. In a river. Again she was there for several day or at least in water for several days before she was discovered. We know this because of the condition of the body. No ID, no marks, scars, or tattoos. Police are trying to make a connection by dental records and DNA."

"Charis will make the initial contact and request their cooperation. Ethan will join her on this case. How does July 11th work for this one?"

All agreed. Greg was at the bottom of the board.

"Case number six. The lock 12 victim. Right in our back yard. Female, age looks to be early to mid-twenties. The police haven't released much information but the case is only a few days old. The only thing they mentioned besides the fact that she had zero ID, is she wore a medical alert bracelet. It appears the young woman was diabetic."

"Trey will open the doors with the Montgomery County Sheriff's office and with the state police. Mary, Jack, and I will be his soldiers. We will report back by July 11th. Have I missed anything?" No one spoke up. "Alright then. Ethan and I will work on this tomorrow and have it e-mailed to you by the end of the day."

"Allow me to thank all of you. This is voluntary work for all of us and we should keep in mind what our priorities are. First and foremost is to find out who is harassing Charis. Secondly, to see if we can find out what happened to Lilijac. The others fall into the good Samaritan category. We will do what we can to find a common thread. All they have in common now is that they are unknown, no one is looking for them, and they were found in water. When I say that aloud, it seems like more than it should."

"Now, everyone grab your coats because I am taking you all out for dinner!

"Greg, we have two other children," Mary said.

"They can come too!" he replied.

"Greg, it's like eight-five degrees out there," Charis added.

"Okay, so what?" Greg said.

"We don't need coats, Dad," Jack added.

"Right. That's just an expression. Haven't you ever heard it?"

"Many times, Greg," Trey answered, "always when it's cold outside."

"Alright, ball-busters! No dessert!"

Chapter 23

July 6, 2016
Quicksburg, VA

Doc Flanders was up early. He had loaded the young man's body into the hearse, which in this case was a twelve year old retired Cadillac ambulance. Bright yellow and white. The name decals were removed and the emergency lights had been deactivated. It didn't have many miles though and it ran like a top.

He was on his way to Shenandoah Memorial Hospital in Woodstock, about a twenty mile drive north along I-81. He had called ahead to make sure they had a technologist available to take some radiographs. He knew from previous experience that not all Radiologic Technologists were made equal. Not many of them were cut out to spend an hour or two with a cadaver. Especially one that was dragged out of a river after soaking for a hot week.

Doc didn't ordinarily require post-mortem x-rays but he had nothing else to go on. He was holding off on opening the guy up until the x-rays were taken. Removing the internal organs can distort the images, decreasing the value. He cleaned the outside of the corpse the best he could and gave it a good going over with spray deodorizer. He even added a butt plug to prevent seepage.

He was assured by the department manager that someone would be available but the earlier they got there, the better it would be. He was also advised to use the staff entrance thereby avoiding the waiting room. He guessed no one would want to go next after seeing somebody come out in a body bag.

He started the hearse about twenty minutes before moving the body from the cooler to the car. It took a good while for that bloated vehicle to cool down on a normal day and today was not going to be normal. The weatherman predicted the temperature would get up around a hundred by 2pm with possible thunderstorms in the early evening. He did not want to have to drag his client through a downpour.

He believed he was in good shape. He was on the road before seven o'clock and he was making good time. The temp in the car was comfortable and outside was a balmy eight-six. The car didn't have a radio so he pretty much talked to himself most of the way there. But before he knew it, he had arrived. He pulled up to the emergency entrance to unload. He had an acquaintance who worked in the ER who came out to give him a hand.

"Morning, Doc! You're up early."

"So are you Fred, no rest for the wicked."

"You got that right. So what did you bring us today?"

"I'm sure you heard about this on the news, Fred. This is the young man they pulled from the river down in Quicksburg a couple days ago."

"You're right, I did hear about that. No ID on him. Did you get a fix on him yet?"

"Not yet, I'm afraid. That's why we're here. To see if he can tell us something from the inside."

"Gonna do a CT scan, Doc?"

"Not me, Fred. I don't know how to interpret those things. A few simple x-rays should do it."

"I hear you Doc. Come on, I'll help you wheel him down to Medical Imaging."

"You're a good man, Fred. I don't care what they say about you."

"Don't believe everything you hear, Doc."

"I hear you, Fred."

Doc and Fred wheeled the cart down the employee corridor to the imaging department where there were a couple of very reluctant techs waiting to do their thing.

"Hey kids," Doc said, "I appreciate y'all taking care of this. I don't need too much. AP views head to toe and a lateral skull. How long you think that will take?"

"That depends on how many times we need to stop to throw up," one of the tech's joked. "Give us thirty five to forty minutes, Doc."

"Heck, that's nothing, fellas. I'll wait by the film processor and take a look as the come out."

"Where have you been, Doc, off the planet? We haven't used film for like five years now. Everything's digital now."

"I read about that a while back. I guess I was thinking we were a little behind the rest of the world down here in Shenandoah County."

"We are. The rest of the world has been digital for twice as long."

"Come with us. We'll set you up in front of a computer screen and you can view them as we take them."

"That sounds real good, but how am I gonna look at them back at the office?"

"We can give you a disk that you can load on your computer."

"That ain't gonna work fellas, can you make me a hard copy?"

"Sure we can, Doc. Anything you need."

"So just to be sure I've got this right, you're gonna make digital images and then convert them into regular film for me."

"That's exactly right, Doc."

"And that's progress?"

The boys just looked at each other and began wheeling the cart toward a procedure room. One of them looked back.

"Coming old man?"

"Right behind you!" Doc exclaimed and hurried to catch up.

Chapter 24

Hilton Head Island, SC

"Good morning, Dear." Shelly greeted her husband, "you were up really late last night. Is it the writing?"

"Good morning, Shelly," Dean said as he took the cup of tea from her. "Thank you. I'm just trying to figure how all of this illustrating works. Sometimes I will get a response just minutes after I send a request and other times, it takes hours. I was expecting something yesterday afternoon and when it didn't arrive by bedtime, I became a little worried."

Dean was reluctant to share the whole story with Shelly for several reasons. While he knew she would understand and be sympathetic toward the girl, she would also think that he was stuck in his previous life. Better for her to think he was having trouble adjusting to his new interest.

"What kind of turn around do they advertise?" she asked.

"Up to twenty-four hours for the single line drawing and forty-eight more for the full colorized version. Modifications requests can take an additional twenty-four."

"And are they keeping their end of the bargain?"

"Yes. I guess she just spoiled me with the first couple of correspondences."

"Perhaps she has had an influx of requests lately. I'm sure she will catch up.."

"I'm sure you're right, Shell. Patience was never my strong suit."

"Give yourself time to adjust. Perhaps a walk along the beach this morning will calm you down. I can put your tea in a travel mug for you to take with you. I would join you but I have plans with Anna."

"Shopping?"

"If you must know, I am driving her to a medical appointment in Bluffton."

"I'm sorry, is everything okay?" His tone changed from challenging to compassionate."

"Nothing that a little shopping after the appointment won't cure."

"Not fair," Dean said.

"Isn't it Kenny who always said, *don't ask the question if you can't handle the answer?*"

"Yes, good old Kenny," he answered.

"Here is your walkabout tea. Breathe deeply and enjoy your stroll!"

Shelly gave him a kiss and headed for the door. Dean was putting his second beach shoe on and was ready to follow her when he heard his tablet calling him. He dropped his second shoe and hobbled back to the living room where the tablet rested on the coffee table. He hurriedly open it, entered his password, and opened his mail. Sure enough, it was from Audra.

Dean downloaded the file to his software and opened the layers. He clicked on layer four not even bothering to look at the illustration. The usual pastel background and white lettering caused his heart to flutter a little just like it used to when he was on the heels of a perpetrator. He enlarged the image.

There are no windows to the outside. I am taken outdoors about once each week for thirty minutes. Indonesian? I think I am American. Most of the others are too.

American? Dean pondered. That explains the smooth English but where are they? Was he looking at Americans held captive at home or abroad? He needed something solid that would define that, but what? He knew that the FBI handled both domestic and foreign cases. He could reach out to one of the several agents he worked with in the past but he afraid to get others involved. Would that further endanger Audra?

He decided he would try a few more hidden messages before sharing the case. They seemed to be getting away with their game so far. Dean added a new layer five and penned a new inquiry.

Is Audra your real name? What do you see when you go outside? How long have you been there? How old are you?

Dean sent his hidden response under the title: Can we soften the characters just a little? You're doing great!

He sent the email off not knowing when he would receive a response. He began working on the next installment of the story. At the rate he was going, he may need a few more stories. Within just a few minutes, he received another email. He was becoming very proficient at processing the files.

Audra is the only name I know. I think I have been here about ten years. I don't know my exact age. Maybe thirty? The outside is beautiful. Fresh air, blue sky, green hills, deep valleys.

It didn't sound like she was in the desert. Why wouldn't she know her age or if Audra was her real name? Was brainwashing part of the initiation? If she can see hills and valleys, why can't she run? She could be tethered somehow. He needed to keep pushing.

Dean created another job. A continuation of the story line, just a short paragraph to justify a new illustration. He sent off the request and waited for a response. It came almost immediately. It wasn't from Audra.

Chapter 25

Montgomery County, NY

Sheriff Bentley gave his boys their orders and drove his cruiser back to the station. He greeted the desk sergeant on duty, filled a cup halfway with coffee and walked back to his office. He sat in his chair and turned toward the window. The view hadn't changed. It was pretty enough with the nicely cut lawn and the thick trees. In the late autumn and winter he could see beyond the trees and had a view of RT. 5s and the hills on the other side.

He was just about to pick up the phone to call the manager of the Dunkin Donuts when an incoming call rang through.

"Sheriff Bentley."

"Hello, Sheriff, this is Doctor Lanford returning your call."

"Doctor Lanford, thank you for calling back."

"I'm sorry you didn't get through right away, that seems to be happening a lot lately and I can't tell you why. I don't know about you, but I really don't like playing phone tag."

"I am with you there, doctor, and thanks for the apology. That's something you rarely hear."

"You're welcome. Now how can I help you today, Sheriff?"

"I'm not sure you can, but I'm not known for my patient personality and sometimes I just need to do something. I know it's only been a few days but I'm really hungry for information on the body we drew out of the Mohawk. I have read your preliminary report and I guess I was hoping there might be a secondary."

"I understand your frustration Sheriff. Do you mind if I call you Judd? That whole Sheriff thing seems so impersonal on my part."

"Please do," Judd responded.

"Thank you. And you can call me Al."

"Paul Simon."

"Very good, Judd! Are you a fan?"

"Always. I was a little confused by the whole South America thing but I worked through it and now I enjoy it. So I shall call you Al."

"Excellent. Glad we got that out of the way. Let me share what we have. Outwardly, the body did not show signs of recent traumatic injury aside from the ligature marks on the upper thighs. There was no evidence of suffocation by strangulation or other means. There was no evidence of head trauma."

"Internal examination showed a variety of inflammation. This type of inflammation can be caused by any number of pathological processes such as liver disease and certain types of cancers. So we now know that this person died from the inside out."

"Can resting in warm water cause that type of inflammation?" Judd asked.

"Not really. Once the body dies, the metabolic processes slow down and then stop. We know that this person didn't drown because of the absence of water in the lungs. She was dead prior to ending up in the water.

Unless there is some opening into the thoracic or abdominal cavity, what is inside stays inside and outside elements stay out. That can change if the degree of decay creates openings but that wasn't the case here."

"Probably a dumb question," Judd said.

"Not at all!" she answered, "I want to give you the junior high school standard response of *there are no stupid questions* but I've been around long enough to know that it is not true. I've heard some really dumb questions but yours is not one of them."

"I think what we have here is exposure to a chemical or chemicals that were probably ingested. I have a few guesses as to what they may be but I would rather wait until I have all the toxicology tests back rather than guess. Can you hold on a few more days? I promise to contact you just as soon as I have the results. If you find yourself needing to talk before then, please feel free to call me. In fact, I will give you my private mobile number so that you can bypass the main desk."

"Just when I was giving up on society's desire to offer excellent service, you come along and convince me that I may be wrong. Thank you for restoring my hope for our future."

"Thank you, Judd. It was a pleasure speaking with you! We will talk again soon."

Judd hung up the phone. He couldn't remember the last conversation he had that made him feel inspired. He pulled out the card with the DD manager's information on it and dialed the number.

"Hello."

"Hi, is this Joe Stern?"

"Yes, what can I do for you?"

"Mr. Stern, I'm Sheriff Bentley. We were investigating a possible crime scene today near your store on Riverside Drive and I was given your number by Kaycee."

"Crime scene? At my store?"

"No sir," I said near your store. Just west of your parking lot, we found a set of tire tracks which may be linked to a crime. The reason I'm calling is I would like to have a look at your surveillance footage for the last few days. Would that be possible?"

"Of course, Sheriff. I will be at the store tomorrow morning if that works for you."

"That would be fine. What time is good for you?"

"I will be in around 6:00am and will probably stay until 9:30 or 10:00."

"I will meet you there at eight. I appreciate your cooperation, Joe."

"No trouble Sheriff. See you in the morning."

Judd didn't know what he did to deserve this day and he wasn't going to ask.

Chapter 26

High Falls, NY

Greg arrived at the hospital before 7:30 for an 8:00 am meeting. The long weekend left him plenty of things to catch up on but all in all, it seemed to be a fairly calm holiday from the healthcare perspective. He plugged along, reading his email and making follow up phone calls. The morning flew by.

He was meeting Ethan for lunch to compile their notes from the weekend meetings and to plan their next moves. As expected, Ethan showed up five minutes early. Greg could hear him talking to Kathy in the reception area. As he listened to their conversation, Greg flashed back to his first visit to High Falls Hospital.

Kathy was the first person he met. She was the administrative assistant to Alex Winfield the CEO. Greg was sent there to do a routine investigation into a sudden, unobserved death. Something that happened with relative frequency in hospitals. He thought he could review the case, draw a sensible conclusion and be home before dinner. He could never imagine that a short time later he would be asked to take over as CEO.

Ethan reminded Greg of himself. He was confident and charismatic. There was no doubt in Greg's mind that Ethan would achieve any goals that he set for himself. He could even envision him taking Greg's position when he was done with it.

Greg walked out to the reception area to rescue Ethan. Not that he really needed rescuing but Greg remembered how hard Kathy came after him all those years ago and how close he came to giving in. Kathy was confused and under an extreme amount of pressure then. Once the ordeal ended, she became a different person. Greg always knew she was worth her weight in gold as an assistant.

"I see you're right on time, Ethan. Kathy, would you ask dietary to send over a couple sandwiches, please. Would you like anything in particular, Ethan?"

"Whatever you're having is fine," he replied.

"Okay, Kathy, two liver and onion sandwiches."

Greg could see the color draining from Ethan's face.

"Just kidding, Ethan. How about turkey, cheese, lettuce and tomato? I'll have mine on wheat bread, no mayo."

"That sounds much better, Mr. Webster. Thank you."

"I will take care of that right away, sir." Kathy said.

"Excellent. I think we will sit in the conference room today. Let's get started young man while we wait for our lunch."

Greg walked into the conference room and Ethan followed. Greg sat at the head of the table and Ethan took the first chair to his left. There was a pitcher of water and glasses on a silver platter in the center of the table. Greg poured them each a glass.

"I think we should begin talking about our assigned cases and save the paperwork part for after lunch," Greg began.

"That would be fine, Greg. I don't need to be back in the department until two o'clock."

"Perfect!" Greg opened his notebook. "Okay, it looks like we have case number five which is finding out what happened to Lilijac MacNamara after she was discharged from St. Luke's Hospital in Utica. If I recall you're story correctly, she was discharged two days prior to your meeting with her father."

"That's correct. After that, I checked local cemeteries, hospitals, rehab centers and even nursing homes. No one had heard of her."

"I am going to make a request for her discharge summary from St. Luke's," Greg replied. "I know a few people over there who may be able to help us. If that fails, we may be able to have Trey help us from a law enforcement angle. I believe you also said you haven't had any further contact with her parents."

"Also correct," Ethan said. "I called and I dropped by the house but no one ever responded."

"You said that she attended church with her parents. Do you know what church that was? My thinking is this, maybe we can track her parents down through the church."

"I don't remember the name but I know it was south of here. Someplace pretty rural. Hold on.."

Ethan retrieved his cell phone from his pocket and opened the map app. He selected his current location and the map zeroed in on it. He widened the view until he could see a thirty mile circumference with High Falls in the center.

"Here, she said it was between Jordanville and Richfield Springs. Somewhere just off Rt. 167."

He left the map app and surfed the web for churches near Jordanville. To his amazement, one church was listed but it was Russian Orthodox. He did the same thing for Richfield Springs and found about twelve more.

"The only thing listed near Jordanville is a Russian Orthodox Monastery. Richfield Springs has a dozen churches including Mennonite, Presbyterian, Catholic and the rest are Fundamentalist Christian and one non-denominational."

"Do the names of any of them sound familiar?" Greg asked.

"No. I'm sure she said it was north of Richfield Springs, close to Jordanville. But there is nothing on the map and no listings on the internet."

"Did Lilijac ever mention any friends or classmates that went to the same church?"

"No," Ethan replied, "in fact, she said she didn't know another soul there."

"Where did Lilijac live, Ethan?"

"She lived a couple miles from me on RT. 144."

Greg picked up the phone in the conference room. "Kathy, would you please connect me with Lacey Meadows at the county records department. If you reach her, please transfer the call here. Thank you."

"An old friend of mine," Greg said. Did you meet her at the party?"

"Not that I'm aware of."

"She would have been the woman in her forties walking around with a man almost twice her age."

"I did see them but I didn't get to meet them. Are they a couple?"

"They are. Bill was the head of security and maintenance here when I first visited. He is a good man and he was extremely helpful to me during our investigation. Lacey was one of the victims. She was the only one that survived. Years later, while we were investigating the university bombings, Bill and Richard worked together to help solve the case. Richard was retired by then and Bill had lost his wife so they both had time on their hands and I was able to convince them to work together.

"I thought there was a good chance they would kill each other but they both came out of it better then they went in. Bill and Lacey met right after that and really hit it off. I think it's more about friendship and companionship than romance but love is love. Anyway, Lacey is still working at the records department and she is always willing to lend a hand."

"It's hard for me to believe," Ethan exclaimed, "that both of those things happened to you. I mean, what are the odds?"

"I think both of those things happened because of me. The episodes would have happened either way but they happened to me because I chose to get involved. The first time, I couldn't imagine that I would be in any danger. The second time, everything was happening so far away from here that I didn't feel directly involved at all. Once it came to Syracuse, I knew that somehow I was deeply involved without even knowing it."

"It's not that I'm looking for things like this, I just can't hear about them and do nothing. Some people volunteer, others contribute financially to causes and I try to figure things out."

"There are worse things you could be doing." Ethan said, "I admire you and I want to be involved."

Kathy opened the door. "I have Lacey Meadows on line one."

"Thank you, Kathy." Greg picked up the line. "Good afternoon, Lacey. How are you today?"

"I'm great, Greg. Nice party the other day. We are so happy you invited us!"

"Are you kidding? You and Bill are part of the team and we couldn't and wouldn't have done it without you. Lacey, If you don't mind I have Ethan Baylor in my office and I would like to place you on speaker."

"That would be fine, Greg."

"Are you there, Lacey?"

"Yes, I am. Hello Ethan. I'm sorry we didn't get the chance to chat at the party. I've heard so much about you."

"Thank you, Lacey, I am sorry as well. Hopefully soon," Ethan replied.

"What can I help you with today, gentlemen?"

"Lacey, I know you won't believe this but I'm conducting an informal investigation and as usual, I need your help."

"Well, first of all that is no surprise and secondly, I am always happy to assist you."

"That's very kind of you, Lacey. I was wondering if you could find out if Gloria and Alfred MacNamara still own the house out on Rt. 144.?"

"Do the know the house number?" Lacey inquired. Greg looked at Ethan.

"I'm not sure," Ethan replied but it was just down the road from my childhood house which was 3810."

"Okay, that will narrow it down. Let me check the map and pull the file." They could hear the clicks of her keyboard in the background. "It looks like we have a house at 4062 RT. 144 that was owned by the MacNamaras until about three years ago. They sold it to a couple with the last name of Hilton."

"Lacey, can you tell if the MacNamaras bought another house in the area?"

"Sure, let me check." Again the sound of the keyboard clicking away. "I don't see any new deeds filed with that name. That doesn't mean they're not still around. They could be renting or, they could have just moved to another county."

"Is there any way to tell if they're still alive?" Greg asked.

"I can check the death certificates for Herkimer County. If they died while they were living in the county, we should be able to find it. Hold on." A moment later she came back on the line. "I do not see one for Albert but it looks like Gloria passed away seven years ago."

Ethan entered the conversation again. "Lacey, would there be any forwarding address in any of your records for Alfred?"

"That's a good question, Ethan. If we needed to forward any records after the sale of the house, we would have requested a forwarding address. Let me have a look." A few minutes passed this time. "I have good news and bad news." The good news is you were right, we do have a forwarding address. The bad news is that it is a P.O. box."

"Well, that a start!" Ethan said.

"It's P.O. box 366, Richfield Springs, NY 13439."

"What else can I help you with?" Lacey asked.

"I think that's it for now. You have been a great help." Greg replied.

"Well, if you think of anything else, you just let me know."

"Actually, I just thought of something. Do you have a death certificate for Lillian Jacqueline MacNamara?" Ethan asked.

"Let's see," she said as her fingers went to work. "Nothing for her."

"Thank you, Lacey. We will be in touch soon. Oh and tell Bill we may need his help soon. We may be putting the band back together!"

"The Blues Brothers!" Lacey guessed.

"Good call, Lacey. Jake and Elwood ride again!"

"I will let him know. See ya, fellas."

The call was disconnected.

"She seems so nice. And very helpful."

"She is a miracle girl. She was so close to death and she pulled through. And she has never forgotten for a minute just how fortunate she is."

"Jake and Elwood huh?" Ethan said.

"Yeah, it was a movie from a long time ago."

"Oh, I know the movie. I just can't see you as Jake or Elwood."

"That's because I'm old now but back in the day.."

"Nope, I'm not buying it." Ethan remarked.

"Alright already," Greg said. Here is what I think we should do. I think it's time for a road trip. We will check out the post office and look for a church between Jordanville and Richfield Springs. What do you think?"

"How soon can we go?" Ethan asked excitedly.

"What time can you leave work today?" Greg asked.

"I can be ready by 3:30," he replied.

"Make it 3:45. Now, let's create this flow chart for the rest of our team."

Chapter 27

Quantico, VA

Charis returned to her office after the long weekend. She left High Falls at 5:00am to make the 6:30 flight out of Albany. Airtime to BWI was about an hour and a quarter which left her plenty of time to get her car out of the parking garage and drive to Quantico by 9:30.

Everything seemed to move along without a hitch. She didn't have time to swing by her apartment first but she had laundered a few things at Greg's house that made it doable.

During the flight, she had checked her email, updated her project list, and submitted it to her boss. So even though she was getting in a little later than she preferred, she was still ahead of schedule.

She booted her desktop computer, entered her credentials and created a to do list for the day. First on her list was to call her dad. She dialed his number.

"Good morning, sweetheart!"

"Good morning, Dad, how are you?"

"I'm fine. How was your trip up north?"

"It was great, Dad. I was around so many nice people all weekend and it was really refreshing to get away. I made some really good friends up there and it's such a beautiful part of the country. It's a much slower pace compared to here."

"Well, anything is slower than Washington!"

"That's true. Hey, did you mention to anyone that I would be traveling this past weekend?"

"Gee, I don't think so. The only people I was with were Danny and Skip. We met for lunch on Saturday. I guess I may have mentioned it but I don't remember a big conversation about it. Why do you ask?"

"Well, it's probably nothing and certainly nothing for you to worry about. Hey, I was thinking about coming by this week for a quick visit. I can't stay but I would like to see you for a couple hours. Would that work?"

"I would drop everything to spend some time with you. Just tell me when and I'll be available."

"How about tomorrow after work?"

"Sure. What time will you be getting here? Can you make it for dinner? I'll get takeout from Kwon's."

"I can most likely be there by 7:00. Is that too late?"

"No, seven would be perfect."

"Alright, Dad, I'll see you then."

"I look forward to it, sweetheart. Be safe."

"Okay, Dad. I love you."

"I love you too, Charis."

Charis felt good about that being off her list. It had been a while since she last visited her dad and while this wasn't the reason she was looking for, it was good enough.

She began her next task which was reviewing the child abduction case in Bowling Green. She had the transcripts from the local police, clips of news coverage from various TV stations and the interview she had conducted with the child's mother via telephone. She compiled everything together in one file and attached a confidentiality statement. Then she opened an email to Trey Lawrence. She was stepping a little out of bounds by sending it to his personal email account but they all agreed that was the best scenario.

"Good morning, Trey. As promised, I have enclosed the file we discussed. Any help you can provide is appreciated. I enjoyed seeing everyone this

weekend, especially those in our special group. We should have a name for our group, don't you think?" Have a good day! Charis."

She hit the send button and checked number two off her list. Next was a review of the case of the unidentified body in Custer, South Dakota. The FBI was not the lead agency on this one. The Custer Police Department was lead agency along with the Custer County Sheriff's Department and the South Dakota State Police.

She had a copy of the Sheriff's report along with the results of the autopsy. She had spoken once to the sheriff in charge immediately after she received notification. She hadn't received any follow up reports. She jotted down the sheriff's name and phone number on a piece of scrap paper, picked up the phone and then realized it was not even 7am in Custer. She thought about hanging up and decided to make the call anyway.

"Sheriff Moran."

"Good morning Sheriff, this is Special Agent Charis Andrews, FBI. I hope I didn't wake you."

"Maybe two hours ago, Special Agent but not this time of day," Moran replied.

"Excellent! I was wonder if you have any news about the unidentified vic from the river. I haven't seen anything come across my desk for a while."

"You know, I'm almost to the office. Can I give you a call in about an hour?"

"Of course, Sheriff, I'll be here. Thanks."

Charis was pleasantly surprised that the sheriff was awake and on the job so early. She was also confused that he was almost to the office yet she didn't hear any road noise.

Chapter 28

Custer County, SD
Sheriff Moran set his phone down on the bedside stand and rested his head back on the pillow.

"The FBI wants an update on the river case."

"I heard. What are you going to do?"

"What am I going to do? What are you going to do? Your department is lead on this."

Det. Doreen Hillabrandt turned on her side to face the sheriff. "I don't believe my department is going to do a whole lot about it. We will chase some obscure leads around for a while but we won't find any evidence. A body shows up in a river and nobody is looking for it. There aren't any identifying marks and all we can do is try to match a dental record or wait for DNA. Who gives a shit?"

"What if they send someone out here? What if they send Agent Andrews out here to nose around?" He asked.

"Then we may have to find out just how special Agent Andrews is."

"What do you mean by that?"

"You know, you may have to use your manly charm to lure her into our bed. It's been a while since we've had a good threesome.

"Doreen, it was just a few weeks ago."

"You mean that whore you arrested? That was way too easy and she was fair at best. I'm ready for someone that hasn't ever been with another women. Someone I can teach even if it does mean we have to rough her up a bit."

"And you want it to be an FBI agent? Do you know how crazy that sounds? How much hell you would bring down on us?"

"Hey!" Doreen shouted, "you're the one that pursued me, remember? You're the one that had to have me. You're the one that wanted to add a little variety to the bedroom. Well, bringing home bar room drunks and hookers isn't enough for me now. If you want out, you just say so. You can run back home to your frigid little wife any time you want. I won't have any problem getting one or more of your deputies to take your place."

"You're talking nonsense now, Doreen. You're going to extremes. Why can't we just go after a woman who is not law enforcement? Why do we have to take that risk?"

Doreen threw her naked body on top of his, her breasts just inches from his face.

"Because the higher the risk, the greater the reward."

She reached between her legs and grabbed him and stroked him until he was hard. When he tried to enter her, she jumped off.

"You had better get going, Sheriff, you have to give that nice FBI lady an update. Don't keep her waiting."

Lester Moran picked up his uniform and walked to the bathroom. He cursed himself for getting involved with this woman but he knew he couldn't help it. She brought excitement into his benign existence. And he knew he could take her at her word. She would have him replaced before sundown and he couldn't live with that.

When he was dressed, he opened the bathroom door and walked over to the bed. He bent over to kiss her and realized she was finishing by herself. He turned and walked out.

He made sure no one was looking before walking to his car. He didn't bring the patrol car home anymore, it would be too easily noticed if someone was driving by Doreen's place. So, every morning at 5:00am, he would drive his car to Doreen's and stay until after 7:30. He would then drive to the office where he would park his car.

When his wife inquired about the car situation, he told her the county had changed their policy and he was no longer allowed to keep it at home. It was also a way for him to make sure she wasn't following him. They only owned one car.

On the drive from Doreen's to the office, he was trying to create a story for the FBI. He would just tell her the truth. Sort of. He would say they didn't have any new leads. No one has come forward and so far the medical examiner hasn't found anything. Lester knew they haven't been looking very hard but Special Agent Andrews wouldn't know that. He figured they probably didn't care too much either. She just needed something to tell her boss.

He pulled into his parking place, shut off the car, grabbed his hat and proceeded to the building. The desk clerk greeted him and told him the medical examiner had called. The clerk handed him a note with the return number. Moran took the note and headed to his office.

He sat down, pulled a bottle of scotch out of the bottom drawer of his desk, took a long swallow, and placed the bottle back. He dialed the phone and it was answered immediately.

"Hello, Doctor Short here."

"Good morning, Doc you asked me to call?"

"I did indeed, Sheriff. I have some news about your victim. The lab results are back and there are some very interesting findings."

Moran didn't know whether to be excited that he would actually have something to report to the FBI or nervous that he could be incriminated.

"Terrific, Doc, what do you have?"

"I believe your victim was poisoned. We are not exactly sure of the chemical component just yet but I am certain that it was ingested. Secondly, this young woman who was approximately twenty-five years old, was recently pregnant."

Sheriff Moran's pulse quickened. He could feel a nervous sweat beading up at the top of his spine.

"How can you tell Doc? I mean, when you say recently, does that mean she was with child when she died?"

"No, she aborted the fetus sometime before her own death. My guess would be several days at most. We found placental tissue and fetal remnants in her uterus. I am sure that whatever poison she had in her system caused the spontaneous abortion. Someone this sick would probably be seeking medical care. She may not have known she was pregnant but she must have known she was sick."

"So you're saying we should check with local medical facilities?"

"That would seem like a good place to start. Once we know what substance we're dealing with, you may have other leads to chase. I will contact you as soon as we get the results. We should also have DNA results in another week or two."

"Hopefully, the DNA will tell us who she is," the sheriff stated.

"If we're lucky, Sheriff, it will also tell us who the father is. I've got to run now. We'll talk soon."

Chapter 29

July 7, 2016
Hilton Head Island, SC

Dean flopped down on the couch. The message he just received took his breath away momentarily. He was still clutching his tablet and looked at the message again. It wasn't from Audra and it wasn't hidden within a picture. It was on a chat page.

Dear customer, we thank you for using our site and we hope the work we provide is exceeding your expectations. We are sorry to say that we cannot continue to accept your project as individual requests. Customarily, once you have sampled our work, we would expect you to submit the entire project at one time. This allows better use of the artists time and also saves you money.

Please submit the remainder of your project so that the artist can provide a final project cost. Once we receive payment in full, your artist will turn your project around in four days. Should you require changes, you will have an opportunity to submit those all at once.

Again, we thank you for using ArtJobDepot for your project.
Management.

Dean began to play out all the possible ramifications of this event. He wasn't sure if this meant they were busted or was it simply routine procedure. He did remember that the costs were broken down by the image but he didn't remember if there was a package deal.

He went back to the company's home page and carefully browsed through the many illustrators. All of them listed *as low as* pricing per image. He also noticed that a subscriber could in fact ask for an estimate for a complete job when the project involved multiple images.

He selected Audra's site but he didn't find the same wording. Maybe he was reading too much into this. He wondered what would happen if he tried to contact Audra directly. He could try but he didn't want to endanger her any more than she already was.

He didn't have many options. He decided he would just ask a simple question without sending an image. So, he opened Audra's page, clicked on *Contact this artist,* and typed this note.

"Audra, what would be the price for the remaining ten illustrations?"

Within seconds, he received a response.

We will discuss this with the artist and get back to you shortly. Thank you. Management.

Audra was taken out of the loop. He had reached the end of what he could do by himself. If a response came back with a package price, he would pay the fee and see what happens but he had to put plan B in motion now. He picked up his notepad, turned to a blank page and began to list his prior contacts.

Chapter 30

Quantico/McMInnville, TN

While Charis was waiting for a call back from Sheriff Moran in South Dakota, She decided to make contact with Martin Ballard in McMinnville, Tennessee to grease the skids for Mary and Greg.

Martin carried the title of detective but Charis was well aware that in small towns across the country, law enforcement often embellished their roles. It was likely that Detective Ballard was also Chief Ballard and most probably, Officer Ballard. When he personally answered the call, she mentally added clerk to his resume.

"Detective Ballard, this is Special Agent Andrews. How have you been?"

"Hello, Special Agent Andrews, I have been well, thank you. And how about you?"

"Keeping busy. Hey, anything new on the river body case?"

"In fact, there is. We just received the information recently so I haven't had time to relay it. The medical examiner filed a revised report of his findings based on lab results that came in after he completed the autopsy."

"That's usually how it works, detective. What did they find?"

"They believe the adult female victim died from ingestion of poison. That substantiates the M.E.'s finding at autopsy. There was massive organ involvement, inflammation is how he stated it. The lab also reported the presence of calcium carbonate in the lung tissue."

"Calcium carbonate is chalk, right? Charis thought aloud.

"I'm no chemist, Agent, but I think you're correct."

"Do you mine calcium carbonate in your neck of the woods?"

"I don't know of any plants nearby," he replied.

"Detective Ballard, I need you to fax me everything you have on the case. I'm adding a couple assistants to my team just to focus on your case. Their names are Greg and Mary Webster. They are consultants with the FBI and I would appreciate any help and cooperation you can afford them."

"That sounds fine, Agent Andrews."

"Besides the pathology and lab reports, have you made any progress with the investigation? Any leads, surveillance video, eyewitnesses etc.?"

"Nothing, I'm afraid."

"Have you been able to determine where the body entered the water?"

"No, we followed the roads nearest the river on both shores for a few miles upstream but didn't find anything."

"Is the river large enough to accommodate a flat bottom boat?"

"I'm sure it is."

"Have you tried looking from the river towards shore."

"Our department doesn't have a flat bottomed boat."

"Alright Detective Ballard, I'm going to contact an FBI field office near you and have them search the water for some clues. I'll put you down as the contact."

"Do you really think that's necessary, Agent? I mean no one has reported her missing and no one has come looking for her. It seems like a waste of resources at this point."

"Detective, a human body has washed up on shore in your jurisdiction. You now have evidence that the woman was poisoned. Maybe her family doesn't know she's missing yet. Perhaps she lived alone. She may well be someone's mother, daughter, sister, or grandmother, and even if she's not, a crime was committed and we will solve it. Now, do your job! I expect that fax in the next fifteen minutes."

Charis hung up the phone. She could feel her blood pressure climbing. *It was less stressful being shot at than dealing with an incompetent asshole*, she thought.

She sent Mary and Greg a text informing them that she had made contact and forwarded the name and number. She also told them she would send over the updated file shortly.

She looked down the rest of her list. She needed to be out of here by noon if she was going to catch her flight to Bowling Green. There were three more things on her list and one of those was dependent on the return call from Sheriff Moran in Custer County.

She went back to check her email while she waited. He had ten more minutes or she was going to call him back at which time her blood pressure would go even higher.

There were several internal communications and just two external ones. The first external email was from dballard@mcminnvillepd. She opened it and found the attached files which included the new report from the M.E. She copied the file and embedded it in a new email to Greg and Mary.

The second note was from dmadris911@hcomm.net. She usually didn't open mail from addresses she didn't recognize. She was ready to delete it when her eyes went to the subject line again. *Do you remember me? I need your help. Possible MHT.*

She did remember him. They worked on a case a couple years back involving several teenage girls who had been taken from a catholic school in Mexico. Eight girls were taken across the border via a tunnel by a faction of Mina De Calcio cartel.

They made their way east to New York where the intent was to rent or sell them. The Human Trafficking Task Force in New York received an anonymous tip just a day before they were to arrive in the city. Detective Dean Madris contacted the FBI requesting help.

Charis was assigned as leader of the team of agents sent to New York to coordinate with Madris in setting up a sting. Madris was going undercover as a buyer. He played the part of a wealthy but under the radar business professional who was looking for ownership of a teen girl. He was mid-fifties and handsome, and he nailed the part perfectly.

She opened the email, read the details, and responded. Of course she would help. Details would be discussed later in the day. Right now, she was calling Sheriff Moran.

She dialed the number for the Custer County Sheriff's Department rather than the number she called earlier. She wanted to know if he was just avoiding her. If he was in the office and hadn't called back, she would be pissed.

"Sheriff Moran."

"Glad to see you made it to the office, Sheriff. I'm sure you were just about to dial my number so I thought I would save you the trouble. Do you have time to chat?"

"I am having a busy morning but I can take a few minutes."

"Look Lester, we are supposed to be kept abreast of what's going on with this case. That shouldn't require a call from me to get the information, but, here we are. So let's have it."

"I'm not in the mood to be pushed around today, Agent Andrews. Who do you think you are, to tell me how to handle my department?"

"You keep up with that attitude and I will become your worst nightmare. Let me tell you what happened to the last leader of a local law enforcement agency who refused to cooperate with an FBI investigation. He is now working for a funeral home. He didn't get unemployment, he didn't get early retirement, he lost his pension, his home, and his wife."

"Hey Lady, I was voted into this office by the public."

"And one call to the Custer County Board of Supervisors and you will be let go for dereliction of duty. You are supposed to be investigating a crime. You are partnering with the Custer Police Department and the FBI. You are not only letting down your voters and the people you're employed to protect, but your careless attitude is also a poor reflection on the rest of us."

"You know what Sheriff, forget about it. I'll get my information elsewhere.

Charis hung up the phone and started an email to Mary and Greg.

"There has been a snag making contact in Custer. It may not happen today. I'll you know for sure. Sit tight."

Charis looked at her notes from the case and found two other contacts to call. She took the next one on the list. Detective Doreen Hillabrandt. She had time for one more call and this was it. She dialed.

"Police Department, Coldwell."

"Officer Coldwell, Special Agent Andrews, FBI. I would like to speak with Detective Hillabrandt, please."

"Hold please."

"What in Hell was wrong with people today?" Charis asked herself.

"Agent Andrews, nice of you to call. How can I help you?"

"Detective, I was hoping you would have an update about the river case."

"Not much news, Agent, we have been following up a few leads but nothing has materialized. The sheriff's office has taken the lead on the case."

"No, they really haven't. I just spoke with the Sheriff and he has nothing, nor has he been doing anything. Have you been in touch with him?

Doreen found this question amusing and wanted to blurt out the truth just to piss her off. *"You might say that, in fact I held his dick in my hand this morning!"* She didn't vocalize the thought.

"No, I haven't spoken with him lately."

"I see. I guess I'll just make a trip out there myself and see what I can find. Let's say Friday afternoon, shall we? I will expect you and Sheriff Moran to clear your calendars for the weekend. Be prepared to move a few rocks to see what we can uncover. I'll see you both at 1:00pm."

Charis didn't wait for a response. She hung up and let her pressure climb once more. She created another email for Greg and Mary. She also remembered that she needed to call Dean Madris and that could not wait until tomorrow.

Greg and Mary,

"It looks like I'm going to make a trip to Custer later this week. I'm attaching the file but don't expect to find much. For some reason they are really dragging their feet out there. I'll be in touch."

Doreen immediately called Lester Moran.

"I don't know what you said but she's on her way. She arrives Friday afternoon. It should make for a fun weekend! Remind me to thank you later!"

Chapter 31

Quicksburg, VA

Doc Flanders was amazed by the technology. He wasn't comfortable with it, but truly amazed. He was sitting on a stool inside the control booth of the x-ray room. The techs were busy positioning the victim and changing the digital cassettes. They would come behind the booth to make the exposure and ten seconds later, the image was on the computer monitor in front of him.

The images could then be enlarged, lightened, darkened, zoomed in on and any number of other post-processing technical marvels. Not only was he impressed with the quality of the images, but he was also surprised at what they were demonstrating.

The extremities showed old, healed fractures of both humeri, wrists and both distal lower extremities. The ankles looked like they had been clubbed intentionally. There was no doubt in Doc's mind that this man had been abused as a child.

The skull was intact, the left side of the jaw had a healed fracture of the mandible and the teeth displayed a mish mash of decay, disease, and haphazard repair.

The chest demonstrated several old and a couple of recent rib fractures while the lungs were mildly radiopaque, consistent with long term inhalation of some particular substance.

The abdomen is what caught the doctor's attention the most. The entire small bowel and colon looked as though it was filled with barium. He was aware that it was not uncommon to find a similar condition in poor children in the Appalachia region of the US. The young without enough food would ingest the soil which was rich in barium sulfate. The inert properties of barium sulfate would not cause harm to the body unless it resulted in a blockage of the intestine.

When the radiographs had all been obtained, Doc and the boys wrapped the body back up and moved him to the cart. Wheeling him back to the ER entrance, one of the fellas said, "did you find what you were looking for, Doc?"

"I don't know that I was looking for anything in particular, but we sure found a lot. I thank you fellas an awful lot. I know that wasn't easy but the information you provided will help solve this case."

When they reached the exit, Doc shook hands with them both. Looking them in the eyes, in his most sincere voice he said, "boys, be good to each other and don't ever strike your children."

He wheeled the gurney outside where his buddy was waiting for him. As they loaded the body inside the bright yellow makeshift hearse his friend said, "are you okay, Doc?"

He patted his friend on the shoulder and replied. "I will be son, I will be."

Doc placed the envelope of radiographs on the passenger seat, buckled in and began his drive back to Quicksville. He now knew what specimens he would need to collect when he performed the autopsy.

Chapter 32

Hilton Head Island, SC/Quantico, VA

"Hello."

"Good morning, Dean, it's Charis Andrews."

"Hi, Charis, thanks for calling back. I didn't expect a response this quickly."

"Are you saying that I or the FBI are slow to respond?"

"Of course not, but I'm living in the south now and people only have two speeds, slow and stop!"

"In the south? When did that happen?"

"The minute I retired."

"Good for you! Are you a beachcomber now? The old guy with the Gilligan hat and 70 sunscreen carrying a metal detector?"

"I do not wear a Gilligan hat! I really enjoy the view and the sound of the ocean and I do try to walk on the beach each nice day but I'm not your typical retired person from up north."

"I believe you. So, if you're retired, why are you poking your nose around a possible MHT?"

"It wasn't by design, I assure you. I had this idea that I would try to write a children's book. I came up with a decent story and tried to find an illustrator. They all wanted a fortune and I wasn't prepared to drop that kind of coin on an idea that promises little or no return."

"An online search brought me to this website that coordinates independent artists with potential customers. The site seemed legit and the prices were much less than half of the other guys.' I found an artist profile I liked and requested one illustration."

"At the same time, I purchased a new tablet and a digital pen along with a digital software program. My hope was that I could learn to draw my own illustrations. Not easy! I did find out however that these digital drawings are done in layers like the cells in the old cartoons. When I received my first sketch, it contained seven layers. I separated them and found that the fourth layer contained a hidden message that could only be seen by taking the layers apart."

"It sounds complicated, Dean. You call this retirement?"

"It seemed better than joining a poker club at the time. Anyway, the message was *help me, please*. Once a cop, always a cop, right? So I copy the multilayer image and add a new layer five and I ask a few simple questions. We have now exchanged several notes and I got a few answers. I'll send you a summary of what I have so far. The thing is it sounds like there are many Americans being held against their will."

"Do you know where?" Charis asked.

"No, she only gets outside for a few minutes each week and whatever she is being held in has no windows. That will all be in the summary. The critical thing is my last note must have been intercepted. The last response I received was from management. I tried again and my message bounced right to management again."

"If what you're saying is true and what she is saying is true, this could be a huge case of human trafficking! We need to get other people involved."

"I know, I had Kenny from my office in New York do a little legwork but they couldn't find anything. I didn't want to get more people involved because I was afraid of exposing her to harm but now I think I may have done just that."

"Dean, I'm going to think about this for a minute and then put a proposed team together. I want you to be a silent part of that team. You can do all your tasks from home and your name won't be listed. I will just copy you on everything. Does that sound fair?"

"That sounds great, Charis, thank you!"

"Okay, get that summary off to me ASAP. I'll be back in touch in a day or two. I have some traveling to do but I'll keep working on this while I'm moving. It was good talking to you, Dean. By the way, what's the story about?"

"It's about an underprivileged girl who wants to become a cop."

"I like it already. I will be your first customer but I want it signed by the author!"

"It would be my pleasure. Be safe out there, Charis."

Charis ended the call. Her sixth sense was telling her that something weird was brewing. The way the day started would definitely support that feeling.

Chapter 33

High Falls, NY/Richfield Springs, NY/Jordanville, NY

Ethan was waiting outside Greg's office at 3:35pm. He knew he was early but he figured he could talk with Kathy until Greg was ready. He liked Kathy. She seemed very professional and reliable. The Physical Therapy Department did not have its own secretary, just a registration clerk. Whenever he needed something typed or mailed, or collated, he would ask for Kathy's help. She was always happy to comply.

Kathy seemed to be about Greg's age and she was very good looking. He had heard the rumors of her involvement with the Chief Financial Officer who killed those patients years ago. It was believed that her involvement was romantic in nature and that she had nothing to do with nor any knowledge of what transpired. The story was rarely talked about and never confirmed nor denied by those who would know.

It didn't matter now, many years had passed and Kathy was adored and respected by all who knew her. Ethan did feel sorry for her in the sense that she probably carried some guilt by association, at least for a while. She was not married and rumor suggests that she has never even dated since the event. He knew how that felt.

Greg's door opened at exactly 3:45.

"Are you ready young man?"

"Yes Sir!"

"Kathy, Ethan and I will be out of the office for the remainder of the day. We are heading south through some pretty rural areas so there may be times when we are not within range of a cell tower. If you need me and I don't answer, leave a message and I will return the call as soon as we are back in service. If something comes up that you can't handle, call Dr. Shand."

"Don't worry about a thing, Greg, I have it under control. Have a safe and fun trip guys!"

"Thank you," they said in unison.

"I'll drive," Greg said.

"Are you sure?" Ethan answered.

"Yes. Do you have a problem with that? Do you not trust my driving abilities?"

"It's really more about what kind of music you're going to subject me to."

"Not to worry, son, I thought we could just sing our own songs on the way. Who needs a radio, right?"

"Exactly what I was afraid of." Ethan mumbled under his breath.

"What's that?" Greg said.

"I said exactly, sir."

"Excellent! This should be fun!"

"Did you let Mrs. Webster know you were going to be late getting home?"

"I certainly did but thank you for thinking about that. Are you sure you wouldn't like to marry one of my daughters? You can have your pick. The younger ones would have to wait a while but you can stake your claim now."

"That's a very kind and generous offer sir, and any man would be lucky to have any one of them. Honestly, at this juncture of my life, I am not considering a relationship."

"Ah that old *are you married or happy* thing, right?"

"No sir. I think one can be, in fact, should be both married and happy. I'm just not ready to find out."

"You are a smart man, Ethan. What do you say we go directly to the post office in Richfield Springs first and then work or way back home through Jordanville? We should have plenty of daylight left."

"That sounds good to me, chief."

It was a pretty drive with little traffic once they left the boundary of High Falls. The road was winding and undulating but not severely so. It was a perfect summer afternoon. The sun was still high in the sky, with moderate temperature and low humidity. They passed plenty of farms and thousands of acres of both planted and undisturbed fields. The sweetcorn plants were about twenty inches tall, the grass was surrealistically green and the occasional solar farm and windmill stuck out like a sore thumb. They discussed how advancements in energy technology was a double edged sword.

They were on the road for about thirty minutes when they reached the peak of a hill and began their descent on the other side. All at once, seemingly directly in front of them, they could see several milk colored towers topped with shiny, golden onion domes.

"What is that?" Ethan asked. "It looks like India in the middle of nowhere."

Their view from the top of the hill was well above the height of the structures and each turn in the countryside exposed a new angle.

"I'm not sure," Greg answered. "Should we have a look?"

"Sure, if you can find the start of the yellow brick road!"

They continued along the tortuous path for another six or seven minutes. When they reached the bottom of the valley, they noticed a very small sign that proclaimed a Russian Orthodox Monastery and an arrow pointing to the left. They continued a thousand feet more and found themselves in front on what looked like a large classroom building on a college campus.

"Did you know this place was here?" Ethan asked Greg.

"I've never even heard of it," Greg responded. "It's amazing! You don't think this is the church Lilijac talked about, do you?"

"The description of the location seems right but I'm sure she said it was a fundamentalist church."

"Alright, then I say we leave this for another time and keep on the path to Richfield Springs."

"I agree," Ethan responded.

Greg kept driving and in another fifteen minutes they were driving down the main street of Richfield Springs. There was a school, several businesses and a small, quaint downtown. They parked in the lot of the post office, turned off the car and rested a minute.

"How do we do this? Ethan asked.

"Well, I'm not sure. I guess we tell them the information we were given by the Herkimer County records department including the PO Box number and ask if it's still rented by the same person. There can only be three answers: yes, no or I can't tell you. If it's a no, we are done. If it's yes, we ask a follow-up question although I don't know what that would be at the moment and if the answer is I can't tell you, we ask who can. Does that sound like a plan?"

"Yes," Ethan replied, "except for the middle part about the question we don't know."

"It will reveal itself to us at the right time," Greg responded.

The men opened their doors and exited the vehicle. They stretched their legs while looking up and down Main Street. After a moment, they headed toward the door.

"Look trustworthy, Ethan."

"How do I do that?"

"I don't know. Look like me."

"What does that even mean? I don't look like you."

"Just put on a friendly, trustworthy smile."

Greg looked at Ethan, "that's a fake smile. You look like a little kid in a toothpaste commercial."

"I guess I can't smile on command."

"Just act naturally and let me do the talking," Greg said.

They walked into lobby of the post office which was actually fairly large for a small town. There were two windows open. The one on the left was staffed by an older gentleman. There was a younger woman at the window on the right. Ethan could hear the wheels turning in Greg's head trying to calculate which attendant would supply the most information. Ethan would have gone for the young woman. Greg played it just the opposite.

There was one person in each line. When it was their turn, Greg approached.

"Good afternoon. I was hoping you could help me. My name is Greg Webster and I am the administrator at High Falls Hospital. I have been trying to find a friend of mine from several years ago. I contacted the Herkimer County Clerk's office and they were able to tell me that the last address they had for him was a post office box here. If I gave you the name and the box number, could you tell me if it is still active?"

"You were the guy who solved the hospital murder case up there."

Greg smiled even wider.

"That was me, nice of you to remember."

"How can a hospital administrator let something like that happen right under their nose?"

"I wasn't the administrator then, I was an investigator with the state health department. Once I was on the case, it took just a few days to solve the case and apprehend the killer."

Ethan looked behind him and the line had grown to five people. He checked the other line and the window had closed.

"Do you really know this guy you're looking for or are your just on another case?"

"You got me there, Mitch." Greg had read his name tag.

"I don't think I can help you, son."

"Please, Mitch, there is a young girl missing and a young girl already dead. You can help us try to put an end to this. All we need is a yes or no. The name is MacNamara and the box number is 366. Please just tell me if that box is still active under the same name. What can it hurt?"

"It can probably hurt my retirement. It can hurt my reputation, and it can hurt my pride." He never took his eyes of Greg. "Now if you don't mind, there are several behind you that would like some real service."

"I understand," Greg said. "Thank you for your time." He turned to walk away and Mitch said,

"Don't forget your paper!" Greg looked back and the man was holding up a small, ragged edged piece of scrap paper. Greg moved back to retrieve it. He quickly glanced at it and gave the man a wink.

Ethan followed Greg outside.

"What was that all about?" Ethan asked.

Greg handed him the slip.

Ethan read it aloud.

"Yes. 8667 HWY 167."

"His home address?"

"That's what I'm guessing," Greg answered.

They got back in the car and drove out of town following the signs for RT. 167 north. Ten minutes later they pulled up to the address. The house sat back quite a way off the road. There was a long gravel drive leading up to a small, single story, older home. There was no garage and no vehicle parked in the driveway.

"It doesn't look like anyone is home." Ethan said.

"I agree. Do you want to break in?"

"You're kidding, right?"

"Yes, I'm kidding. We let the authorities handle that stuff. Right now, there is no reason to get the authorities involved. Let's go back to the town and have an early dinner. We can run by here again on the way home."

"I like the way you think boss."

They found themselves back on Main Street. There was an open parking spot in front of a place called Some Like it Hot.

"What do you think, Ethan?"

"It looks good to me. Perhaps the parking spot right out front is an omen."

"That could be. It could also be that they have lousy food!"

"One meal in a lifetime, right?" Ethan replied.

"That's what every poisoned person thought just before they died," Greg added.

"Boy, you really know how to spoil a person's appetite."

"Just kidding. I'm sure it will be fine. You eat first."

"Coward!"

The restaurant had a welcoming appearance from the outside. There were two large windows facing the sidewalk, a center door, and three steps up from the walkway. The inside was just as nice. It wasn't fancy but it was well decorated, clean and very homey.

It was probably well before the usual dinner crowd arrived and there were just two occupied tables. A waitress who looked to be in her late forties walked over to greet them.

"Just the two of you?"

"Yes ma'am," Greg answered.

"Right this way." She led them toward the back of the moderately sized room to a table for two. When they were seated she said, "Where are the ladies tonight?"

"This is the end of a business trip," Ethan answered. "It was getting late and we thought we would catch a bite before the drive home."

"Where is home?"

"High Falls," Greg answered.

"That's a nice place," she responded. "I don't know if I would want to be a patient in the hospital there but I do like the area. What kind of work do you boys do?"

They looked at each other and Greg gave Ethan a little wink.

"We work in the energy field, you know alternate fuels like solar and wind."

"How interesting. My name is Brenda. Let me get you some water and I'll be right back to tell you about our specials." She handed them each a menu and walked off.

"Brenda is a bit forward, don't you think?" Greg stated.

"I think it's that small town charm. Everyone wants to know everyone else and that includes strangers," Ethan replied.

Brenda returned with two glasses and a pitcher of ice water.

"Tonight we are featuring linguini with clam sauce, filet of beef medallions with a red wine reduction and chicken fajitas. Everything except the fajitas comes with salad and fresh baked bread. The fajitas come with fresh pressed tortillas. You are also welcome to anything off the regular menu. I'll give you a few minutes to think it over."

"Impressive menu for a small town restaurant," Ethan exclaimed.

"That it is," Greg replied as he studied the menu.

"Isn't it funny that we are only an hour from home yet neither of us have ever been here?"

"Ethan, I would bet that if we were to draw a circle with a sixty mile radius around High Falls you would find many places we have never been. We tend to ignore our immediate surroundings for the more exciting places outside of our purview."

"I wouldn't take that bet. I think you're right. But look at what we may be missing. Like that monastery we found today! Who knew?"

"That was pretty cool. I can't wait to Google that place when I get home!" Greg replied.

"Alright gentlemen, have you made a decision or can I answer any questions for you?"

"I would like the filet medallions," Greg responded.

"And I have decided on the fajitas," Ethan added.

"Excellent, I will get this order in right away."

"Brenda, after you place the order, would you be kind enough to answer a few questions?" Greg asked.

"I would be happy to try. I'll be right back." Thirty seconds later, she was standing at the table. "Shoot!"

"Do you know a man named Alfred MacNamara who lives out on 167?"

"I meet a lot of people here but I don't always remember the names. That one doesn't ring a bell."

"That's okay, let's try another. Are you familiar with a Christian church somewhere between here and Jordanville?"

"Now that I can help you with. There was a young girl who used to work here maybe three years ago. She couldn't ever work a Sunday because of the church conflict. I understood, I used to attend church awhile back and I didn't like to miss it either. This seemed like more of a cultish attachment."

"How do you mean?" Ethan asked.

"There were also two or three nights a week that she couldn't stay past six o'clock because she needed to be at church. So, she took the breakfast and lunch shift most of the time. She was polite but very quiet. I couldn't tell if she was just shy or intentionally closing herself off."

"Have you ever attended that church?" Greg pursued.

"No. I have a friend who tried it once but they never went back. She said it was like being a goldfish in a tankful of sharks. Not very welcoming and you didn't want to turn your back on them. I hear people talk around town here and there are some rumors that some folks who started attending there just disappeared after a while. Most people assume they just moved away, probably to get away from them."

"It seems strange that someone would move because they had a bad experience at church," Greg said.

"Strange seems to be the right word for that place. If you want to check it out, it sits on a side road off Rt. 167 just shy of Jordanville. It's called the Valley Church of Redemption. You won't see a sign for it on 167. There is a small wooden cross that sits at the intersection. It will be a right hand turn heading north. Alright, I'm going to check on your order."

"Thank you, Brenda."

"Wow!" Greg exclaimed. "Have you ever heard of a church that was not welcoming? How do you build a congregation?"

"Maybe it's by invitation only," Ethan replied.

"Like a country club?"

"Maybe. Members invite people they know who they think will fit into the group. I think I've read about that happening in different periods of history."

"We need to check out that church," Greg followed, let's see if we can find it on the way home. It's right off the same road Alfred lives on."

"Here you are boys!. What else can I bring for you?

Chapter 34

Quantico, VA/Bowling Green, KY

Charis managed to get out of the office on time, make it to the airport on time and catch her flight to Bowling Green. By 2:30 pm she had landed. It was a short flight but she used the time wisely, arranging for a team out of Knoxville to get a flatbottom boat out to McMinnville.

She also sent an email to Trey Lawrence to tell him she was on her way to Kentucky to continue her investigation of the child abduction. She would send him a report later with items that he could follow up on.

She would spend the afternoon with the Bowling Green Missing Persons Task Force, a division of the B.G.P.D. and be back in the air by 8:00 pm. With any luck she would be back in her own bed before midnight.

Charis had a rental waiting at the airport and made her way to the police department downtown. She arrived a good twenty minutes before the start of the meeting. She used the ladies room and found a seat around the large oval table in the conference room.

She checked her email again and found a response from Trey acknowledging her message. She had also received a new internal message from her boss.

"I know you're on the road and that you have a full plate, Charis, but this came in and it looks like the same M.O. as your other unidentified.

Please contact Sheriff Til Sweeney in Quicksburg, VA asap. His number is attached.

A few more people had arrived for the meeting so Charis went out to the hallway to make the call.

"Shenandoah County Sheriff's Office, this is Deputy Swart. How may I help you?"

"Well Deputy, your greeting is a breath of fresh air. I'm Special Agent Charis Andrews with the FBI in Quantico."

"Thank you, Special Agent Andrews, what can I do for you?"

"I'm calling for Sheriff Sweeney."

"Yes ma'am, he right here. Please hold. Til, FBI for you, line one"

"Sheriff Sweeney."

"Good afternoon Sheriff, Charis Andrews, FBI. I was just assigned your case. I am just about to enter a meeting in Kentucky so I only have a few minutes to talk but I promise I will call you back as soon as possible. Give me a quick summary if you can."

"Good afternoon, Special Agent. We had a body wash up on the shore of the Shenandoah a few days ago. It's an adult male roughly thirty years old without any ID or identifying marks. We received word today from our Medical Examiner that has us concerned."

"It appears that this young man was possibly poisoned and prior to autopsy, Doctor Charles Flanders had full body x-rays done. Both the lungs and the intestine show a radiopaque substance. During the post, Doc took some samples to send off to the lab. In the meantime, he is a bit of a mineralogy buff and tested the samples in house. He believes the colon contains Thallium and the lungs contain Calcium Carbonate."

"Sheriff Sweeney, I am going to send you an email with my contact information. Please send me a copy of the doctor's summary asap and tell the M.E. to treat the body as hazardous. I'm sure he knows what to do. I will call you back just as soon as I can."

"Will do, Agent Andrews. Thank you."

"Thank you, Sheriff."

This was big. Charis didn't know the exact dangers associated with

Thallium but she knew enough to be concerned. She sent a quick note off to her boss to bring him up to speed. She also told him she would fly from Bowling Green to Quicksburg before coming home.

She needed to contact the Webster team as well but that would have to wait until after the meeting which was ready to begin. She re-entered the conference room and reclaimed her seat. The room was just about full.

Leading the group was Detective Stan Woburn of the Bowling Green Police Department. Representatives from several other agencies were there including The Kentucky State Police, the Warren County Sheriff's office and the FBI.

The overview hadn't changed much since the last gathering. They had interviewed students, parents, bus drivers, teachers and administrators. They viewed all available surveillance footage with the exception of one camera which was disabled at the time.

Charis raised her hand.

"Yes. Agent Andrews."

"Do we know what caused the camera failure?"

"It looks like the camera was offline. It tested fine."

"How did it get offline?" Charis asked.

"We were not able to determine that."

"Do we know when it went offline?"

Detective Woburn scoured his notes. "It went offline at 10:00 am that morning."

"So we know it went offline at 10:00am but we don't know why or who took it offline. The system doesn't keep a record of who accessed the control panel and at what time? Doesn't that seem strange? We have one camera that went down one hour before the girl was abducted and no one finds that to be more than coincidence? I'll bet that camera was pointed at one of the main entrances."

Woburn checked his notes again. "It was the door to the staff parking lot."

Charis was on a roll. "do we have the attendance list of the staff for that day?" Were all of the staff present for the entire day?"

"We don't have that information," Woburn answered.

"How do we get that information right now?" she asked.

"School is probably out for today. We can try first thing tomorrow," Woburn said.

"This girl could be dead by tomorrow if she's not already. Not good enough. Call the principal, the superintendent, call the president of the board of education if you have to but we need that information now!"

Woburn passed that task onto one his assistants and continued the meeting. A half hour later they had copies of the staff schedule, the absentee list, the substitute list and an early dismissal list.

Charis was looking at her lists trying to find anything that didn't line up. It didn't take long. She noticed that one substitute teacher was scheduled to come in at 11:30 am. She knew that could be to cover for a teacher that had an afternoon medical appointment or something similar but it was worth following through on. She jotted down the name and moved on.

She pulled a new list that was for the following day to look for absences. Sure enough, the teacher that needed coverage the afternoon that Samantha disappeared also called in sick the next day. Again, it could be related to a medical time off.

The teacher's name was Elliott Powers. He was a first year science teacher at the junior high school. She needed to see the background check on this guy and she needed to know if he had access to the security system.

Everyone else was looking over their lists, some were chatting while doing it. She approached Woburn and requested a private conversation with him. They went out to the hall.

"Detective," she began," I need to see the background check that the school obtained on Elliott Powers. We also need to know if he has security system clearance. Also, please obtain his home address."

"Where are you going with this Agent Andrews?"

"I'm not quite sure yet but my gut is telling me something."

"I'll make the call. In fact, come with me and we will make the call together."

"Thank you, Detective."

Charis followed Woburn down the hall to his office.

"Have a seat, agent."

He went around his desk, sat down and made the call.

"Mr. Sheldon, Detective Woburn again. I'm here with FBI agent Andrews and we would like to ask you a few questions. Can you tell me about a teacher by the name of Powers?"

"I'll try," he replied, "he just joined us this year. What do you need to know?"

"Is there anything in his background check that stands out? Also, would he have the ability and access to take a security camera offline?"

"Let me pull up his file. One moment."

Woburn and Charis stared at each other.

"I have it here. He does not have clearance to the security system. As far as the background check...that's odd" Sheldon said, "I don't see a background check in his file."

"Isn't that mandatory now, Mr. Sheldon? Charis asked.

"Yes, it is. I'm not sure why I'm not seeing it."

"Let's move on, Mr. Sheldon," Charis said. "Do you have a home address for him?"

"Yes. 2115 North Cumberland Avenue."

"Is that in Bowling Green?"

"No, Three Springs, just a little south of here."

"Do you know what make and model car he drives?"

"Let's see...we issued a parking permit for a 2014 Dodge Challenger."

"Color?"

"Black," he answered.

"Mr. Sheldon, is Mr. Powers married?"

"I hope not! He seems to be quite taken with another employee here."

"And who would that be?" Charis asked.

"Jeffrey Ketterman."

"What does Mr. Ketterman do there?"

"He works in the I.T. department."

"Does he have access to the security system?"

"I believe he would, yes."

"What is his address, please. Also, the make and model of his vehicle."

"Okay, hold on…here it is. Biltmore Farms, Apt. B-27, Biltmore Avenue,

Bowling Green. He drives a black 2015 Nissan Altima."

Charis nodded at Woburn. He knew she meant they had enough information.

"Thank you, Mr. Sheldon," Woburn said, "we will be in touch." He hung up.

"I'll contact the police in Three Springs and put them on alert."

"Don't mention an address or names," Charis said. "Leaks happen. Choose a meeting spot nearby and tell them to wait for us. We will need backup as well. Also, we need to send a couple teams to Ketterman's address here in Bowling Green. I don't think they would keep the girl in his apartment. My guess is if she is still alive, they have her at Powers' place."

They went back to the conference room and gave an update. All of the units present were told not to release any specifics until we were at the meeting place.

An hour later, Charis and a team of twelve officers from various units were at the predetermined meeting place which was a strip mall parking lot a half mile from the house. Woburn was in radio contact with his units at the apartment complex. There was no evidence of the black Nissan.

Woburn gave the order for both units to move in and await his next command. Charis' group drove quietly through the neighborhood. They had cruisers parked at both entrances to the street that the house was on plus a couple on the block behind the house.

2115 North Cumberland Avenue was in an older neighborhood and the houses were spread out a bit. The house belonging to Powers was a two story wood sided structure with a large covered front porch. There was a good twenty yards of lawn between the houses and there was a two car garage on the left side. The black Nissan was parked in the driveway. If the Challenger was there, it was in the garage.

It was still daylight so there weren't any lights on in the house. Woburn called the landline number listed for the address.

"Hello." A male voice answered.

"Hi, this is Bob Marley, I'm calling for Jeff Ketterman."

"Hold on, Jeffrey, it's for you."

"Who is it?" they could hear him ask in the background.

"Bob Marley."

"I don't know any Bob Marley. Get a number."

"They're both here" Woburn said covering the phone. He gave the signal for his people to move in.

"I'm sorry, Jeff is busy. Can I take a message?"

"Well, yes. Please tell him to put his hands up and face the wall."

"What are you tal....."

The front and back doors both flew open at the same time. Officers in protective gear streamed in yelling *"Police. Put your hands up!"*

Powers stood in the kitchen with the telephone still in his hand. Ketterman was coming out of the back bedroom. Officers had both men on the floor in a few seconds.

Charis stepped over Ketterman into the bedroom. The young girl was gagged and tied to the bed.

"I'm Agent Andrews, you're safe now."

Charis released the gag and untied the ropes holding her down.

"Are you alright?"

Samantha started crying but she nodded her head. Charis held her tight and assured her everything was going to be alright. Charis and Woburn accompanied Samantha to the hospital where her parents were waiting for her. They were allowed to see her for a few minutes before the doctors began their examination.

Samantha denied that she was sexually assaulted. She said that except for being bound and gagged, she was not treated harshly. She had no idea why she was abducted. Based on her testimony, a rape kit was not necessary. She would be held for a few hours and released to the custody of her parents.

The crime scene investigation unit would thoroughly check the house for evidence and clues as to the purpose of the kidnapping. Both Powers and Ketterman would spend the next several hours being interrogated separately with no doubt that one would turn on the other.

For Charis, her work was done here and she would change her evening flight. She wouldn't be going home though. She was heading to Quicksburg, Virginia to investigate that case. It was a short flight from Bowling Green to Shenandoah Regional Airport. There was only one flight and it was leaving in forty-five minutes. Once in the air, she would call Sheriff Sweeney to tell him she was on her way. She would also contact Greg and Trey and fill them in. First, she needed to find a hotel room near Quicksburg.

Chapter 35

High Falls, NY/Jordanville, NY

"That was a great meal!" Greg exclaimed.

"Mine was excellent as well. You don't expect much when you order Mexican food from a non-Mexican restaurant but it tasted really authentic."

They were in the car heading toward Rt. 167. It was 5:45 pm when they left downtown Richfield Springs and only a ten minute drive to the MacNamara place. They still had a good three hours of daylight left.

"Hey, that Brenda was a piece of work. She loved to talk!" Ethan said.

"She gave us some good information though. I'm glad it got busier in there, otherwise we may not have had a chance to eat," Greg replied.

"It shouldn't be much farther!" Greg exclaimed, "keep a look out."

Ethan stared at the road ahead of him.

"I think it's right up here on the right."

Greg slowed down. "Right there," he said. He pulled off the side of the road.

"There's a car in the driveway and it looks like a light is on in the living room."

"Should we stop?" Ethan asked.

"If we're going to do it, it may as well be now." Greg answered.

Greg pulled into the driveway but not all the way to the house.

"Let's not give him a reason to hide," he said.

"Let's not give him a heart attack either!" Ethan replied.

"That's a valid point, Ethan, it's your call."

"Oh, we're out of the car, let's just keep walking."

It was fifty yards from the car to the front door. As they neared, they listened for a dog barking or perhaps a security alarm. They didn't hear either. They stood on the front stoop and could see Alfred sitting in a recliner in the living room. It looked like he was reading a very small newspaper.

"Here goes," Ethan said as he raised his fist.

He knocked lightly. MacNamara didn't stir.

"I hope he's not dead," Ethan said.

"Let's wait and see if he turns the page," Greg offered.

They waited for five minutes.

"Maybe he's sleeping, Greg."

"Or maybe he's just hard of hearing. Knock harder!"

Ethan gave the door several good raps this time. Alfred was startled. He peered out the window with his eyes squinting almost shut.

"I guess his vision isn't any better than his hearing!" Greg chuckled.

It took a long minute but Alfred hobbled over to the door.

"Don't say it, Greg."

"What?" Greg asked all innocent like.

The door opened with a deafening squeak.

"Maybe that's why he can't hear," Greg said. "I think my hearing is gone too."

He stood there on the other side of the screen door with no obvious intention of opening it.

"What do you boys want?"

"Good evening, Mr. MacNamara, it's Ethan Baylor."

"Who?"

Greg was motioning for Ethan to speak louder.

"Ethan Baylor!" he shouted. "I was friends with Lillian. Do you remember me?"

"Lillian who?" he responded.

"Your daughter, Lillian."

"I'm sorry, I don't have a daughter."

"You are Alfred MacNamara, aren't you?

"That's right."

"You had as daughter, Lillian. She had a stroke about ten years ago. I was with her."

He didn't say anything. He stood staring at Ethan for a bit then backed up and started to close the door.

"Please, Mr. MacNamara, don't close the door. I need to ask you a few questions. Please!"

The door continued to close. It squeaked shut. Alfred turned off the light and disappeared into the darkness of the rear of the house. Ethan stayed there, staring through the door at nothing. He was obviously disappointed.

"I'm sorry, Ethan."

"What do we do now, Greg? I need to know what happened to her."

"We will find out, Ethan, I promise. Just not this way. We can't make him talk and to try again would border on harassment. We will find out. Let's go."

They turned around and Greg put his hand on Ethan's shoulder and held it there until they reached the car. Ethan opened his door but didn't get in right away. He just stared back at the house.

Neither man said anything as they drove up the road. No more than a thousand feet from the end of Alfred's driveway was the cross. It was at the intersection of Rt. 167 and Hicks Rd. Greg slowed down. Ethan looked up and it was then that Greg could tell he had been crying.

"We are going to find out what happened to her Ethan, even if we have to follow every back road in the state. Let's start with this one. Greg turned right on Hicks Rd. They quickly reached another intersection that looked like it ran parallel to 167. He couldn't go straight and wasn't sure whether he turn left or right.

"Which way, Ethan."

"Either way. We have a fifty-fifty chance."

Greg turned left on what according to the sign was Henderson Rd. In two hundred feet there was another right turn. Hicks Rd.

"Why do they do that?" Ethan asked.

"Because someone wouldn't negotiate for a small piece of their property."

"This church is hard enough to get to, they really don't need to be nasty to people as well." Ethan added.

"You're right. It seems to me that they are doing more to keep people out than bring them in. What are you doing Sunday?"

"Really? You want to attend a service?"

"Why not?" Greg answered with a question. "We can ask Mary and Jack to come so we will look like a family. What better way to find out what they're all about than to try to become part of the flock?"

"Hey, I'm up for it." Ethan stopped for a moment. "There it is."

Greg slowed the car and looked where Ethan's eyes were pointing. Greg stopped the car. Off to the left they could see a large, nicely kept set of buildings. The property was vast with no other homes or farms nearby. There was a twelve foot tall wrought iron fence guarding the campus with a double door gate that appeared to be closed.

They pulled the car into the very end of the drive and got out. It was still at least an hour before dusk but the numerous tall trees staged around the structures gave the feeling of night. They could now see that the driveway was circular, entering where they stood and exiting nearly seventy-five yards further down Hicks Rd. There was another closed gate at that end.

In the center between the two gates sat what looked to be the main church building. It was very large with a three story rotunda facing the front. There were six wide concrete steps leading to the solid wooden doors. The windows on all three levels of the rotunda were the size and shape of gun turrets one would find in an old castle. They appeared to be three feet tall and perhaps only eight inches wide. They were enclosed with what appeared to be black glass.

The rotunda continued one hundred feet into the air forming the steeple. The foundation was made of large multifaceted stones and every-thing above was deep red brick. The rotunda looked to be a nearly complete circle before it joined with the front facing wall.

From there, it was difficult to say how deep the building was but it was at least sixty feet wide on each side of the rotunda. Set back along the sides of the main building were two identically shaped structures. Just two stories above ground, they seemed dwarfed by the church.

The landscaping was beautifully designed but practical. The plantings were far away from the exterior walls of the buildings with wide walkways in between so that the entire perimeter of the building was clear and walkable.

"Ethan, we have got to come here Sunday. This is magnificent!"

"Greg, how do they afford to maintain a property like this if they chase everyone away? It would take a congregation of several hundreds if not thousands to pull this kind of money from a collection plate."

"Maybe they're part of a regional or national church organization. We won't know until we do some research. We will look into it before we come back. Do you see a sign anywhere that lists their schedule?"

"There is something over there to the left. It's near that bench under the tall maple." Ethan said.

"I can't read it from here. Who would put that information behind a locked fence? Once again, not really inviting."

Ethan reached into his pocket and pulled out his phone. "Maybe I can enlarge it enough to see what it says."

He zoomed in as far as he could and took the picture. The lettering was blurred. He zoomed out a little and took another. It was clearer but not large enough.

"Nothing we can see now but I have a software program that I use to enhance photos. I'll try it when we get home."

"I don't think there is too much more we can do now. I guess we should head out," Greg stated.

They turned to walk back to the car when Ethan heard something. He stopped. He began walking again and the noise was back. He looked around but couldn't see anything. He began again but the sound was gone.

Back in the car, Greg asked if he was okay.

"Yeah, I just thought I heard something but I guess not."

They made their way back to Rt. 167 looking at everything along the way. There was nothing to indicate this place existed. The trip on Rt. 167 was delightful. The undulating hills where aglow with the blaze of the setting sun. When they were just a few miles from home Greg's phone rang. It was Charis.

Chapter 36

Bowling Green, KY/ Quicksburg, VA

Charis made it through airport security in a heartbeat. Working for a federal agency has its advantages. The aircraft was a little smaller than she was accustomed to but it was comfortable. After the captain, who appeared to be about fourteen years old gave the permission to use electronic devices, she found a hotel not too far from Quicksville and booked a room.

She proceeded down her list. The next call was to Sheriff Sweeney to tell him she was on her way. They were to meet for breakfast at a local diner and trade notes. Then they were off to meet the M.E. at his office.

Her next call was to Greg Webster. He answered on the first ring.

"Hi, Charis, how are things in Bowling Green?"

"I have left Bowling Green and am on my way to Quicksville."

"Charis, would it be alright to place you on speaker phone? I'm driving with Ethan."

"That's fine."

"Charis?"

"I'm here," she replied.

"Hello, Charis."

"Hi, Ethan, are you working late tonight?"

"We are just returning from an investigative mission to Richfield Springs and Jordanville."

"They sound about as rural as where I'm heading."

Greg jumped into the conversation. "Hey, we may not be in Kansas anymore but we had a great meal and met some interesting people. It was a good afternoon."

"How was Bowling Green?"

"It was fine, nothing exciting really, just took down two kidnappers and rescued a young hostage."

"In one afternoon?"

"It wasn't anything they couldn't have done without me if they knew how to ask the right questions and who to ask them to. I'm really losing my faith in law enforcement. I would take your volunteer possie any day of the week."

"Is it that they don't know how to do the job or that they just don't want to?" Greg asked.

"Some of both, I think. There just doesn't seem to be any sense of urgency anymore. They're afraid to inconvenience people and they are a little bit lazy."

"It seems to me that goes beyond law enforcement, Charis, I see it in kids coming out of college who are looking for jobs. They don't seem excited! If they can't be enthusiastic at an interview, what are they going to be like on the job six months from now?"

"You're right Ethan, I think there is a huge sense of entitlement right now. It's getting harder to deal with. I actually had a sheriff tell me to stay out of his business today," Charis told them.

"Ouch! That couldn't have gone well. Is he still alive?" Greg asked.

"If I could have slapped him through the phone, I would have. I'll be seeing him later this week, maybe I'll just shoot him. My gift to the world."

"Take a deep breath now, Charis, this too shall pass. Where will you be later this week?"

"The metropolis of McMInnville, Tennessee. I'll be arriving Thursday afternoon. My way of thanking the nice sheriff for being so polite. And I will be in Custer on Friday and possible working through the weekend. A gift to them for being so sweet to me on the phone."

"McMinnville? Are there any vowels in that name? It kind of rolls off the tongue funny." Greg joked.

"I think the population is ten and one of them is dead. That's what I get for trying to prove a point. I dish out punishment for him and end up punishing myself. Anyway, enough about me. What's happening on your end?"

"Ethan and I decided to track down Lilijac's parents again. Our friend Lacey Meadows gave us some helpful information that led us to Richfield Springs. A nice man at the post office gave us a tip and we were able to find Lilijac's father. Unfortunately, he wouldn't talk. In fact, he denied having a daughter."

"That's a little strange, isn't it?" Charis replied.

"It gets even more strange," Greg said.

"Our waitress tonight was very chatty. We asked her if she knew of a church near Jordanville, which is where Lilijac told Ethan she used to go with her parents each Sunday. It turns out that this gal had a friend who had attended that church. Just once. She was freaked out by it. She gave us loose directions and we found it. It's right around the corner from Alfred MacNamara's house."

"This place is a fortress, Charis. It's like a smaller version of the Capitol building in Washington except that it's made of stone and brick. It has a twelve foot fence around the entire perimeter and locked gates at each driveway entrance. There are no signs marking its location and no postings stating when services are."

"Greg, do you know the name of the church?"

"We were told that it is the Valley Church of Redemption." Ethan chimed in.

"I've never heard of it. Must be a one only," Charis speculated. "Hey, my dad is very interested in the history of churches in the US, I'll run it by him."

"Great! We will see what we can find out on the internet as well. Hey Charis, did you know there is a Russian Orthodox Monastery in Jordanville? It's in the middle of nowhere but it beautiful."

"I do know that. I had forgotten it until just now but we studied that as a case history. I think it's called the Holy Trinity Monastery and the Holy Trinity Seminary. If memory serves me, it began around 1930 and was completed sometime in the 1950's."

"Why would you study churches at the academy?" Ethan asked.

"The cold war," Charis responded, "our government had eyes and ears on everything Russian. Think about it, what better place to infiltrate our borders during that time? It turned out to be nothing but the timing was awful for those poor immigrants who just wanted a place to worship."

"You amaze me, Charis."

"Me too," said Ethan.

"Well, I am equally amazed by the two of you! So what's your plan?"

"The Webster family is going to church! Mary and I, our two adult sons Jack and Ethan, and our parents Richard and Marilyn."

"Do any of those other people know that?"

"Not yet, but I think I can persuade them."

"No doubt in my mind."

"That is, if we can find out what time the service is!"

"Good luck with that."

"Thanks. Hey Charis, are you alright? Any more calls?"

"No calls since the weekend. I'm good. I'll be seeing my dad tomorrow night and we will check out his phone. It will be good to see him anyway."

"Nice. Do me a favor and send me your itinerary for the rest of the week. Someone should know where you are."

"That's very thoughtful of you Greg, I will send an email with that information. Alright, young men, and you too Greg, I need to make a few more contacts before this puddle jumper touches down. I'll be in touch soon."

Greg and Charis said goodbye and the call ended.

"How can somebody be so kickass and so nice at the same time?" Ethan asked, not really expecting an answer.

"It happens once in a blue moon. Look at me!"

Ethan turned in his seat to look at Greg. "Where is the kickass part?"

"We will have the discharge summary from St. Luke's tomorrow."

"You were able to get it? That's great news!" Ethan exclaimed. "I apologize. I do see the kickass part of you."

Chapter 37

Somewhere over western Virginia/Hilton Head Island, SC

"Good evening, Dean, I'm sorry to call so late. I hope I didn't wake you."

"Wake me? I'm retired Charis, not dead. Thanks for calling."

"Anything new on your end, Dean?"

"I received a quote for the completion of the book but it from management, not Audra. They want three-hundred and they will turn it around in three days."

"Dean, I think you should do it. It will give you a chance to evaluate the artwork to see if it compares with Audra's. If it does, we will know she is still alive. It will also complete your book."

"Just what I was thinking. I already sent off the payment."

"Let me tell you what we are proposing on my end. I spoke with my boss and he is putting a team together. It will comprise mostly of people who work behind the scene like data tracking and internet specialists. They will be attempting to follow the trail from your order to the artist."

"You will be receiving a request for information from Kathleen Gerherty. She will leading the back office team. I will be copied in on everything that transpires and so will you. If you have any questions, call me directly. Does that sit okay with you? I would love to put troops on the ground but we don't yet know where to put them."

"That sounds great, Charis. I really appreciate your help."

"I appreciate you getting involved. You could have just looked the other way."

"No, I really couldn't have."

"I know that. You're a good man, Dean. I hope you have a restful night."

"Thanks. Goodnight, Charis."

The captain announce their final approach and asked that communication devices be turned off. She complied. Eight minutes later, they were at the gate. There were only about fifteen people on the plane out of a possible thirty seats. She was surprised by how smooth the flight was.

Charis pulled her carry on from the overhead, her computer bag from under the seat and made her way to the front of the aircraft where she thanked the teenager flying the plane and the cabin crew, which was a team of one.

She descended the narrow flight of stairs on to the tarmac and proceeded to the terminal. She arrived at gate number one which was also the only gate. She followed the sign for rental cars and found the desk about ten feet on the other side of the sign. *"You've got to love small airports,"* she said to herself.

Her choice of rentals was a Ford Fiesta or a GMC pickup truck. The truck was better equipped so she chose that. The sales agent at the counter directed her to the rental lot. She went to the end of the hallway and out the door. The truck was sitting in space number two. The furthest space was number four which was probably fifty yards from the aircraft she just flew in on.

She opened the back door and placed her bags on the seat. When she opened the driver's door, a step slid out from under the frame. She stepped up and in she went. She started it up and familiarized herself with the dashboard. She coupled her phone with the Bluetooth audio and entered the hotel's address. A map came up on the display. It looked like she was just off I-81 about 38 miles south of Quicksburg. Her hotel was another twenty minutes north.

She saw a sign for a Wendy's off of I-81 just a few miles ahead and decided to stop. It would be too late to get something by the time she reached the hotel and did not want to be faced with a dinner from the vending machine. She had more than her share of those.

She ordered a salad to take back to the hotel and a small frosty to eat on the way. She liked the way the truck handled and was impressed with the accessories in the center console. She set the bag on the passenger seat and the frosty in one of the four cup holders. She left the drive thru and headed back toward the interstate. It was still early enough to call her dad so she though he might appreciate her checking in.

He picked up on the first ring.

"Hello pumpkin, how are you doing?"

"Hi Dad, I'm fine, a little tired I guess but fine."

"Rough day?"

"Long and rough, I guess. I'm in western Virginia now. I started the day in Bowling Green and I'll spend a good part of the day tomorrow in Quicksburg."

"What's in Quicksburg, honey?"

"Not much by the looks of it. Actually, that's not fair, I haven't even seen it yet. It doesn't look like much on a map though."

"I guess crime has no boundaries my dear."

"You're right about that, dad."

"So, does this mean we need to put off our date tomorrow?"

"No way, dad. I'll be on the road by 3:00 pm tomorrow and I'm just a couple hours away. You order the Kwon's and I will be there by 7:00. I Promise!"

"You've got it kid. Just let me know if anything changes."

"It won't! Hey dad, do you know anything about the Valley Church of Redemption?"

"It sounds like an independent, doesn't it."

"That's what I was thinking too, but you're the expert. Do you mind kicking it around a little and we can talk about it tomorrow?"

"Not at all. I like a little homework now and then. I'll see what I can dig up."

"Thanks Dad, you're the best!"

"My pleasure sweetheart. You try to get some rest tonight."

"I will dad. I'm almost to the hotel. I'll let you know when I'm on my way tomorrow. I love you!"

"I love you too. Goodnight Charis."

She reached her hotel just a few minutes later. She dragged her bags and food inside, checked in and went to her room. It was a typical room with one king bed and a decent bath. It was clean and the mattress was firm. She was tired enough to sleep on a bed of nails.

She washed up, put on her pajamas and pulled the salad out of her bag. Along with the plastic wear, a piece of literature fell to the floor. She put it all on the small table and sat in the chair next to it. As she ate her salad, she picked up the brochure. It was a discount coupon for a local attraction.

It actually looked like it could be fun. Shenandoah Caverns contained seventeen rooms and passageways whose formation began millions of years ago. There was also a café, a giftshop and America's smallest post office on the grounds. She promised herself she would check it out someday when she had the time.

She finished her salad and discarded the trash. She was about to throw out the brochure as well but decided to put it in her computer bag. She brushed her teeth, turned down the covers and turned out the lights. She was asleep for all of ten minutes before her phone rang.

When she answered, she could immediately hear the buzzing in the background.

"Hello," she said softly.

"Detective Andrews," the deep, altered voice said, "this is your last warning. Go back to solving real crimes and leave the petty things alone. I wouldn't want to see something bad happen to such a pretty girl."

The call ended. Charis had forgotten to send Greg her itinerary. She decided to get up and do it right then. With her computer open and a second wind, she decided to do a little research.

Chapter 38

July 8, 2016
Montgomery County, NY
"Good morning Sheriff Bentley, nice to see you again."

"I appreciate you meeting me Mr. Stern."

"You can call me Joe, Sheriff. Can I get you anything? Coffee and donut perhaps?"

"No, thank you Joe. I think we should just get started."

"Right this way." Off the right side of the kitchen in the back was a small office. "Why don't you have a seat Sheriff while I set this up." He set a laptop computer on the desk in front of Bentley.

"This device is hooked up to the surveillance replay system. There are three data boxes for you to fill in. The first is the beginning date and end date. The second is the time that you want to start and the last is the time you want to stop. The date fields are DD/MM/YYYY and the times are military so 00:00:00 thru 23:59:59.

"Do you know where you want to begin?"

"I think we should look at July first from 10:00 pm to 6:00 am, Joe."

Joe typed in the data.

"Once you have the parameters set, you just hit the play button here. You can go at normal speed, up to eight times normal, and you can reverse with the same speed options. You control that with the forward and back keys. Now this is just for camera two, which is the one in the back. We can also switch to camera one if you find something and want to see it from a different angle. Once you freeze a frame, you can zoom in on it."

"Do you have any questions, Sheriff?"

"I think I've got it. It may take a few minutes to get the feel of it."

"Alright then, if you need me, I'll be just outside the door. Are you sure I can't offer you something to eat or drink?"

"I think I would like a coffee, black please."

"Coming right up."

Joe left the office and Judd pressed the play button. The video started and the angle of the camera looked perfect. Judd realized that if his guess about when the body would have entered the water was wrong, it could take days of watching to find out what kind of vehicle made those tracks.

He tried speeding up the playback but anything above 2X was too fast for him to keep up. Joe came back with the coffee.

"How is it going?"

"This may take a while."

"I know. If you don't find it right away, I can make a copy of the timeframe you're interested in for you to take with you. You may need to download the playback app which is free."

"You just made my day, Joe. I don't have the patience for this kind of work."

"See what you come up with in the next thirty minutes. If you hit a dead end, I'll make the copy."

Judd turned back to the computer and took a sip of his coffee. He liked it. His phone rang.

"Sheriff Bentley."

"Judd, it's Cliff. We have identified the tire make and size that made those tracks."

"That was fast, Cliff!"

"We got lucky. It's a very popular model. The problem is that it is a very popular model."

"You mean there are a whole lot of vehicles wear those sneakers."

"That's right but we can narrow it down a bit. That model is only two years old and it's designed for light trucks so we can probably rule out sedans and many SUVs. Our office is running a report now that should give us a list."

"It's a place to start, Cliff. That's more than we had a few minutes ago."

"That's right, Judd. Do you have anything else?"

I'm at the donut shop now looking through surveillance footage. It could take a while."

"I hear you, If you need any help, let me know."

"Thanks, Cliff."

Judd went back to the video and his phone rang again.

"Sheriff Bentley."

"Good morning Sheriff, this Al."

He liked her voice.

"Good morning Al, are you missing me already?" Judd joked.

"Must be, I called you didn't I?"

She could take it and dish it out. He liked that too.

"The fact is I have some more information for you. Some of the labs came back early. I'm afraid my hunch was correct. Judd, the girl was definitely poisoned but here is the scary part, the poison is Thallium."

"Like the metal Thallium?" Judd questioned.

"Yes. This was once known as the poisoner's poison. It's colorless and tasteless so it's easy to add to food without the victim knowing. It can take some time for it to work depending on the dosage. Small doses over a long period of time would make the victim think they were developing an illness. Large doses can cause gastrointestinal issues including diarrhea and vomiting as well as neurological disorders. Death can occur within hours, weeks or months."

"That sounds like arsenic," Judd said.

"They are very similar and they are both heavy metals. The difference with Thallium is the ability to spread from the host. It can move from person to person, it can infiltrate the air and water. It's highly toxic, Judd."

"What does this all mean in general terms, Al?"

"It means that we need to be careful. If more bodies show up, we need to treat them as hazardous materials. Everyone from first responders to funeral directors need to take precautions. Professionals usually take routine precautions anyway. I, for example, am protected by the clothing, mask and gloves that I wear. For others, like you for example, can come into contact with a body before you are aware of the consequences."

Do I and the others need to be tested?" he asked.

"I think it would be wise. Coming into contact with a person with this poisoning briefly will probably not be harmful but there is a simple blood test that can be performed to give us some peace of mind."

"And if someone tests positive?"

"There is also a simple treatment. There is one other thing, Judd. The substance in the girls lungs is something different. Calcium Carbonate."

"This one I know, chalk right?"

"Yes, chalk is one form but calcium carbonate can be found in a variety of materials including many that we find in the home. It's in everything from antacids to paint. It makes up about four percent of the earth's crust and is found all over the world."

"Did this contribute to her death?"

"That's doubtful, Judd but it could be a clue. In order for that amount of calcium carbonate to be in the lungs, it would have to be inhaled over a fairly long period of time, especially if it was in small quantities."

"So, some research into where she might have inhaled calcium carbonate dust could provide a clue as to where she has been. And what about the Thallium? Could that be a clue as well?"

"Well, it could be a clue but it's going to be a much more difficult one to trace. Thallium salts which is what we have here, used to be promoted as rodent and insect killer. It was available for purchase up until 1984. It is still in use in some manufacturing processes but it's closely controlled."

"What are some of the symptoms of Thallium ingestion, Al?"

"The first signs would include digestive issues and maybe a headache. That would be followed by fatigue and disorientation, confusion and even passing out. It robs the body of potassium which eventually leads to cardiac issues. Are you feeling disoriented or confused?"

"Yes, but no more than usual," he joked again.

"A sense of humor is a good sign. I'm not saying you should but if you think it is prudent, ask your doctor to check for Thallium in your blood. It he or she asks why, tell them you may have had a brief exposure to it."

"I am going to get word out to other law enforcement agencies."

"Good idea. I have already notified the CDC and the Poison Control Center."

"Al, thanks for letting me know. It is really a pleasure to work with you!"

"With you as well, Judd. Be safe."

Judd needed to call some people who were close to the body. He also needed a copy of the surveillance footage.

Chapter 39

Somewhere

It was morning and Alpha Sam was enjoying his tea and biscuit. The warm but dark wood in the office was in stark contrast to the early sun breaking through the window. He looked around at the beautiful grounds and thought about a walk around the perimeter.

The ringing of the phone interrupted his peaceful thoughts. He moved slowly without concern that the ringing would disturb anyone else.

"Hello."

"Good morning, Alpha Sam, this is Myron Hawkins."

"Yes, Myron, what can I do for you?"

"I'm afraid I have some troubling news. The FBI will be paying a visit to Quicksburg today."

"Do you know why?"

"I'm pretty sure it has to do with the body found in the river recently."

"And is your resource trustworthy?"

"Oh yes."

"What do you know of this situation, Myron?"

"Only what I read in the papers and now from my resource."

"Has your resource disclosed any particulars?"

"Not yet, but I am monitoring the situation."

"I see. Let me know when you have more details Myron. Thank you for the call."

"Yes, sir."

The Alpha was not happy, nor alarmed really. He just felt a sudden anxiousness. The kind that a walk wasn't going to relieve.

He picked up the receiver and dialed three digits.

"Yes, your Highness."

"In ten minutes, I would like to have one of the morale services resources brought to my chambers. Perhaps a garnet this time."

"Yes, your Highness. Any particular requests?"

"Thirties and clean."

"Of course, your Highness."

The Alpha walked to the bathroom to get ready. He despised nothing more than having to pause in the middle to pee. After relieving himself, he went to the bedroom, removed his clothes and put on his silk garments. He moved to the chest of drawers and pulled out some ligatures just in case.

From the night stand he removed a prophylactic and placed it on the bed. Moments later his guest arrived. He opened the door and welcomed her and the handler.

"Your Highness, this is Lana and she is delighted to be your guest this morning."

"Thank you Marcus. Good morning Lana, it's so nice to see you."

Lana didn't say anything and didn't acknowledge his presence. She started straight ahead.

"Should I expect any trouble, Marcus?"

"I don't believe so sir, Lana has been given a cocktail that should keep her very relaxed for several hours. If you wish, I could stay for a few moments just to be sure."

"I think we should be alright alone. Don't you think so Lana?" He placed his hand on her back and guided her to the bedroom. "You're dismissed, Marcus."

"Thank you, sir. Have a good morning."

"I believe I shall."

Chapter 40

Hilton Head Island/Crystal City, MO

Trey searched the state police database for a contact in the Missouri state police who might be able to answer some questions about case number two which was the 14-18 year old male body that washed ashore in a small tributary of the Mississippi River near Festus on June 3.

By calling the Springfield office he was able to track down the lead detective who worked out of the Festus barracks. His name was Laroy Climm. The desk officer put Trey right through.

"Good Morning Detective Lawrence, this is Detective Laroy Climm, what can I do for you?"

"Hello, Detective, I have been working some cases with the FBI including one up here in New York that is very similar to yours. I was asked by Special Agent Charis Andrews to reach out to you to see if we could share notes."

"I would be happy to, Trey. Where do we begin?"

"How about if I tell you about mine first."

"That would be fine."

"On July 3, we had a body get wedged against the upriver side of lock twelve of the Mohawk River. It was a young female with no identifying marks or other identification. While she was found in the water, the coroner has ruled out drowning as a cause of death. She has some dental issues that will make cross-referencing a real challenge and she did have what appeared to be ligature marks on her upper thighs."

"That sounds real familiar, Trey. Our vic was a young male found in the water in a small tributary just west of the Mississippi in Crystal City which is just a stone's throw from Festus. No ID, no marks to speak of and bad dental work. Drowning was also ruled out. Some lab tests came back about a week ago that said the boy had calcium carbonate in his lungs and some heavy metal in his colon. The M.E. here says it was poisoning of some sort."

"We're about a month behind you on the date the body was found so I haven't seen a final report from the coroner. Laroy, have you determined where the body entered the water? Any useful surveillance footage?"

"To be honest Trey, we don't have a whole lot to go on. I think DNA is going to be our best bet."

"Let's keep each other up to date on any progress, Laroy. I'll send you my contact information. By the way, I have an FBI approved consultant working on my team by the name of Ethan Baylor. If it's all right with you, he may check in from time to time on my behalf."

"That would be fine, Trey. I'll look for your contact information and I will stay in touch."

"Thanks, Laroy."

Chapter 41

Montgomery County, NY

"New Your State Police this is Detective Alvord."

"Good morning, Cliff, it's Trey Lawrence. Do you have a minute?"

"Sure, Trey, how are you?"

"It's all good here, thanks. You okay?"

"I am, it's a little busier than I would like it but other than that, I'm fine."

"That's great Cliff. Listen I wanted to talk to you about the body found at lock twelve a few days ago. I understand you've been working with Sheriff Bentley on the case."

"That's affirmative."

"Cliff, I've been working with an FBI agent on some other cases and I believe there may be some consistencies with yours."

"Can you hold just a minute, Trey, I have another call coming in. I hate to do it to you but I'm a bit short handed here at the minute."

"Go on, I'll wait."

No music on hold, no advertisements to apply for cadet school, just silence.

"Hey Trey, I have Sheriff Bentley on the other line and think we should join him in on this conversation. Is that alright with you?"

"Of course."

There was a click on Trey's end and then all three were connected.

"Trey, I have Judd Bentley here with us and he was just telling me something I think you should hear."

"Good morning, Sheriff," Trey said.

"Good morning Detective. Cliff tells me you're working with the FBI on some similar cases. Are they local?"

"No sir, there Is one in McMinnville, Tennessee, one in Custer, South Dakota and one in Crystal City Missouri that we know of. All found in a river, all there several days before they were found and none of them have anything to go on besides poor dental work and a hope at DNA matching."

"Do you have more than that?"

"I'm afraid we do. I just spoke with Dr. Amelia Lanford in Albany. She has determined that the young lady we found died from Thallium poisoning. Now, this stuff is difficult to trace but in can be environmentally toxic and contact with others including first responders can spread the stuff."

"Judd, in what part of the body was the Thallium found?"

"The intestines."

"Holy crap!" Trey said.

Cliff snickered. "Nice pun? In the intestines, holy crap!"

"I guess that is a little funny," Trey agreed. "No pun intended. Anyway, I just got off the phone with a trooper in Festus, Missouri who said they got the report from their M.E. Now I have another question for you, Judd. Did Dr. Lanford mention anything about the lungs?"

"Yes, she found calcium carbonate."

There was silence for a minute as they all tried to connect the dots.

"The vic in Missouri had the same thing." Trey told them.

"With your permission fellas, I would like to talk to my contact at the FBI. I think she needs to add our case to the others. I mean, what are the odds that these are not connected?"

"I think you're right, Cliff," Judd said. "I'm on board with it."

"Listen fellas, I need to be upfront with you about something. Do you remember the High Falls Hospital killings and the hospital bombing in Plattsburgh, Burlington and Philadelphia?"

"Of course, you were involved with both of those if I recall." Cliff said.

"That's correct. You will remember that a group of volunteers led by Greg Webster really solved those cases. Well, they have been volunteering on these cases as well. They aren't directly involved or in any danger, they just provide some legwork that is less innocuous than a call or visit from a law enforcement official."

"I remember them, a pretty smart bunch of citizens." Bentley added.

"That they are. Anyway if you're not opposed I would like them to keep working at this. They would be happy to take on tasks that would free us up for other things. I'm not asking you to work directly with them. If you have a need, bring it to me and I will assign it. I will do the coordination on my end."

"I have no problem with it," Cliff responded.

"Nor do I," added Judd. "In fact, I have something they can do right now! I picked up a copy of the surveillance footage from the donut shop but it could take hours to review it."

"Send me a copy Judd and I'll get someone right on it."

"That's awesome, Trey. It's on its way."

"Alright fellas, I am going to contact Charis Andrews at the FBI and bring her up to date."

Trey hung up and dialed Charis' number. It went directly to her voicemail. "Charis, I have some news for you. I hope you're having a good day."

Chapter 42

Quicksburg, VA

Charis found her way to the Broken Egg diner and arrived ten minutes early. There were a few spots open right in front of the building but she knew better than to get herself hemmed in so she backed the truck into a space off to the side.

It was one of those low profile diners, the kind that came premade in sections and delivered on a flatbed truck. She guessed it had been around since the sixties and could make a fair guess at what the interior looked like. She envisioned red seat coverings on stools at the counter and the rest in booths.

The counter and tabletops would be grey Formica that had a design consisting of different colored boomerangs pointing in various direction. There would either be a jukebox at one end or little ones in each booth. They would no longer work and the song selection would be from the late sixties into the early seventies.

She would bet money that Conway Twitty and Loretta Lynn would be represented. The waitresses would be wearing pink dresses about knee length with darker pink aprons. They would be wearing white nurses shoes and skin tone stockings.

The silverware would be a mixed bag of old, new, and in-between and the water glasses would be shaped like the old Coca-Cola glasses used in the old soda fountains. The napkins just might be real cloth. The plastic lenses over the lights would be yellowed and the type and wattage of the bulbs would vary greatly.

The ladies room would have a wall length mirror that was rusting around the edges and the stall would have at least one number she could call for a good time. The Sheriff would want to sit at the counter and would draw special attention.

It was time to find out if she was right. She slid out of the truck, locking it on her way to the entrance which was on the right end of the building as you face it. She had one last guess as she approached the door. A bell.

She tugged on the door and sure enough, it rang. There were three empty seats at the counter as well as a couple available booths. She didn't see anyone in a Sheriff's uniform so she took a seat at the counter.

A middle aged woman in a pink dress, pinker apron and white shoes walked up the other side of the counter. She was very shapely and very pretty for her age. Her makeup was expertly applied. *Southern women know how to look good,* she thought to herself.

"Good morning, my name is Del. What can I start you out with, darlin'."

"Good morning, Del. How about some black coffee."

"Coming right up."

She walked halfway down the counter, retrieved a cup and picked up the coffee pot on her way back. *She's been doing this a while.* She set the cup and saucer in front of her and poured quickly and accurately.

Del handed her a menu and said "everything is good. The breakfast special is a killer."

"That means the breakfast special is extra-good? Charis asked.

"No, I mean it will probably stop your heart! Any fat you can name, it's in there."

"I appreciate the warning." Charis replied.

She was studying the menu while the multi-brightness yellow lights flashed above her. She was taking her time, hoping the sheriff would walk in so they could order at the same time. Del came back to top off her coffee.

"Well hey sheriff," Del said.

Charis turned her head to the right, toward the door and he sat down at the open stool to her left. Del brought a cup and filled it with coffee.

"The usual, Til?" she asked.

"Let's let the lady order first, shall we?" he said looking at Charis.

Hi, I'm Tilman Sweeney and you must be Charis Andrews. It's a pleasure to meet you," he said extending his hand.

She swiveled her seat toward him and stuck out her hand.

"The pleasure is mine," she responded.

"You can't go wrong with the southern style French toast," Til offered.

"And what makes it southern style?" Charis questioned.

"It's made with peach and cinnamon swirl bread and topped with homemade warm cinnamon maple syrup. You can have a side of bacon, country ham, Scrapple or grits."

"I will try the French toast but no sides, please." Charis said to Del.

"The usual for me, Delilah."

"Coming right up," Del said and walked the order to the window.

"I like this place, Sheriff, it has a nice feel to it," Charis commented.

"It's simple but it's home," he responded.

Charis liked this man. He seemed kind and smart in a quiet way. He was in his mid-fifties, she guessed, maybe 6'2" and a firm 190 pounds. His hair was just beginning to grey at the temples and his hat, when it was on, looked natural, like he was born to wear it.

He reminded her of a young Matt Dillon with his dimpled cheeks and just the faintest crow's feet starting to develop, but only when he smiled.

"There you are Sheriff, country ham and grits, and for the lady, the French toast, no sides."

"Much obliged, Delilah. And aren't you looking pretty today!"

"I look the same as every other day, Til but I appreciate the compliment."

"Delilah, I want to introduce you to Charis Andrews. She is here from Washington to talk about the young man that came ashore a while back."

"What a pretty name, Charis, it sure is nice to meet you! Are you a reporter?"

"Some days I wish I was but no, I'm with the FBI."

"The FBI? Like an agent? Are you packing?"

"If you're asking if I carry a weapon, the answer is yes."

"Good Lord, your daddy must be proud of you."

"Oh, he is. My mother was too, although it worried her a lot."

"You said she was proud?"

"Yes, she passed a few years ago."

"I am sorry to hear that. I'm sure she is watching over you right now."

"Not all the time, I hope. I mean, I hope she doesn't see everything I do."

"Oh honey, I know what you mean. I think our loved ones only see what we want them to."

"Well I feel much better now. Thank you Del!"

"Y'all go on and eat your breakfast before it gets cold."

"She's lovely, Sheriff Sweeney. I think she is sweet on you!" Charis teased.

"I've known Delilah forever. She hasn't had the easiest go of it. I would describe what we have as a friendship. We care about each other and watch out for each other but I think deep down, we know we will do better without the true romantic side of things."

"Sometimes it's worth the try even if things don't work out. At least you don't look back twenty years later and think *what if we had.*"

"I like you Agent Andrews. You have a sweet spirit. I knew it the minute I spoke to you on the phone. Do you ever have intuitions like that?"

"I do. I don't know if I developed that being a cop or if I always had it and it's what makes me a better cop. Anyway, I had a vision before I came in here this morning. I knew the seats would be red and the countertops grey. I knew the waitresses would wear pink dresses and white shoes. I knew the lights would be different brightness and that the lenses would be yellowed. I also believed there would be at least one jukebox and that Conway Twitty and Loretta Lynn would be on it. I haven't confirmed that yet but I will when I walk to the ladies room to see if there is a rusting mirror and a number I can call for a good time."

"That's a vivid sense of imagination," Til said.

"Oh, and the jukebox won't play." She added as she walked toward the ladies room. Passing the jukebox on the way.

The mirror was the full width of the counter. In the stall, she could read the plethora of graffiti as she sat. There it was, For a Good Time Call

701-555-DICK. She wondered if she should write it down. She decided not to. She washed up and returned to the dining room.

Sheriff Sweeney was standing at the jukebox.

"Well, was your intuition right?"

"One hundred percent so far," she exclaimed. Is there some Loretta on there?"

Til dropped a quarter in the machine. Nothing happened.

"Just as I said, "Charis bragged.

Til tapped the machine with his knee and it came to life. The light came on, the speaker hissed and the records rolled by. The carousel stopped and the record dropped. The tone arm swung over and lowered to the record. Loretta and Conway were singing As *Soon as I Hang Up The Phone*.

Til smiled, "ninety eight percent is pretty good."

He walked passed her, left the money on the counter and gave Delilah a wink.

"I think we have work to do, Agent Andrews."

Charis stepped quickly toward the door that Til was holding open, pausing just once to put a twenty on the counter and say goodbye to Del.

"Til already took care of it, honey." Del said.

"I know, I want you to have that. Thank you!"

Once outside he said, "follow me to the station. We can park your vehicle there and you can ride with me."

He didn't wait for a response. Charis climbed up into the cab of her rental and followed his cruiser. It was only about a mile to the station. A very small building just off the main street.

"Park it anywhere," he instructed. There were only three spaces in the parking lot and he occupied one. The other was taken by another cruiser.

Charis backed the truck perfectly between the two cars, knowing he was testing her. She got out carrying her computer bag and got in his car.

"Nice job parking! He said.

"Park anywhere?" she questioned.

"There are five more spots on the other side of the building," he replied.

"I thought you were testing me."

"Now why would I do that? I am impressed though."

"I'm going to take you over to Doc Flanders' place. He can answer any question you have about the body. After that, we can discuss next steps. It's about a ten minute ride so if you need to check in, feel free.

Charis took out her phone and checked her messages. She had a missed call and a voice message from Trey. She listened to the short message and called him back.

"Good morning Charis, I didn't expect to hear from you until later but I'm glad you called."

"There is a little break in the action, Trey. What's up?

She sat silently while he explained what he learned from Cliff and Judd in Montgomery County and Laroy in Festus. She told him where she was headed and promised to call immediately after they were finished with the visit.

"Sheriff, that was call from a state trooper in upstate NY. They have a similar situation with similar findings. I don't think it's coincidental."

"Please call me Til, Charis. So there is a similar situation in New York. How do you think the two would be connected?"

"Well, there's more. There are reports of the same thing in Crystal City, Missouri, and quite possibly in McMInnville, Tennessee."

"You say possibly. Does that mean there is something different about that one?"

"I don't know yet. The circumstances are similar but I am not getting the cooperation from the P.D or the sheriff. I'm scheduled to go there on Thursday but that may be too late.

Til pulled into the parking area of the M.E.'s office.

"This looks like a one man show," Charis said.

"It is. Doc Flanders is a smart man, probably the smartest man I know. He could be working in any major city in the country but he chooses to be here."

"Why do you think that is?"

"He would feel stifled in a big city. He knows he would be expected to perform a dozen autopsies in a day which wouldn't allow him to use his analytical mind. Besides, the city could never hold him. He needs to be near the wilderness. He's really a down to earth guy. He doesn't feel he's any better than common folk around here."

"It sounds like you're very lucky to have him."

"Amen to that, Charis. Let's go meet him."

It was a one story building built on a slightly elevated parcel of land just off the main road. There were no signs indicating what the building was used for. The exterior was light grey vinyl siding with white trim. There was a front door that was reachable via a sidewalk that originated off the driveway on the right side of the structure. The driveway was three cars wide with a portico that was two cars deep. The portico had several columns on the right that held up the large roof which was attached to the building on the left. Essentially, six cars could be parked beneath the portico.

From the front, it resembled a funerial home. Til pulled under the portico next to a hideous bright yellow, aged Cadillac hearse. There was a double width entry to facilitate the arrival and departure of wide loads.

Til pressed the doorbell which rang loudly, even from outside. A man with uncombed hair, thick spectacles and a white lab coat opened the door.

"Sheriff, welcome. This must be Agent Andrews. Please come in. It's very nice to meet you." They shook hands.

"Please call me Charis, Dr. Flanders."

"Of course, and you may call me Charlie. May I get you a beverage?'

"None for me, thank you," Charis replied.

"I'm all set, Doc, we just finished up at the diner."

"Splendid. Let's go this way then."

Flanders led them from the small reception area through another double door that accessed a wide corridor. There were several rooms on both the left and the right sides. They entered the second door on the right which opened to an anteroom. There was an interior door that opened to a large procedure room.

"Before we proceed, I must insist that y'all put on protective clothing."

He handed them each a heavy paper jump suit, a surgical head covering, a surgical mask, gloves, paper booties and goggles.

"You can't be too careful. Thallium can be prickly so we don't want to spread it around. All the gear I gave you is worn right on top of your street clothes. No need to disrobe."

It took a few minutes for them to prepare. When they were ready, Doc opened the inner door. Charis could feel the cool air immediately. She also felt like they were in a vacuum. The lights were very bright and very white.

"This room is equipped with a positive flow laminar hood which exhausts all of the contaminated air through a series of filters. By the time the exhaust reaches the outside, it is ten times cleaner than our regular atmosphere."

Doc walked toward the far wall which had a very familiar look. It was stainless steel with three small, hinged doors all at the same height. The doors were marked 1, 2, and three from left to right. After the third small door, there one large, regular height door.

He opened the regular sized door and walked through.

"Follow me please."

Inside the door, the temperature dropped drastically. They were in the cooler. Looking to the left, Charis could see that the three smaller doors contained retractable carts for bodies to rest on. The carts were empty. Straight ahead was one moveable cart that held a body.

"If you don't mind, I could use a hand wheeling our young man into the procedure room."

Charis held the door while Til and Doc wheeled the body through it. The large room had stainless steel counters all along one wall with a huge sink in the middle. The exam table was about eight feet long with a motorized top moved three feet in either direction. The table ran perpendicular to the counter.

"We are not going to move the body from the cart today," Doc explained, "The examination of the body has been completed but I wanted you to see what effect long term ingestion of Thallium can do to a body."

He locked the wheels of the cart and positioned a large surgical light over the body. He then carefully unzipped the plastic bag to expose almost the entire corpse. Charis was surprised that she didn't notice the smell of decay. The body appeared very grey even under the bright light.

"As you can see, the internal organs have been removed for examination and that the torso has been closed."

"Nice job with the suturing, Charlie! I don't think I've ever seen a neater closure."

"Very kind of you to notice, Charis. I did spend a short time in a plastics rotation. Didn't like it. I just want to point out a few things. If you look at the scalp, you will see that much of the hair has thinned out. Some would believe that to be the effect of being in the water for so long but that's not the case."

"Alopecia is a common and sometimes one of the first signs of Thallium poisoning. In fact, it was used as a depilatory until they realized the adverse effects. Now in slow poisoning, alopecia will be a sign. In high dose poisoning, the victim will be dead before the hair has a chance to fall out."

"Where does the Thallium come from, Charlie?" Charis asked.

"That's a great question, one that I wish I could answer unequivocally. Thallium exists in the earth's crust but it is not very useful or harmful in its natural state. It's when it is a byproduct of another process that it is broken down into Thallium salts which can then find their way into the body via water, air or contact with the skin of a victim."

"So what would one of those processes be?" Doc asked.

"Another good question. It is usually found during the smelting process of other heavy metals such as silver, lead and gold. During these processes, workers could be exposed if the area was not well ventilated. Somehow, they discovered that rats and insects that ate the Thallium died so it became the poison of choice in many countries, especially in big cities where rodents were a huge issue."

"It soon became the poisoner's poison. It was odorless, colorless and tasteless so it was easily administered without detection. It wasn't long before it became the choice of doing away with unwanted relatives. The victims illnesses mimicked other diseases so no one expected foul play.

The greedy who were not happy with killing just one husband raised a flag. When the second or third husband died with the same symptoms, bodies started being exhumed and that's when the link to Thallium poisoning was uncovered. There was a woman in Australia who poisoned so many she was known as Aunt Thally."

"Here is something else I want you to see. It doesn't seem to be related to the cause of death but if you find it elsewhere, it could be a valuable clue."

He picked up a remote control and pointed it at the large TV mounted on the wall.

"It will be easier to show you the photos I took rather than having you look in our guys mouth. This is the upper set of teeth. You can see that he is missing a couple, which is not unusual. But look at the dental work that was performed on the ones that remain. They look like they soldered together. I have never seen such unprofessional work and trust me, I've seen the worst of the worst."

"Here is a picture of the lower set. There is evidence of gum disease which may or may not be related to the poison. But the shoddy workmanship leads me to believe that repairs were either done by the owner or a non-dentist. Perhaps someone who dropped out of dental school after the first semester but thought he knew enough."

"Do you think someone like that could be working in a regular setting?" Til asked.

"No, Til. Perhaps there is an underground network of medical providers who prey on the poor. It would only take one regular customer with these results to blow the whistle. He or she would be shut down immediately."

"I have two more things to show you," Doc said as he pointed to the TV once more. "Here are some radiographic Images I had done before doing the autopsy. The first is a picture of the abdomen. Typically, the colon is not easily definable on a plain x-ray. We can see gas patterns and perhaps some well-formed stool but if you look here, the entire small bowel and colon is visible. It's as if the person were given barium for an upper GI series or a barium enema."

"This is a result of the Thallium traveling through the digestive tract. The heavy metal properties of the Thallium match that of barium sulfate in its ability to be radiopaque meaning the x-rays can't pass through. It's another easily noticeable sign if someone knows to look."

"I have two more findings to share with you."

The image on the screen changed.

"Here are a variety of radiographs taken of the skeletal structures. Notice that here in the wrists, upper arms and lower legs are multiple healed fractures. Many of these were caused in this man's youth. They are not from childhood accidents."

"Abuse!" Charis exclaimed.

"Yes, I'm afraid so. Look here at the ankles. This is intentional clubbing or hobbling as they use to call it. A long ago practice used to keep prisoners from escaping. So you can add abuse to your profile."

"Here is the last thing I want to point out. This is a chest x-ray. You will notice the white haze in the lungs. This is not pneumonia. This is a result of chronic inhalation of calcium carbonate."

"Where would someone inhale large amounts of calcium carbonate?" Charis inquired.

"Perhaps in a stone quarry, a gypsum plant or at a pharmaceutical company where they make antacid. Millions of years of seashells have been buried in layer upon layer of the earth's crust. Calcium carbonate is a product of the breakdown of all those shells. Teachers and students have been breathing chalk dust for decades."

"This is the same chalk dust that is in his lungs?" Til asked.

"Essentially, yes. And I thought my teachers asked me to clean the erasers because I was being rewarded. Some reward. Anyway, they stopped using calcium carbonate chalk years ago. This didn't kill him. He may have developed emphysema if he lived long enough."

"Charlie, are you aware that there are several cases now in several states of bodies washing up in rivers that cannot be identified?"

"I was not and quite honestly, that frightens me. We need to establish protocol for what to look for when examining these bodies. I would be happy to write it for you."

"That is extremely generous of you Charlie. When you have it ready, I will make sure it is distributed it to all law enforcement agencies around the country."

"Do you any other confirmed cases?" Doc asked.

"One. Upstate New York," Charis answered. ....

Chapter 43

High Falls, NY

Greg and Ethan were in his office searching the internet for information on the Valley Church of Redemption. They couldn't find a website. They did find a half dozen links to posts. There were comments by various people half of whom were relaying stories that they had heard about the place.

"The strangest people I ever met."

"I know someone who went there and they were totally confused about their beliefs and what purpose they served as a church."

"People here say it exists but I've never been able to find it."

"I went once, we arrived halfway through the service. What church starts a service on the half hour? They weren't friendly but I thought that was because we arrived late. If you're planning to go, the service begins at 11:30."

"I found it once but didn't go in. It looks really cool though. By the way, it's just off 167 on Hicks Rd. in Jordanville."

"There we go, Ethan, now we know the time."

"Don't you find 11:30 a bit odd, Greg?"

"Maybe they take a break for lunch," Greg replied.

"Right. That's when they eat their uninvited guests!"

"I doubt they eat their guests, Ethan, besides, they can't eat six of us at once!"

"Have you ever heard of leftovers?" Ethan said. "Do you even know there will be six of us?"

"Well Mary and Jack are on board and I've invited Richard to meet us here this morning. He should be here any minute. While we're waiting let's see if anything is happening with our cases."

Greg closed the internet and opened his mail. There were messages from Charis and Trey. He opened Charis' first. He read it aloud.

"Lots to talk about. Can we have a group conference at 2:00 pm today?"

"Are you available, Ethan? I can move my 2:00pm to 3:00."

"I will make myself available, Greg."

"I'll call Mary and get her onboard."

He responded in the affirmative to Charis and opened the one from Trey.

"Hi all, breaking news on the body found in the Mohawk. Not public yet. We can talk about it on the 2pm with Charis. Also, I need someone to work with the Montgomery County Sheriff's office for a day or two. I thought Bill Dillon would be perfect. Greg can you make the call and let me know if he's available? See you all at 2:00!

"Ethan, let's hold on updating our chart until after the group call. You can head back to your department for now. I'll call you if I need you sooner."

Ethan opened the door to leave just as Richard Ingraham was ready to knock.

"Hi, Dr. Ingraham."

"Hello, Ethan. Goodbye, Ethan."

"Hey, Richard, come on in. Thanks for stopping by."

"It's always a pleasure, Greg. I kind of miss the old place."

"And the old place misses you too. Have a seat. I have a favor to ask of you and Marilyn."

"Mary isn't pregnant is she?"

"No. Why would you ask that?" Greg said.

"It sounded like you were gearing up to ask us to be Godparents."

"Your mind works differently, doesn't it, Richard?"

"It seems normal to me," he replied.

"I want you and Marilyn to go to church with us this Sunday."

"And you think my mind works differently? Do know how long it has been since I've attended church?"

"Not exactly but it sounds like you're overdue."

"Where is the rub?"

"Alright, Ethan and I want to attend this church in Jordanville. This is the one that Lilijac's parents took her to. We thought if we looked like a family, we would be less suspicious."

"If anyone there knows me, you're going to seem more suspicious," Richard answered.

"Who is going to know you down there?"

"Are you kidding, I've had many patients from Jordanville and Richfield Springs. I'm a bit of a local legend around here, you know?"

"Alright, even if they recognize you, it's been a long time. They don't know that you're a non-church guy."

"Alright, but you're taking us to lunch after church."

"If were still alive," Greg said under his breath.

"What's that?" Richard asked.

"I said I know the perfect place."

Chapter 44

High Falls, NY

Richard left the office while Greg's phone was ringing.

"Yes, Kathy," Greg answered.

"Greg, I have Chris Goodman on the line. He wants to know if you have thirty minutes for him today. He says he doesn't think it's urgent but that you would be very interested in what he has to show you."

"I can meet him at lunch time in the conference room. Kathy, could you.."

"I will order lunch for you both, Greg."

"Thanks, and will you push my two o'clock to a different day please? I'm expecting a call from Charis Andrews."

"Yes, sir."

Greg couldn't imagine what Chris Goodman had to show him. Perhaps it was a new IT project that would save the hospital some money. Chris was very creative when it came to running the Information

Technology program. In the few years he had been there, he implemented several procedures that improved operations and reduced cost.

He had a little while before the meeting and used it to call Bill Dillon. He knew there would be a good chance that Bill was out for a walk this time of day. Lacey would be working and Bill did everything he could to keep busy while she was gone.

"Hello."

"HI Bill, it's Greg Webster. Did I catch you at a bad time?"

"Not at all, Greg, I'm stretching my legs down by the river. What can I do for you?"

"Bill, I received a note from Trey Lawrence just now. It seems that Sheriff Bentley needs some assistance and Trey thought you were just the guy for the job."

"I would be happy to help. Do you know what the job entails?"

"I'm afraid I don't have the particulars, Bill but I'll ask Trey to have the Sheriff give you a call. Okay if I give him your number?"

"Of course."

"Thanks Bill, I'll talk with you soon."

Greg had just enough time to use the restroom before his noontime meeting. When he returned to the office, Chris Goodman was in the conference room. He had some equipment with him but it didn't look new.

"Hi Chris, did you bring me a gift?"

"I'm not sure, Greg but I thought you needed to see it."

"It looks like an old computer tower."

"That's exactly what it is. We found it in storage. We were cleaning out some old stuff and came across this. Before we send the retired equipment for recycling, we make sure the hard drives are clean. If we are unable to clear them, we smash them."

"So what's so special about this one?" Greg Asked.

"When we fired it up, we found some disturbing files."

"How far back do these files go?"

"Back to the Alex Winfield days or more specifically, Barry Miller."

"Barry was the CFO responsible for the propofol murders. Are you saying this is his work computer? It appears to be one of them."

"He had more than one? Why?"

"Well, he had his business computer and then he had this one. I'm sure the I.T. department never knew anything about it. That's not to say someone inside didn't help him set it up. I just don't think anyone knew what he was using it for. I think It's probably best just to show you, Greg."

Chris took just a few minutes to set the tower up to a keyboard and monitor. It took the computer a good three minutes to boot up.

"You will notice that the operating system is old by today's standards so the speed and the quality of the video is not great, but it's good enough to see what is happening."

"Chris, how do you know for sure that this belonged to Barry Miller?"

"First, he used the same login that he used to sign into the hospital system. Secondly, review of the connection records suggests that the IP address was listed as Barry's office. Lastly, we are also able to prove that Barry used his phone to receive the data remotely."

"Do we know where the video feed was coming from, Chris?"

"Yes. We know the camera was positioned in the morgue."

"The morgue? Why the morgue? Was he watching Seike perform the autopsies?"

"Sometimes. He was also watching other activity."

"What other activity would be taking place in the morgue?"

"See for yourself, Greg." Chris pressed the play button.

Greg was stunned. He watched file after file of video that showed various men having sex with dead patients. He was feeling sick to his stomach and lightheaded. He could not believe what he was seeing. There was no discussion in the room.

Greg recognized some of the players as hospital employees but several others were complete strangers. The date and time stamps showed that this practice went on for several months or more. At some point, the angle of the video changed suggesting that the camera had been moved.

Chris paused the video and looked at Greg for direction.

"How much more is there, Chris?"

"There is over twenty hours total."

"Who else knows about this, Chris?"

"Just Eric. He was the one that found the computer and brought it to me."

"Has he seen what's on it?"

"No. You are the second one to see it."

"Chris, I need a few days before going to the authorities. I would like to review the testimony of everyone involved in the murders as well as all the witnesses. Are you okay with that? I promise that I will let the authorities know that you brought this to my attention today."

"Greg, I did what I needed to do. Use your discretion regarding what happens from here. I trust you to do the right thing. You were here and know much better than I about the people involved and the roles they may have played."

"I appreciate that, Chris. What's the best way to protect this equipment until it's turned over?"

"Do you have a lockable cabinet that only you have a key to?"

"I have a pretty deep drawer in my desk, do you think it may fit in there?"

"Let's find out," Chris said.

Chapter 45

Bentonville, VA

Leland Hadwell was preparing for the monthly, Wednesday noontime gathering. As Supreme Leader, this was his service and it was his time to lead the leaders of the organization. Sunday services were for the Alphas and Omegas and they would make his audience today.

It was an added expense to bring them all together each month but it was a necessity if he was to keep the others on a short lead. They needed a constant reminder of their purpose, their mission and their mantra.

"Redemption is for today and every day. We are all redeemers."

He was dressed in his most precious silks as he made his way to the chamber. It was a long walk from his quarters in the church complex but the changing room was just a few yards from the door to the inner sanctum.

He could hear the soft music from the chamber making its way through the seams of the heavy wooden door. This was not the eighteenth or nineteenth century hymns that were typical of Anglican churches. There was no booming pipe organ or grand piano. The songs were created for the church by members over the fifty years since their founding. They were written for stringed instruments performed by quartets or sextets.

He opened the door and the sound grew louder but still soft and controlled. Everything revolved around control. The chamber was aglow with candlelight with soft electrical light illuminating selected areas including the altar and the pulpit.

The chamber was round with curved pews that faced the altar. The high ceilings afforded a practical balcony at the back, above the main entry doors. This contained the small group of musicians who were to be heard but not necessarily seen. There were few distractions at the front of the chamber.

There was a noticeable absence of statuary. This church did not recognize Christ as the redeemer or son of God nor Mary as the mother of God. All men were considered equal and capable of providing redemption. All men.

Leland closed the door behind him and took his seat in the oversized velvet chair. The black cloth signifying power and purpose. He sat for the remainder of the song while his subjects stood both still and silently, heads bowed.

When the song ended, Leland continued to sit, ensuring that his followers remembered who was in charge. He sat for a full minute looking over his subjects who were absolutely still with their heads still bowed.

"Please be seated, brethren. I am glad that you can be here to celebrate this service with me. I trust you all had a chance to enjoy the Independence Day weekend. We would be remiss by not recognizing the birth of this great county, especially being this close to Washington. For those of you who were once connected to Washington, we thank you for doing your part.

"As you know, we will be recognizing our fiftieth anniversary come fall. Let us give thanks to our founders."

Redemption is for today and every day!

The congregants responded:

We are all redeemers!

"You have all heard this before but it must be said frequently. For if it is not the first thing on our minds, it may be the last and we would all suffer because of it.

What is redemption? The Christian version tells us that our redemption is eternal. That by Jesus Christ dying, we will be given eternal life. That when He comes again, He will raise the dead who believe in Him and take them to heaven.

What happens to the people who are suffering now? Are we to believe that they will be overlooked while alive? Left to suffer immeasurably? Why, when we can offer them redemption from their pain and suffering now?

The Christians promise healing and hope but only if we believe enough. Have we not all known people who believed and prayed for miracles for themselves or loved ones only to die waiting. Did they not have faith enough to receive healing?

Their scriptures tell us that God created everything. The heaven and the earth. That means he was around from the beginning, that he created this planet that is hundreds of billions years old. And we are to believe he created it for man. Yet man only appeared perhaps twenty thousand years ago.

Would you bake a cake for a celebration billions of years from now? If you knew all things, would you wait billions of years to bring forth your greatest creation?

He created heaven and earth in just six days, which included man. A few thousand years later, he sent His son with the sole purpose of dying for our sins. Necessary only because Adam and Eve disobeyed His order to avoid the forbidden fruit. But He knew they were going to defy Him because He knows everything. He was testing them.

Why wait thousands of years before sending the solution to sin which He set up in the first place. Wouldn't a loving, all knowing father build a garden in which all the fruit was good and safe?

There are eight billion people on the planet and many religions. Many of those religions predate Christianity. The numbers supporting the theory of creation don't stand up. Believers will tell you that you must have faith that the numbers are correct even if they don't make sense to us.

How do we explain the unexplainable? Faith. Have faith that God has a plan and that we mere humans could never understand it so therefore, we should never question it.

We look at thing differently, don't we brothers? We believe that waiting for God to intercede is ignoring our responsibilities to each other. Faith in God and the afterlife provides comfort to those who cannot believe that when we die, we do not simply die. How greedy to want to live forever in spirit form at the cost of ignoring the human tragedy that is right before us.

Brethren, many people would not understand the work we do. Many will continue to choose a different story of where we came from and where we are going. We will never change that nor is it our mission to do so.

Our mission is to care for the lame, the injured and the lost as best we can. To give them a sense of purpose while they are still here, rather than waiting out their altered existence until they die, often alone and miserable. With us, they are a part of a community. It may not be everyone's vision of perfect or even better, but we believe doing something is better than doing nothing.

We are all redeemers. We take people who are broken and offer them a home and rehabilitation. They will, in the vast majority of cases, not return to the outside world. However, they will be given jobs according to their strengths. They will be fed and bathed, kept dry and warm. We become their family.

Be proud of the work we do! Be strong in your convictions! Follow our path of righteousness and prosperity. Do not divert from the path because to do so has consequences. No tricks, no forbidden fruit but there are rules. Rules that protect us individually and as a group.

There are also great benefits. I know you have all partaken in the vast pleasures available to our faithful. You have been chosen. You are the special ones. You have been invited inside the door to the kingdom. Protect your privilege.

I invite you all to be my guest for a light lunch and relaxation. Thank you for coming.

Chapter 46

Quicksburg, VA

"I didn't think I would see you two back here today!" Del exclaimed.

"Are you saying you're not happy to see me twice in one day?" Til joked.

"You're usually here twice a day, I'm just surprised she was willing to come back with you."

"I have a little time to kill and I was actually getting hungry again. Besides, it's my turn to buy. How about a booth this time, Sheriff?"

"That's fine with me, Charis. Del, we'll be over there by the jukebox."

"Coffee?" Del asked.

They both affirmed.

Til waited until Charis was seated before he climbed in across from her. The coffee arrived as soon as they were seated. Del also brought menus.

"Raise a hand when you're ready."

She walked away. The place was nearly full but it was almost noon.

"Dr. Flanders is every bit as smart as you said. He blew me away. How does he keep busy here? It's such a small area."

"Quicksburg is small but Shenandoah County takes up a lot of territory and we have our share of violent crime and suspicious deaths. Most of it seems to be family related. Just a lot of poor people looking for a way out."

"So Doc is the county M.E.. That makes more sense."

"He also lends a hand with surrounding counties when he can. What looks good to you, Charis?"

"How are the burgers?"

"Very good. They grind it fresh right here. Never frozen and locally raised."

"And the fries?"

"Grown local as well. So is the lettuce and tomato. All organic as well."

"You sound like a spokesperson," Charis added.

"I like to be an advocate when I can. It's all true and I wouldn't say so If I didn't know firsthand."

"You sold me!" she said and raised her hand. "I hope you know what you want."

Til just smiled. Del hustled over to take their order.

"What'll you have kids?"

Charis spoke first.

"I would like a bacon cheeseburger, medium rare with fries."

"Sweet or white?"

Charis stared blankly.

"Fries honey, sweet or white potatoes?"

"Oh, white please."

"Any cheese or gravy?"

"Straight up!" she answered.

"Til?"

"The usual. Have I told you how pretty you look today, Delilah?"

Del shook her head, took their menus and walked away.

"Til, what else do you have on this case? Any entry point or surveillance cameras in the area?"

"There aren't any cameras where the body was discovered. It was almost directly under the interstate. That's a pretty rural area and there aren't any buildings around."

"Where is the most logical place upriver to dump a body?"

"There is a road off route 11 that passes over the river between here and there. It called Caverns Rd. We can take another look after lunch if you have the time."

"I'll make the time but you said another look."

"Yes, my deputy was already out there but he didn't find anything. It's worth a shot though."

"Have you spoken to your team up north?"

"Mostly by text since I've been on the road. We have a conference call scheduled for 2:00 pm today."

"Is everything alright, Charis? You have a serious look in your face."

"I guess it's just the seriousness of the business."

"Maybe, but it's been serious since you got here and I haven't seen that look yet."

"I've been receiving threats. Telephone calls from a burner phone. The caller is using voice altering technology but it's always the same voice. I've had several calls telling me to stop looking for people who may not want to be found."

"What does your superior say?"

"I haven't told him about it?"

"Why in the world not?"

"Because I think someone on the inside may be involved. I found a note on my desk with a similar sentiment and someone flattened my tires in the parking garage at work."

"When was the last call?"

"Last night, at the hotel."

"I'm sorry, Charis, I wish you had called me."

"I appreciate that Til but if someone wanted to hurt me, they've had plenty of opportunities. He or she is trying to get me to back off of something but I don't know what. He said I should know and last night he said it was my last warning."

"Do you think it's about this case?" Til asked.

"The calls started before I came here so I didn't think so but now that we have similar cases in various states, I'm rethinking that. But how are they connected?"

"I'm not sure but it seems like they must be. What else did the caller say?"

"He said *go back to solving real crimes and leave the petty things alone.* Then he said, *I would hate to see such a pretty girl get hurt.*"

"Was he talking about you?"

"I'm not sure. One other time he was referring to a toddler. I was at a party in High Falls and somehow he knew I was there. He called me at the party asking me if I was *enjoying my time away and it would be a shame if that little girl was hurt.*"

"And you think he knows because he works for the FBI?"

"No one else knew except my father and he would never say anything. I'm going to see him tomorrow to make sure his phone and home aren't bugged."

Del returned with the food. Til's *usual* turned out to be the same thing Charis ordered.

"So you really do know about the burgers."

"Yes, I do. I wouldn't steer you wrong. Now eat fast so we can go check out that river in time for you to make your call."

Chapter 47

High Falls, NY

Greg didn't touch his lunch. When Chris left the conference room, Greg asked Kathy to have the conference room cleared of the food. When she saw that very little was gone, she asked Greg if he was alright.

"Just a loss of appetite, Kathy, nothing to worry about. Please hold my calls until Charis calls at two. Oh, and ask Jim Larkin if he could come to see me. Now would be good."

She knew him better than to believe that, but she let it lie. She also knew that he would talk about it when he was ready.

Greg went to his office and closed the door. He sat behind his desk and leaned back in his chair. He was trying to digest what he just witnessed. He never really knew Maury Slater until he visited his funeral home during the university murders more than a decade later.

Could Slater and Barry Miller have been working together? He supposed it was possible. Other employees had been involved. But if they were working together, why would Barry be videotaping him? Maybe Maury was a decoy. Sure, if Barry was drawing heat, he could leak evidence that Slater was molesting deceased patients. That would make it look like Slater was the killer and the motive was his sick sexual fetish. But what about the other guys?

There was a knock on the door.

"Come!" Greg said.

"Mr. Larkin is here to see you."

"Come in, Jim, thanks for coming on short notice."

"No problem, Mr. Webster. What can I do for you?"

"Jim, this is going to sound strange to you but I need to ask you a few questions about the propofol murders. I know I questioned you at the time and you were very helpful in getting a conviction of Dr. Seike."

"Okay Chief, I'm happy to answer anything I can."

"Jim, were you ever aware of any video cameras in the morgue?"

"I never saw a camera. What I do remember is finding a hole in the wall behind a shelving unit. I was cleaning and restocking supplies and I found a hole that was only about three quarters of an inch across."

"I reported it to maintenance but when they came the next day, the hole was gone and the wall was patched and painted. It bothered me for quite a while but I could never prove anything."

"Jim, what do you remember about Maury Slater?"

"Maury was okay sometimes but very strange at others. He seemed to be a bit of a loner until he hooked up with Lynette just before he left here. There was one thing I never understood about Maury. He always had money and he drove a sweet car that he could never afford working here."

"Could he have inherited money from a family member?"

"I suppose he could have, I didn't know him that well."

"Jim, aside from what you testified to, can you remember anything strange going on in your area?"

"Not that I recall."

"One last question, Jim. Did Barry Miller ever stop by the morgue?"

"Yes, I do remember him coming by every once in a while. Dr. Seike would usually ask me to run an errand or take a break when he stopped by. I figured it had to do with using too many supplies. Mr. Miller had a reputation of being a miser."

"Unfortunately, that comes with the job he had. Jim, if you think of anything else, just call Kathy and ask for a few minutes of my time. I appreciate you coming by and we all appreciate the work you do."

"Thank you, Mr. Webster. By the way, everyone here loves working for you."

"That's nice of you to say, Jim. Have a great day!"

When Jim left his office, Greg closed the door and tried to put some of the pieces back together. Who were the other men in the videos and where did Maury get his money? Many of the men were friends of his who shared his taste in women. Then it hit him. Maybe just maybe he was selling the services of the dead. That would explain the men and the money. It was a place to start. Right now he needed to focus and prepare for the call from Charis.

Chapter 48

Quicksburg, VA

Charis and Sheriff Sweeney made their way from the restaurant down Quicksburg Rd., underneath I-81 and up Rt. 11 north. Til made a left turn on Caverns Rd and stopped just short of the bridge crossing the North Fork Shenandoah River.

He pulled off the road onto the gravel shoulder making sure he allowed enough room for Charis to exit the passenger side. They walked toward the end of the bridge and check out each bank. Not seeing anything they walked beneath the bridge. Til went down first and offered a hand to Charis. She took it.

When they reached the water's edge, they scoped left and right looking for any disturbance in the grass.

"I don't see anything on this side, do you?" Til asked.

"No, I don't but what do you see across the river?"

Judd went back to the cruiser and came back with binoculars. Raising the glasses, he focused the lenses on the opposite bank. He handed them to Charis.

"Have a look," he said.

She zeroed in on the area just to the left of the bridge.

"I see some disturbance in the soil to the left of the bridge."

"So do I. Let's go."

He assisted Charis back up the hill. They got in the car and took off across the bridge. Til parked just on the other side. They got out and walked to the top of the bank. There was a definite flattening of the grass.

"Wait here and I'll check it out," he said.

Til walked well outside the flattened area. He reached over and felt beneath the grass.

"I can feel the ridges of tire tracks, Charis."

"Can you get a forensics crew out here, Til?"

"Yes, but they have to come from Harrisonburg. That could take hours."

"Will putting tape around the perimeter do any good?" she asked.

"It's better than nothing. There should be a roll and some stakes in the trunk."

"Stay there," Charis said, "I'll get them."

Til wondered how Deputy Swart missed this. Then he remembered who he was talking about. He would have a chat with him when he got back to the office.

"Here we go, Sheriff."

"How would you like to be my new deputy, Charis?"

"How would you like to be mine?" she said back.

"Right," he said. "Hand me a few sticks."

It only took them a few minutes to place the tape. When they got in the car, Til placed a call to the state police in Harrisonburg. They would try to have someone out there before sundown.

Deputy Swart was hiding across the bridge. He could see that they were about done so he quickly backed away from the bridge and sped out of there. He pulled out his cell phone and called Alpha Sam.

Chapter 49

Quicksburg, VA

Deputy Alan Swart had never called Alpha Sam directly. They had met each other many times but he was not considered an insider. He was nervous but he knew Sam would want to know.

Sam was enjoying his company when the phone rang. He did not want to stop what he was doing but if and when his phone rang, it needed to be answered.

"You must excuse me," he said to his guest, "I won't be long."

He left the warmth of his bed and wrapped his robe around his generous torso. The phone was in the other room.

"Hello," he said almost out of breath.

"Alpha Samuel, I am sorry to bother you but I have new information."

"And who am I speaking with?"

"Brother Alan Swart."

There was a moment of silence while Sam tried to force his memory to place the caller.

"What is your information, Brother Alan?"

"The FBI agent is nosing around with Sheriff Sweeney. Just a few minutes ago, they found the entry point in the river."

"I see. This is not good news, Brother, I was told that you had taken care of that."

"I thought I had. I did the investigation and I told the sheriff that I didn't find anything. He wouldn't have looked again if it wasn't for that Agent Andrews."

"But you did nothing to cover the tracks?"

"You couldn't see the tracks, they were almost under the bridge!"

"Well, someone saw them and now we need to do something about that. What will happen next?"

"My guess is that Til will call Harrisonburg and ask for assistance. It will take them hours to send someone."

"Do we have any brethren at that location?"

"You mean within the state police?"

"Yes, that is what I mean."

"Not that I am aware of."

"Alan, there is nothing to worry about. I do need you to do something for me though."

"Of course, Sir, anything."

"That's the spirit. I need you to go back there right now and either fill in those tire tracks or disturb them so that they cannot be traced."

"Yes Sir. I will take care of it."

"Excellent. In return, I would like to invite you to dinner tonight. I'm having a few close friends over and I would like them to meet you. I would like to show you off a little. Someone with your positive attitude is an inspiration and you should be celebrated."

"It would be an honor, sir."

"Good then, we shall see you at six sharp! And Alan, drive your personal vehicle, we wouldn't want to draw any unnecessary attention. Park around the back and I will see to it that the back door is open for you."

"I will be there by six. Thank you."

Deputy Swart was excited. He had been attending faithfully but was never asked to look behind the curtain. He knew a few people who had and while they didn't talk about specifics, they said it was life changing. They couldn't get enough of it.

But first, Alan had things to take care of. He needed to get a few buckets and fill them with dirt. He would drive by the county's sand and salt dome for the fill but he wasn't sure where he would find the buckets. He thought *maybe they had some at the diner. Maybe the grease for the fryers came in pails.*

It was getting to be almost two o'clock, surely the lunch crowd would be gone by now. He was just a few minutes away. When he drew close, he slowed down. He could see Til's cruiser in the parking lot. Andrews was getting out of the car. He drove past them and took a left turn at the next intersection, hoping he wasn't noticed.

After ten minutes, he returned. Til's car was gone and he assumed Andrews had left as well. He went inside and was greeted by Del.

"Afternoon, Deputy, It's a little late for lunch. Did Til have you off chasing gangsters again."

"Hi, Del. I had lunch already. I find myself needing a few empty buckets. You wouldn't have some hanging around now would you?"

"Going to the beach, Deputy?"

"No beach, I'm getting ready to do a project at home. You know, mixing cement to point up the steps."

"Let me look in the kitchen, Alan."

She was only gone a few seconds and came back with three, two gallon pails.

"That's all we have for now, I'm afraid. We should have more empties by the weekend."

"I think these will do, Del. Much appreciated."

"Have fun with your project."

Alan walked out. *"Smaller than I was hoping for,"* he thought. *"But who wants to carry a five gallon bucket full of sand?*

Chapter 50

On the road to Quantico, VA

Charis sent Greg a message asking if he could initiate the call because she was going to be on the road. At 2:05, she received the call. The interior of the truck was extremely quiet which she was thankful for.

"Hi, Greg," she said when she was asked to join the group.

"Hello Charis. Mary, Jack, Trey and Ethan are also on the line."

"Hi everyone'" Charis said.

They all echoed their hellos.

"Okay, Charis, it's your party," Greg said.

"I can bring you up to speed on what's happening on my end and then we can all take turns. Feel free to interrupt whenever you find it necessary. I just finished with Sheriff Sweeney in Quicksburg. We had a great morning."

"Did you get any work done?" Greg chimed in.

"That's it for you Greg. Raise your hand from now on."

"A lot of good that will do, this is not a video conference," he replied.

"Exactly!" she said.

"Anyway, we had a very productive morning. We met with the M.E. who is extremely knowledgeable and thorough. He came to the same conclusions as Dr. Lanford up there with a few additions.

The male victim down here showed multiple signs of abuse from years earlier. Things like healed fractures. He had even been subjected to hobbling at some point."

"It sounds like he was held against his will and his captors wanted to make sure he wasn't going to run." Trey added.

"We agree. He also displayed some dental work gone wrong. Before beginning the autopsy, Dr. Flanders had the foresight to take the corpse for full body x-rays. This of course showed the fractures but also identified heavy metal in the intestinal tract and moderate silicosis in his lungs."

"Thallium and calcium carbonate?" Trey asked.

"That's right."

"The same thing we are finding here," Charis answered.

"Are we working with the theory that these bodies all started out in the same place?" Jack asked.

"Good question, Jack. One theory might be that the bodies were moved from a central point and that makes sense, but why move them all over the place?"

"To complicate things," Ethan said.

"Yes, Ethan," Charis responded, "that certainly clouds things a bit but at great risk of getting caught. It has been done before but the bodies are usually spread out in a small regional area. Maybe fifty to a hundred miles. Moving a body halfway across the country is logistically difficult."

"And why are they all dropped in a river?" Mary asked.

"To delay being found." Trey answered. Several days in warm water can make it difficult to obtain fingerprints and footprints. It can also make the autopsy more difficult and less conclusive."

"We need to be thinking about the similarities across these cases. The poisoning is one thing but the inhalation of calcium carbonate is a bit more complex."

"Perhaps," Greg interrupted, "they all worked for an employer who was afraid to be exposed for OSHA violations or by the EPA for harming the environment."

"That's the way we need to think," Charis said. "Who would have incentive to make these people go away?"

"How would the abuse fit into that scenario?" Jack asked.

"It could be coincidental," Trey added. "I'm certain there are plenty of adult workers out there who were abused as children."

"Very true, Trey, but what about the teenager found in Crystal City, Missouri? He wouldn't be old enough to work and even if he was, could he have worked long enough to demonstrate lung disease?" Ethan suggested.

"Good point, Ethan. We need to keep this kind of thinking going," Charis said. I think with what we now know that we need to find more ways to link these cases. Dr. Flanders developed a post-mortem protocol to furnish to the medical examiners. It includes full body x-rays. We need to know if there is evidence of abuse and if they show signs of heavy metal in the colon and calcium carbonate in the lungs.

The FBI and CDC have this information but I want you to all have a copy. Posting on official sites is fine but we don't know how long it takes for people to notice it. For each body we have and for each additional one that comes in, we need to hand a copy of this protocol to the M.E."

"I am on my way back to Quantico now. I will be having dinner with my father tonight at which time we will discuss the possibility that his phone and/or home has been bugged. In addition, I have asked him to delve into the Valley Church of Redemption. I'll see if he has been able to find anything."

"What's up on your end?"

"Hey Charis," Greg said, "Aren't we forgetting the number one priority? Have there been any more calls?"

Charis was hoping this wouldn't come up but she should have known that Greg wouldn't let it go.

"Funny you should mention that. I received a call last night. I was in the hotel and had just turned off the lights. It was the same voice, using the same altering software. He said it was my last warning, that I should be solving real crimes and that it would be a shame to see a pretty girl get hurt.”

“Well I think you should have led with that one, Charis!” Mary said.

“Mary is right Charis, protecting you should trump everything else.” Greg added.

“Charis, is it time to get your boss involved?”

“I can’t Trey, not until I know if it’s coming from inside.”

“What can we do, Charis?” Greg asked.

“When he called the night of the party, he said it would a shame if something bad happened to that little girl. I’m sure now that he was talking about Destiny. Last night, I thought he was talking about me but he may still be implying that he would go after Destiny.”

“I want to be sure she is protected. Do you think they would consent to staying at the safehouse for a short time?”

Greg stepped up. “What safehouse, Charis?”

“I know, Greg, I shouldn’t have kicked you.”

“It’s okay for now,” he replied. Veronica and Destiny might go but Charles and Priscilla would need to stay and work the farm. That would leave them vulnerable.”

“I have an idea, Dad. I’m at the farm during the day anyway, what if I just stay overnight as well? Perhaps Ethan could spend the nights at the safehouse with Veronica and Destiny, and Richard and Bill might be able to assist during work hours.”

“Jack has a good idea, Greg. I can fill in the gaps with local law enforcement.” Trey added.

“I don’t know, Jack, I promised your mother I wouldn’t put you kids in jeopardy again.”

Mary spoke up. “Thank you, Greg, I love you for saying that but we are all family now and we need to look out for each other. It doesn’t sound like that big of a risk.”

“Charis, promise me that if the shit hits the fan, everyone can go to the funhouse. I mean the safehouse.”

"I promise. And if starts to look there is more of a real threat, we will put an agent there."

"Ethan, are you on board with this?"

"Absolutely."

"Alright, I will talk to the Chalmers," Greg said.

"Settled. Trey what is new in your investigation?"

"We have essentially the same information you do. The state police are close to identifying the type of tires that were on the vehicle that we believe may have created the tracks behind the donut shop in Fultonville. We also have surveillance footage from that shop that may help. Bill Dillon is assisting the Sheriff by reviewing the tape."

"That's excellent!" Charis exclaimed. "We found tracks along the river outside of Quicksville also. They should have them cast by this evening. Boy, if we had a match that may move things along."

Anything else?

"The Webster family is going to church on Sunday!"

"So you told me," Charis replied.

"I wasn't sure everyone else knew," Greg said.

"I didn't know," Trey said, "but I guess I didn't need to."

"We found the church that Lilijac's parents used to take her to. We are going to conduct an undercover investigation, Trey. The place is so far off the beaten path that it is virtually unfindable. No signs, no website and no postings. An odd way to build a congregation, don't you think?"

"I think it would be odd enough to keep me away," he said. "Why do you want to go there?"

"Because we can't find any other connection. Well, that's not exactly true. We did find her dad, who by the way, lives around the corner from the church, but he denies he even had a daughter. Our last hope is a discharge summary from St. Luke's Hospital in Utica. I should be receiving that by the end of the day," Greg added. "There is one other new thing Charis but you and I will need to take that conversation offline."

"I'll stay on when the others sign off."

"Thanks, Charis."

"Alright everyone. Hey, listen, the dates we set up for everyone to check in, just forget about them. We are up to speed so let's just do this again on Friday afternoon."

All agreed and everyone but Charis vacated the call.

"What's up, Greg?"

"I have some disturbing news about the propofol murders."

"Wow, I thought that one was well behind you."

"That makes two of us. The killer, Barry Miller, left behind a computer which until now has rested in a storage unit that the hospital owns. It must have been taken there after Barry left the office.

"Anyway, this thing shows up in my office yesterday and is loaded with video files of men having sex with the dead patients."

"You have got to be kidding me! Necrophilia?"

"That's right. I had all I could do to keep from throwing up."

"Greg, do you recognize any of the faces?"

"Just one. Do you remember the owner of the funeral home in town that I went to see when we were investigating the university bombings?"

"Yes, I remember you telling me a funny story about him."

"Well, he left High Falls Hospital right after the propofol case ended. He was employed as an orderly."

"He was abusing the corpses?"

"Yes, but so were other men. None of them recognizable to me. So if it was just him getting his warped rocks off, that's one thing. But if he was, let's say renting the corpses, that opens another can of worms."

"Why would you think he was pimping them out?"

"I didn't at first. I thought that perhaps he had some friends who were into the same thing. But then I talked to a guy who was working here at the same time and he told me Maury always had money and that he drove a car that was way above his pay grade. It just seemed to click."

"So do you think he and Miller were in it together?"

"I think Miller knew Maury was doing this and I think he was taping him as a way out if Miller ever got caught."

"Interesting. Miller was looking for a get out of jail free card and Maury was the fall guy. It's plausible, Greg."

"How are you going to find out?"

"I'm not sure yet but part of it may involve talking to Maury."

"Be careful, Greg, that is dangerous territory. You can't really accuse him or threaten him with the video. That would be considered extortion if it doesn't go through the proper channels."

"You're right. What if I just follow him around a bit?"

"Do you think he may still be doing this after all these years?"

"Why not, he got away with it once, maybe it's easier and less risky doing it out of your own funeral business."

"Good point. How do you gain entry?"

"For now, I don't. I just find an inconspicuous place to park and take some video of my own. Just to see who is coming and going."

"I guess that's harmless enough. Keep me informed though, Greg, and don't do something stupid!"

"Me? Stupid? Don't answer that. Alright now what about you? Do you think you're safe?"

"I'm not a hundred percent sure, but I think so. If someone wanted me out of the picture, they have had a thousand chances to do it."

"Besides going to your Dad's tomorrow, you are going to Custer, South Dakota on Friday. What about tomorrow?"

"I'm not sure right now. I'm going to call McMinnville, Tennessee after we hang up. If I don't get the answers I want or they don't co-operate, I may catch a plane there tomorrow. I'll let you know."

"Promise?"

"I promise."

Chapter 51

US RT. 211 Toward Quantico

Charis decided she would go to McMinnville, TN the next day. She would spend a good part of the day there and then continue on to Custer, SD. She dialed Detective Martin Ballard's number to give him the good news.

"Ballard."

"Good afternoon, detective, Special Agent Charis Andrews, are you having a good day?"

"I've had better," he said.

"I'm sorry to hear that. I guess it's just the nature of the job sometimes. Listen, I don't want to make your life any more difficult but I have decided to come out there tomorrow. I should arrive in McMinnville by 11am and be gone by 3pm. Any luck with the boat?"

She already received a message from the office that the boat was delivered and in a short period of time, they located the entry point.

"Yes, your boys found the spot that the body most likely entered the water. They made the concrete impressions and were out of here in no time."

"That's great! Do you see what you can do with the right attitude and a little planning? Anyway, I would like to speak with the medical examiner on the case tomorrow, Can you arrange that please?"

"Yes Ma'am."

"Perfect, I will see you late morning tomorrow."

Charis hung up. She was going to be home in plenty of time to stop at the office and her apartment before going to her father's for dinner. She was excited to see him. She dialed the airline.

Chapter 52

Quicksville, VA

After taking Agent Andrews back to the diner to get her truck, Sheriff Sweeney returned to the office. He noticed that the other cruiser was out. He really wanted to have a talk with his deputy regarding the less than adequate job he did investigating the river.

It was shoddy work but it also made Til look bad in the eyes of the FBI. He knew Andrews wasn't the type to tell anyone at the office but he was also aware how she felt about the other crews she was working with, especially in Custer.

He tried to radio Alan Swart but there was no response. He waited a few minutes and tried again. Still nothing. He looked at the call log to see if he could determine where his deputy might be based on incoming calls. There was nothing unusual. He checked the outgoing calls as well but nothing seemed suspicious.

He got back in his car and drove to the diner again.

"Howdy, Sheriff, three times in a day and it's not even dinner time yet," Del greeted him.

"Your lucky day Delilah! I knew you would be off shift soon and I just needed to see you once more."

"Sit down and I'll bring you some coffee."

She set the cup and saucer down and poured from the decaf coffee pot.

"It's late, you want to sleep tonight, don't you?"

"I don't know, do I?"

"Don't go teasing me Sheriff, my feet are killing me and I'm not in the mood."

She brought him a piece of peach pie.

"This will have to be your sweetie today."

"You are a heartbreaker, Delilah. Hey, has Alan been in today?"

"He was here just a short while ago. He needed buckets for a project he was fixin' to start at home. It couldn't have been five minutes after you dropped off that nice young lady."

"That seems strange to me," Til said, "I've never known him to be the home project type."

"There are a lot of things that seem strange about your deputy, Til."

"How do you mean, Delilah?"

"It's hard to define, he just seems different. He doesn't come in as often as he used to and when he does he meets up with a few fellas I don't recognize. They always stop talking when I approach the table. A few times though, I've heard them talking about redeemer or redemption, or something like that. My guess is he's caught up in a church thing."

"That doesn't sound like a bad thing, Delilah."

"I'm not saying it is, I'm just telling you I have noticed a change in him."

"Hasn't made him any smarter, I can tell you," he replied.

"I think I may take the pie home with me, D. I may need something sweet later," Til said as he winked.

Outside the diner, Til radioed once more. Still no response. He drove back to the office.

Chapter 53

High Falls, NY

Greg left work early so that he could drive out to the Chalmers' place and talk to them about the safehouse and security at the farm. But first, he decided to take a run by the funeral home. He heard what Charis said and he agreed. He just wanted to scope out a spot where he could observe without being seen.

The Mease funeral home was just outside of town. Mr. Mease had left the business to Maury when he retired. Greg had only been there one time, during the university bombing crimes. He found Maury to be a bit of an ass kissing moron. He remembered how frustrated he was getting with him just asking simple questions.

Driving up to the place brought back memories. The color of the exterior was different now and it looked like they had added a crematorium around the back. There were two cars parked in the driveway near the side entrance. He jotted down the make and model and plate numbers of each car.

He backed out of the driveway and headed back the way he came. There was a hardware store across the street and just west of the parlor. He should be able to park there without drawing any undue attention. He was done for the day. He found his place for reconnaissance and he had a couple of plate numbers. He planned to stop by each day at whatever times he could to monitor the traffic in and out.

About fifteen minutes out of town he pulled into the Chalmers' driveway. He parked his car in front of the barn. The door was open but the barn was empty. The cows were still out in the fields.

He walked up toward the house and was greeted by a German Shepard who looked a little pissed at him. He stopped his forward motion and began speaking softly. The dog wasn't buying it. He believed if he turned around, the dog might attack. If he continued toward the house, he was sure he would become more aggressive.

It seemed Greg's only choice was to stay where he was and hope that someone inside heard the commotion. *"I'm bringing biscuits from now on,"* Greg thought to himself. He was careful not to keep eye contact with the animal. He was sure he just read this somewhere. The Shepard continued to bark. Finally, after what seemed like an eternity, Priscilla stepped out the side door of the house.

"Laddie! Heel!" The dog backed up a few steps then held his ground. Priscilla walked toward them. "Come here, Laddie. Good boy, come on."

Laddie turned to meet her and sat down at her feet.

"It looks like you have a new family member," Greg said.

"That, we do. Sorry about that. He's a bit protective."

"That's a good thing, right?"

"Most of the time," she replied.

They walked toward Greg, Priscilla's hand on Laddie's collar.

"This is Mr. Webster, he won't hurt us."

Greg put his hand down, palm away from the dog. Laddie sniffed Greg's hand and then his legs. When Laddie came back to smell his hand again, Greg turned it and pet him gently.

"That should do it. A friend for life," Priscilla said.

"How are you Priscilla?"

"I'm fine. What brings you here today?"

"I was hoping to get a few minutes with you, your dad and Veronica. I have something I would like to talk about."

"They are all here somewhere, come on in."

Greg could tell that Laddie didn't think it was a good idea. He growled his disapproval as they moved toward the house. Veronica was preparing dinner while Charles was entertaining Destiny in the living room.

"Company, everyone!," Priscilla announced.

Veronica turned from the sink and went to give Greg a hug. Charles came into the kitchen carrying Destiny.

"Welcome!. Let go give Uncle Greg a hug," Charles said.

"It's great to see you all again. I know it's been just a few days but I can never get enough."

"Greg would like to talk with all of us, Dad."

"Of course. Let's sit in the living room." They all followed the patriarch and claimed a seat. Destiny was set on the floor to play.

"What is it, Greg?"

"Probably much of nothing, but because we have all been through this before, I don't think we should take any chances. Charis has been receiving threatening phone calls. The odds that they are connected in any way with us is close to zero but she did receive one the evening of the party so whoever is making the calls, was aware of the party and may have threatened to harm Destiny."

"Why Destiny, Greg?" Veronica asked.

"Exactly, that's why we're not very concerned about it. It is most likely that Charis is getting too close for comfort with one of her cases and is being warned off. She is not involved in anything having to do with any of us."

"So, what do you need us to do?" said Charles.

"Charis suggests that Veronica and Destiny stay at the safehouse for a few days. It's really a beautiful place and not far away. You will be treated like royalty. I knew that neither you Priscilla, nor you Charles would consent to leaving the farm so we would like to add a little additional security at the homestead."

"What does that look like, Greg?" Charles replied.

"First of all, I think you have a good start to your security team with Laddie. Secondly, in addition to Jack being here during the day, he could spend the nights as well. Trey will also provide some backup when needed.

Ethan will spend evenings and nights at the safehouse with Veronica and Destiny. I'll ask Richard and Bill if they can cover during the day. Charis can have an agent standing by when necessary."

The room became very quiet while they all thought about it.

"Greg," Charles began, "I trust you and your team enough to follow your recommendations."

The others voiced their consent.

"Will I be able to visit Destiny at the safehouse?" Charles followed, "We have become very close and I'm not sure how either of us would handle the separation."

"It would probably be alright, Charles. I know they frown on a lot of coming and going when the safehouse is active."

"Dad," Priscilla said, why don't you stay at the safehouse with the girls. I'll be fine here with Laddie and Jack. It sounds like the only potential target is Destiny."

"What do you think, Greg?" Charles asked.

"I thinks that's a fine idea. Can you give Jack a few lessons on how to handle your shotgun?"

"We will begin in the morning," he replied.

"Alright. If everyone is on board, I will get it organized." Greg said.

When he stood, Laddie came over and sat in front of him. Greg squatted to pet him and realized the friendship started now.

When Greg arrived home, he talked it over with Jack and Mary. They were fine with the plan. Mary offered to make the calls and put a schedule together. Jack liked the idea of spending more time at the farm. He found that he enjoyed the hard work more than he imagined. He also enjoyed the company of Charles and the girls. Especially Priscilla.

Chapter 54

Quicksburg, VA

Til Sweeney was in the office awaiting the arrival of his deputy. He had finally tracked Alan down on the radio. Alan didn't offer an excuse and Til didn't demand one over the phone. He just told Alan he needed to see him in the office asap.

The deputy arrived at 4:20 pm, a good hour after Til made contact.

"You wanted to see me Sheriff?"

"Have a seat Alan."

Alan could tell Til was upset.

"Alan, I tried to get you on the radio for over an hour today. I don't really care what you were doing or where you were but you need to respond to radio calls. That's why we put one on your vest. The thing that bothers me more Alan is that you totally messed up on your assignment at the river."

"What do you mean, Sheriff, I did go look at the river and I didn't see anything."

"How hard did you look, Alan? I was there less than five minutes and spotted it from the other side of the river! Did you look from both sides? Did you look with binoculars?"

"I didn't look from one side to the other, I just looked as I walked each side."

"Did you go close to the bridge, Alan? The tracks were underneath the bridge."

"Why would someone drive under the bridge when they could just toss the body over the railing?"

"Have you ever lifted a dead body, Deputy? Do you think you could even lift a hundred and twenty pounds high enough to through it over the railing?"

"I suppose I could if I had to!" Alan raised his voice. He stood up in a display of guilt and frustration.

"Alan, you need to relax and sit back down."

Alan came around to Til's side of the desk. He was pacing anxiously, like a kid who knew he had lied, was caught and was about to get the belt.

The sheriff looked down at Alan's feet. The cuffs of his pants had grass and dirt on them but his shoes were clean, as if just polished.

"Alan, I'm going to ask you one more time to sit down and get control of yourself." The deputy took a few deep breaths and followed the order.

"What has gotten into you, Alan? You seem strung out lately."

"I don't know, Sheriff. Nothing I guess."

"Well, it looks like a lot of something to me. Is everything alright at home?"

"Mostly. Ma is on my case about going to church so much. Can you imagine? A parent upset with a child who goes to church?"

"I guess it depends on what's happening as a result of all that going," Til responded. "Is that what this obvious change in you is about?"

"I'm a little nervous because I've been invited to dinner tonight. It's the first time I've been asked to attend. It's kind of a big deal. Mama doesn't understand. She thinks going to church on Sunday should be enough. She don't see that it is a social event for me. I don't get out much Sheriff and I enjoy the people there."

"Well, it's good to get out and socialize, Alan, but be aware that people notice the change in you and ask yourself if that change is a good thing. If you believe it's right for you, then others will just have to accept it. But if it is getting in the way of your thinking or your actions, you may need to re-evaluate.

For example, if you are losing focus on your duties to the county, that could hurt you. Those tracks should have been an easy pickup but you missed them. Were you distracted by church events?"

"I don't think so, Til, I just missed them and I'm sorry."

"Alright. I'm going to make a note of it, Alan. I won't put it in your file right away bit it could end up there if I see you slipping. And I don't want to catch you not answering your calls again. Do we have an understanding, Deputy?"

"Yes, Sheriff, we do."

"Okay, go on home and get ready for your church dinner."

When Alan stood up, Til checked his legs again. He decided not to push the issue at the time. He had dished out enough for one day. After checking the call log and email, Til removed his pie from the fridge, turned off the lights and closed the office door. He heard the phone ringing and quickly reopened the door.

'Sheriff Sweeney. Say that again please. Yes, alright. I'll be there in twenty minutes."

Til closed the door and left the office. He was heading back to where he and Charis had found the tracks.

Chapter 55

Montgomery County, NY

Sheriff Bentley received a call from Bill Dillon. He had found what they were looking for. Judd raced his car from Fonda across the bridge to Fultonville with the emergency lights on and an occasional siren.

When he arrived at the office, Bill Dillon had not only found the place in the tape they were looking for but had printed an enlargement.

"Here you are Sheriff. We can't see a plate number but we know what type vehicle made those tracks. We also know the day and time. I have jotted down the date and the beginning and end times so that you can easily review the video."

"That's great Bill! We owe you a huge debt."

"Catching the guy will settle the bill," he responded.

"If there is anything else I can do, just give a call, Sheriff."

"I will. Thank you!"

Bill left the Sheriff's office feeling useful. He realized those moments were few and far between.

Judd Bentley called Cliff Alvord at the state police station.

"Clint we Identified the vehicle. It's a black, 2016 Mercedes Benz Sprinter 2500."

"You got that on the video? Any plate? He replied.

"Couldn't see the plate. We see the driver as he got out of the van but only from mid-chest down. It looks like the passenger door is open as well so we're probably looking at two people."

"I was just cross referencing what we have on the tire marks. Michelin makes an LT 245/75R that matches our measurements and would fit that van. If we only had some proof that a body was dropped there. For all we know, the two guys went fishing in the dark."

"It's still more than we had an hour ago. How many of those vans are on the road?" Judd asked.

"I'm guessing a bunch, but we can narrow it down by point of sale. I'll start checking the Department of Motor Vehicles database. It may take a while."

"Thanks, Cliff."

Judd's next call was to Trey Lawrence.

"Hey Trey, Judd Bentley."

"What can I do for you Sheriff?"

"I was hoping you could get a message to Agent Andrews to let her know we found a vehicle make and model. Maybe she could pass it on to law enforcement in the other places."

"Send me the details and a photo if you have it and I'll get it to her right away. I don't suppose you have a plate number."

"You can't have everything!"

"I hear you, "Trey said and hung up.

Chapter 56

Albany, NY

Dr. Lanford was ready to call it day. She checked her email one last time and found a message from the FBI with copies sent to law enforcement offices, the CDC, EPA and M.E.s across the country. It was titled *Recent Victim's Found in Rivers. *Environmental and Occupational Health Warning!"*

To whom it may concern,

Multiple states are reporting bodies found in rivers that contain hazardous materials. The primary concern is the presence of Thallium. Please follow universal precautions when handling, moving and examining these victims.

Secondary:

Please verify the presence of calcium carbonate in the lungs.

Tertiary:

Please conduct whole body radiographs with particular attention to:

1. Radiopaque substances in the GI tract and chest.

2. Recent new or old, healed fractures as well as any other signs of abuse.

3. Dental caries and improper dental repairs.

Please report any findings as a response to this message.

Amelia dialed the imaging department.

"I need stat imaging of a corpse I'm holding in the morgue. You will need to dress in protective clothing and follow HazMat protocol. I will wait for the images."

"So much for an early evening," she thought.

Chapter 57

Quicksburg, VA

There were two Virginia State Police vehicles parked on the far side of the bridge. One was a cruiser and the other, a work truck. Til advanced slowly across the bridge. He pulled as far onto the shoulder of the road as he possible could.

A uniformed officer approached as he got out of the car.

"Sheriff Sweeney, I'm Lieutenant Brown. I'm sorry to call you out here this time of day," he said as they shook hands.

"I appreciate you being here, Lieutenant. What do we have?"

"Well, it looks like the tracks were recently filled in."

"It would have to be very recently. I was out here just a few hours ago."

"Come have a look," Brown said.

They went down the shallow decline toward the water's edge.

"This is the spot," Til said. "It was just two grass topped ruts when I found it earlier."

"There is good news here Sheriff. While whoever did this filled the depressions, he did a pretty poor job of it. My boys think they can remove the loose soil mixture and still get an impression."

"That is great news!" Til exclaimed. "Why would someone go to all the trouble of covering their tracks, especially in daylight and then do a lousy job? Doesn't make sense to me."

"I've been thinking about that. I believe the person was either lazy, crazy, or following an order."

"Or maybe all three," Til followed.

"There is another thing that seems odd, Sheriff. Why wouldn't this person just destroy the tracks with a shovel? Why bring soil from somewhere else? All they did was lay this mix on top of the bent grass which left the tire marks virtually untouched."

"You keep referring to a mix. Do you know what the mix is?"

"I believe I do," Brown said. "I think it's sand and sodium chloride."

Brown grabbed a handful and held it out to Til.

"I think you're right, Brown, that's what it looks like to me too."

"So, where does one get sand and halite?"

"From a highway salt dome," Til answered.

"Right again, Sheriff."

"I'll bet it was from our county road treatment site. I think I may have a clue about who did this."

Til was remembering how defensive Deputy Swart was and the dirt on the cuffs of his pants. *But why?*

"Lieutenant Brown," said one of the workers, "I believe we have enough of that soil removed to allow for a good print."

"Alright then fellas, go on ahead." Brown ordered.

"Sheriff, we don't need to keep you any longer. Go enjoy your evening and I'll call you when we have the details. It could take a day or so."

"I appreciate that, Lieutenant. Thanks for your help."

Til walked back to the cruiser. He didn't know what Alan was up to but he was pretty sure he was behind this. Til set out to find him.

Chapter 58

Quantico, VA

Charis parked in the garage at headquarters and took a good look around before getting out of her car. She locked it and released the strap holding her gun in the holster. She walked briskly with her bag in one hand and the other near her hip.

When she reached the elevator, she made sure it was empty before getting in. When it arrived at her floor, she stood with her back to the controls until the doors were fully opened. She proceeded as if she were entering a building where gunfire was expected.

When she determined that the hallway was clear, she proceeded to her office. There were still several people at work and she greeted them as she passed by. She looked down the hallway toward the boss' office but it was dark.

She opened her door and turned on her lights. It looked exactly like she left it with the exception of a folded and taped note in the center of her desk. She started her computer and checked her voice mail while she waited for it to boot up.

She had no new voicemails that needed immediate attention. She sat back and opened the note. The handwriting was familiar, the same as the first note she received. It was written on FBI notepad paper that every employee in the building had access to.

"Welcome back Agent Andrews, I hear that you had a successful trip. Let it go now. These bodies are not important. You should pay more attention to the living, including yourself and that little cutie up north. I wonder who will have your office when you're no longer here. A pity really, but you do have one chance to redeem yourself. Let sleeping DOGS lie."

She folded the note and placed it in her bag. She opened her email and scanned the list. There was one from her agency regarding the proper handling of victims with possible Thallium poisoning. She read it and moved on, happy that the word was out.

The next was from Greg telling her that the Chalmers were on board with the security plan. She would make the arrangements for that after meeting with her father.

The last note she planned to open was from Trey Lawrence. The folks in upstate New York had a positive ID on the make, model and tire size of the vehicle in question surrounding the Lock 12 body. She would get this information out to the other locations right away.

Trey also requested her itinerary for the next two days including the players she would be meeting with. She didn't think it was necessary but she complied with the request.

Having satisfied her mental checklist, Charis closed the lights and her door and headed back to the garage. She started her car remotely as soon as she entered the garage. She could hear the engine come to life and she could see the running lights come on.

She was just about ready to unlock the door when she heard a loud noise. It sounded like a pistol shot coming from five or six cars away. She could hear a car squealing it's tires on the level below her. She was ducked down behind the car next to hers. She laid flat on the ground and looked beneath the other parked vehicles, searching for foot movement.

Not seeing any, she rose back to a squatting position. She raised her head slowly and carefully to the window level and peered through the glass. There was no evidence of anyone else on her level. She quietly moved between cars, passing her own until she found where the noise had come from.

As she approached, she could smell the gunpowder from the cherry bomb that had exploded on the concrete. There was an eight inch charred area on the floor and remnants of the wrapper.

She made her way back to her car and found a note beneath the driver's side wiper blade.

"Last Chance!"

Chapter 59

Near Quicksburg, VA

Alan Swart parked in the back of the church as directed. There were only a few cars in the lot. The gate in the perimeter fence had been open just like on Sundays. The place looked different at night. He could hear what sounded like a large window fan blowing.

He was fifteen minutes early but he didn't think anyone would mind. He exited and locked his car and walked to the rear entry door. He had never entered the building any way but through the front. It was dimly lit and a little eerie.

There was a doorbell but he wasn't sure if he should use it or just knock on the door. He rang the bell. He couldn't hear anything through the thick wooden door. He didn't want to seem like a pain so he just waited rather than ringing again.

The door opened and a man in all black greeted him.

"Welcome Brother, please come in."

Alan enter a room that was roughly twenty feet square. To the right were benches with red velvet seats. Straight ahead was another large door that was closed, and to the left was a staircase that wound its way up past the high ceiling.

"We will be meeting upstairs tonight, Brother Alan, please follow me."

Alan was both nervous and excited. The entire area was paneled in golden oak including the stairs which had treads of plush red carpeting. When they reached the landing, Alan could see through the banister to the entryway he just came through.

When he looked down the hall to his left, he was awestruck with the beauty and breadth of the place. The corridor reminded him of a conference he once attended. It was thirty feet wide with small sitting areas that seemed to go on forever. On each side, large oak doors guarded rooms that he could only imagine.

About halfway down the hallway, his greeter made a left turn into a similar sized corridor. It was shorter than the last and at the end, he could see people gathering. There were perhaps only a dozen who all seemed to be dressed the same.

When they got closer, he could see they were all men and they were wearing robes of the same color. Each had a red martini style glass in his hand. As he approached, they began walking toward him. In turn, they welcomed him by name and introduced themselves. First names only, preceded by Brother.

Alan was overwhelmed by the attention. His experience of life had been much more solitary. His mother was wrong about his church habit, this is where he belonged.

At once, the double doors on the left of the expansive gathering area opened. He could sense a rushing of air surrounding him, catching him off guard. There was a sweet yet dank smell that he couldn't place. It reminded him of the ocean, like sea spray.

He walked in with the others guiding him. The room reminded him of a small ballroom with a high ceiling, red carpeting and white high-backed, ornate wooden chairs with an ivory finish. In the center of the room was a round dining table set with the finest silver and crystal he had ever seen. At least fourteen chairs surrounded the table.

At the back wall of the room stood an altar, backed by what appeared to be black glass. It was still early enough to be light outside but no light penetrated the windows. Along the side walls were several doors with additional seating in between.

He could smell food cooking from behind one or several of the doors. It was wonderful. He senses were in overload. The men began seating themselves. Alan didn't know where he should perch so he just waited until everyone else was settled. There were just two seats left open. One with its back to the door and the other directly across the large table having its back to the altar.

While he was trying to decide, the door behind him opened and in walked Alpha Samuel. He was wearing a much fancier robe that the others making Alan feel even more out of place.

The men all stood and Alan turned to face the host, who was now walking toward him.

"Brother Alan, our guest of honor, we welcome you the Redeemer's Round Table Dinner."

The men clapped in a unified syncopated rhythm. It was three claps and a rest on the fourth. Alpha Sam raised his hand and the clapping came to a sudden halt.

"Brother Alan, you will now be escorted to the Vestry where you will receive your celebratory robe."

Samuel nodded to one of the men who then left his place and put his hand on Alans back, guiding him toward the altar. Alan followed his guidance.

When they reached the small room to the left of the altar, the gentleman opened the door and the two entered. There were three cubicles with hooks for hanging clothes but no curtain.

In one of the cubicles hung a long robe in a multitude of colors. It glimmered as if it were electrified.

"This is your robe, Brother Alan. It is required that you remove all of your other clothing before getting into the robe."

"Everything?" he asked with an element of surprise in his voice.

"Yes. Acceptance into the inner circle is a serious matter. Wearing nothing but the robe symbolizes your willingness to leave all your earthly attachments for the cause. Our mission is based on our enduring trust in each other."

Alan began disrobing, hanging his clothes one article at time on the hooks. He was very aware that the other Brother was continually watching him. He finished and reached for the robe.

"Your sox, Brother. I have a pair of slippers for you."

Alan removed his sox and removed the robe from the hanger. He placed it over his head and pulled it down around him. The material was magnificently soft and slippery. He liked the way it felt against his bare skin. The gentle brushing against his genitals was sending little shocks of excitement throughout his body. He was worried that he would become erect and embarrass himself.

A pair of leather sandals were laid at his feet. He slipped into them.

"I think I'm ready," he said.

"Indeed you are, Brother. Let us join the others."

Alan noticed that the Alpha had claimed the seat with his back to the altar which meant he would be seated with his back to the door. The men stood again as he returned to the room.

"All hail to our new Brother!" Alpha Sam shouted.

"All hail the new Redeemer!" the men said in unison.

Alan was escorted to his seat. Alpha Sam rose to speak. As he did, several of the side doors opened and a dozen beautiful women entered the room. They were dressed in some kind of uniform that was shiny yet flimsy. The material was nearly see-through yet glided above their skin as if not touching them at all.

They glided around the room as though they were a ballet troupe. Their arms were flailing softly about their bodies as they moved. They came to within five feet of the table and then whisked away again, back to where they came from finally disappearing behind the doors.

"It is with great honor and respect that we induct our new Redeemer. Brother Alan has proven his allegiance to the church and is deemed worthy of our acceptance.

"Alan, our continued existence is based on trust. We are a brotherhood that believes that redemption is not only in our control but it is our mission. Without this trust we will crumble into dust."

"Do you, Brother Alan, swear to uphold the trust until your very death?"

"I do."

"And do you Brother Alan, promise with your blood and with your manhood to protect and defend our existence forsaking all outsiders?"

"I do."

"Finally, Brother Alan, do you trust your life and your very soul to this brotherhood of redeemers, questioning not the orders given you nor the gifts bestowed but following and accepting on faith?"

"I do."

"Then stand with us."

They all stood in a circle and held hands.

"Brethren, let us celebrate with joy and passion the acceptance of our new redeemer."

"All hail the new redeemer," the men responded.

Alpha nodded to the men on either side of Alan. They all unlocked hands and the two men raised Alan's robe above his waist. Alan allowed it to happen because he believed he was being tested.

"You may sit now," Alpha proclaimed.

They all sat down, Alan with his robe above his waist. The doors re-opened and the women returned carrying trays of food with them. They each had a large platter of delicious smelling food that they set down around the table.

They stood back a few feet from the table and waited. The men all slid their chairs back but remained seated. The girls knelt down, one girl to each man and began to raise their robes. Alan was looking left and right taking in the scene. The men raised their robes chest high while the women began fondling and kissing their private parts.

Alan was aware of his own fullness from watching what was going on around him. Alpha Sam was staring across the table at him. Alan didn't know what to do. Then, he felt a hand on his flesh. He was startled at first but he was trying to trust. He looked at Sam who was smiling.

Alan couldn't see which girl was under the table but it really didn't matter. He was getting lost in the moment just like the others. The movement and noise in the room was beginning to escalate.

"Brethren, let us prove our commitment to trust and to each other by sharing in this communal act and by expelling our seed of manhood."

Alan was looking around the room. A few of the men had helped their woman to her feet and bending them over their chair. Alan was uncertain about what he should do next. He was very content with what was going on under the table but maybe he was expected to follow suit.

More men were standing now, some were facing the woman, some were behind and one of the couples was on the floor. Before long, all the men including the Alpha were standing or on the floor. The sound of sex was overwhelming. Both man and woman moaning in ecstasy. The escalation was reaching a fever point and he could see by some of the men's faces that they were ready to climax. It was like they were all waiting for each other to get there.

Alan slid back, stood and guided his partner out in one coordinated move. She stood up and faced the table, her hands holding her up. He slid into her and reached around her to grab her breasts with both hands. The firm tissue underneath the silky material felt magical and he could feel his excitement rising.

He gazed around the room, feeling like he was watching a movie. All the flesh, all the moaning, he couldn't stand it anymore. He could feel his body shaking, the muscles in his legs beginning to cramp. He held on to her breasts as tight as he could and let loose.

As if choreographed, it appeared that all the men came together. Perhaps that was the point. Solidarity. Many acting as one. He didn't know what just happened but if this was the routine of the inner circle, he would never leave.

Chapter 60

Hilton Head Island, SC/Quantico, VA

Dean and Shelly Madris were waiting for the sun to set at their favorite restaurant on the island. It was a place called Coucher du Soleil and although it sounded French, the cuisine was American coastal.

It was located on the southwestern tip of the island in the South Beach area. The open patio faced the west across Calibogue Sound toward Daufuskie Island and boasted one of the best sunsets on Hilton Head.

It was a clear evening and the temperature was about perfect. Low humidity days were treasured in the summertime and this was a diamond. The fans spread out about the deck created a relaxing faux breeze.

Dean ordered a light beer, one of the six a year he allowed himself while Shelly sipped her margarita. They always ordered hushpuppies as an appetizer and tonight was no different.

They looked over the menu knowing full well that they would order what they always do. She would have the fish tacos and Dean would go with the fried flounder. They would share an order of French Fries because it was after all, a French Restaurant.

The waitress came to take their order just as Dean's phone rang. He looked at the caller ID which simply stated *"Washington."* He knew he had to take the call.

"I'll have the flounder, she'll have the fish tacos, wait fifteen minutes before you put the order in and bring her another margarita." Dean said hurriedly as he walked away.

"Dean Madris," he answered.

"Mr. Madris, my name Phil White, I am a cybercrime agent with the FBI. I was given your number by Special Agent Charis Andrews."

"Yes, Mr. White, I've been expecting a call."

"Excellent. I do have an update for you. The company is legitimate from what we can see. First, I want to assure you that Audra is still alive. We placed an order with her and we have no reason to believe it was intercepted by management."

"That's good news," Dean replied.

"Yes sir. I believe that they have stored your profile so that when you connect, they have it flagged and will not allow it to pass to the artist. So while you were right about them intercepting your requests, it doesn't appear that you caused her any harm."

"Thank God!"

"Yes sir. We tracked the routing from here, meaning your computer and mine to Israel then to Indonesia. From there it went to England and then back to the United States. It appears that all correspondence goes to Israel first which makes sense because the company's servers are there. From there, the messages are routed to the artists all over the world.

It is normal to route traffic through hubs in other places before reaching the final destination, especially when large volumes of data are involved. In this case, we believe the end destination is not Indonesia but right here in the US.

"So you mean Audra is likely sitting in the US somewhere."

"That is our belief, yes sir."

"So this looks like a domestic issue."

"This particular instance looks domestic but that doesn't mean there is not foreign involvement. We have only tracked a few of these artists so far."

"What's the next step, agent White?"

"Finding where in the US the destination router sits. We are still working on that but I wanted you to know your girl seems okay for the moment."

"Thank you so much! Call me anytime, Agent."

Dean disconnected and went back to his table.

"I'm sorry, dear, I needed to take that."

"It's fine, Dean, the food hasn't arrived and the sun hasn't set. Is everything alright?"

"So far."

Chapter 61

Albany, NY

Dr. Al was scrolling through the digital x-ray images on her computer. None of the extremities showed any sign of abuse. The only images of interest were the abdominal because of the Thallium and the chest due to the calcium carbide.

She went through one more time for good measure. She slowed down while looking at the cervical spine and skull. She spotted something but wasn't quite certain what it was or if it meant anything. She magnified the area of interest and looked at it from various angles.

There was just a line of high density in the right side of the skull. When glanced at quickly could be mistaken for an overlay of the parietal bone of the skull. Single dimension images of the skull can be tricky because the front of the skull superimposes itself on the back of the skull so that you're looking at both on top of each other.

She had a thought. Because she found the cause of death, in this case poisoning during the torso part of the autopsy, she didn't have a good reason to open the skull. Now, she wished she did. She could do it now but she had a better idea.

She got back on the phone to Imaging.

"Medical Imaging, Denise speaking."

"Denise, this is Dr. Lanford. What are the chances of getting an MRI at this time of day?"

"I think Larry just left for the day. Let me put you on hold for a minute."

Music on hold. She thought it might have been Stairway to Heaven played on a pan flute.

"MRI, this is Larry."

"Oh Larry, I am so glad you're still here," Dr. Al exclaimed.

"Can we pretend that I'm not?" Larry asked.

"Ordinarily Larry, I would help you out and look the other way but this one is really important."

"Sure. What do you have?"

"MRI of the brain, T-2 weighting."

"What are you looking for Doc?"

"Sclerotic plaque."

"Is the patient here?" He asked.

"In body only," she answered.

"Cadaver?"

"Yes. If you come down here, I will help you transport and wait with you while you do the exam." She offered.

"I'm on my way."

Dr. Al went to the cooler and pulled the body which was still on a cart.

Chapter 62

Quantico, VA

Charis took a few pictures with her cell phone of the note and charred area of the concrete floor. She got in the car and headed toward home. She took a roundabout route to make sure she wasn't being followed.

When she arrived at her building, she parked on a different floor of the garage than usual. She parked one floor higher, thinking that fewer people would be taking the elevator down than up.

She found a spot as close to the elevator as possible without being hemmed in by a wall or other cars. After a thorough inspection of the vehicle's perimeter, she made her way to the elevator.

The walk to her unit was unincumbered and quick. She just needed a shower and some fresh clothes and she would on her way to her Dad's house. She put the key in the lock and paused suddenly. The piece of clear tape was not where she had left it. Someone had moved it. She took a credit card out of her purse and measured the distance from the bottom of the tape to the top of the card. It was off by more than an inch.

She unholstered her gun, turned the key in the lock and opened the door quietly. She stepped in and locked the door continually canvassing her surroundings. She looked right toward the kitchen and approached pointing her weapon to the space between the island and the wall.

She turned around and headed toward the hallway to the bedroom and bath. The doors were both open as she had left them. She checked the bathroom first. There was no place to hide except the closet. The shower was a glass enclosure. She opened the closet door. Nothing. Re-entering the hallway she swept left and right. The doors to her bedroom and office opposed each other.

She had to choose which to peruse first. She knew that the wrong choice could result in taking a bullet in the back. Her gut told her to check the office first. She swung to the right, arms extended and swept the room. She opened the closet but found nothing.

Her bedroom was the last room. She approached slowly. She could see most of the room from the doorway. The dresser and bed were clear. Now, she needed to make a full swing to the left to face the closet doors. With her gun trained on the door in one hand, she used her left to pull open the door.

As soon as she pulled, the door flew open with the weight of something behind it. Her years of training told her to hold fire until she knew what or who she was shooting at.

A box came flying off the top shelf and slammed to the floor just missing her feet. There was no one in the closet. She examined the box which contained personal keepsakes, the contents of which were now scattered across the floor. There was a string tied to the inside handle of the door that must have been anchored to the box.

She took some photos and returned to her office. She didn't see any notes on the desk. She unlocked her desk and pulled out a small electronic device. She also removed a dusting kit. The small device was used to sweep for bugging devices. She would use the dusting kit to check for fingerprints.

While she was there, she booted her computer. While it was waking up, she scoured the apartment for listening devices. She found two. The first was in the kitchen underneath an overhead cabinet. The second was in the office adhered to the back of the large monitor connected to her desktop computer.

Charis took the dusting kit to the front door. Using gloves, she removed the tape and dusted it. On the sticky side, she immediately saw a nearly full print come to life. She set that aside and removed and dusted the listening devices. The perp was more careful placing these so there were no prints to be found.

She returned to the office and pressed the icon for wireless connectivity. She selected Bluetooth and searched for devices. She found one that didn't belong to her. There was one other device somewhere in her apartment. She didn't have time to do another search of the place, it would have to wait until later.

She preserved the evidence she collected and prepared to shower.

Chapter 63

Near Quicksburg, VA

The girls hurried off as soon as their work was finished. Four men entered the room carrying hot washcloths and towels for the men to clean up with. When done, the men carried on like nothing had happened. They turned to the platters of appetizers that the girls had brought out earlier.

Soon after, the same girls returned delivering a hot plate of food for each gentleman. They didn't speak or smile. They just did their job and walked away. Alan realized he never even saw the face of the girl.

After dinner, the men were treated to dessert and drinks. There was very little conversation happening at the table. The desserts were pre-plated and delivered to each individual. Alan noticed his dessert was different than the rest. His drink was also in a different glass.

Alpha raised his glass.

"A toast, he said."

Everyone raised their glass.

"To Brother Alan, welcome to the inner circle. You have shown that you can trust and be trusted. We honor you with the traditional drink and dessert reserved for new members. To Alan!"

"To Alan!" the others refrained.

"To the bottom!" Alpha proclaimed.

Everyone drank the entire glass with one draw. He didn't know what he was drinking but it tasted great. Once seated again, they each ate their dessert.

"Brethren, it has been an honor to guide you in tonight's celebration.

As is customary, I will be giving Alan a personal in depth tour of our magnificent facility."

They all rose as Alpha raised a hand to Alan.

"Please join me."

Alan walked around the table to meet Alpha Sam who then walked him back to the dressing area.

"You are in for a treat, my friend. Not many get to see the inner working of the church."

"I'm looking forward to it, Alpha Sam! Alan exclaimed.

"Go ahead and get dressed. I'll be waiting right outside the door."

"I'm sorry, Alpha Sam, is there a restroom I could use?"

"Of course, it just over there."

Alan's stomach was bothering him. He figured he just wasn't used to all the rich food.

When he was done, he met Sam in the hall.

They didn't go back through the dining room. Instead, Sam led him to a corridor behind the vestal. It was a long, dimly lit walk which ended at an elevator. Inside, there were eight buttons indicating eight levels and they were apparently at the top. Sam pushed the bottom labeled with the letter I.

Alan could feel the elevator going down and it triggered an uncomfortable feeling in his belly. He was also developing a slight headache.

"Let's start at the bottom and work our way up, shall we?" Sam said.

Alan didn't answer. He felt a bit tongue tied. He found himself pressing his back against the elevator wall to steady himself.

"What was in that drink? He asked.

"Did you like it?" Sam asked.

"Yes, it was very good but I think it has made me a bit drunk."

"Oh, I'm not surprised." Sam said.

"It contains several shots of alcohol along with exotic fruit juice and some minerals. It has quite a kick."

"I'll say," Alan replied.

Alan was having trouble focusing on the level indicator light on the elevator control panel. He was feeling very dizzy now and thought he would pass out if he wasn't able to sit soon.

The elevator came to a stop at level I. When the door opened, bright lights from the room ahead almost blinded him. He had to squint to see anything. There was a sign directly across from the elevator door, *Infirmary.*

"Is there a place I could sit for a minute?" Alan pleaded.

"Of course, just down the hall here. Would you like to use the restroom again?"

"Yes, I think that would be wise."

"Come right in here."

Sam was holding the door to a rather large bathroom. There was a toilet with straps straight ahead. Alan rushed toward it, undoing his pants as he moved. He quickly turned and sat just in time. At that moment, another man entered and helped Alan get strapped in. Alan just stared ahead, he couldn't control his eyes. His peripheral vision told him there was an open shower in the room with a huge drain in the center. He closed his eyes, not able to keep them open any longer. He could hear sounds but could not make out what they were. The last thing he remembered was the sound of the fan. Just like the sound he heard when he entered the building.

Chapter 64

Quicksburg, VA

"Sheriff Sweeney."

"Hello again, Sheriff, this is Lieutenant Brown."

"That was fast, Lieutenant, I didn't expect to hear from you until tomorrow."

"And you probably shouldn't be. We have not begun to analyze anything yet but the mold came out so clean and defined that I took a few pictures of it. I know you're working with the FBI on this case so I thought this might give you a head start. I'm sending them over the wire right now."

"Thanks, Lieutenant. I will be sure to forward them right away."

Til could hear the tone of the incoming email and opened it right up. Brown was right, the detail in the photos was spectacular. He forwarded the file to Charis.

He would ordinarily share news like this with Deputy Swart but he didn't want to bother him in the middle of his dinner. He also knew there was a slim chance of him answering.

Til's phone rang. It was Charis.

"Good evening Charis, it sounds like you're still on the road."

"I am on my way to my father's house. Til, I just received your photos of the tracks. I'm sending them off to Trey Lawrence in New York, he should be able to tell if it's a match. I wish we had a picture of the vehicle that left them."

"So do I, Charis. I guess we're lucky to have the tracks. I think my deputy filled in the ruts after we left there. By the time the troopers got there they were covered with dirt."

"Why would he do that?"

"I think he was embarrassed that he missed them. He has been acting a little strange lately anyway."

"Til, when I arrived at headquarters, there was note for me. Same old stuff. But when I got to my apartment, I noticed someone had been there."

"More notes," he asked.

"No note but he left a message. He rigged the closet so that a box came crashing down when I opened it. I also found two bugs."

"Are you okay?"

"I'm fine, just pissed."

"Charis, you need to bring the department in on this. You are putting yourself at risk."

"I can't, Til, I feel like I'm getting close. I can handle myself and we have a plan in place to protect the others. I think I have a fingerprint of whoever broke into my place."

"Where did you find that?"

"I always leave a piece of clear tape on my door jamb. It was in a different place when I came back. The idiot didn't want to wear gloves I guess, and he didn't realize the back of the tape would capture a perfect impression."

"He probably thought it would be a red flag if he was seen in the hall wearing gloves. Who has the print now?"

"I do. I'll run it later. Thanks for the tire print, Til."

"You still off to Tennessee tomorrow?"

"Yes, and South Dakota on Friday. I will be glad when this week is over."

"I'm sure you will. You take care of yourself, Charis."

"I will. Thanks Til.

She pulled to the side of the road just long enough to forward the photos from Til to Trey. She was twenty minutes from her dad's place.

Chapter 65

Dale City, VA

Rennie Andrews answered the door and took the delivery of Kwon's from the driver. He thanked him and tipped him fairly. He could feel the heat from the contents and the familiar smell was amazing. He placed the entire bag into the microwave oven. He didn't turn it on, he wanted the food to stay warm and he found the small but insulated space of a microwave did the trick.

Charis called a few minutes earlier to say she was twenty minutes out. He was excited to see her. She always kept so busy it was difficult for her to spare the time. It was even worse before she convinced him to move to Dale City. Her office was just thirty minutes away now so even when she had just a few moments to spare, they could get together.

The doorbell rang. He looked through the security hole into the hallway. It was her. He opened the door with a big smile on his face.

"Come in, darling, I'm so happy to see you!"

"Thanks, Dad, you too."

They gave each other a big squeeze.

"You look thinner, Charis, have you been eating regularly?"

"I don't know if regularly is the correct word, but I eat when I can. I do okay. I can smell the Kwon's though!"

"It's ready when we are. What can I get you to drink?"

"You wouldn't have any Irish Mist, would you?"

"I picked up a bottle just for you. I thought you might like one."

"You're the best, Dad. On the rocks please."

He went to the kitchen and filled two short but heavy crystal glasses with ice. She joined him. He broke the seal on the bottle and poured the golden fluid slowly over the ice. They could gear the ice crackling. He place a swizzle stick in each glass and handed her one. The both knew to stir for a minute or two.

"Cheers, my girl!"

"Cheers, Dad."

"Have a seat Charis and I'll bring the food out."

She did and he plated the food and delivered it to the table.

"This looks great, Dad, thanks for doing this."

"Anything for my little girl! So, what are you involved in now?"

"I'm not even sure if I know, Dad. We have had some bodies show up in rivers in several states between New York and Missouri. At first they seem isolated but now I'm convinced they are connected somehow."

"Is that why you are interested in the Valley Church of Redemption?"

"No, I actually think that's the one case that is not connected. We are looking into that for a friend of ours in High Falls. He is a friend and employee of Greg's whose high school girlfriend disappeared ten years ago."

"So what makes the others seem connected?"

"Well, a lot actually. Let's talk about it after dinner, Dad. I'm happy to discuss it with you, but I need to do something first and that can wait until after we eat. This is really good! Just as I remember it."

So they continued to talk while they ate but they refrained from talking about business. It was more about her Dad's volunteer work and his cronies. Of course the conversation eventually turned to Charis' romantic life as it usually does. She assured him that he would be the first to know if and when there was any sign of romance.

When they were finished, Charis helped her dad clean up the kitchen. She poured them each another half glass of Irish Mist and set them on the counter to chill. She put the leftovers in the fridge and started to throw the bag in the trash when she saw the receipt in the bottom of it.

"Dad, do you want to keep the receipt for the food?" she said as she pulled it from the bag.

He took it from her and looked at it.

"This isn't a receipt, Charis."

"What is it?"

He handed it to her. She read it and whispered in his ear. He nodded indicating he understood. Charis went to her bag and pulled out the bug finder.

"Who are you rooting for this year, Dad? Are you still an Orioles fan?"

"Through thick and thin," he answered.

Charis was moving slowly and quietly throughout the room. She could see the indicator jump just a little every now and then but she couldn't find any listening devices.

"How do they look?" she asked.

"They're five and a half out of first but that doesn't mean much this early in the season."

She continued moving around the apartment. The only place she pick up any signal was in the center of the dining room.

"We should go to a game sometime," she said."

"I would like that! It's been a long time since we went to a game together."

Charis stopped at the edge of the table and raised the device toward the ceiling. She pulled out a chair and stood on it.

"I know, Dad, I'm sorry about that. We will make it happen this year. And I mean soon."

She was getting a much stronger signal now. She released the glass globe from the ceiling mounted light fixture. Taped to the mounting bracket, where it wouldn't cast a shadow, was a small microphone and transmitter.

She loosened the tape and pulled it down. She carried it to the sink and threw it in the dishwater.

She did one more sweep around but didn't detect any more.

"We can talk now."

"Why on earth would someone bug my home?"

"I have a guess, Dad and if I'm right, your phone is tapped as well."

"When did you have that light fixture replaced?" she asked.

"It was just before the holiday, the first of July maybe."

"Did you get a new phone as well?"

"No, same phone as always," he answered.

"Do you always have it on you?"

"Yes. Wait a minute. About three weeks ago, I met the guys for coffee and I realized I didn't have my phone with me. I worried that I may have dropped it somewhere but when I got home about an hour later, I realized I had just left it behind. I didn't think anything of it."

"It's alright, Dad, it happens to all of us. May I see it?"

Rennie handed her the phone. He was still using an older style flip phone. She opened it and looked through his call history. For each incoming and outgoing call, there was another number right below it. All of his calls were being forwarded to another number.

"Here is the problem, Dad, Your calls were connecting to a third party every time you place and received one."

"How does that happen?" He asked.

"Do you remember you used to tell me stories about the old days? You usually did it when I had been on the phone too long. You told me that in your day, you had party lines. You could be on a phone call and someone in the neighborhood would pick up and try to dial a number and you could hear the clicking of the rotary dial."

"I do remember that story. You would talk to your girlfriends for hours."

"It wasn't always girls, but yes," she replied.

"I had a hunch!" he said.

"I'm sure you did. Anyway, in this case, someone came in here and changed the settings on your phone so that when you dialed or received a call, it would automatically connect to a third number."

"Can you tell what number they were connecting to?"

"Not right now, but the phone company can tell me that. I will work on that tomorrow. For now, I am going to reset your phone so that doesn't happen anymore."

"So each time you and I talked, someone was listening?"

"Either listening or recording. I haven't seen it done this way in a long time. This person has been around the block once or twice."

"Have I compromised your safety, Charis?"

"You did not do anything, Dad. This is not your fault. It just explains how someone knew that I would be in New York and Quicksburg and Bowling Green. Dad, who installed your light fixture?"

"It was gentleman, maybe forty-five years old. I would say six feet, a few extra pounds around the middle."

"Was he with the maintenance department here?"

"No one I had seen before. No, he couldn't have been. I bought the fixture myself at Blythe's Hardware. They sent the installer."

"That's good, Dad, I can run with that. Now, tell me about the delivery guy from Kwon's. Was it the same guy?"

"I didn't catch a good look at his face, Charis, I was so excited that you were on your way."

"That's fine dad. Did he look about the same height and build?"

"I believe he was. I should have paid more attention. I did notice that he had some greyish white powder on his shoes."

"Okay, another good tip. Do you have some tape?"

"Scotch, packing or duct?" he asked.

"Duct would be perfect."

Charis took a six inch piece from the roll and walked to the entry. She opened the door and could see just a slight bit of residual on the carpeting. She bent down and placed the tape sticky side down. She pressed it for a few seconds and then withdrew it. She closed the door and went back to the table.

Using the light from her cell phone, she examined the tape.

"There it is!" she exclaimed. "So, I am interested in hearing what you found out about the Valley Church of Redemption. What's for dessert?"

Chapter 66

Dale City, VA

Myron Hawkins watched Charis enter from the parking lot. If she had moved her father to a place with a parking garage, spying wouldn't have been this easy. But it was thoughtful of her to move him closer to work.

He was having a good time listening to their conversation, that was until it stopped. She apparently found the bug in the light. He heard some scratching sounds and then it went dead. Hopefully, she didn't have any clue about the phone. She was sharp but probably too young to come across this old technique.

It wouldn't take him long to plant another bug now that he had the key to the place. The old man got out at least once daily unless it was raining. He was kind enough to leave the house early on those days so that Myron wouldn't miss work.

If he needed to, he could always drop a more powerful device in the ceiling. A small hole in the floor of his apartment and he could pass the wire right down to Rennie's ceiling. He had to wait two months to get the apartment right above him.

It was time for him to check in. He dialed but no one answered. He thought he must have dialed incorrectly so he tried again.

"Valley Church of Redemption, we are currently unable to answer you're call. Please call again later."

That is so weird! He thought. He would try again later.

Chapter 67

Crystal City, MO

Det. Laroy Climm was on his way to church when his personal cell phone started buzzing.

"Hello."

"Hey Laroy, it's Myron Hawkins."

"Hi, Myron, what's going on?"

"I just called Alpha Sam in Quicksburg and there was no answer. Have you heard of anything happening over there? It is so unusual, in fact, I have never had a call go unanswered."

"Maybe he is just indisposed at the moment, if you know what I mean."

"I know what you mean, Laroy but he always has someone covering the phone for him."

"Alright, Myron, I'll tell you what I'll do. I'm on my way to church as we speak so I'll ask around and see what I can find out. I'll give you a shout back."

"Thanks, Laroy."

It seemed a little strange to Laroy too. He felt certain there was a reasonable explanation for it. He pulled through the open gate and around to the back of the building. He rang the bell and almost immediately, the door was opened for him.

"Good evening, sir."

"Good evening Edwardo, which room is the meeting in tonight?"

"That would be the Sires Room."

"Perfect," he replied.

Laroy had been in most rooms at the church over the ten years he was a member. It took the better part of two years before he was chosen for the inner circle. What a night that was. He thought the initiation was a little hokey at first but he went along and he was rewarded for it. Having a badge probably had something to do with his selection. He was invited by a superior on the force. That gentleman had long since retired but was still quite active in the church.

He did like the Sires room. It was probably his favorite. It was dimly lit with a soft but lusty feel. It reminded him of a gentlemen's club from years gone by. It was a bar, a restaurant, a strip club and a whore house all in one. There were few rules but the ones they had, you didn't want to break.

He witnessed someone disobeying a rule once. It was another cop, from a nearby city. He was heavy on the bottle and one night, he treated one of the girls a little rough. At some point he slapped her across the face.

From out of nowhere, a half dozen men swooped down on him and dragged him off. A few seconds later, things were back to normal. We never saw him again and no one ever talked about it. Why ruin a good thing?

He entered the Sires room. It wasn't very busy yet. It typically started hopping at around 8:00 pm. It took the boys a little while to get loosened up. A few drinks and some snacks seemed to help. It would be at least 7:30 before the girls started mingling.

He had run into "girls of the night" before. On the outside, he wondered about how they got where they were. Was it something they were forced to do to survive or was it by their own choosing? They never seemed truly happy.

In here, for the most part, the girls seemed genuinely happy. There were a few that appeared quiet or perhaps medicated, but the majority seemed content. There was never any talk about them personally, that was rule number one. There was very little conversation and there didn't need to be. You knew why you were there and they knew why they were there.

There were girls of all ages, all shapes and all ethnicity. They all seemed to be American. If someone had a particular preference, they could make a request.

Laroy was looking around the room for Alpha Timothy. He wasn't always there but he would usually make an appearance at some point in the evening. He sat in a booth near the back of the room. There were no TVs in this room. Come to think of it, he had never seen a TV anywhere in the facility. He ordered a drink from the waitress who was not to be confused with one of the social girls. Everyone here had a specific job. To confuse them could violate one of the rules.

Just as his drink arrived, another brother climbed in the bench across the booth.

"Brother Laroy, good to see you!"

"Brother Steven, how are you?"

"I'm fine now. This place is such a respite from the outside world."

"That it is, Steven. Are you looking forward to the evening?"

"Oh, yes. I wish they had these meetings every night of the week!"

"Now wouldn't that get a little tiring?"

"I would like to find out." Steven replied.

"Everything in moderation, right?" Laroy reminded him.

"Yes, Brother, I forgot myself for a moment."

"No harm, it is our nature to want more. But when I think of all we have, I am more than satisfied. By the way, have you seen Alpha Timothy?"

"No, I haven't seen him tonight but it's early. He will probably stop around."

"No doubt. I am going to mingle a bit, Steven. Have fun!"

Laroy grabbed his drink and walked off. He was on his way to the rest room when he saw Alpha Timothy coming through the door.

"Alpha Timothy, I was wondering if I might have a word with you."

"Of course, Brother Laroy. Let's step out for a moment."

Alpha led the way and Laroy followed him back outside into the hallway. They found a little nook near a window where they could have some privacy.

"What is it, Brother?"

"I received a call just a short time ago from Brother Myron in Virginia. He tried reaching out to Alpha Samuel but didn't receive an answer. He was worried that something may be amiss."

"I was in touch with Alpha Sam earlier today and I can assure you all is well. He did have a special meeting tonight with a new recruit. I'm sure he is just taking care of business. Please thank Brother Myron for his concern and assure him there is nothing to worry about."

"Thank you, Alpha Timothy."

After the Alpha walked away, Laroy went outside to make the call.

"Hello, Myron, Laroy here, I just spoke with Alpha Timothy and he assures me all is well. There was a special function tonight and Alpha Sam is probably still tied up. Is there something you need to talk about?"

"I just wanted him to know that there has been a disruption in my eyes and ears. The FBI agent is getting closer and it's going to be more difficult for me to track her."

"Do you know if she has us on her agenda?"

"There has been no mention of Crystal City as yet."

"That's good news. Where is she headed next, Myron?"

"McMinnville tomorrow and Custer on Friday."

"Are they aware?"

"Yes."

"Then Myron, I wouldn't worry about her. She will meet her match in Custer."

"I'm sure you're right, Laroy. It's been nice talking to you. Thank you!"

"Anytime, Brother Myron."

Chapter 68

Albany, NY

The MRI unit was singing it's song consisting of the deep buzzing notes followed by the high pitch staccato intermittent tones and then back to the low buzzing again.

Every thirty seconds a new image would appear on the computer screen in the operator's booth. Dr. Lanford was sitting beside the technologist. The science inside the donut shaped gantry was using magnetic energy and radio frequency waves to electronically slice through the cadaver's cranium.

The first image taken at the apex of the skull showed mostly bone. Each subsequent picture highlighted more brain tissue and the bone was limited to the outer surfaces. It was during the sixth image that Dr. Al found what she was looking for.

Present in both the left and right hemispheres of the brain were multiple areas of sclerotic plaque.

"There they are," Dr. Lanford said. This girl was suffering from Multiple Sclerosis long before she was poisoned. I think we had her age wrong too. I think she is closer to, if not more than 30 years old.

They completed the scan, moved the girl back onto the cart and wheeled her back to the morgue. When she was secured in the cooler, Dr. Lanford thanked the tech and went to her office to call Sheriff Bentley.

"Bentley."

"Hi Judd, It's Amelia Lanford. I'm sorry to bother you. Would you have a minute to talk?"

"Yes, of course."

"I have new information on our girl."

"Really, I thought we had learned all we were going to."

"I ordered the whole body x-rays as indicated by the FBI. On a plain film of the skull, I noticed an area that looked too dense to be bone so I ordered an MRI tonight. Judd, this young lady also had MS. That doesn't change the fact that she was poisoned and that was the cause of death. What it may change is how you investigate the crime."

"I'm not sure I'm following you, Al."

"First of all, this new diagnosis probably puts her age closer to thirty to thirty-five. Secondly, in addition to the diabetes which we already knew, she was probably seeking care for the MS or at least for the symptoms."

"So we should be asking around about a patient with this particular co-morbidity who may have missed an appointment or two."

"Yes. I know it's like finding a needle in a haystack but you may cover some ground by starting with insurance companies. They can probably do a search by sex, age and co-morbidity."

"That's a good idea, Al. Why are you working so late tonight?"

"So that I can make you work late, I guess. Sorry about that."

"It comes with the territory."

"I guess it does. Have a good night, Judd."

Chapter 69

Dale City, VA

Charis decided to run the fingerprint before having dessert. Once she had photographed it and posted it, she could sit back and wait for a match. Rennie had made Charis her favorite, apple pie served with vanilla ice cream.

"Okay Dad, I am ready to hear the results of your research. Tell me everything about the Valley Church of Redemption."

"Let me begin by saying that they are by far the most difficult church to find information on. I will try to qualify that by saying that the early years are somewhat searchable. The church had its humble beginning in 1976. It was founded by a former senior member of the Mormons by the name of Grady Braxton.

Braxton's father was a Mormon as well so he was well bred in the religion. The elder Braxton practiced polygamy when it was popular so Grady grew up in the presence of many maternal figures.

When the church became more rigid about the life choice, Grady decided to part ways with Utah and head east. He began his first church in Cody Wyoming. He created his own brand of religion and developed his own doctrine. They didn't profess alliance with any God and believed more in the theory of evolution.

He believed and taught that men were the stronger sex and therefore were in charge. He liked the idea of polygamy and carried that forward in his doctrine. He believed that our humanity demanded caring for the less fortunate and the infirm.

As the church grew, he continued to move east and south. Once he established a church, he would assign an elder as the leader or Alpha. The Alpha would assign an Omega or director as his assistant. Women were not allowed to hold any office or title in the church. His second church was in South Dakota. The whereabouts of the newer churches is not documented.

The church raised its money by collecting a tithe of a family's income. They would also accept donations from families who have an infirm member. It wasn't mandatory but encouraged.

What began as Church of the Redeemer in 1976 became the Valley Church of Redemption sometime in the mid-1990s. It was at that time that they changed their membership process to "by invitation." They couldn't say "invitation only" because they would lose their non-profit status.

They limit drop-ins by keeping a low profile. You won't find a website, billboard, brochure or obituary that lists the name, address or phone number for one of their churches. Members invite friends and family to interview for membership. You will never find one of their churches in a city or on a main road.

I have found a few web posts of people who have stumbled upon the church and were turned off. But I haven't found a single post of a former member. It seems like once you're in, you never want to leave.

"Dad, if they take care of the infirm and less fortunate don't they have to report to a state or federal agency or be licensed by some organization?"

"I think if you're caring for someone out of the goodness of your heart and you are not billing insurance companies or accepting state or federal funds, you can circumvent the usual requirements."

"Do you know how their corporation is formed?"

"I'm not sure they are incorporated. "I can't find any records under the name of the church or Grady Braxton, "her father said.

"They must buy supplies and food. How about utilities like gas and electricity?"

"You would think so, Charis, but I couldn't find anything. As I said, the minimal data available is old."

"Is it your theory that your friend's girlfriend is or was in the care of the church?"

"All we know is that her parents used to take her to a church which she didn't have fond memories of. We have tracked down her father who denies that he ever had a daughter but lives around the corner from the church. The church is in the middle of absolutely nowhere and Greg and his family plan to visit this Sunday."

"Well, I wish them luck."

"Thanks for doing the research, Dad. I'm going to have my agency look into it. There must be some records, somewhere. Hey Dad, do you mind if I crash in your spare room tonight? I don't think I have the energy to go home."

"It's your room dear, you can stay any time you like."

Charis kissed her dad goodnight, washed up and took her laptop to bed. She signed into the FBI internal site and browsed her email. There were two new ones.

The first was a note from Det. Laroy Climm in Festus, Missouri. He had the results from the DNA on their victim. The young boy was a match to an uncle on his father's side. There was no parental or sibling match in the database. Climm was going to interview the uncle if he could find him.

The other information from the genetics test showed that the boy had a genetic defect of chromosome 21 called Trisomy 21. The term Trisomy means that there is an extra copy of the chromosome, in this case, the twenty first. The common term for this condition is Down Syndrome.

The second notice was from the bureau. It found a match of the fingerprint. Charis would try to track the culprit down in the morning when she was on a flight to McMinnville by way of the Chattanooga airport.

Chapter 70

7/9/16

Quicksburg, VA

Alpha Sam was below deck in the infirmary. Alan, the new recruit didn't make it through the night. His body was cleaned and wrapped in a protective sheath.

Sam had arranged to have the vehicle brought down to the transport bay. The medical assistant, Malcom, wheeled the cart down the long corridor to the bay where the van was waiting. They slid the specially designed cart into the recessed bed of the van and locked it in. Then the power sliding faux floor drew over it.

The van pulled forward and waited until the garage door opened and then drove away. Alpha Sam watched as the van drove the half mile to the other end of the property, all underground.

When the driver arrived at the other end, an operator would open the elevator door, allow the van inside, close the door and push the button for the surface. When the driver reached the surface level the door would open automatically and the van would proceed out the gate at the back of the property.

No one would notice the van exiting the elevator or the gate. Outbuildings and clever landscaping concealed everything. The driver had his orders. No dumping the body in the river this time. The black, unmarked vehicle would take the back roads into nearby Timberville, a small town with a funeral home operated by a church Omega.

The church had helped the member update his business and prepare licensing guidance for a crematorium. The home was located outside the small village and the environmental impact was considered negligible.

Once there, Alan's remains would be placed in the furnace and an hour later, he would be swept into a small box. His ashes would be spread in a remote location.

It was still before 7:00am when Sam arrived back in his suite. On the walk back, he took the time to visit a few classrooms and the tactile learning center where the training took place. He never ceased to be amazed by the quality of work nor the scope of the project. But now, it was time for morning tea, a biscuit and to stare out his window.

Later in the morning he would have someone from Morale Services come by for a visit. He could really use a spa day. Perhaps the hot tub followed by a massage. He would choose later whether it would be a two or four hand massage.

Chapter 71

Quantico, VA

Charis was in the office by 6:45 am. She wanted to follow up on the fingerprint she turned in the night before. She seemed to be the first one in the office. The outer door was locked and all the lights were off.

Once she entered, she locked the door behind her. She took a quick look around in the vicinity of her office. It looked clear. She didn't find any new notes on her desk. She booted her computer and thought about what the day would look like.

Her flight was scheduled for 8:30 am which meant she would need to be on her way to the airport in less than thirty minutes. She needed her feet on the ground in Sheriff Ballard's office by 11 am. She would meet with the ME at 12:30 and be back at the airport before her 6:00 pm flight to Custer.

The computer came to life. She entered her credentials and went right to the results page. The page that loaded on her screen took her breath away. It didn't show a driver's license photo or a rap sheet.

There was a message that said the file was locked. That meant that the fingerprint belonged to a government employee. She would need her supervisor's approval to release the information. She wouldn't be able to do that until later if she wanted to do it at all.

For all she knew, it could be her supervisor's print. The risk factor was high and she needed to tread carefully. It would probably have to wait until she was back in town.

One thing left to do. She picked up the evidence bag containing the tape with the powder from her desk.

She turned everything off, closed her door and walked to the exit dropping the bag in the evidence collection bin on the way.

There were just a few people starting to arrive for work. Charis got to her car without interference and found no messages on her car.

She needed to stop by her apartment quickly to retrieve her travel bag. This time the tape on the door was just where she had placed it. She ran in, used the restroom and grabbed the bag. It was always packed and ready to go.

She rushed out, got in her car and headed toward Reagan International. It was too early to make calls but she had two hours on the plane to respond to email. It seemed like two weeks had passed since she was in Bowling Green but it was just a couple days. She couldn't wait for the weekend.

Chapter 72

High Falls, NY
Greg sent a text to Kathy asking her to reschedule his first meeting.

He told her he would be in by ten o'clock. He was out of the house by 6:30. Mary and the girls were still sleeping and Jack had spent the night at the farm.

He left a note for Mary telling her he needed to look into something and he would call her later in the morning. He placed a cranberry muffin and a napkin in a paper bag and carried along his hot thermal coffee mug.

He pulled into the parking lot of the hardware store just before seven. They were just opening the doors for business. He chose the parking space that gave the best view of the funeral home. He rolled his front windows down and grabbed the binoculars from the passenger seat.

It looked quiet over there. He didn't really expect to see much his first time out but it was a start. He guessed that the front part of the house was for business and the upstairs rear would be the living quarters. He wasn't even sure that it was the Slaters who lived there.

From the road to the canopy over the side door was seventy-five feet, he guessed. To the left of the driveway, there were four parking spaces where lawn used to be. The driveway continued under the portico to a four car garage. The doors were all closed.

He knew from his previous experience there that the majority of the parking was on the right side of the building. He put the binoculars down and opened the bag and removed the muffin. He took a bite and washed it down with a mouthful of coffee.

The muffin was actually pretty good. Jillian had made them the evening before. She was beginning to have an interest in cooking and baking and he was happy to be one of the judges. Jillian seemed to respond to his ever positive evaluations.

Greg turned the radio on and tuned it to a local news channel. It was going to be a little cooler than usual for this time of year. Westerly winds out of Canada were sweeping down through Lake Ontario. Highs were expected to be in the low eighties. That explained the lower than normal temperature he was experiencing this morning. *Perfect for a stakeout.*

He wondered how long it would take him to become bored. He tried listening to music but it was too early for the noise. He reclined his seat a few degrees and took a few deep breaths. That seemed to calm him down.

He put the lenses back up to his eyes just in time to see a vehicle come around the back of the house. It was a black high roof van with a NY commercial plate with the number B783447. He pulled a pen out of his pocket and wrote the number on the paper bag without taking his eyes off the vehicle.

The sun was still low in the sky and he was having difficulty seeing the driver's face through the glare on the windshield. As the vehicle move closer to the end of the driveway, he could see the Mercedes emblem on the hood. He had no idea what year it was but it looked new.

The driver turned left in the direction opposite Greg. He never got to see the face. He was deciding between following the van or continuing observing the funeral home. He decided to stay put. He could ask Trey to trace the number later.

"Could be anyone," he thought. *"Maybe an early delivery of supplies or someone in the house going off to work. Maybe that's the van they use for transporting bodies from hospitals and nursing homes."*

He gave his mind permission to let go of it and just continue watching. He sat there for another forty-five minutes and no one came or left. He was ready to shut the stakeout down for the morning when the van returned. This time, as the vehicle approached the home, he could see the driver.

He hadn't seen Maury Slater in years but the guy driving looked familiar. Greg was willing to bet it was him.

"So what?. What do I do with that information? The guy runs a business, he has the right and the need to be out and about."

Greg thought he would wait another twenty minutes and then head out. Just when he was ready to give up, a car turned into the driveway and pulled around to the back of the house. It was a late model Cadillac sedan in a creamy white color. The driver was a male who looked to be in his late forties or early fifties. He managed to get just the first few letters of the plate FTD 2. The car was gone before he could get the rest.

"Grasping at straws," he said to himself. *"Enough for one day."*

On his way back to the hospital, he received a call from Charis Andrews.

"Hey Charis, what's going on?"

"Good morning, Greg, I am on my way to McMinnville, TN. I'm trying to finish out my week of fun and games. I'm in the air and at a safe level so they let me make phone calls."

"How nice! It's always good to hear your voice. Have you made any progress? Our team is still willing to help you out, we're just waiting for your call. By the way, the Chalmers are on their way to The Haven. Richard is going to keep them company during the day and Ethan will be spending the night."

"I guess I can say we're making some progress," Charis said, "no arrests are pending yet but it sure looks like the murders are linked. I received a message last night from Trey and one from the folks in Custer both stating that while Thallium killed their victims, they also had other health concerns."

"Really," Greg asked, "the same conditions?"

"No, Custer was Down Syndrome but the girl in the Mohawk had MS. The body in Quicksburg, Virginia showed signs of long term physical abuse but the ME didn't mention any other conditions."

"Any commonality with the calcium carbide?" Greg followed.

"Not yet," she answered.

"And how about you, Charis, any more threats?"

"Yes. Not only that but my dad's phone was tapped, his apartment was bugged and so was mine. The reason I looked was because I had noticed that someone broke in. The good news is I was able to pull a fingerprint from my door. I also have a lead on who may have entered my father's home and placed the bugs."

"How long will it take to match the fingerprint?" Greg asked.

"I already have a match. I can't access the file because it's sealed."

"What does that mean, exactly?"

"It means that it is probably a government employee. I need my supervisor's approval to have the file unlocked."

"So it may very well be someone inside, just as you thought. It looks like you don't have any choice but to go to your boss now."

"I know. I hope it's not his print!" Charis exclaimed.

"If it is, he will just blow the whole thing off and deny access. You will know one way or the other."

"Right. I plan on calling him next. So what's new on your end?"

"I just finished my first stakeout of the funeral home."

"What did you find out?" Charis asked.

"The only thing I found out for sure is that I do not have the patience for surveillance work. I was bored after ten minutes."

"Most people don't realize how difficult that job is. Especially when you're alone. Did anything happen?"

"Maybe," Greg responded. I watched a van leave the home at seven am. It came back forty-five minutes later. Twenty minutes after that, a Cadillac pulled in and parked around back. Is that enough to make an arrest?"

"Sure! You can arrest the first guy for going to get coffee and donuts and the second guy for showing up for work," she joked.

"I did get plate numbers. I thought maybe Trey could run them just for kicks."

"That is a much better idea, Greg."

Charis paused a minute.

"Greg, what color was the van?"

"Black. It was a Mercedes, one of those high roof ones. Why?"

"Video footage from the donut shop by the Mohawk captured a black van. They also had a tire track which matches the tires used on the Mercedes Sprinter 2500. Call Trey right away, Greg. This may be more than a coincidence."

"I'll try him right now, Charis. Safe journey!"

"Thanks. Greg, Please ask Trey to call me when he's finished with you. Oh, and Greg, I found out some stuff about the Valley Church of Redemption. My father did a bunch of research, well let's say he tried to do a bunch of research but there is not much information out there. I'll send a summary to your email in a little while. Just be careful."

"Ten-four."

Chapter 73

Hilton Head Island, SC

Dean and Shelly had just come in from their morning walk on the beach. It was a beautiful sunrise and the low tide gave a wide berth of sand. By 10 am it would be too hot for a fast-paced walk.

They kicked off their sandy beach shoes, replaced them with slippers and went to the fridge for a cool drink. Shelly had a lunch date with some of the neighborhood women and Dean thought he would get started on the manuscript for his next book.

"Dean, I'm going to take a quick shower," Shelly advised.

"Okay, Dear."

Dean opened the slider to the patio just a few inches so that he could hear the waves coming to shore. He was really getting used to life at the shore. He picked up his tablet and found a surprise. The preliminary sketches were waiting for his review and approval.

He was told it could take three days but here they were. He opened the file and downloaded the images to his software. They were single line drawings but they were all there. If he liked what he saw, he would just send a note with his approval and the cells would be colorized.

The message was from management so he didn't know if Audra had drawn them or if the job was sourced to someone else. He opened the first one. The sketches of the characters looked just like the earlier ones. He looked to the right border where it showed the levels. There were only three.

He opened the next and did the same thing. Three levels. He tried the third image and got the same results. There were ten images in all. He opened the fourth and there were four images. He was hoping for a hidden message.

He didn't find any white writing on a pastel background but the image was different. The main character was wearing sunglasses. There was a reflection on the lenses that demonstrated what the girl was looking at.

He enlarged the image to see if he could make out what the reflection was. He had no idea. It looked like long pointed teeth. Some were pointing up and others down but they didn't have a regular alignment.

He went on to the rest of the images but nothing else jumped out at him. He thought about his options and realized he didn't have any. All he could do was approve the job and wait for the full color version. That is what he did.

He attached a note saying: *"So far, so good. I can't wait to see them in color!"*

He pressed the send button and off they went. He looked at the image again. Not a clue. He closed out the program and opened a new text document. He was thinking about his first line when his phone rang.

"Hello."

"Good morning Mr. Madris, this is Phil White. Did I catch you at a good time?"

"Yes, good morning Phil. How is the investigation going?"

"That's why I am calling, Dean, we have traced the signal to a server in Missouri but then we lost it."

"What does that mean, Phil?"

"It means that we can see signals going to that router and we can see them coming back but we can't get anything past that router. It looks like it ends there.

"So you believe the server is in the state of Missouri?"

"That's the way it looks. It enters the US through a group of exchange servers in Oregon. The data is then transferred to another bank of exchange servers in Utah and then on to somewhere in the St. Louis area."

"We are trying to track the IP addresses in Missouri but it's going to take a little more time."

"How much more, Phil?"

"That I don't know Mr. Madris, it could be five minutes or it could be five days."

"I see," Dean replied. Is there anything I can do?"

"Probably not without raising suspicion. Have you had any more contact with the artist?"

"Yes, I received a message about ten minutes ago. They sent the rest of my sketches. I can't tell for sure if they were drawn by Audra but they look extremely similar to her work. The message was sent from Management."

"Dean, do you mind if I take over your computer for just a minute. I may be able to see the IP address that initiated the message. If so, we may be able to pin the location down a little more."

"That's fine. What do I need to do?"

Phil talked him through the sequence. In five minutes, Phil had what he needed and the call ended.

Dean decided to send a message to Charis Andrews. He didn't know if any of this new information was valuable to her or not but she would know best.

Chapter 74

High Falls, NY

"Detective Lawrence."

"Good morning Trey, it's Greg Webster. I just got off the phone with Charis and she asked me to follow up with you. She also asked me to tell you to call her when we are finished. I know if I waited until we were done, I would forget."

"That was a lengthy hello, Greg. How are you doing?"

"I'm fine, thanks. I wanted to tell you that I was staking out a funeral home this morning."

"Planning ahead?" Trey joked.

"Not at this place! Anyway, I have my reasons and I can't share what they are at this moment but I promise that when I can share it, you will be the first, second or third person to know."

"That sure makes me feel special, Greg. Alright, skipping your little secret about why you're spying, tell me what you found."

"Charis thought you might be interested to know about the black Mercedes high roof van that pulled out of there at 7 am."

"You have my attention," Trey said.

"It was gone for forty-five minutes and returned. There were no markings and no side windows with the exception of the driver and front passenger. The driver was a male around forty-five and the plate number is B783447.”

“That’s good work, Greg.”

“There’s more. Twenty minutes after he returned, a white Cadillac turned into the driveway and pulled around the back. I couldn’t see either driver get out from my position. I only have a partial plate for the Caddy. It’s FTD2 something, something, something.”

“Partial is good, now we only have to look for 999 different registrations but that’s a start!” Trey replied.

“Are you being a wise guy?”

“Just busting on you a little, Greg. What do you think the person in the Caddy has to do with it?”

“I’m not sure any of this has to do with anything,” Greg answered. “I am quite frankly more interested in the Caddy than the van but don’t ask me why.”

“Yep, you already made that clear.”

“Trey, can you run the plates and let me know what you find?”

“I will get on that right away,” he answered.

“Hey Trey, I’m worried about Charis. She is still getting threats and her apartment and her father’s apartment were broken into. She found transmitters in both and her father’s phone was tapped. She’s on the road for two days and someone knows her travel plans.”

“That worries me too, Greg. You know she doesn’t like to ask for help. She did send me her itinerary just in case. I’ll keep in touch with her while she is gone and why don’t you do the same? She will answer one of us sooner or later.”

“Sounds good. Trey, have you ever heard of the Valley Church of Redemption in Jordanville?”

“I can’t say I have.”

“Okay, just wondering.”

“I’ll get back to you a little later today, Greg. Thanks for the heads up!”

“You bet.”

Chapter 75

Custer, SD

"Where are going so early, Sheriff?" Det. Doreen Hillabrandt asked. "It's only 6:45. You seem distracted."

"I am a bit distracted," he answered. "We have the FBI coming to-morrow Doreen, doesn't that worry you?"

"And what do you think they will find, Lester? They have a dead body they can't identify, big deal. They may find fault with the way our offices handled the investigation but they can't arrest us for that."

"What if they find out more information from the body?" he asked.

"Like what, Lester? We saw the preliminary report from the ME, what else do you think they're going to find?"

Lester knew what else the Doc found but he wasn't going to tell Doreen about it. If the DNA from the pregnant victim showed the father as someone other than him, he wouldn't need to say anything. If it was him, he was going to need a new plan.

"I don't know, Doreen, probably nothing. It just worries me. And with you wanting to abduct Agent Andrews to use as a sex toy for a couple hours, I'm just really nervous, okay?"

"Who said it would be just a couple hours? I may want to keep her for days or maybe forever if I really like her."

"You're crazy, Doreen. You have lost your mind. I've got to go."

"Come back to bed, Lester. I'll make it worth your while," she said in a sexy, childish voice. "Come here, I know you like sex when you're upset. I like having sex when you're upset. You get a little mean side to you."

She had the covers turned down and was touching her naked body. He had all he could do to resist. But then he was afraid to resist because she would be mad that he walked out. He felt trapped. He supposed what he had to do could wait. It was probably too early anyway.

He looked at her and she knew she was close to reeling him in. She changed her pose now, exposing more of her backside. He wanted to run but he couldn't. He knew he should, but he wouldn't. She held the power over him but if he was going to lose, he was going to do it on his terms.

He pulled the belt from his pants and took off all his clothes except his hat.

Holding the belt he growled: *"On your knees, bitch!"*

It didn't take him long and he didn't make sure she was finished first. This was for him. The moment he was done, he knew he had made a mistake. He felt ashamed, like a kid being bullied at school. He had to find a way out of this.

He pulled himself out of the bed, gathered his clothes and walked into the bathroom. She was yelling at him through the door to get back to bed. He looked in the mirror and saw the nine year old boy whose mother yelled constantly. Chiding him for every little thing.

When he was dressed, he opened the door and walked right past her. She screamed at his back: *"Don't you walk out on me again, Lester. I will have you replaced, you bad little boy! I'll be someone else's toy tomorrow you wimp!"*

Sheriff Moran walked to his car still hearing her scream at him. He drove away. He knew he had to do something. He couldn't live like this anymore.

Lester needed to go to church. He headed south on Sydney Park Road and then east on Hazelroot Cutoff. A couple miles down the road he made a left hand turn on Devils Hill Road. About a mile in, he turned right down the long driveway to the Valley Church of Redemption.

He was a long standing, valued member of the church. His father was an Omega when he was a young boy. When his father died, he was fifteen years old. His mother had always been a nasty woman and not just to him. He remembered feeling sorry for his father and often wondered why he put up with it.

Alpha Micah came to him shortly after his father passed and invited him to become a member of the inner circle. Lester had met some members but never one as young as he was. Years later, Micah told him he worried about his future, especially being alone with his mother. He would need to mature quickly but if he was agreeable, he could live a very rewarding life with the church.

They made him study and pushed him toward a career in law

enforcement. The church needed strong people like him out in the community to protect the church members. He was told it wouldn't be easy at times but well worth it.

Alpha Micah had helped him file for emancipated minor status with the church being his sponsor. The family court judge was a member also and his application received immediate approval. That same day, Lester moved into the church.

Now he was back, too early in the morning and he hoped that Alpha Micah would still welcome him. He had nowhere else to turn if he didn't.

Lester pulled around to the back of the church, parked and walked to the door. He hesitated before ringing the bell. He hoped he was doing the right thing. He pressed the button.

Chapter 76

In The Air Over Eastern Tennessee

Charis heard the pilot announce that they were starting their decent into Chattanooga Airport. She figured she had fifteen minutes tops to call her boss.

"Paul Jenner,"

"Good morning Paul, It's Charis Andrews."

"I know, Charis, that's why I have my secretary ask who's calling."

"If you knew, why didn't you just answer hello Charis?"

"It too early for a wiseass, Charis. Are you still in the air?"

"Getting ready to land."

"How can I help you?"

"Paul, I tried to run a print last night and the file was blocked. I need your authorization to open it."

"I'll need to review it and then let you know. Are you reachable today?"

"Yes, I will be in and out of meetings but nothing that can't be interrupted."

"Let me have the case number Charis and I'll take a look."

"Thanks, Paul."

She gave him the number.

"I've got it, Charis. I will get back to you within the hour."

He hung up. "*Paul is all business,*" she thought.

She packed her gear into her carryon bag and readied herself for landing.

It was a smooth flight. She found that she was taking a liking to the smaller regional jets. There were easy to board and deplane and the staff seemed more friendly and less hurried. She walked to the front of the plane, thanked the kid who just graduated nursery school for flying her there safely and deplaned.

At least there was a real, enclosed jetway at this airport. It was still very small but nice. As she guessed, the car rental desk was a one minute walk. She opted for a pickup truck again. She was out the door in under five minutes which pleased her because she had an hour and fifteen minute drive to McMinnville.

She had reread the file on the plane and really only had two things to accomplish: slap the Sherriff and speak with the ME. She threw her bags in the back of the cab and set the GPS for the Sheriff's Office in McMinnville. It looked like two turns over the seventy miles. One onto Rt. 111 and then onto RT. 8.

She was on the road for fifteen minutes when the boss called back.

"Hello Paul."

"Charis, are you sitting down?"

"That's usually how I drive, Paul."

"It's not good news."

Chapter 77

Quicksburg, VA

Til was late getting to the diner. Delilah greeted him as usual.

"Kinda late aren't you, Sheriff?"

"I am, Delilah."

Something was up. She brought him coffee and placed her hand on top of his. "I'm ready to listen when you're ready to talk."

She walked away and let him be. She made sure the other customers had what they needed for a while. After several minutes of not touching his coffee, she came back.

"What is it, Til? Can I bring you something other than coffee?"

"The coffee is fine D. You haven't seen Alan this morning, have you?"

"No, the last time I saw him was yesterday when he came by for those buckets. Is he alright?"

"I haven't seen him either. We had a talk late afternoon yesterday in the office and I sent him on his way. It was a serious talk but I thought we were okay when he left."

"What about his house? He said he was working on a project."

"I stopped by there, his mother hasn't seen his since five last night."

"Does he have the patrol car?"

"No, that was in the parking lot this morning."

"What's your next step?" she asked.

"If I don't hear from him by noon, I'm going to report him missing."

"What can I do, Til?" Delilah asked.

"You said that Alan would meet up with some guys from church now and then. If they come in again, would you let me know right away?"

"Of course, Til. Can I get you some breakfast?" she asked tenderly.

"I think I'll just go with the coffee today, but thanks."

"Then it's going to be a hot one," she said as she pulled the cup away. "I'll pour you a fresh cup."

Chapter 78

High Falls, NY

Greg was back at the hospital well before 10am. He had already called Mary and explained his early departure. He had a few minutes before his first meeting was to begin so he had Kathy ask Ethan to come to his office.

"Ethan, come on in," Greg said. "I received the discharge summary from St. Luke's and I thought we could read it together."

"I appreciate that, Greg, that's very thoughtful of you."

Greg opened the manilla envelope and removed three pages. He skimmed and read at the same time, slowing down at the important parts. He barely touched on things like date of discharge, age and address. The summary was on the third page.

"Female patient, age 17 was discharged against medical advice to her father. The proposed plan of care was to discharge her to a rehabilitation center where she could have her health monitored while receiving moderate to intense rehabilitative services including physical therapy and occupational therapy, plus speech and cognitive therapy. The final disposition of the patient, to the best of our knowledge, is home."

Further on Greg read, *"copies of the complete inpatient chart was requested by the father and delivered as requested. The father also signed the DAMA form."*

"So she was never taken to a rehab facility?" Ethan asked.

"We don't know that for sure. Her father could have taken her somewhere, perhaps even out of state."

"Greg, does it list her insurance carrier on that report?"

"Let's see…Yes. She was covered by EmPath. I think I know where you're going with this. If she was readmitted to another facility, the insurance company would have been billed. I am going to ask Medical Records to call and find out."

Greg sent an email to the manager of the Medical Records department with the request, including the policy number from the discharge summary.

"We should have an answer on that today, Ethan. I'm sorry we didn't find more."

"Hey, we do what we can. I really appreciate you your effort."

"I'm happy to do what I can. I'll call you when I hear back from MR."

Ethan walked out leaving Greg a minute or two to check his email. At the top of his list was one from Charis that arrived just moments before. The heading was, *"Summary of unofficial investigation of VCOTR."*

Greg didn't have time to read it now. Kathy popped her head in.

"Can you take a call from Trey Lawrence?"

"Send it in."

"Hi Trey, what do you have?"

"The black van is registered to Mease Mortuary, LLC. The white Cadillac is registered to a Stanley Wiloman who lives in High Falls. He has a clean record."

"You wouldn't happen to have a photo of Stan, would you?"

"I have a copy of his driver's license," Trey responded.

"I wish you had one from fifteen years ago," Greg said.

"I can request a copy of an old photo from DMV. Do you have something to compare it to?"

"I may have. Let me have a look and if I think we have a match, I will be ready to tell you what I think is going on."

"That's a deal, Greg. I'll get right on it."

"So Trey, what does the black van mean?"

"It may not mean anything but we are going to take a look. If the tires match, we are probably going to take a close look."

"You will enjoy working with the owner if it's the same guy I talked to last year."

"I think you're being facetious."

"You'll see. Thanks Trey!"

Greg hung up the phone and thought about the note from Charis. He would rather dig into that than attend another meeting discussing long term disability but he had a job to do. As he prepared to leave the office, he had another thought.

He ran back to his desk and jotted down a note.

Names, age, sex and dates of all bodies released to Mease Mortuary over the last year. He circled it and left the office.

Chapter 79

Custer, SD

The solid wood door was opened by Brother Jeffrey.

"Good morning, Brother Lester, how can I help you?"

"Good morning. I was wonder if I could see Alpha Micah for just a few minutes."

"This is his meditation time and he usually doesn't want to be disturbed. Can you call again later, this afternoon perhaps?"

"No, this can't wait until this afternoon. It is really important and time sensitive. Please ask him to see me."

"Come in, Brother. I'll see what I can do."

Lester entered the foyer while Jeffrey closed the door behind him. Lester looked around the room at the beautiful oak furniture with red cushions but he was too worked up to sit.

Jeffrey quickly ascended the half spiral staircase to his left. Lester knew Jeffrey was heading to the third floor to the Alpha's chambers. Lester had been there before. It was not customary for anyone but the Alpha and his invited female guests to enter his quarters.

It was many years ago when Lester was just a boy of fifteen years when he first saw it. He couldn't believe that one man could live in such an extravagant space. As he grew and became more aware of the world around him, he would compare the Alpha's quarters with pictures he had seen of a penthouse apartment in New York or Los Angeles.

He was aware that everything seems bigger when you're a child but he would guess, from memory, that is was at least three thousand square feet on one floor. He never saw all of it, the bedroom and bathroom were off limits of course. There were probably other private sections of the apartment as well.

He could only imaging what went on behind those closed doors. Once he was old enough to partake in the physical rewards of the church, he would fantasize about what went on back there.

Jeffrey was coming down the stairs.

"Alpha Micah has agreed to see you but he needs twenty minutes. He asked that you be taken care of while you wait. May I have some food sent for you or perhaps a young maiden?"

"That's very kind. Perhaps just a cup of coffee if it's not too much trouble."

"Right away. Come upstairs and we will find a comfortable place for you to rest."

Lester followed Jeffrey up the stairs and toward the back of the structure. There were several doors close together on the left of the hall. He opened the first and stepped in. Lester followed him into a small but very cozy room that had a table for two near the back and a daybed along one side.

Lester took a seat at the table facing a small window that looked out over the back of the property. It was beautiful. He could see three workers off in the distance tending to one of the many gardens.

He had been around long enough to see most of the complex both inside and out. He was amazed how smoothly it all flowed. Everyone seemed content here. It was like they were comfortable in whatever their role was. It appeared that that had all they wanted and needed.

The door opened and a woman he guessed to be in her mid-fifties entered carrying a tray. She had a very pleasant way about her. She seemed unhurried yet efficient. It was like watching the calm flow of a small stream on a breezeless day.

She set a cup and saucer on the table and poured the coffee. The aroma woke his senses. She placed a small sugar bowl and a carafe that held no more than two ounces of cream next to it. She returned to the tray and came back with what appeared to be a bran muffin on a plate with whipped butter on the side.

She did all of this silently and joyfully. Before she turned to leave she said,

"May I be of any further service to you, sir?"

She met his eyes for just a moment and then looked away.

"What is your name?" he asked.

"They call me Martha, sir."

He thought that was an unusual response.

"But is that your name?"

"Yes, sir."

"Thank you, Martha."

He watched as she left the room just as smoothly and silently as she had entered.

He felt so comfortable, so cared for. He tried the coffee. He guessed it was French roast, made in a French press. It was dark and rich. He added a little cream and stirred, noticing how the white and the black swirled together before they both disappeared.

He cut a small wedge from the muffin and spread the soft whipped butter on it. It was perfect. There was just enough spice and just the right amount of bran making it dense without being heavy. It was still a little warm inside.

For as anxious and upset as he was upon arrival, he felt relaxed and satiated now. He looked out at the workers again. He imagined the smell of the soil as they turned it over and the warmth of the early morning sun.

He was almost startled when the door opened. It was Jeffrey.

"He will see you now, Brother. Please follow me."

They moved down the corridor toward the back of the building. There was another small window at the very end. Just before they reached it, there was an elevator off to the right. They boarded and went to the third level.

Lester was having flashbacks of his first time there, leaving his mother to fend for herself much like his father had done. They were still married but he spent all of his time at the church and she resented it but Lester knew that if his father was around more, he probably would have killed her.

They reached the double doors that entered the Alpha's suite. There were no other doors around and no other hallways. This was a destination, not something you passed on the way to somewhere else.

Jeffrey knocked and then entered without waiting for a reply. Lester was once again amazed by the vastness of the space. He was standing in the entryway which was at least twelve feet deep. Straight ahead was a beautiful painting with a gilded frame. It occupied most of the wall.

To his left, set back at least ten feet was another wall. About eight feet down the wall was another double door. To his right, the foyer opened into a sitting area that was a good thirty feet deep and forty feet wide. The walls were a rich cream color, the floors were deep gold and cream colored marble with several plush Persian rugs laying beneath the furniture.

There were three sofas in the room all pure white. There were at least a half dozen accent chairs that were mostly high back, Queen Anne style in crimson. The side tables were made of glass and gold and there was a long buffet table immediately to his right. It has a rounded front, was made of art carved wood painted white with a thick marble top.

It's curve matched the outward curvature of the opposite exterior wall that had at least ten, eight inch wide by eight foot high darkened windows that looked short compared to the height of the ceiling. The view was over the back of the property.

From the far side of the long sitting room was a wide corridor. It was from there that Alpha Micah appeared. He smiled as he made his way between the sitting are and the buffet.

"Brother Lester, it is so good to see you. Thank you Jeffrey."

Micah took his hand as Jeffrey let himself out. Lester and Micah hugged.

"It's good to see you Alpha Micah. I'm sorry for showing up so early."

"We've known each other a long time, Les, I trust that you have something that can't wait. Please sit down and relax."

"Thank you."

The men took positions at the end of two sofas that opposed each other. In between was a gold and glass coffee table.

"How can I help you, Les?"

"I'm afraid I have fallen into some trouble and I need your guidance."

"I'll do my best. Go on."

"You may already know this but I have been seeing a woman outside of my marriage. I am neither proud of nor ashamed of that. The problem is that this other woman is a control freak and has a grip on me that I can't explain nor enjoy."

"This would be the detective in Custer?" the Alpha asked.

"Yes, but how did you know?"

"Lester, you can't manage a project of this magnitude without having eyes and ears on the outside. You should know that because you are one of them."

"Of course, I'm not sure what I was thinking."

"You are obviously emotionally upset by this situation and that is what may be clouding your thinking. It's understandable. Love and even lust can trap a man in uncontrollable jealousy that can become an addiction."

"Yes, Alpha Micah, that is what it feels like, an addiction. I have grown to hate this woman but I can't envision her with anyone else. It is eating me up!"

"What do you hate about her, if I may ask?"

"I hate the way she treats me. She is demanding, unreasonable and insulting. She knows she has me hooked and she uses that as leverage."

"But she gives you what you can't get at home?" Alpha asked.

"That's part of it. She has a nasty way of exciting me. But it's not all about the sex. I've had exciting sex right here, several times. There's something else about her."

"She reminds you of your mother," Alpha said.

"I hated her too. I hated the way she treated my father and I despised the way she treated me."

"I know. I was there. Your father knew that as well. He knew that he needed to get you away from her. That's why you're here."

"Yes, and I am forever grateful. There is a peace that I find here that doesn't exist out there."

"Lester, some of us turn into our parents. Some children who were abused become abusive parents and spouses. It's what they are used to. But it doesn't have to be that way. Many troubled children become strong, successful and nurturing adults.

"I think you are used to being controlled and belittled and so you feel a familiarity with it. That is not unusual. You may think *"why would I do that? I wouldn't subject myself to that again,"* but it does happen, Lester and it happens more than we care to admit."

"Somehow, you need to break that chain. You need to do it and the sooner the better. If you don't, the chain will eventually snap and come back and hit you in the face, taking you out."

"I know you're right, Alpha Micah. There is more to the story. Det. Hillabrandt has become fond of bringing an outsider into the bedroom."

"Do you mean as a replacement or an addition?"

"An addition. And not a male. It's always a female and I suppose I should enjoy that but it still makes me jealous."

"Of course it would. How can a man possibly compete with another woman. If she wants another woman in your bed, she is diminishing your edge. A woman who goes along with another woman because she is trying to please her husband is doing so out of love and acceptance. It is more of a sacrifice than a desire. The same would hold true if she wanted another male to join you. But when the woman chooses a woman or a man chooses a man, they have just doubled your competition and your jealousy goes off the chart."

"You make a good point, Alpha. There is one more complicating factor. A couple of months ago, I was with a young lady here. It was delightful but I think she was furloughed. I think she may be the one that was found in the river."

"Certainly, no one can connect someone from here with you, Lester. I know the girl you're speaking of. It was discovered that she had a health issue that she wasn't going to get beyond. We did the sensible and honorable thing."

"I am not questioning your judgement, Alpha, I am sure you handle all of your affairs appropriately. At autopsy, the ME discovered the girl was also pregnant." Les said.

There was silence for a long moment as Micah digested what he just heard.

"You're afraid you may be the father?"

"Yes, sir."

"I am sorry, Lester. We are very careful about controlling that factor. Any women chosen for reproduction are secluded from the morale services team. All the others are protected against pregnancy. I will look into this at once."

"Again sir, no judgement. It does leave me to wonder about what I will do if they trace the DNA to me."

"Is your DNA on file anywhere?"

"Yes. It is in the federal database as a law enforcement officer."

"So, if it turns out that your DNA is found, you are going to be suspected of the murder. Even if not proven, you will lose your job and life as you now know it," Alpha proposed.

"Yes, sir."

"Lester, I feel responsible for this. I will make it right somehow. Would you be willing to live here and work here? It's a rather enjoyable place to be."

"I'm sure it is. I always feel very comfortable here, Alpha. How would that work though? Somebody is going to be looking for me."

"Of course, but they won't find you here. You will simply disappear. Everyone will think you ran off because of your guilt. After a while, they will project that you have done yourself in. In a few months, they will stop looking."

"But I am never able to leave the grounds?" Lester asked.

"Not true at all, Lester, Believe or not, our employees do get to travel. It may not be any place you want or any time you wish, but we try to give our people time off every three months. Plus we have almost anything one would want right here on the premises."

"One of the rules however is that you can never see family again. That just wouldn't work and that is why we recruit people who don't have family. It works out for all of us. We become each other's family."

"Well, I surely fit into the no family rule," Les replied.

"Will you accept my offer, Les? If you are the father, you come to me."

"I graciously accept, Alpha Micah. Thank you."

"You are welcome. You can choose your job. We would be delighted to have you. Now, what do we do about that bitch detective?"

Chapter 80

McMinnville, TN

Charis passed the sign welcoming her to McMinnville, the county seat of Warren County. Population 13,659. She really enjoyed the ride getting here. It was rural but beautiful. She was looking for the downtown restaurant where she was going to meet Det. Martin Ballard for an early lunch.

Ballard said it was two blocks west of the Barren River on Main Street. She found it. It was three blocks by her calculation. It was a charming downtown, the one everyone pictures when they think about small town America. She found a parking place just around the corner, grateful that she beat the lunch crowd.

The place was called "Fry Me A River" and it looked cute from the outside although a little modern for an old town. She walked into a nearly empty dining room. She was five minutes late and the detective still wasn't there. She worried that he showed up early and left when she wasn't on time.

She could hear voices coming from the kitchen but no one rushed out to meet her. She gave them the benefit of the doubt that they didn't hear her come in. She said hello in a slightly raised voice. A young lady appeared from behind the swinging saloon doors.

"Hi there! Are you here for lunch?"

"Yes, I am."

"Will it be just you?"

Charis wanted to say she felt minimized by the term "Just you" but she bit her tongue.

"No, I'm expecting someone to join me. Would you happen to know Detective Ballard?"

"Marty Ballard?"

"Yes, Martin Ballard." Charis replied.

"I know him. We call him Officer Ballard."

"He's not a detective?"

"He might be. Can I get you a beverage while you're waiting?"

"Yes, a diet cola, please."

"Coming right up!"

The girl was cute and perky. Charis didn't think she was old enough to be working or riding a bike without training wheels for that matter. She wondered what was going on with her that everyone looked so young. For a second she thought it was because she was aging but she dismissed that possibility.

"Here you go, ma'am. Oh look, there's Officer Ballard now."

Charis stood up to meet him and held out her hand.

"I'm agent Charis Andrews."

"Detective Martin Ballard."

They shook hand, he didn't smile.

"This is a pretty little town you have." Charis offered.

"We like it."

"This is going to be a long afternoon," Charis thought.

"So, Detective Ballard, can I call you Martin?"

"The folks round here call me Marty." He replied with an annoying disdain.

They probably call you asshole and who knows what else when you're not around. It's nice to meet you Marty, you can call me Charis."

"Okay."

"I should just kick his ass and get it over with but he is pretty big and he probably had a weapon somewhere. Although it would take him a minute to get the bullet out of his front shirt pocket."

"Marty, do you have anything new on the case?"

"No, not really. I mean your fellas with the boat found the dumping place and found the tire track. Other than that, I don't have anything."

Including a brain! Calm down. "Tell me about the spot on the river."

"It was about a half mile upriver from here." He replied.

"Okay. Is there anything unique about that spot?"

"No."

The waitress came back to take Ballard's drink order.

He'll have a ginkgo biloba milkshake. Charis said in her head.

"I'll have a beer," he said.

"I'm sorry Officer Ballard, we don't serve beer until after noon time."

That's when both hands of the clock point straight up. She would have said it but she didn't think either of them would understand.

"Alright then, just some water."

"Would you like to hear the specials?"

"Yes, please," Charis said before he had a chance to answer.

"Today we have the fried catfish sandwich with chips or fries and the fried trout platter. That comes with fries and coleslaw."

"May I look at a menu, please?" Charis asked.

"I'll have the catfish sandwich," Marty answered, "and don't go cheap on the fries."

The waitress brought a menu. Charis gave it a quick look and confirmed her theory. If it didn't come from the river, it wasn't on the menu.

"May I please have the chopped salad without the fried catfish? And the dressing on the side please."

She placed the order and delivered Marty's water.

"Marty, are we still meeting the ME at 12:30?"

"Yes."

"If we hurry and eat, would we have time to run by the spot on the river."

"Yes."

"Great."

Charis hoped the food wouldn't take too long to arrive or too long to eat. The excitement of the conversation was more than she could handle.

Chapter 81

High Falls, NY

Maury Slater had just walked his guest to the back door. His wife Lynette was tidying up the room in the basement. She didn't expect another guest today but in this business one ever knew for sure. Her years of nursing experience proved useful in providing an aseptic environment for their business but it was her girliness that added to the pleasure of the customers.

She had mastered the art of cosmetology. She provided hair cutting and styling and received regular praises from all customers about her application of makeup and not just from the men.

At first, she was somewhat alarmed. She had suspected Maury was different right from the start but she fell in love with him anyway. He seemed cocky but she knew it was a cover up for the loneliness he felt. She knew what it was like to be different too.

Shortly after they got together, he opened up to her and told her about his attraction to the deceased. He described how he too was offended by it when he interrupted Mr. Mease in the act. It took a considerable amount of talking before Harold had convinced him that it was okay.

It took a while for Lynette to adapt to it as well but she never criticized Maury for it. Everyone had their faults and who was she to judge. She had one rule that Maury had to accept. They were in it together. He could not partake on his own. She needed to be informed and allowed to either witness or join in.

It wasn't long before she understood Maury's attraction and she felt they created a closer bond because of it. The business side of it was a bonus. She had no idea there was that much interest in necrophilia. She had heard about it and then read about it but never anticipated its popularity.

Her job was to ready the subject and clean up afterward. He managed the customer base and guided them through the process. On the rare occasion that the customer was a female and the subject was a male, they reversed duties.

Business activity varied based on how many funeral contracts they received but lately they were busy. They averaged three per week which was enough considering the time involved and the coordination required to host large groups of family and other visitors on top of the "rental" line. There was also the periodic disposal of a church member.

They had joined the church a few years back. Another businessman in town had invited them to a Sunday gathering. They were aware that being active in community increased their referrals so they gave it a try.

The church facility was amazing, the leadership appeared sincere and open. Maury chose to attend a men's night gathering a few weeks later where the Alpha ask him to serve on the inner circle. He learned that someone in his position would be very helpful to the church and that the congregation would in turn support his business.

This wasn't the typical men's gathering. They withheld the morale services feature until after Maury had left. They needed him and didn't want to scare him off. It was several months before Maury was exposed to the many other benefits of membership. When he was, he didn't participate but rather talked to the Alpha about his agreement with his wife.

Alpha offered a private session with him and his wife. If they wanted in, they could both attend the mixed night gatherings that were held periodically. They agreed to giving it a try and they loved it. They became a very active couple in the church family.

Maury returned after seeing his customer out. He proceeded to the basement and set the cash on the counter next to Lynette.

"We're having a good week, Maury. Was Stan satisfied?"

"Very, he commented on how nice she looked. I believe "life-like" were the words he used."

"It is a lot easier when they are freshly departed," Lynette replied. "By the way, I like the concealer you ordered."

"That's great. Hey, I got a call to make a pickup at the church. Would you like to ride along?"

"Sure," she answered, "let me forward the landline to my cell phone and I'll be ready."

Maury went out to the car to tidy it up. If there was anything laying on the floor, it could prevent the faux floor from sliding properly. Lynette come out just before he finished.

"I'm ready," she said.

They hopped in the van and pulled around the home toward the road. They turned left, heading out of town.

Across the street, Trey Lawrence was taking some photographs of the vehicle. He could follow it but he wanted to be there when it came back. He wasn't in any hurry besides, he didn't want to steal Greg's thunder on this. He also had a few other things to do.

Chapter 82

McMinnville, TN

Charis had worked with some members of law enforcement that she believed were subpar but none as incompetent as Marty Ballard. She experienced run ins with cavalier cops, righteous cops, and dumb cops but this guy took the cake. Except perhaps for that misogynistic idiot FBI agent in Vermont, Taylor Summers.

She walked the river's edge, found the spot, found nothing unusual and left. Her meeting with the medical examiner went well, pretty much the same as the others. Same findings and he had already read and followed the FBI notice regarding handling and diagnosing victims.

He played by the rules and seemed thorough and proactive. She found herself with some welcomed spare time before having to return to Chattanooga to catch her next flight.

She sat in the park near where her car was parked. She called her boss at work.

"Agent Andrews, how is it going in McMinnville?"

"It's actually lovely here, have you ever been to McMInnville?" she replied.

"Yes, my wife is a fan of botany. If it grows, she knows, or at least wants to. How did your investigation go?"

"Nothing unexpected or useful. The ME was helpful but the detective, I had to shoot him and throw him in the river. He sank to the bottom immediately."

"Like a box of rocks, I get it. Let me tell you what we have here, Charis. When I'm done, I want your opinion on what our next steps are."

"Okay, Paul."

"Your print belongs to Agent Myron Hawkins."

"That's why I couldn't access his file." Charis said.

"Correct. Here is some other information. The substance on the tape you sent us is calcium carbonate."

"Jesus Paul, tell me had Thallium in his desk and we can wrap this up right now."

"We haven't found anything in his office, Charis. The fingerprint is powerful but the dust on the tape could be from anywhere or almost anything. Calcium carbonate is everywhere."

"So, he planted listening devices in private homes, he broke into these homes and he has trace minerals consistent with the material found in the lungs of the victims. What do you think our next move is?"

"That's why I want your opinion. If he is the one who has been harassing you and you feel as though you are in eminent danger, we can hold him but only based on the fingerprint. Everything else is speculation at this point. He would probably walk, until we come up with something else."

"Like my murder, Paul?"

"That would certainly seal the deal but I was thinking more in the line of putting a tail on him to make sure that doesn't happen. If I call him on it now it would be like letting him off the hook."

"I know you're right, Paul, it's just a little personal this time."

"That's why I want you to weigh in, Charis."

"It's not just me Paul, I'm worried about Destiny Chalmers too."

"She is at The Haven, right? We can protect her there. I can call in Sanchez."

"Michael is a good man," Charis replied, "I trust him."

"And how about you? Would like a partner for a few days?" Paul asked.

Charis thought about it then decided against it.

"Not necessary, but thanks. Now that I know who my ghost is, I'm not as worried about him. I can take care of myself. Why do think he is after me? I have never worked with him, I haven't seen him outside of office meetings and I've never even run into him at the coffee pot."

"He is vested in a case you're working. This current one has the highest profile. I'm not sure what the connection is, but we will be looking into that," Paul said.

"Do you know what his schedule is for the next few days?" Charis asked.

"He has been working a possible drug case out of western Virginia. His travel receipts have been in the I-81 corridor between Harrisonburg and Roanoke. We will keep an eye on him."

"Let's go with that, Paul. You watch him and I'll watch my back. I have a few things left to do before I make the drive to catch my flight so I'll sign off for now."

"Be careful, Charis. Hey, is Fry Me A River still there?"

"Yes, you know of it?" Charis asked.

"My wife wanted to go. It was the most fattening meal I ever had but I liked the name." Paul hung up.

Charis checked her notes to see if she had any loose ends. Everything looked to be in fair shape except for Crystal City, Missouri. She hadn't received an update in a while. Custer, South Dakota to St. Louis, Missouri would get her halfway home. She could fly out of Rapid City to St. Louis Friday evening, spend half of Saturday in Crystal City and be home in time for dinner Saturday night.

She called Detective Climm to set it up.

"Laroy Climm."

"Detective Climm, this is Agent Andrews, FBI."

"Hello Agent Andrews, how are you doing today?"

"I am well, thank you. I know this is short notice but I would like to spend some time there Saturday morning. I wasn't planning to but I'm in the neighborhood, so to speak and it would make sense to do it now. I know it's a weekend and I apologize for that."

"Of course, Agent Andrews, I will make myself available. I assume you would like to speak to the ME as well?"

"Yes, I would. I think three hours total would be enough time. If we begin by 9:00 am, I will be out of your hair by noon."

"I will take care of it," he said." Is there anything else I can arrange for you?"

"I think I can take care of the rest. I appreciate your help, Detective."

"My pleasure, Agent. Safe travel."

She thanked him and ended the call. *I had better let some people know,* she thought and began creating some emails.

Chapter 83

Crystal City, MO

Laroy Climm had barely ended the call with Charis Andrews before he started dialing the number for Alpha Timothy. It took three rings but he answered.

"Alpha Timothy, Brother Laroy, do you have a moment to talk?"

"Of course, Brother Laroy, how can I help you?"

"The FBI will be in Crystal City this Saturday. I just received a call from the lead agent on the case."

"Do you know what her intent is?"

"She wants to go over my notes and meet with the ME."

"Does that present a problem, Brother?"

"I don't have many notes. We pulled a body from the river, no ID and not much else to go on. The ME part will go fine." Laroy answered.

"Have you interviewed possible witnesses, checked for security cameras in the area, you know, routine police work?"

"No, I didn't think it would get this far."

"I see," Timothy replied.

"There is a chance she will never make it here, she is supposed to be in Custer tomorrow and I don't think Sheriff Moran will have much tolerance for her."

"Let me make a few call, Brother Laroy. See if you can make up a few notes in the meantime. If she does arrive, you will need to show her something. Thank you for letting me know. We are having some brothers over tomorrow evening, why don't you join us and bring your notes? We can review them quickly and then blow off some steam together."

"That sounds great, Alpha Timothy, what time?"

"We begin at 6:30. As always, use your private car and park in the rear. Someone will be tending the back door. See you then."

Laroy found great comfort in speaking with the Alpha. He was always so calm and collected. He felt like he owed Myron Hawkins a call.

"Hello."

"Myron, this is Laroy in Festus. Guess who's coming to town?"

"It's too soon for Santa, so my next guess is Charis Andrews."

"You win a prize, Brother."

"How do you know, Laroy?"

"She just called me. She said she was in the neighborhood, could be here Saturday morning."

"That's good to know. She is probably going to stop on her way back from Custer," Myron added.

"If she makes it out of Custer!" Laroy exclaimed.

"She needs to be stopped somewhere, Custer is as good a place as any," Myron replied.

"I tried to get her to back off," Myron said, "I gave her several warnings. She's just a hard nut to crack."

"I think it will be over soon, one way or the other," Laroy projected.

"Maybe if I had followed through on my threats sooner, we wouldn't be in this predicament" Myron added.

"Hey Myron, I just had a thought. "What if something came up at home that she would need to return for?"

"You mean like business related?"

"I was thinking more along the lines of something personal."

"Right! If something happened to her father, she would drop all this and run home. That's perfect and he is an easy target. Great idea, Laroy. If we don't hear anything from Custer tomorrow, I'll pay her dad another visit."

"That's excellent, Myron, now I won't need to come up with any phony police reports. I will contact you after I speak with Brother Lester in Custer tomorrow."

They hung up and Myron began thinking about a plan.

Chapter 84

High Falls, NY

Ethan was in his office looking over the map and documents he had been preparing. No one asked him to, but he just had a gut feeling that there was some common connection that everyone else was overlooking.

A map of the United States was spread out over the desk with an index card containing the details of each case standing behind the location. The furthest west was Custer, SD., followed by Crystal City, MO, McMinnville, TN, Quicksburg, VA, and Tribes Hill, NY.

He used a compass to draw a circle fifty miles in every direction from the point where each body was found. Then he used a computer map to zoom in on the area of interest.

No one knew for sure when the bodies entered the water so it was difficult to define how the murders occurred, chronologically. Going by the date they were found and assuming it was the same persons or persons, the path would have begun in Tennessee, moved to Custer two days later, Missouri two days after that, Then upstate New York one month later and Virginia two day after that.

The first three would have been nearly impossible to pull off without flying from place to place. That meant that the culprit or culprits had a private plane or traveled by commercial aircraft. He would ask Trey to look into getting the data for the same person boarding aircrafts to those three destinations during that time frame.

"Why wait a month between numbers three and four?" He asked himself. There were only two to three days between victims four and five but central New York to Virginia is drivable in that amount of time.

The bodies were both male and female ranging in ages from fourteen to fifty-five. *"Probably not a typical serial killer pattern,"* he thought.

"So what is the connection?" He asked himself. Some were northeast states and some were mid-west. There were no trains that covered all those areas. The bodies were all found in rivers but not the same river. He worked a little longer but couldn't come up with a common trait. He looked through the available information online for each city and county that they were in to find a common denominator. He didn't come up with anything.

Checking his email, Ethan found a message that Greg had forwarded from Charis. It was a summary of the research her father had done on the Valley Church of Redemption. He opened the attached file to discovered several pages of information.

As he delved into it, he realized that much of the information was old. The wasn't much at all from the last few decades. Again, he was stymied by the ability of any church to remain solvent without anyone knowing they were there.

He performed a mini summary in his mind as he went along.

A Mormon guy created his own church, the first in Cody, WY, the second in SD, probably more in between but certainly one in NY. They tolerate, if not encourage polygamy, they care for the infirm, the company hasn't been found on paper and they do all this without buying as much as a single roll of toilet paper.

Not much to go on, he thought. He wondered what prompted them to change their name, adding "Valley" in the 90's. The eastward movement interested him. It seemed to coincide with the pattern of the crimes. *"Could the church be a clue?"* He didn't see how.

All in all, he didn't have much more than he had an hour ago. He decided to send Trey a message.

Trey, Is it possible to find out if a single passenger or group of passengers flew between Rapid City, SD., Chattanooga, TN., and St. Louis, MO. Between the dates of May 25 and Jun 5 of this year? Not sure about which order they would have flown. Thanks, Ethan.

Ethan had some work he needed to complete before lunch so he placed his investigation on hold.

Chapter 85

High Falls, NY

Trey had been sitting in the parking lot of the hardware store for well over two hours after the black van departed. He kept busy getting caught up on other cases and managing his email. He received one from Charis and one from Ethan. He opened them in the order that he received them.

Charis had finished in McMInnville and was going back to Chattanooga to get a flight to Rapid City. She would rent a car, drive to Custer and find a hotel for the night. She also included her itinerary for the next day.

She was meeting with Sheriff Lester Moran at the county courthouse at 9:00am. Then, she would meet with the medical examiner and Detective Doreen Hillabrandt at a place to be determined. She included the office and home addresses for both.

He opened the message from Ethan. He read the request and thought that Ethan might be on to something. He placed a call to the office and opened a task. He should hear something by the end of the day.

Trey could see a car coming from the other direction beginning to slow down. He watched it turn into the driveway and stop. The brake lights were still on. He snapped a picture of the vehicle and zoomed in to take another of the plate.

The driver didn't seem to be in a hurry to get out. He started running the plate through the DMV. A moment later, the black van returned. When the driver in the first car noticed the van behind him, he pulled around the back of the house. The van followed.

He couldn't see any of the action going on behind the building from where he was. He grabbed his camera and dashed across the busy road. He walked down the shoulder toward the right side of the building where the parking lot was located. He went as far as he could down the road until he had a view to the back.

The van was backed up to a ramp. One man and one woman pulled the stretcher from the van, released the legs so that they extended to walking height and proceeded up the ramp. There was obviously a body in the bag on the stretcher. There wasn't any indication of the driver from the other vehicle. He must have gone in ahead of them.

Trey snapped a few more pictures of the van and the other car and walked across the highway. When he reached his car, the results of the search were available. It was a 2014 Toyota Camry registered to Alton Smith whose address was listed as Rt 167, Jordanville.

He didn't see any arrest record. *"Maybe he was just planning a funeral for a loved one,"* he thought. He was done for today. There were other things he needed to do.

Chapter 86

High Falls. NY

Greg received an email from Trey Lawrence including another driver's license photo of Stan Wiloman. This one was from 2002 which would be helpful in comparing to the man in the video. He also received a new license photo of a man named Alton Smith. *Check this one while you're at it.* Trey wrote.

There were a couple of things Greg needed to do first. He dialed the number for Charles Chalmers.

"Hello, Greg."

"Charles, is everyone settled in at the Haven?"

"Yes, this place is wonderful. The girls are already playing in the pool."

"Excellent," Greg replied. "Ethan will be there after work to keep you all company and I will stop by later on as well. I'm going to stop out at the farm first to check on Priscilla and Jack. Do you need me to bring anything back for you?"

"Not that I can think of Greg but I'll ask the girls."

"Just give me a call if you think of anything."

"Will do. Thank you Greg."

Greg was ready to review the tape again. He pulled the computer tower out of his desk drawer and hooked it up to his monitor. When the cables were connected, he booted the system and went to get a cup of coffee. He asked Kathy to keep people away for the next couple hours.

On the way to the cafeteria, he ran into Ethan.

"How is it going, Ethan?"

"Hi Mr. Webster, everything is swell."

"Swell? Who are you, Dennis the menace?"

"Who is Dennis the menace?" Ethan asked.

"Never mind. Hey, I will see you at the Haven around seven. Are you going right from work? Did you pack a bathing suit?"

"I was going right from work, now I guess I'll go home to get a bathing suit first," Ethan explained.

"Don't worry about it, that place has extras of everything. I am so certain of it that if they don't, call me and I will stop and get one for you on my way."

"That's cool, thanks!"

"You're welcome. Catch you later."

Greg chatted with a few associates in the kitchen as usual and then made his way back to his office.

"Don't let anyone through that door, Kathy."

"I won't sir!"

"Greg knew she was being sarcastic and he also knew no one would come through his door.

He signed in using the temporary password he was assigned and sipped his coffee while his other hand found the file. He clicked to open it. He closed the drapes behind him and turned off the lights. The image needed all the help it could get.

When he reached a segment that included a man other than Maury, he paused the video. He used the still feature to hold a frame that was in focus and sent the image to his printer. It was tedious work much like the stakeout. It took him just one day to realize that he could eliminate police work from his bucket list.

After printing five images, he turned on the light and compared them to the driver's license photos. The printed images resulted in even more degradation. There didn't seem to be a match in the first batch of five.

Greg fast forwarded to the next location. It was apparent that the camera and recording device were activated motion sensors which helped immensely. Greg didn't need to watch hours of nothing happening. He pressed the play button again and stopped as each new man entered the scene. At least one of them looked like a repeat customer.

He printed off five images, turned the lights back on and did a comparison. He wasn't sure if the light of the scene had changed but something made these images a little sharper. The old driver's license image of Stanley Wiloman seemed like a match for one of the players.

Greg jotted down the date and time of the video. He continued on. It wasn't quite as difficult to handle the second time around but it still bothered him. He was making progress. If he could find just one more person who was in both the morgue all those years ago and at the funeral home now, it would probably be enough to open an investigation.

Forwarding the playback, he was focused on finding the guy in the second license that Trey had sent. It could take him weeks to review twenty plus hours of video and the odds that the second guy would be in the first hour were stacked against him.

He made a silent promise to himself that he would work at it until four o'clock. He was hoping to be out of the office and on his way to the Chalmers place by four-thirty.

He took a quick break to call Mary to give her the updated plan and to see if she and the girls would like to go along. He knew she would accept the invitation because she loved the place.

The last time she and the girls were there, they had a ball or at least until Mary found out about the explosion at Syracuse University. The memory of that day flooded back to Greg but not in a bad way. He was injured badly but he watched his son Jack become a man that day. He was always a responsible young man but the way he handled himself during that time assured Greg that he was a natural leader and a good caretaker.

Jack saved the lives of countless students as well as his dad that day. He had his mother's good looks but Greg's innate ability to see things. Greg always thought his own gift was just curiosity. Over the past few years, he realized that it was more and he knew Jack had it too. Even Jillian showed signs of it toward the end of the University Murders.

For Greg, it felt like things would reveal themselves. If was as if when looking at a page of printed words, everything would fade to background except the words he needed to see. If it was something he heard, he only retained the critical facts. In a life and death situation, he had cat-like instincts. For him, an empty stage and new overhead projector still in the box equaled bomb and that equaled take cover.

Greg was brought back to the present by his phone ringing.

"Greg, sorry to bother you but Medical Record has the results of the search you requested."

"Patch them in, Kathy. Greg Webster."

"Mr. Webster, this is Charlene, I have the results of your requests."

"Great Charlene, what did you find?"

"The first was a call that we made to EmPath Insurance Company regarding Lillian MacNamara. According to their representative, their coverage of that subscriber ended when she was signed out of St. Luke's."

"Charlene, does that mean the company dropped her?"

"No sir, according to them, the primary subscriber, in this case her father, had her taken off the policy."

"Did they list a reason for the request?"

"Yes, the father said his daughter was no longer in need of coverage."

"That doesn't sound right. It's certainly in conflict with the prescribed course of treatment listed in the discharge summary. Okay, how about the other request?"

"Yes, you had asked for the number of deaths from High Falls Hospital with a disposition of Mease Mortuary over the last two years. That number is one hundred, sixty-seven. That number was down eighteen percent from the previous two years."

"I would expect that decrease. It's attributed to the rise of offsite hospice facilities and people opting to spend their final days at home."

"Yes, sir."

"Thank you Charlene, good work."

Greg wasn't sure how any of that applied to the current situation but he had a feeling that time would prove that it did. He went back to reviewing the video.

Chapter 87

On the road to Chattanooga, TN

Charis was only fifteen minutes out of McMinnville when she spotted a two sided billboard. ***Your visit isn't complete without experiencing Cumberland Caverns and the magnificent Ruby Falls.*** The picture for the ad featured the falls with a caption that read ***More than 1100 feet below the surface.***

It looked like another great place to visit when she had the time. It wasn't going to be today. She had other things to do once she was in the air. She turned on the radio and searched for some music she could tolerate. There was a station that featured songs from the seventies and eighties that caught her attention.

Charis took in the scenery and sang to the music. She realized how much physical beauty surrounded her. A much needed departure from the ugliness presented through her work. She was really developing a fondness for rural America. She could see herself living in a place like High Falls someday.

It would be a long while before she reached retirement age but she could put in for a transfer. Thinking about getting out of the political influence and absurd traffic of the D.C. area sounded inviting. She would have to think about bringing her dad with her though. She would like that but she wasn't sure he would. He had already been uprooted once since Charis' mom passed and he had finally developed a network of friends. She made a mental note to call him from the plane.

Charis was nearing the Chattanooga Airport when her phone rang.

"Good afternoon, Greg, how are things up there?"

"All good as far as I know, Charis. Where are you?"

"I'm just about to pull into the Chattanooga Airport," she replied.

"Gate 29? Can I give you a shine?" Greg joked.

"It's a good thing my father listened to a lot of music when I was young or that joke would have been as flat as a pancake. Actually, it was still flat."

"I tried," Greg said. "Okay Charis, what do you know about crematories?"

"I know to stay away from them for as long as possible," she answered.

"I share your sentiment but I'm asking what you know about them from a regulatory standpoint."

"If I had to guess, and I do because I really don't know, I would say they fall under the purview of the Department of State and/or the Environmental Protection Agency."

"Nothing under Health and Human Services?" Greg asked.

"I think if you're looking for a crematorium it's a little too late for HHS."

"Good point," he replied.

"Why do you ask, Greg?"

"This funeral home here in town. I think he is back to his evil ways and was wondering what he had to do to get credentialed to add a crematorium to his business. Plus, I want to know who inspects them and how often. I want to nail this guy and I'm not sure "dating his clients" will result in more than a slap on the wrist."

"What makes you think he is still at it?" she asked.

"Trey and I have been staking out the place. We each captured photos of guys going in and out. We also had plate numbers for their vehicles so Trey sent me driver's license photos and I think I have one of them on tape from years ago."

"Ah, have you been watching porn again?" she asked.

"Not by choice, believe me. But I am doing it and I think it's paying off. I'm trying to make a match to one more player before turning it over to Trey."

"Good luck with that," she said, "I hope you get the guy."

"Thanks. Hey, you be careful out there!" Greg demanded.

"I will. I need to run but I will talk to you soon, Greg."

"Okay, Charis, safe flight."

It took Charis all of fifteen minutes to return the car and make it through security. She was at her gate with plenty of time to spare. She walked around the small terminal for a while to stretch her legs. She purchased a coffee and a snack and headed back to her gate. On the way she passed an electronic billboard.

The ad rotated about every thirty seconds. These things always made her feel like she was in the most charming place in America. There were hotel ads, restaurant ads, and one for Lookout Mountain which looked like fun. The next ad caught her attention.

It was another ad for Cumberland Caverns and Ruby Falls. The pictures were incredible. She wasn't crazy about being underground and she would never try real spelunking, squeezing through tiny openings to get to the next room, but the thought of touring a cavern interested her.

She decided she would add it to her bucket list. She realized she really didn't have an organized, written list anywhere but it might be time to start. Maybe she was feeling that age thing again.

The overhead announcement told her the plane was ready for pre-boarding so she walked a little faster toward her gate. She could see the aircraft through the window and realized it was another small regional jet. That was okay with her, she liked the small feel and the speed of boarding and deplaning.

She handed the gate attendant her boarding pass and walked down the tunnel to the plane. She was fully expecting to see "junior" seated in the Captain's chair propped up by a booster seat. She was right. She couldn't actually see a booster seat but she imagined it was there somewhere. She looked at the right side chair and sure enough "junior" brought along his younger brother to help him fly the plane.

I guess that's why they serve alcohol on airplanes. At least the pilots are too young to drink. Why don't they just close the cockpit door before boarding so that the passengers can imagine real adult pilots up there?

She found her seat, just three rows back on the side that only had one seat. The other side of the isle had two. *No middle seats on this plane. I like that but how do they make their money?*

She buckled her seatbelt and waited patiently for the plane to back away from the gate. *I hope they remembered to latch the luggage compartment.* She didn't know why but she always thought about that when she boarded a flight.

Ten minutes later, she was in the air. *I guess the captain can reach the pedals after all.* She closed her eyes and rested unit they reached cruising altitude and was allowed to turn on her computer and use her phone.

Flight time to Rapid City was two hours and forty minutes. She would use the time to catch up on paperwork once she called her father.

"Hello,"

"Hi Dad, how are you doing?"

"I'm fine, Charis. Where are you jetting off to today?"

"On my way to Rapid City, picking up a car and then driving to Custer. I should be there well before dark."

"Are you spending the weekend? There are many exciting things to do out there."

"Not this time Dad, I'll save them for when you come with me. I'm ready to travel for something other than business. Are you ready?"

"Honey, anytime you're ready, I'm ready. I'm not convinced it will happen but I'm happy to hear you talking about it. What's on your agenda tonight?"

"Find a hotel room, some dinner and rest. I'm starting early tomorrow and hope to be out of here by early afternoon. I'll be stopping in Festus, Missouri tomorrow evening for meetings on Saturday. With any luck, I'll be on a mid-afternoon flight back home."

"Who has your back out there, Charis?"

"I've got my back, Dad. If I need help, I have lots of friends. Don't worry about me. Are you alright? Any visitors or repair people coming around?"

"Not today, Sweetie. I'll be fine, you keep your head in the game, okay?"

"Yes, Dad, head in the game. I'll talk to you soon, Dad. I love you."

"I love you too, my girl. Get some rest!"

"Goodnight, Dad."

She was a little verklempt, an unusual situation for her. Her dad was getting older. He was still in great shape and she never really thought about losing him. She didn't think about losing her mother either but it happened anyway.

Charis opened her laptop and checked her email. There were several, but one was from the office.

Charis, Myron Hawkins did not report for work this morning. He is also not answering his phone. I sent a police patrol to his address we have on file but it appears he moved out a few months ago and didn't register a new address with the Bureau. We will keep looking. Watch your back. Paul.

Charis was not surprised, he probably had some suspicion that we were on to him. She didn't think he would be following her across the country but she was worried about the folks in High Falls and her father. She sent an email to Greg and the others asking for a conference call at 7 pm.

She sent her dad a message to not answer the door for anyone. She said it was just a precaution and she asked him to stay at home the rest of the day. She opened Paul's message and wrote a response.

Not feeling good about this Paul. Please have someone check on my father's place and make sure Michael Sanchez is on his way to The Haven. I also need home addresses for everyone I'm meeting with over the next two days. Thanks, Charis.

Kids flying the plane became the least of her worries.

Chapter 88

High Falls, NY

Greg had reached his limit reviewing the video. It was only 3:45 but he couldn't endure any more. He thought he found a match for the second driver's license photo. He felt confident enough that he could turn the evidence over to Trey Lawrence.

"Kathy, I'm heading out for the day. You know how to find me."

Greg walked back into his office to secure the computer in his desk and noticed a new email. It was from Charis and the entire team was copied.

Urgent. Conference call at 7 pm eastern. Please RSVP. I will initiate the call.

Greg sent his reply, locked the computer in his desk and left. He needed to get home, pick up the girls, visit Chalmers' farm and be back to The Haven before 7 pm.

He called Mary to make sure they would be ready. Twenty minutes later he was loading them into the car. He was still good on time.

They rolled into the Chalmers' driveway at 5:15.

"What is that?" Mary asked.

She was pointing at the large dog walking toward them.

"That's Laddie!" Greg exclaimed. "He won't hurt you. He seems to be a good watchdog but he warms up quickly."

Greg got out of the car first and Laddie came running around to meet him. Greg stood still for a moment to allow Laddie adequate time for a sniff test.

The dog nuzzled up against him. "Come on Laddie, let's get the girls out."

Laddie followed Greg excitedly to the passenger side of the car. He opened the door and Laddie put his head in Mary's lap. She petted and praised him. He then did the same for the back door and Jillian and Jocelyn climbed out. Laddie was excited to see everyone and they all became quick friends. The dog led the way to the house, announcing their arrival with deep, incessant barking. Priscilla and Jack came out the side door to greet them.

"How is life on the farm?" Greg asked.

"It's great! Jack replied. "We just finished getting the girls back in the barn. Come on in."

"Jack, take drink orders while I check on the milking. I'll join you in a few minutes," Priscilla said.

Everyone followed Jack and took their rest in the living room.

"What can I get you to drink?" Jack asked.

Mary and Greg asked for regular milk while Jocelyn and Jillian requested chocolate.

"I love this place," Jocelyn said, "It's so cozy."

"It's the stereotypical farmhouse from the old television shows," Greg added.

"If you say so, Dad," Jillian commented.

"It's okay, Greg, I remember those shows," Mary said in support of her husband.

Jack returned with the drinks at the same time Priscilla walked in. They joined their guests in the living room.

"Jack, did you see the email from Charis?" Greg asked.

"No, we have been busy the last few hours. Is something up?" Jack replied.

"She has requested a conference call at 7 pm tonight. She labeled it as urgent. We will be at The Haven, would you like to join us?"

"I guess we can get our chores done by then," Priscilla said, "I would love to see it!"

"I would too," Jack said, "I missed out on that the last time."

"Let me make a call," Greg said. Just to let them know we're coming."

"Jack, are you and Priscilla going to be okay here?"

"I think we're fine, Mom. Laddie is a great early warning device as well as a protector. Mr. Chalmers gave me some shooting lessons yesterday so I think we're ready. Besides, we are not a likely target."

Greg walked back in. "They are expecting us between 6:30 and 7:00. You can bring your swimsuits if you want to use the pool."

"I guess we will meet you there around 6:45," Jack replied.

They all finished their farm fresh milk, said their goodbyes and got back in the car. Laddie escorted them outside. On the drive over, They were talking about how well Jack and Priscilla got along. Jocelyn said, "I think they're hooking up."

"What! You mean like hooking up, hooking up?" Greg asked, not willing to believe it.

"I mean having sex," Jocelyn replied.

"I know what you mean, Jocelyn, I just don't agree with you. Jack is there to work and protect and that's all."

"I don't know, Greg, he was acting like more than a hired hand," Mary interjected. "Is it so hard to believe that they like each other more than just friends?"

"They're just kids for crying out loud!" he said.

"Greg, our son is twenty years old, he is not a kid anymore. And with all that Priscilla has been through, she stopped being a child a very long time ago."

Greg didn't want to admit that his children were adults.

"Alright, I guess I can admit that they could be more than friends but I don't buy the hooking up idea."

"Dad, they're close in age, Priscilla is a beautiful girl and a nice girl, not to mention that she is the proverbial farmer's daughter," Jillian said.

"Don't let Mr. Chalmers hear you talking like that, he may just go after Jack with the shotgun himself."

"I doubt it, Greg, he knows Jack is a hard worker and he's good man. Priscilla could do worse."

"I know, I'm just having a little fun with you. If Jack and Priscilla become a thing, they would have my support as long as Jack finishes school."

They made the remainder of the ride in quiet solitude. When they arrived, Agent Michael Sanchez met hem in the driveway. He waved them through to the rear parking area and followed the car.

"It's the Webster family, welcome back!"

"It's good to see you again, Agent Sanchez," Mary said.

"Hello, Michael, you're looking well."

"Hi Greg, are you staying out of trouble?"

"I guess not or you wouldn't be here," Greg said, joking.

"Some of us are just drawn to it like a moth to a flame. It's in our DNA. My, look at how those girls have grown in year. Let's see that taller one is Jillian and this here must be Jocelyn. It's nice to see you again."

"Thank you Agent Sanchez," they both said.

"Let's get you into the house, they are expecting you."

The entered through the enclosed porch at the rear of the house. Standing just inside the main entry were Ellie and Patrick Millen.

"Welcome back Mr. and Mrs. Webster. Hello girls. Do I need to go over all the rules again or do you remember from last year?" Ellie asked.

"We remember," the girls replied.

"And you, Mr. Webster?"

"She's got your number, Greg." Mary said.

"I will behave, I promise," Greg replied.

"Come in please. I have kept dinner warm for you. You may eat any time you wish. I know you have a meeting scheduled at 7:00 so we have set up a speaker phone at the dining room table. Feel free to eat and work if you prefer. The bar is ready for you in the sitting room and dinner is on the buffet. If there is anything you need, don't hesitate to ask."

"Thank you Ellie, Patrick, you folks haven't aged a day!" Greg said.

"After what you went through, you don't look so bad yourself!" Patrick replied. "Mrs. Webster, you look lovely as always."

"Thank you, Patrick," she replied.

Greg just rolled his eyes.

"My son, Jack and Priscilla Chalmers will be joining us as well. They should be here momentarily," Greg added.

"We are expecting them. Charles, Veronica and Destiny are upstairs changing out of their swimwear. They have had a busy afternoon," Ellie informed them.

"I'm going to the bar. Anyone else?" Greg said.

They all followed. The place looked just as he remembered it. The security and comfort it provided would never be forgotten. From the sitting room, Greg could see Jack's car approaching the parking area. Michael greeted them and escorted them to the back patio. The received the same warm welcome from the hosts and were given a quick tour. When they returned, everyone gathered in the dining room.

The only exceptions were Veronica, Destiny, Jillian and Jocelyn. They decided to take their meal to their rooms.

Everyone was seated by 6:55. The phone rang at 7:00 sharp.

Greg answered and placed Charis on speaker phone. He announced everyone who was seated at the table. Charis was surprised but happy that they were all there.

"Hi everyone," Charis began, "I asked for this meeting because I believe our alert level has elevated in the last eight hours. I would like to tell you what I know and then have everyone provide an update.

Let me start by saying that I have arrived in Custer and it is really nice out this way. The traffic was heavy driving up here, but that stands to reason being summer and all, and that I'm just a few minutes away from Mount Rushmore.

Alright, I now know who has been harassing me. I was correct about it being someone inside the Bureau but my boss doesn't appear to be involved. Agent Myron Hawkins left the notes as well as his fingerprint on my apartment door. He installed listening devices in my apartment as well as my father's while disguised as a repairman.

It was recommended that rather than arresting him for the break-ins, it would be better to put a tail on him and see what else he is up to. Well, before they had him, he was in the wind. He didn't report to work, is not answering his phone and apparently vacated his listed residence several months ago.

Based on all that, it seems he has had a long term plan in place. To me, that says something bigger is out there. I still don't believe that any of you are the primary target but it would make sense to continue to take precautions.

I have a meeting tomorrow in Custer and one last meeting in Festus, Missouri on Saturday. That will conclude visits to each location where a body came ashore. With the exception of New York and Quicksburg, VA, I must say that the others seem odd.

I haven't found the level of cooperation I would expect from a federal investigation. The guy in McMinnville barely spoke and the sheriff in Custer just blew me off on the phone. I don't expect much tomorrow or Saturday for that matter. Please tell me you guys have some ideas."

Ethan was the first to speak.

"I have been spending time looking at geography, trying to make a connection. The timing and the patterns don't make any sense, especially if you're trying to connect the cases to one person. The three most westerly would have had to use air travel to cover that much territory in just a couple of days assuming the bodies were in the water for a similar period of time. According to what I know about the medical reports, the bodies were similar in their decomposition.

I also looked at industry connections amongst all the areas but couldn't find a common denominator."

"Hey Ethan, Charis interrupted, In each of the places I've visited so far, I found advertisements for caves or caverns. Someone do a quick search of cave near Custer and Festus."

Greg had his tablet with him and began a search. Jack pulled his out as well.

"Charis, there are caverns very near both Festus and Custer."

"Okay, Charis said, "finally a link. It may not mean anything but it's something."

"Charis," Jack said, "I think I have another link. All of these caverns offer tours. Most caves have stalactites and stalagmites which are made of limestone. And what is limestone made of?"

"Calcium carbonate, "Greg answered.

"So how long does a person need to be in a cave to show signs of calcium carbonate in their lungs?" Charis asked.

"I think we need to ask an expert about that, Charis," Greg said.

"Would caves also be a source of Thallium?" Jack asked.

"I don't think so," Ethan answered. "I did some research on that topic and while it exists in the earth's crust, it is in very small amounts. It is more likely that the Thallium used to poison our victims was produced as a byproduct of smelting."

"So are we talking about silver mining or gold mining or what?" Mary asked.

"It could be from the mining of iron ore in which all of the above can be found," Greg replied.

"Charis, how do we explain the timing of the killings? There was a month between the first three and the last two," Ethan asked.

"I'm not sure, Ethan. We have had serial killers commit several acts in a close span of time and then take months or even years off before committing the next murder. Maybe they think the police are getting close or maybe they just get tired of it."

"Hey, can I jump in here?" It was Trey.

"Hi Trey, go ahead," Charis said.

"I think we need to find one more connection. There has to be one more thing they all have in common. Maybe the killings go way beyond the ones we know about. Maybe we're looking at some sort of cult, you know, a larger group that share a common belief or mantra."

"Then why aren't more bodies showing up?" Jack asked.

"Maybe were not looking in the right places. Across the country, we have hundreds of unidentified bodies every year. People that go un-claimed for one reason or another. How do we know some of these aren't related?"

"I guess we don't but wouldn't the MEs be finding the poison?" Charis responded.

"Maybe poisoning isn't the only M.O." Trey replied.

"Fair enough." Charis said, "I can ask the FBI to gather information on unclaimed bodies over the last year. We will see if we can find a connection. What else is going on?"

"It's Trey again. Greg, I received your email regarding the funeral home. I think we have two positive IDs that link the Slaters to the men in the videos. I'm tied up for the next couple of days but how about if Monday, we stop by and have a talk with Maury. Nothing accusative, just a chat."

"That sounds good to me," Greg replied. "Charis, you told me earlier that crematories fall under the Department of State or the EPA. Do we know anyone, and when I say we I mean you, who can tell us when the last time Mease Mortuary was inspected and what that report shows?"

"I will put the request in tonight, Greg. I will have an answer by noon tomorrow." Charis replied. "What else do we have, folks?"

"Charis, what can we be doing for you? We are all concerned about your safety," Mary asked.

"Keep looking for the other connection. The sooner we have that, the sooner this all goes away. I will be alright until then. Hawkins wouldn't be crazy enough to try to get on a flight with the Bureau looking for him. I suppose he could drive but South Dakota is a long way from Virginia.

I had better run along now, lots to do before bedtime. Good luck everyone. Enjoy The Haven and call or text if you need me."

They all said their goodbyes. The team continued to work on resolving the questions they had. Greg excused Jack so that he join the others in the pool.

"Mary, how would you like to do a little undercover work?"

"What cover did you have in mind?" she said seductively.

"Hold that thought," Greg replied.

"Hey, I'm still on the phone here!" Trey chimed in.

"And I am sitting right here!" Ethan added.

"Mary, behave yourself, for now," Greg said. "I mean at the funeral home. Perhaps you can pay them a visit pretending to be shopping for a funeral. Tell them you have an aunt in a nursing home and you've been told she doesn't have much time. Tell them your aunt is a stickler for cleanliness and you would like to see the prep room and the crematory."

"Why would I need to see the prep room if she's going to be cremated?" Mary asked.

"Because you're going to have a viewing first, just one visiting session so her old cronies can say goodbye."

"I don't know Greg, I'm not very good at pretending."

"Sure you are Mary, you've been with Greg all these years, right?" Trey joked.

"I guess you're right, Trey. But I still don't feel very comfortable about it."

"I'll do it," Ethan spoke up. "I can do it. I'll use the same story you just described. I'll be in and out in an hour."

"Perfect," Greg replied, "you can call first thing in the morning and get an appointment. I will be in my position across the street keeping an eye on things."

"Hey, Starsky and Hutch, be careful. They are currently suspects in a murder, and they have sex with dead people. You don't want to be on either end of that," Trey said seriously.

"You didn't say there was a potential for sex!" Mary exclaimed, "May I reconsider?"

Greg gave her a stern look while Ethan and Trey laughed.

"You can play dead at home later," he added.

"Darn, I was hoping for something new," she said.

The guys were laughing even harder.

"I need to go," Trey said. I will be busy on another project but keep me posted."

"Trey, on Monday I would like to officially turn over the evidence I have in my possession surrounding the Slater case."

"Okay, I will call you Monday morning. I'm looking forward to hearing about your day in church anyway," Trey responded.

"Wow, I almost forgot about that. We need to come up with another story for that," Greg said. "Mary, you have a wild imagination, why don't you work on that?"

"I will. Something about the married woman in search of a pastor?"

"You know, a black shirt and a small piece of white cardboard and I can become a priest!" Greg teased.

"Would you hear my confession, Father?" she replied.

"TMI!" Ethan shouted.

"I'm hanging up now!" Trey exclaimed.

"Let's all go take a cool swim," Greg said.

Chapter 89

Hilton Head Island, SC

Dean and Shelly Madris had just been seated. They brought their drinks from the bar with them. It wasn't a special occasion, just dinner out. The restaurant was located in the northwest corner of the island and had earned the bragging rights as one of the best places to view the sun setting.

There were many things they loved about the island but the top two were sunrise and sunset. At first they thought the newness of watching the sun do its thing would wear off, but it didn't. Dean thought it was from all the years living in a place where the sun was only visible when it was straight up in the sky. The rest of the time it was blocked by the skyscrapers.

He finally understood why ancient civilizations depicted the sun in so many ways. It provoked thought of the splendor and the fragility of life. Sitting next to Shelly while he witnessed it made him feel connected. He felt sorry that they didn't have children to pass it on to.

The Seascape specialized in fresh seafood as did the majority of the other two hundred plus eateries on the island. Summertime was busy on HHI but it also brought a sense of inclusion. People from all over the world came and brought a global feel in contrast to offseason which is made up mostly of snowbirds from the northeastern US.

There is a saying that 9 pm is midnight on the island. That seems to be true except for summertime. Dean guessed the average age dropped about twenty years during summer. He and Shelly tailored their social hours so they could avoid the intense heat of the day.

Shelly ordered shrimp cocktail and pan seared grouper. Dean chose the blackened flounder on a bed of spinach and a side order of hushpuppies. He thought about Kenny every time he ordered hushpuppies which was every time they went out. As much as Kenny liked his donuts, he would love jalapeno hushpuppies even more.

After the orders were placed, Dean raised his glass. "To you, my dear, for all that you have given me and all that you have sacrificed for me. I love you!"

Shelly raised her glass with a tear in her eye and a smile on her face. "I have never loved you more than I do right now. Thank you."

They clinked glassed and sipped their drinks. Dean's phone vibrated in his pocket. He just looked at Shelly.

"It's alright, Dean, answer the call."

"Hello."

"Mr. Madris, it's Phil White."

"Hi Phil, do have something new?"

"We found it, Dean. The terminus of the messages between you and Audra is in Crystal City, Missouri. We are attempting to triangulate the exact location now. I would think that by tomorrow, you will know where Audra was when she sent those messages."

"That's great news, Dean. Where do we go from here?"

"I will contact Agent Andrews and give her an update. As soon as we know the precise location, I'm sure she will send a team out there to investigate. I will notify you when we have something."

"Thank you, Phil."

"That sounds like good news!" Shelly said. "Would you like to tell me all about it?"

Dean just gave her the deer in the headlight look. He was busted.

Chapter 90

Dale City, VA

Rennie Andrews was just finishing a few dinner dishes when he heard a key turning in the lock of the front door. He went into the bedroom withdrew his pistol from the closet and retreated to the bathroom. He dialed Charis' number. When she answered he whispered "Moochie, mute your phone."

Charis followed his directions. Moochie was Charis' pet hamster when she was a child. After Moochie died at the ripe old age of two, Moochie became the code word for trouble. It was something Charis insisted on once she became an agent.

She couldn't hear anything but she remained patient.

Rennie was in the shower with the semi translucent curtain closed. The lights were off. He listened carefully and cocked the weapon. The door opened just a crack, allowing a thin chard of light to enter the room. It was just enough to illuminate the image of a man in the mirror above the vanity.

Charis could make out the sound of a door opening.

Rennie remained still and calm. He could see that his intruder had a gun in his hand as well. Rennie backed as far away from the curtain as possible so that he had room to raise his weapon without brushing against the curtain. The man disappeared for a moment. Rennie thought he was probably searching the rest of the apartment.

Charis was listening to silence.

Rennie heard soft footsteps returning toward the bathroom. The door opened wider this time and he could see the entire image of the man in the backlighting from the bedroom. The man turned toward the shower and raised his weapon.

Rennie fired one shot that hit the man in the right shoulder. His body twisted to the right from the impact of the slug. He came back to face the curtain again and raised his right arm but more slowly this time. Rennie fired a second shot that caught him in the right side of the chest.

The intruder slumped to the floor with his back against the vanity. Rennie opened the shower curtain ready to fire again if necessary. The man was passed out sitting on the floor, his gun lying next to him.

Rennie got out of the tub, kicked the gun away from the intruder and picked up the phone.

"Charis, did you get all that?"

"My God, Dad, are you alright?"

"I'm fine dear. The bathroom is a mess but I'm okay."

"Is he dead?" No, I can see him breathing. I had better call an ambulance though."

"Okay Dad, you call rescue and I'll call Paul. He will meet you there. Don't let the police take you away until Paul gets there."

"Alright Darling."

"Do you recognize him, Dad?"

"Yes, he's the guy who installed my light. Hey Charis, thanks for the warning."

"I really didn't think he would come around but I'm glad you were prepared. Go Dad, I'll talk to you a little later."

Rennie looked at the man while he called 911. When he hung up, he pulled some towels from the closet and applied compresses to the wounds. He sat on the edge of the tub and watched him. He was beginning to stir a little. His eyes opened and closed slightly.

"I knew you would be wearing a vest, that shot was just to take you down. I wouldn't expect to play Pickleball anytime soon though."

He wasn't sure that the man was comprehending anything he was saying but Rennie always wanted to make a wiseass comment like that.

The medics arrived and hauled the man away along with a police escort. Two officers waited with Rennie until Paul and a forensics team arrived. The police were content with Rennie's story and didn't make him go to the station. Paul was sure the FBI would take the lead because of Myron Hawkins' status as an agent.

After the police left, a cleanup crew came to tidy up. They did a good job and the small caliber bullet didn't exit the back of the shoulder so the blood splatter was minimal.

Rennie could now roam freely from his apartment. He called his cronies to see if they wanted a nightcap at their local hangout. He wanted to share his story with them. They probably wouldn't believe it.

Chapter 91

Quicksburg, VA
Delilah knew how distraught Til was over the disappearance of his

deputy. When her shift was over at the diner, she called and invited him to dinner. He was reluctant to accept because he believed he should be out doing something to find Alan. Slowly, and with the promise of helping him look, she coaxed him into it.

Delilah lived in a double wide manufactured home in a pretty mobile park just a couple miles from the diner. The home certainly showed a woman's touch both inside and out.

Til knew she was a hard working woman and it showed. The front entry was beautifully landscaped and the exterior of the house was well maintained. She had been married to a man who didn't appreciate her but she stayed with him anyway, always determined to make things work.

He took to drinking the last three or four years of their marriage and put her through the ringer. Toward the end, he lost his job and she ended up working twice as hard to make up for it. He got in trouble with the law a few times, mostly disorderly conduct, and Til tried to help him out. He soon learned that you just can't help some people.

It was a little over two years since he took off in a drunken stupor and wrapped his truck around a tree. Til was the first on the scene and Del was the second. The emergency crew extricated him and got him to the hospital but he lasted just a few hours.

Til waited with Delilah at the hospital and when he expired, he brought her home. It was a long night. Delilah begged him to stay with her and he did. He held her while she cried and he listened as she said that she did her best to love him. She talked a long while about how she had wasted her life on a man who lost the need and desire to love her back.

She wanted to be held in more ways than one that night but Til wouldn't do it. He couldn't do it. He would be all the friend he could be but the line had to be drawn. He believed there was a right time and place for everything and more importantly, an absolute wrong time for some things. For a long time after, Delilah saw him differently. He wasn't sure if she was embarrassed or disappointed or maybe both, but she wasn't as warm for a while. He figured she just needed to grieve in her own way and on her own time.

He would offer to help her out around the house or fix her car when it needed it but she was going to be self-sufficient. She wasn't going to be beholden to any man again. He understood.

When she started working so many hours at the diner, he would see her almost every day. The barrier she had built was slowly breaking down. It was almost a year before he felt comfortable teasing her about little things but when he did, she began to respond.

It was as if the teasing was so innocent that she didn't feel threatened. He kept it light for a good while but over time it became more flirting than teasing. There was sexual inuendo on both sides but neither one taking a step to move past it.

It was just recently that Delilah would joke about him taking her out. Til felt like a schoolboy, not knowing how to handle it. He wasn't sure she was serious. He figured it was safer to let her make the first real move.

Til parked the cruiser on the driveway behind her car. The front porch light was on. Til felt some fluttering in his abdomen but he couldn't tell if was nervousness about this moment or his worry over Alan's sudden disappearance.

He made his way to the door and knocked quietly. He could hear music coming from inside and it was a very warm night so she probably had the air conditioning on as well. He knocked a little harder. She opened the door.

Til was so used to seeing her at the diner in her uniform that he was taken aback by her appearance. She could see that he was a bit stunned so she opened the screen door for him as well. Once inside, she closed the doors behind her.

"Good evening, Til, I am so glad that you decided to come over. I know you have other things on your mind, but you still need to eat. You look handsome tonight, Til."

"I look the same as I do every day, D, but you look really different!" He exclaimed.

"In a good way or bad?" she questioned nicely.

"Oh, you look great! I mean, you always look great, D but there is something different tonight. You are as pretty as a picture."

"Thank you, Tilman, I feel pretty tonight. I can't remember the last time I dressed like this but I'm sure it was years ago. Hasn't been much need lately. Thank you for giving me a reason to dress pretty again!"

She stood before him, posing as if she were a model. She was wearing a sleeveless dress that fell about three inches above the knee in a summery, flowered print. Her shoulder length hair was let down and she wore natural colored sandals with a medium heel. She had applied just a touch more makeup than she would wear at the diner.

"I think you look stunning, Delilah."

"Thank you," she replied. "Dinner is just about ready. What can I get you to drink?"

"Anything would be fine, "he replied.

"Sweet tea?" she offered.

"That would be perfect, thank you."

Til followed her into the dining room. He was admiring the view as he detected just a hint of perfume in her wake.

"You smell nice too, D."

"I think that's the pot roast, silly," she replied.

"That smells good too," he said, "but I think I know the difference between dinner and perfume."

"Maybe you should come closer and make sure," she suggested.

He walked over to her. She raised her head, giving him clear access to her neck. He leaned over and placed his face very close to her neck. He didn't want to move and she was not about to make him. She slowly moved her arms in an attempt to hug him but he thought she was cutting him off.

"Til, come back here. Smell my neck again." He did as he was told. When he bent forward, she grabbed his arms and placed them around her torso.

"Isn't that better?" she asked.

He didn't reply, instead he opted to pull her arms around him.

"I know your mind needs to be elsewhere tonight, Til, I just want you to know how I feel about you. It's how I've always felt about you but I wasn't ready. I'm ready now if you are."

"I have been ready for years, Delilah, I've been waiting on you and I was prepared to wait for as long as you needed," he replied.

She pulled away so that she could look into his eyes. Neither let go of the embrace.

"You are a patient man, Til Sweeney and I love you for that. The waiting is over."

They slowly moved their heads toward each other. Their lips stopped just short of touching, both of them acknowledging that as soon as they kissed, the course of history would forever be changed. They were both eager to take that chance and they did.

"I feel like I've been waiting my entire life for that kiss," he told her.

"And I feel like I have been running away from it forever," she admitted.

"Now, let's sit for dinner and talk about what we can do to find your deputy."

Til sat at the table while Delilah fixed a plate for each of them. When she set his down in front of him, he thanked her and stared at it for a moment.

"Is something wrong?" she asked.

"No, not at all. It looks delicious. I'm just trying to remember the last time someone cooked a meal for me. It has been a while."

"Is it something you could get used to?" she asked.

"There's no doubt in my mind, as long as it's you doing the cooking."

"That's sweet," she said as she bent to give him a kiss. "Alright, dig in and let's talk about Alan. Did he have any other family beside his mother?"

"Not that I'm aware of. I really think the best place to start is that church he has been going to. He was headed there right after our last conversation. He seemed very excited about it."

"Did he say where it was located?" Delilah asked.

"No, did he ever mention it to you?"

"Not directly," she replied, "but I did hear him talking about it when those other guys came in."

"How often were they there, D?"

"I would guess every three or four weeks."

"Can you think of anything that could be a clue to finding one of them?"

"There wasn't anything about them physically that would set them apart. You know what though, I think one of them drove a truck with a logo on the door."

"Like a business or delivery truck?" Til asked.

"Yes, a delivery truck. It was an auto parts place."

"Do you remember the name?"

"No, but I can see the truck. It was yellow, the lettering was blue, and I think it was written on a diagonal."

"It sounds like a Johnson's truck." Til said.

"Yes! That's it. Johnson's Auto Parts."

"Good work, Delilah! Now we have something to go on. Do you remember anything about the driver? Did any of the men wear a jacket or a shirt with the logo on it?"

"He wore a cap. You know, a baseball cap. I remember because he never took it off."

"Do you remember what color his hair was?"

"No," she answered, "but I know why."

"Why Delilah?"

"I don't think he had any hair. At least none that showed."

"Thank you, D, that's a big help. And this pot roast is the best thing I've ever had!"

"I'm sure that's a stretch, but you're welcome."

"Del, I wouldn't say it if I didn't mean it."

"You know what, Sheriff? I believe you."

They finished dinner, Til thanked Delilah again and promised he would be back. He needed to run by the auto parts place and check it out. He gave her a big hug and a kiss.

"I'll see you for breakfast at the diner. I hate to leave so soon."

"I understand," she said. "See you in the morning."

Chapter 92

Hilton Head Island, SC

Dean and Shelly arrived home from their night out. Shelly went to the bedroom to prepare for sleep while Dean checked his mail. He was surprised to find another note from Audra.

"Please review the latest colorized version. Let me know if you need any changes. Thanks, Audra."

Dean hurried to open the file and load it into his software. The image he looked at earlier that he thought were teethlike made a lot more sense in color. He could see the changes in the depth of color, mostly gold with some reddish brown and a bit of white.

The panoramic view provided a three dimensional picture of both depth and height. The only thing that added any sort of scale was the window that the artist was looking out of. Very faintly in the window's glass reflection was the image of a young woman peering out through it.

If the scale was correct, he believed there was at least a hundred feet above the window and the same or more below. The teeth he was looking at earlier now became more evident. The artist was inside a structure that was very deep within a cave. The teeth were stalagmites and stalactites.

He picked up the phone and called Agent Andrews.

"Charis Andrews."

"Charis, it's Dean Madris. I have news for you."

"Hello Dean, is this in regard to Phil White's message that I received earlier?"

"Yes, it is, but I have even more now. I just received a contact from Audra. She attached a colorized image of one she sent earlier. I think I know where she is."

"Is it anywhere near Crystal City, Missouri?"

"Well, Phil thinks that's where the destination router is but this has more to do with where you look when you get there. I believe she is in a cave."

"Did I hear you correctly, dean? You did say a cave, right?"

"That's correct. The image she sent was from the perspective of looking out a window at the vastness of a cave."

"Like a glass visitor's center or something?" Charis clarified.

"Exactly! The cave is huge, at least two hundred feet from top to bottom."

"How do you know it's a cave, Dean?"

"I can see the stalagmites and stalactites. She is either in a cave or on another planet. I have not been on another planet but I have been in a cave before. I'm leaning toward cave."

"Dean, I am scheduled to be in Crystal City on Saturday. Phil is trying to find the precise location of the router as we speak so I will check it out when I get there. Good work, Dean!"

"Charis, will you let me know what you find?"

"Of course. As soon as I know, you will know."

"Thank you, Charis. Goodnight."

"Goodnight, Dean."

Charis hung up and pulled up a map of eastern Missouri. She entered "caves" in the search field and pressed enter. There were a few caves in the eastern part of the state but only one close to Crystal City.

She wrote down the address and contacted her boss in Quantico. He answered his cell immediately.

"Hello Charis."

"Hi Paul, sorry to bother you so late."

"No big deal, Andrews, I haven't made it home yet."

"Late night again?"

"Yes, I'm still at the hospital with Hawkins."

"How is he?" she asked.

"He'll live. Your dad is a pretty good shot. Hawkins will require a little surgery to fix that arm and he'll have a sore chest for a few days but he's better than your dad would be if he didn't shoot first."

"My dad is pretty smart that way. I taught him everything he knows," she said jokingly. "Have you been able to interrogate Hawkins?"

"No yet. It probably won't happen until after surgery. I'm guessing some time tomorrow. He's cuffed to his bed and we have an agent outside the door."

"So I'm thinking he timed this to keep me away from either Custer, Crystal City or both. He thought a call from my father would bring me home."

"So what is in Crystal City or Custer that he doesn't want you to find?"

"I'm not sure yet. I do know that the agencies that I'm supposed to meet with have not been very helpful thus far. Whoever is behind this is probably responsible for the killings in Virginia, New York and Tennessee as well."

"So you think law enforcement is in on it?"

"We know that Hawkins is so why not others? By the way, we have a new lead on the artist who may be part of the human trafficking case. I just got a call from Dean Madris. He has been contacted by the artist and he thinks she is being held in a cave."

"A cave? Do you know of any caves that can house a graphic arts department?"

"I do not, but I don't know a lot about caves. All I know is that there are plenty of them. I passed signs for them near McMInnville and Quicksburg, and I found one near Custer and Crystal City. Coincidence? I'm waiting for our guy in I.T. to triangulate the signal in Crystal City. If he finds it before I get there Saturday, I'll check it out."

"That sounds good, Andrews. If I can squeeze anything out of Hawkins, I'll let you know."

"I appreciate that, Paul. Have a good night."

It was getting late and Charis was feeling the stress of the day settling into her muscles. She made herself a cup of tea and gave her dad a call.

"Hi Dad, I thought I would check on you once more before going to bed."

"I'm fine, Charis. I was a little wound up so I met the guys at the bar for a nightcap. I don't think they believed what happened tonight."

"They'll read about it in the paper tomorrow. You will be a local celebrity. All the ladies in your complex will want a piece of you."

"I had better start using the gym then," he replied.

"You're fine just the way you are, Dad. Those ladies would just want your hard earned savings anyway."

"Yes, you're probably right. Hey, I almost forgot, I've done a little more digging around on the Valley Church of Redemption. I may have found one small clue. There was an internet search listing for a dba being filed for a company called VCR LLC. There wasn't a lot of specifics regarding it but the application was submitted in Jefferson County, Missouri."

"Thanks Dad, I'll have someone at the office kick it around tomorrow. I'm going to turn in now, it's been a long few days. I love you, Dad. Good job tonight."

"Thanks, honey, I love you too."

Chapter 93

Crystal City, MO

It was unusual for the Alphas to be called together on short notice but when the Supreme Leader calls a meeting at headquarters, the Alphas drop everything and jump on a plane to get there.

Alpha Timothy welcomed the others to his church in Crystal City. All had arrived via one of the corporate jets. His visitors included Alpha Micah from Custer, Alpha Sam from Quicksburg, Alpha Isaac from Jordanville, Alpha Mark from McMinnville and Supreme Leader Leland from St. Louis.

"Thank you all for coming," Timothy began, "your guest quarters are being prepared for you as we speak. Due to the hour, there will not be any social gatherings this evening but specific, individual requests will be accommodated after the meeting. Please welcome our spiritual father and our supreme leader, Leland Hadwell."

There were chants of "all hail the supreme redeemer."

"Thank you. Please take your seats. I am sorry to have to bring us all together at this late hour but it seems we have a situation that cannot be ignored or delayed. Gentlemen, our very existence is in jeopardy unless we act immediately to dispose of the threat.

By now, most of you have been contacted by our brothers in law enforcement who have been approached by an FBI outsider. What you may not know is that Brother Myron Hawkins has been detained and is currently hospitalized in the DC area.

Brother Myron was apparently in the process of removing Special Agent Charis Andrews from our trail by creating a situation that would force Andrews to return home. He failed to do his job. Now, we must initiate a response that is complex and multifaceted.

Simply getting Agent Andrews out of our hair is not going to be enough. There are many tendrils that are trying to permeate our borders and we must address them all. It will take members from every church to participate and I am relying on you to select the most qualified from your ranks. Our intel has identified our targets and I will be providing a list to each of you with your specific tasks.

Each target on your list will be prescribed with a method of apprehension and the disposition of said target. This will require coordination and precision and failure is not an option. Your people will work in teams and they should know that the rewards will be great for those who achieve their goals.

Alpha Micah, you will be the first to have an opportunity to subdue Agent Andrews. Sheriff Moran will be your primary contact. He will work with Detective Hillabrandt to secure Ms. Andrews and bring her to your church. You will keep her there until further notice. When she is delivered, Moran will assist you in capturing Hillabrandt as well. Moran will then become an employee of the church. You will take custody of all vehicles they arrive in.

Alpha Timothy, you will provide a backup plan in case Andrews makes it this far on Saturday. In either case, she should be sedated and made comfortable but in no way is she to be harmed or molested. She will be mine first.

Alphas Mark, Sam and Isaac, you will receive your list of apprehensions for your jurisdictions. These details will need to take place by the end of Day Monday so we don't have much time. Once Andrews is not responding to her contacts, the FBI will pounce on her last known whereabouts. It is imperative that as soon as she is in custody, we seize her phone and computer and continue to make contact for her.

After Monday, when all is resolved, she can officially go off their radar. They can come looking but they won't find anything. That is the plan as it stands right now. I want you to take the next hour to formulate you own plan and make your contacts. I will remain on premises should you have any questions. Let's get to work.

Chapter 94

July 10, 2016
Quicksburg, VA

The diner was already hopping and it was just a little after seven in the morning. Til could see Delilah darting around the restaurant floor taking orders and delivering food. She was smiling.

He opened the door and the cowbell rang per usual. He could see Del turn her head as though she was expecting it to be him. She acknowledged him with an even bigger smile. Til took an open seat at the counter. Within seconds, she was standing before him.

"Good morning, Sheriff," she said as she set a cup in front of him and poured the coffee. "Don't you look dapper today!"

"I was thinking the same thing about you, D, you seem happy this morning."

"I'm always happy Til, maybe just a little extra today. Let me put an order for you and I'll come back to talk in a minute. What will you have?"

"How about you?" he paused and she started at him silently. "How about you recommend something for me?"

"I recommend something hot and spicy with something soft and sticky on the side," she offered. "Hot sausage and pancakes coming right up!" She winked and walked away.

Til had feelings he didn't think existed anymore. He also felt younger and like he was sitting up taller.

"Alright," Del said walking back to him. "That should hold them for a while, tell what you found last night."

"The place was closed when I got there and there wasn't an afterhours number listed on the door. I'll swing by there when I'm done here," he replied.

"No word from Alan?" she asked.

"I'm afraid not."

"What time does the parts place open, Til?"

"The sign on the door said eight-thirty."

"Well, you have some time to relax and enjoy your breakfast."

"And look at you," he replied.

Del blushed a little and replied, "lucky for you, looking is free."

She walked and he watched. He could feel himself falling faster than he would ever have allowed but he didn't care. He knew she was the one and looking back, he had known it for a long time.

She returned with his plate and set it down along with a decanter of maple syrup. She refilled his coffee while she was there. She was ready to say something but paused when she heard the door open again.

"I think you're in luck, Sheriff, two of them boys just walked in."

Til didn't look right away. He watched Delilah's eyes and followed them. When she looked back down at him, he knew where they were seated without looking behind him.

"Nice work D, let them order and eat. I'll follow them out when they go."

She smiled again and off she went. Sheriff Sweeney poured some warm maple syrup on his pancakes. Soft and sticky.

Chapter 95

Hilton Head Island, SC

Dean was pouring his third cup of coffee when he heard his tablet ding. He carried his cup to the table, set it down and opened his mail. It was another message from the artist. She had sent another image. He quickly moved it to the software and opened it. There were eight layers this time.

The image was the finest one yet, very colorful and detailed. He tapped on each layer and studied how they all fit together. When he reached layer five, he paused and his heart stopped.

"I don't have much time, I think they are coming to move me. I have enjoyed working on your book and I wish you great success. I'm sorry I won't be able to help you with the next one. Thank you for trying! Please don't stop looking for these people, many more lives will be cut short. Check out page eight."

Dean's eyes were welling up and he could barely see but he clicked on page eight. It was meant to be the last page of the book. It was a beautiful drawing of a stream and a waterfall with a tall rock wall in the background. The quality of the image was magnificent.

The way the water was painted made it appear three dimensional. The layers of the huge wall could almost be counted. There were trees and flowers in the foreground and within the falls, he could barely make out the silhouettes of a young couple holding one another. Centered near the bottom of the page were the words:

For Ethan

The End

Dean was distraught. Here was a girl saying her final goodbye and he couldn't do a damn thing about it. He began pacing around the tiny room. He opened the slider to the balcony and walked to the rail. He wanted to scream at the ocean. He went back inside to grab his phone and dialed Charis Andrew's number. It rang three times before she answered.

"Hello."

"Charis, it's Dean Madris, I need your help."

"Dean, it 5:30 in the morning. What's going on?"

"I'm sorry, it's 7:30 here Charis, you must be on the road. I just received a message from Audra. She is saying goodbye. I think she was caught again and she said they are coming to move her. It didn't sound like it was going to be a move for the better."

"Dean, I know we are really close to nailing down the location of the destination router. When we have that, we can move toward it but until then, I don't know what else we can do."

"I know Charis, I'm just freaking out here. I feel so helpless."

"Dean, you were this girl's only hope. You could have easily ignored her but you didn't. You have been working diligently to find her location and resolve her issue. No one else would have done that. This is not on you, Dean."

There was silence and Charis could imagine Dean crying on the other end. She tried to bring him out of it by talking shop.

"Dean, was there anything different about this image or message?"

"It was by far the best drawing of all. So colorful and detailed. It was a different setting this time which surprised me. This image is meant to be the inside back cover page, you know, the one that say's the end. It is a beautiful stream and waterfall and it looks like it's in a very deep canyon.

There appears to be a young couple inside the waterfall but you can only see their outline. They appear to be holding each other. And here is the strangest thing of all, Charis, written just about the words; The End," she wrote, "For Ethan."

Charis almost fell out of bed.

"Dean, do you know how to send me a copy of that final page?"

"I should be able to do that, but why?"

"I need a friend of mine to look at it. It may or may not be helpful but it's worth a try."

"I'll send it right over, Charis. I hope you hear something about the router today."

"I do too, Dean. Don't beat yourself up about this, you did all you could."

"I'll try not to, Charis. Thanks for your help. I'm sorry if I woke you."

"It was well worth it, Dean. I was just getting up anyway."

Chapter 96

Custer, SD

Charis got out of bed, made coffee for herself and thought about what just happened. She thought it was a pretty big leap to connect Dean's Audra to Ethan's Lilijac but she couldn't shake the idea of it. *How would a young girl from upstate New York make her way to Festus, Missouri?*

Transferred from one medical facility to another? Feasible, but if so, there would be a findable rehab facility in that area.

But if she is well enough to produce that kind of work and has memories of Ethan, why would she still be in a facility? Maybe she lost the use of her legs? Wait a minute, she thought, she is being held captive. Even the strictest of facilities wouldn't prevent any contact from the outside. And where does this email order company fit into the story? Forced labor?

She decided not to contact Ethan right away. She couldn't be responsible for his getting his hopes up, especially in consideration of the fact that she may well be dead or gone even if they could find her. She finished her coffee and was preparing to get in the shower when her phone lit up.

It was the message from Dean containing the image. She opened the email and realized he had sent nine images. The first was the composite of all the others. Dean was right, it was beautiful. The remaining eight layers were individual images. She read the hidden note on page five. This girl did appear desperate although amazingly calm. She understood why Dean was emotionally moved.

She enlarged the last page which contained the back inside cover. She was stunned by the clarity and reality of the drawing. It was difficult for her to take her eyes off of it. She closed her eyes and thought about Ethan telling his story that night. It seemed so long ago but it was less than a week.

The picture he painted with his story seemed identical to the image in front of her. She couldn't discount the similarities. She was still not ready to get Ethan involved. She put her phone down and walked to the bathroom. She turned on the shower and caught a glimpse of herself in the mirror.

She was horrified by the image looking back at her. She allowed for the fact that she just woke up and that it wasn't a slow peaceful awakening but this was another kind of awakening. She felt like she had aged ten years over the past week. Her eyes were dark and hollow, her skin appeared to be lacking for blood and she noticed small wrinkles in her skin that were not there the last time she took a close look.

No time to worry about it now. I'm not here to win a beauty contest, focus on the job. She hung her pajamas on the back of the bathroom door and stepped into the shower. The warmth of the water felt great. She thought about the day ahead and realized she was more excited about it being over than beginning.

She forced herself to walk through the process in her mind. She made a mental list of her objectives and the questions she would have for Sheriff Moran. She did the same for Det. Hillabrandt. She had thought about interviewing them together but decided against it. She wanted to be able to compare their answers and the way in which they physically responded to her questions.

She also wanted a tour of the river where the body was found and she would ask each of them to do that. Something smelled fishy and she wasn't even near the river yet.

She finished her shower and took her time getting dressed. She applied just a little extra makeup to help cover the imperfections. It wasn't that she cared what other people would think, she was afraid of walking by another mirror.

She hadn't really packed enough clothes for the trip and the extra stops added to the dilemma. She always brought along a professional looking skirt and top in case there was an impromptu social affair. It happens periodically and the few times she was unprepared, she felt very out of place wearing her usual uniform.

She didn't prefer to wear the skirt while conducting business but it was either this day or the next and she would prefer flying out in slacks. She set up the ironing board and pressed the skirt and a pretty white shirt. She hated the thought of wearing hose on a summer day but it wasn't expected to be that hot in Custer and her legs were Casper white. Usually by this time of the summer, she had a chance to take a vacation which included some time in the sun. Not this year.

She slipped into her stockings, the neatly pressed skirt and buttoned the blouse over the top. The skirt and her shoes were a deep navy blue and the stockings were just a shade lighter. She took the chance of standing before the mirror again.

Her face still showed some of the hard miles but better than before.

She stood before the full length mirror and realized her body was in much better shape. She still had that slightly athletic but curvy body. She was pleased in spite of the fact that no one else had noticed for a very long time. At least no one said so.

Charis applied the smaller holster that held the weapon in the small of her back. She checked the gun and slipped into the holster. She then put on the jacket that matched the skirt. She was ready. She would forego the free buffet and just grab a muffin before checking out.

She settled her account and wheeled her bag into the dining room. She chose a blueberry muffin, wrapped it in a napkin and proceeded to her truck. She was still getting used to looking for a truck but she was seriously thinking about one for her next personal vehicle.

She unlocked her door, threw the bag in the back, the muffin on the center console and stepped up into the cab. She suddenly realized that her entire thigh was exposed when she stepped up. She promised herself that it was either a truck or a skirt. She couldn't have both.

The gentleman sitting in the car two spaces back didn't mind the view at all. She didn't notice him but when she pulled out, so did he.

Chapter 97

High Falls, NY

Greg and Ethan arrived at work early to allow for time to discuss non-hospital business. They met in the cafeteria at 7 am and got in line for breakfast.

"Are you having a good time at The Haven, Ethan?"

"Yes, what a great place! I still don't understand how a place like that exists but I am really glad I have the opportunity to experience it."

"I was lost about that as well but it really isn't that difficult once you understand the background," Greg replied.

"Why do I have the feeling that Charis would be getting ready to kick you again if she were here?" Ethan asked.

"Because she would be! But she is not here and there is no chance that she will be here anytime soon. Don't worry."

"It's your shin, talk away," Ethan replied.

"About ten years ago, there was a group of drug runners who would use that property as a hide out and exchange facility. Prior to that, it was owned by Ellie and Patrick Millen. It was more of a farmhouse then but it seemed to be the perfect place for drug runners who had deep connections in Canada and Mexico, and deep pockets.

They pressured the Millens into selling the property. After the sale was finished, the Millens called the feds and reported what was going on at that property. It was all kept quiet. Local police like to get articles in the newspaper but the feds aren't needy like that. In fact, they avoid it.

No one locally knew about the raid. All the trials were held in federal court and all those convicted went to federal prisons. In appreciation, the FBI made a deal with the Millens. They could occupy the house as long as they lived. It was still owned by the federal government but was registered in their names for tax purposes and to conceal the real owners.

The house had been added to and improved first by the criminals and then by the government using money confiscated in the raid. The information gathered as a result of this raid led to several more raids and arrests across the country.

In total, the federal government made over two hundred arrests and confiscated nearly one hundred million dollars. Every one of the arrests resulted in convictions, most with long sentences. A fund was established to offset the cost of maintaining and staffing the property in perpetuity.

In return for remaining in their home rent free for life, the Millens agreed to host people under protective custody whenever the FBI requires. All of the staff, supplies and upkeep is provided by the government. Most of the time, the house does not have visitors so they have the entire facility to themselves."

"That's a sweet deal," Ethan said, "but do they ever get to have family and friends over?"

"No. Which works out because they don't have any family and they have as many government friends as they need. I've been told that this is one of three such respites in the country. One east, one central and one west. Now, you have to swear that you will never tell another soul, Ethan."

"Did you take that oath, Greg?"

"This is not do as I do, this is do as I say," Greg replied.

"Okay, I've got it."

"Good, now let's talk about the real stuff. I printed a copy of the satellite photos from the FBI before coming here."

Greg pulled several sheets from a folder and laid them on the table.

"In the center of each photo is the area of the river where the bodies were found. You can see that there is nothing that stands out. However, when you zoom out thirty miles from the center of the scene, it's a different story entirely."

Greg pulled five new sheets from his folder and placed them over the other ones. He took a yellow highlighter from his jacket pocket and began to circle areas on each page.

"These yellow circles are where tourist caves exist. Within thirty miles of each body is one of these caves, even right here in New York."

"Are you saying you believe these bodies came from these caves?" Ethan asked.

"No, "Greg replied, I'm just saying there is a cave in close proximity to each body. However, as I read about some of these places, I realize that there are often other caves nearby. They are not all tourist places and many of them are very small. Many are on private land which require permission from the landowner."

"Okay, let's assume for a moment that these people were kept in one of these small caves. Wouldn't their muscles have atrophied while in captivity? The MEs didn't mention that in any of their reports." Ethan followed.

"That's a fair point, Ethan but what if they were taken out frequently to roam around?" Greg replied.

"That would explain it. But why keep someone captive, walk them every day and them kill them with poison?" Ethan responded.

"I don't know, maybe they exceeded their usefulness?" Greg posed.

"As what?" Ethan retorted.

"Maybe they were digging for minerals and they just became ill or tired or just refused to work anymore. It's not something I would want to do for more than a few hours."

"That could be. Why not just bury them in or near the cave? Why drag them to a river?" Ethan asked.

"Well," Greg began, "They either wanted to disguise the real cause of death or they didn't want the body to be found on their property."

"All good assumptions, Greg. What if they were a source of cash and the cash stopped flowing?" However what kind of cash could someone like that generate? I doubt anyone would pay to have a good time with them. If they live in a cave, hygiene is probably not at the top of their priorities." Ethan responded.

"That's true but who would pay to have sex with a dead body? Apparently more than we can imagine." Greg answered his own question.

"You've got me there, boss."

"Alright, let's move out of the box," Greg said. What are other financial reasons that people kill other people?"

They each thought for a few moments. Ethan replied first.

"To get their social security checks. To inherit their property. To take their cigarettes."

"Really? Cigarettes?" Greg asked.

"It's a stretch, but I'm not a smoker. I've heard it's tough to quit."

"Let's put the cigarette in the ashtray for now and go back to social security. What else along that line? How about life insurance?"

"Too risky. And besides, these people are unidentifiable," Ethan said.

"You're right," Greg thought again. "How about disability payments?"

Ethan was thinking of some way to retort that question.

"It's possible, I guess."

"Let's say that I am a doctor and that I certify a patient as disabled. If that patient disappears and I have access to his bank account, I can collect that money for a long time. It happens with family members all the time. Suzy puts Grandma in the attic after she dies so that the SS checks keep coming. Or Bobby doesn't report his disabled wife who died three years ago at home so he can continue to collect the checks."

"That's good, Greg, I think you're on to something. Keep going!"

"I don't know where to go from here. I'm stuck," he replied.

"Let's take a real case," Ethan suggested. Lillian Jacqueline Mac-Namara is sent to rehab but her father, who won't even admit he had a daughter, cancels her medical insurance knowing that she is going to require lengthy, expensive care. Who will take her?

How about a clandestine operation that takes the patient assuming they will have a long term disability, doesn't really provide the care they need but continues to collect the payments?"

"Yes!" Greg said, "and if and when the checks stop, they have no further use for that patient, so they off him."

Realizing what he just said, Greg looked at Ethan and apologized.

"I'm sorry, Ethan, I was lost in a stream of consciousness and didn't realize the impact until it was too late."

"No apology necessary, Greg, but thank you. I am fully aware that Lilijac could be gone. I don't like to admit it or think about it but facts are facts and if she is still alive, it is the facts they will lead us to her. Let's continue."

"So how do we begin to track down insurance fraud when we don't have any names? The bodies still have not been identified and we don't know if they ever will," Greg asked.

"We have one name. I know it's not much but it's a start. As soon as we're done here, we will go to our billing experts and ask for help."

"Let's switch gears for a minute and talk about a plan for Sunday. If we are going to walk in there as a family, we will need to at least have a unified story. We also need to talk about your trip to Mease Mortuary today."

"Okay, let's keep the ball rolling," Ethan said.

Chapter 98

Crystal City, MO

"Sheriff Moran, this is Alpha Micah. Today is a big day, Sheriff, I hope you're ready."

"Good morning, Alpha Micah. I am ready to do what I need to do."

"You have reviewed the plan I sent last night?"

"Yes."

"And you have erased the file from your computer?"

"Yes."

"Do you have any question, Lester?"

"No, sir."

"Alright then. Oh, one last minute change. Your subject is not to be hurt nor enjoyed. Is that clear?"

"That changes things Alpha Micah. Detective Hillabrandt has plans to entertain Agent Andrews before I bring them both to you."

"I understand the disappointment and the difficulty but this is not negotiable. You will have ample time to have your pleasure with her soon but not before she is delivered."

"I see. And what do I tell Hillabrandt?"

"I think it would be best if you didn't tell her anything. You can still use your plan but before the entertainment begins, you will need to immobilize her. Do you have the tranquilizers I gave you?"

"Yes."

"There are extras so give one to the agent and when Hillabrandt is ready to pounce, administer one to her as well. You will just need to be able to get both women to the vehicle. Will you be able to do that?"

"Yes, Alpha."

"If you need assistance, you may ask the driver for help."

"I understand, Alpha. Thank you, sir."

"Great things lie ahead for you, Lester. I know you will enjoy your life with us. I will personally make sure of it. You can have Charis Andrews for your initiation gift. How would that be?"

"That would be wonderful. Thank you, sir."

"Alright, we will see you later today. You are a true redeemer."

Micah hung up and left his chamber to join the others at breakfast. The Supreme Leader was just about to begin the meeting. Micah filled a plate and assumed the seat opposite Supreme Leader Leland Hadwell.

"Gentlemen, please enjoy your breakfast quietly while we review the day's events. Our action plan will be phased-in beginning in just a couple of hours. Our plan is in place, Alpha Micah?"

Micah nodded in the affirmative.

"Excellent. Tomorrow, our plan will continue here in Crystal City. If everything goes as planned today, tomorrow will involve just some house-keeping activities. That is subject to change based on the outcomes of the day. Alpha Timothy, are you ready for either scenario?"

Timothy nodded in the affirmative.

"Excellent. Saturday will include cleanup detail in Quicksburg and McMinnville. Will your people be ready, Alpha Samuel and Alpha Mark?"

They both confirmed.

"Then all that will be left is Jordanville and that plan will go into action on Sunday. I know that Sunday is set aside for family and entertainment but this is an exception for if we do not accomplish our goals, there will not be any more Sundays.

"Please bow your heads for a moment. Giver and author of redemption we ask for your guidance and strength knowing that our belief in redemption gives home and hope to those without either, jobs to those who have lost their way and peace to those who are hopeless. We do this in hopes of balancing the earth. We are all Redeemers."

"We are all Redeemers," they answered.

"Brethren, you may now reap the rewards of your faith and efforts."

The Leader raised his hands and the doors along the side of the room opened. Soft music began to play and women young and old in flowing see-through cloth danced around the gentlemen at the table. None of the men made a move until the Supreme Leader selected his girl. Once he had, they all selected one. There was a perfect number to go around.

Chapter 99

Custer, SD

Charis was a full thirty minutes ahead of schedule. She didn't know how long it would take to find the courthouse or how readily available parking would be. It wasn't hard to find.

She found a place to park right out front. It was a pleasant day already with full sunshine and early morning temps in the upper fifties. The high was going to be just short of eighty. After checking the weather, she once again checked her email. There were zero new emails.

It was 10:40 am in the east so she gave a call to Trey Lawrence. Trey didn't answer so she left a message.

"Hi Trey, just checking in. I am about to begin what could be a day in hell here in Custer, SD, population nineteen hundred. The city is two and a half square miles. It's claim to fame is the early goldrush and a single grey wolf that created havoc for nine years. Of course, Mt. Rushmore is close by too. Anyway, I'll be in meetings until about noon. I'll talk to you soon."

There was a small but pretty park downtown and she decided to stretch her legs for a few minutes. It was still cool enough to make her glad she chose the panty hose. She carried her small briefcase which she was sure would make her stand out in the crowd, if there was one. The streets were pretty much vacant although there was some activity around the one restaurant that she could see from where she stood. *People have to eat.*

She was hoping that breakfast and or lunch with Moran and Hillabrandt wasn't suggested. Her last experience had her envisioning a menu where mountain oysters were the favorite fare. She tried to imagine how many recipes there were for mountain oysters. She decided she didn't want to know.

Another small town downtown. High Falls seemed big compared to Custer but the view was pretty. She looked at her watch, it was 9:50. She figured it would take her less than a minute to reach the courthouse which would still allow plenty of time to be respectfully early. She hoped Lester Moran appreciated being on time more than he liked talking on the telephone.

It was a decent size building for a very small city. She wondered how much governing was needed for less than two thousand people but then she remembered she worked for the federal government. She always believed that Washington, DC could shed tens of thousands of jobs and still get the work done if politicians would think in terms of reality rather than terms for life.

She entered the front door and was greeted by a perky young lady with a delightful smile.

"Good morning," Charis opened, "I have a nine o'clock meeting with Sheriff Moran. My name is Charis Andrews."

The smile immediately disappeared when Charis said his name.

"I see, Ms. Andrews, I haven't seen him yet this morning. Did he say which room you would be meeting in?"

"No, he just said to meet him at the courthouse."

"Okay, I think it would be best for you to wait right up here. There are benches just behind you. May I get you anything, coffee or a bottle of water perhaps?"

"A bottle of water would be nice, thank you."

The girl walked down the hall and turned right at the next corridor. Charis moved to the bench to sit down. As soon as she was seated, the door opened again and a very handsome man walked in. He looked at Charis and stepped in her direction.

"You must be Agent Andrews," he said, "I am Lester Moran."

He held out his hand, Charis stood and greeted him with a handshake. He hand was firm but not overpowering and he was looking directly into her eyes. *This can't be the same idiot I spoke to on the phone.*

He was a little over six feet tall, blondish hair and vivid blue eyes. He wore a blue suit that fit him perfectly. She guessed he was very early fifties at most and he looked like he worked out.

"You can call me Charis," she said, still holding his hand.

"My friends call me Les."

"Les it is," she said smiling. *What in Hell has gotten into you girl?*

"There is a private anteroom off the courtroom that we can use. Can I get you anything?" he asked.

A hotel room, passionate lovemaking and a hot shower? "No, thank you, that nice young lady took care of me."

"This way then." He pointed his arm toward the same corridor the girl went to earlier.

"How long have you been sheriff, Sheriff?"

"I was voted in eight years ago. Before that, I was a deputy and prior to that, a police officer with the city. Hey, I want to apologize for not seeming more helpful on the phone. I was having a really bad day but that's no fault of yours and I am sorry."

"And I apologize for my response. I, too, was having a very bad day. I guess it comes with the territory."

"True enough," he responded.

They reached the room, Moran opened the door and switched on the lights.

"After you Charis."

He pulled a chair out for her. She sat and crossed her legs. Her skirt hiked up some and she could see Les watching her.

"So," he said as he pulled out his own chair. "Where would you like to begin?"

"Let's start with the crime." *Or we can skip that and go right to the hotel. Focus, girl!* "The who, when and where."

"The body was found on the morning of June third by two teenage boys who were fishing on a tributary of the Stockade Lake called French Creek. The creek winds just south of here but the body was found right at the junction with the lake."

"Were there any visible tracts or ground disruption in that area?" Charis asked.

"No, but the ME figured the body had been in the water for quite some time. I don't know if you have ever spent any time on Stockade Lake but the expression around here is the lake has no memory. That means that the status of the lake is very dynamic. It can rise or drop a foot or more in the course of a day.

Tracks left this morning can be gone this afternoon. The lake even has its own tide in some places. As far as we know that body could have entered the water at any point in the lake or creek. You will see what I mean when I take you down there."

"Fair enough," Charis replied. "Please continue."

"Doc Short said the girl was probably sixteen or seventeen. Fingerprints were not obtainable, no identifying marks were found and no one has come looking for her. The ME did say that he found shoddy dental work and this young lady had a cleft palette. He also found evidence of Thallium poisoning and calcium carbonate absorption. There were no signs of forced trauma."

"Pretty much the same as the other cases, Charis replied. "How about DNA?"

"I thought you would never ask," Lester replied. We got the results two days ago. She is not a direct match but we do have a parental match."

"That's great!," Charis exclaimed, "Do we know where that person is?"

"We believe we do and, she is close by. I thought we could make that visit together if you have the time."

"I will make the time for that. Is it the mother?"

"That's what the genetics indicate. Here is what I have in mind. You want to visit the spot on the river where the body was found and you want to speak with the ME, correct?"

"That was my goal, yes." Charis answered.

"Great, I would recommend that we drive separately, we will visit the river, then stop to see the mother and then we'll pay a visit to Doc Short who is located closer to the airport. I'm not sure what time your flight is but we can do all of this and have you out of before noon."

"That sounds like a good plan, Les. Thank you." *No time for the hotel this trip I guess. Stop!*

Alright then, grab your things and we will hit the road. Where are you parked?"

"I'm right out front, the black GMC truck."

"I didn't have you pegged as a truck kind of girl."

"Really, how did you have me pegged?" she quizzed.

"I pictured a Chevy Impala, silver or dark blue. More business like I guess. I also didn't picture you in a skirt and heels but what do I know."

"Is there something wrong with a skirt and heels, Sheriff?"

"Oh no, not in my book and I didn't mean to offend. I think you look great."

"I'm not offended, Les. A little flattered maybe." *Down girl! Stay on your leash. What is wrong with me?*

They walked out the front door together. He was parked just a few spaces down from her.

"Follow me," he directed and climbed into his gold Nissan crossover.

She jumped in the truck not caring if her skirt climbed up. In fact, she was feeling excited. Lester turned out to be nothing like she imagined. He seemed polite and professional, and he was really handsome. *What if he's married? She didn't see a ring. How about keeping your mind on business?*

Charis backed out first and pulled to the side so he could pass. She didn't ask the address or how long it would take. *That's what happens when your mind is in the gutter. Me, gutter? You know me better than that, if I was any stiffer, I would be a Pollyanna doll. Can't a girl fantasize once in a while? Get off my back!*

They left the confines of the metropolis which took all of thirty seconds and were heading west toward the river. He made a right turn on a narrow paved road which wound itself around in a series of switchbacks. They were on this road for a mile and a half when the pavement turned to gravel. She was glad she had a truck.

The curves were following the stream now which was widening as they continued. It was another quarter mile when she rounded a turn and she saw it straight ahead. The Mississippi was as wide as she could see. It almost frightened her to come upon it this suddenly.

Les pulled his car off to the left shoulder and she followed. She pulled up behind him and turned off the truck. He had already gotten out his car and was walking toward her. He opened the door for her. She looked down and her skirt had ridden nearly all the way up her thigh. She tugged at it but it wasn't moving.

She turned both legs, knees together toward the door. He watched as his eyes fixed upon her legs. He returned them to look in her eyes.

"Let me help you, Charis."

He held out his arm and she grabbed onto it and slid out.

"These things should come with a step ladder," he said.

"I agree. Thanks for the help. That wasn't very lady-like of me, I apologize."

"Nothing to be sorry for. There is a path that leads to the area we want to see but it may be messy. I don't mind getting my shoes dirty but your heels are going to dig right in and get stuck. I have a pair of boots in the trunk. They will be way too large for you but you're welcome to them."

"You know what, Les, if you say there aren't any tracks, I am going to take your word for it. I think we will glean more information from the mother and the doctor than we will get from that spot on the shore."

"I appreciate your faith in my judgement, Charis and I agree with you."

"It sure is nice down here," Charis added. "The river seems so big, majestic even."

"It's a mixed blessing really. That river provide a lot of jobs and feeds a lot of people. It also takes the lives of many. Two hours of a hard rain and this area we're standing on becomes a lake. I can't begin to guess the number of people who have been lost in floods over the course of just my lifetime."

"That's the power of mother nature I guess. It's essential one minute and deadly the next," Charis added.

"May I help you climb back in, Charis."

"No, thank you Les, I think I can handle it."

"I know you can, I was just hoping you wouldn't."

He walked back to his car. Charis opened the door and climbed in.

Now he's flirting with me. How delicious! Keep your panty hose on girl, you have important work to do. I know! Stop hounding me! You do know that I am you and you are me, right? You had better get yourself a dog or a cat or something when you get home. Maybe I just need to date once in a while. That would work too, but not today.

They both turned their vehicles around and went back the way they came. Next stop, the dead girl's mother.

Chapter 100

Quicksburg, VA

Til was talking to Delilah, making plans to have dinner again that evening when Delilah looked up and motioned to Til. The boys were leaving. Til let them exit then stood up and walked out behind them.

"Hey fellas, do you have a few minutes?" Til asked.

They paused a moment before the boy with the hat said,

"I'm afraid I'll be late for work. Is it something that can wait?"

"No, I'm afraid it really can't. You can call your manager though and tell him Sheriff Sweeney needs to talk to you and you might be ten or fifteen minutes late."

The kid looked at his watch.

"I guess I have a few minutes before I need to leave," he said.

"That's good, come on over here out of the way of traffic."

Til leaned up against the cruiser knowing that it would intimidate the young men.

"You boys know Alan Swart, right?"

They both nodded In agreement.

"Well, Alan has been missing for a few days. Have either of you seen him?"

"The last time I saw him was right here a couple weeks ago."

"That was the last time for me too," the boy with the cap said.

"I believe you," Til said. "I also know you boys attend church together, isn't that right?

They looked at each other and then they seemed to get nervous.

"It's alright fellas, you can talk to me. Tell me which church and where I can find it."

"I don't know if we can do that, Sheriff," said the boy in the cap.

"Why not?" Til asked.

"We could get in trouble," the other boy replied.

"Trouble how?" Til said, "I don't even know your names and I haven't asked you because I don't need to. You haven't done anything wrong. Not a soul will know you told me, I promise."

"I don't know," said the capped boy.

"Now look here fellas, if you don't tell me then I have no choice but to take your names and maybe even arrest you for withholding information about a crime."

"What crime?" the other boy asked.

"Right now it looks like kidnapping. An accessory to kidnapping, even after the fact is punishable by up to fifteen years hard time. I don't want to see that happen to two innocent young men."

"Look Sheriff, we don't know anything about a kidnapping. The last we saw Alan he was sitting right there eating pancakes."

"I believe you. Did you see him at church last Sunday?"

"Yes, he was there," the capped boy said.

"Okay, you see here we go, Which was it? Did you see him eating pancakes two weeks ago or at church last Sunday?"

"In church," they both replied.

"Guys, we're going to stop this right now. If you can't tell me where that church is, I'm going to take you both into custody. I don't think you appreciate the seriousness of your situation."

"Billy, we've got to tell him. I don't want to go to jail."

"Alright," Billy said, "but you can't tell them we told you."

"You have my word, I already told you that," the sheriff said.

"It's the Church of Redemption and it's a few miles out of town off River Road. "

"I've been on River Road many time and I have never seen that church," Til said.

"There is a right hand turn off River Road and there is no street sign. You go down there another mile or two and make a left. Go another mile and it will be on your right. There is a big iron gate with tall trees planted in front. You wouldn't see it if you weren't looking for it."

"Alright, I'll check it out. What is so special about this church?"

The boys looked at each other and answered simultaneously.

"It's enlightening."

Til dismissed the boys and went back into the diner. He sat back down to a freshly brewed cup of coffee. Delilah came over wearing a smile.

"Did you get what you were looking for?"

"Not yet, but there is hope. What time is dinner?"

"I meant with the boys, wise guy."

"Oh them, yes, I think so. Have you ever seen a church off of River Road?"

"I think there a few churches down that way," she answered.

"This sounds like a few turns off River Road, maybe a couple miles back. It's surrounded by a big iron fence and tall trees. The boys said you wouldn't know it was there if you didn't know it was there. What kind of church is that hard to find?"

"One that doesn't want to be found?" Del responded.

"That sounds about right, D."

Chapter 101

High Falls, NY

Greg gave Ethan the rest of the morning off to visit Mease Mortuary. Ethan was mildly nervous and wasn't entirely sure he could pull it off. There wasn't much to lose, if he got caught, he would just bolt out of there.

He parked in the right side parking lot and walked up the front steps. He liked the bones of the house and it was very well kept. *Nothing says dying like a neat lawn.*

He took a deep breath and rang the doorbell. He was expecting to hear a sound like the Addams Family doorbell but this was just the opposite. It was a single tone, not real deep and very calming. He wanted to push it a few more times to calm his nerves but the door opened and a pretty woman greeted him.

"Welcome to Mease Mortuary, please come in."

Ethan entered and waited for her to close the door.

"Good morning, I'm Ethan Smythe, with a Y and an E on the end."

"It's a pleasure to meet you Mr. Smythe. My name is Lynette and I am one of the partners here. How may I be of service to you today?"

"My grandmother is near the end of her life. I am her executor and she has asked me to take care of her funeral arrangements."

"I am sorry to hear that, Mr. Smythe, that is a difficult position for a young man to be in. We would be happy to work with you to fulfill your grandmother's final wishes. Was she specific in funeral details?"

"Yes, you could say that Gram was a stickler for details."

"Well that will make your task easier," Lynette said.

"Well, yes and no. You see, Gram was also a stickler for cleanliness and she has insisted that she will leave this earth in the same manner that she lived her life, spotless."

"I see," Lynette replied, "I can assure you that we are sticklers for cleanliness ourselves and that we pride ourselves in all things sanitary. We have received excellent reports from health department inspections and have a triple A rating with the Better Business Bureau."

"I hate to ask this but I feel like I would be disappointing Gram if I wasn't thorough. Would it be possible to review some recent reports?"

"Of course, I would be happy to provide those for you."

"That would be great. She also made it clear that she would like me to tour the facilities myself, prior to making final arrangements."

"That can be arranged as well," Lynette answered.

"Would it be possible to do that today?"

"I don't see why not. We usually leave out the preparation room but seeing as how it is not occupied today, I would be happy to give you the grand tour."

"That is so gracious of you, Gram would like you. She had many mottos as you can imagine. One was to always accommodate others to the best of your ability. Another was to be gracious unto each other as the Lord has been gracious unto you."

"Your grandmother sounds like a lovely woman."

"She is. I'm really going to miss her."

Ethan surprised himself when he felt tears welling up in his eyes. Lynette handed him a tissue, touched his arm gently and remained silent.

"I'm okay, this is more difficult than I thought it would be."

"I understand. Shall we begin the tour before we talk about the details?"

"Yes please, I would like that. I should probably mention that Gram wants to be cremated after her funeral. She never wanted to be buried and she would Like her ashes placed in a bios urn so that she can continue her presence on earth as a tree."

"How lovely. We can accommodate all of that," Lynette assured him.

"Would I be able to tour the crematory as well?"

"Of course, Mr. Smythe that is available today as well. You certainly chose the right day to visit us."

"I guess I did," Ethan replied.

Lynette led him to one of the viewing rooms which was empty of a casket.

"We have two large viewing room, Mr. Smythe, this one and an identical one across the hall."

"Please call me Ethan. You have been so kind that you feel like a friend already."

"Of course. Ethan it is. Shall we continue?"

Lynette led him through the back opening of the large viewing room to a smaller, more intimate setting.

"This is the family room. Family members gather here before the viewing begins, after it is over, and if they just need a moment during calling hours. Do you have a large family, Ethan."

"I'm afraid not. My father was an only child as am I. My father is gone and my mother hasn't had much to do with the family since the divorce. Gram is in her late eighties so I can't imagine many of her friends are left. Most of the visitors will be friends of mine."

"I see," Lynette said. Is there a Mrs. Smythe?"

"Just my Gram. True love has avoided me so far."

"I'm sure it's just a matter of time," she replied. Upstairs, you will find the office and the showroom. In your case, because of the ultimate cremation, you may choose to rent a casket for viewing. I can assure you that the process we use is very sanitary. However, we would be happy to offer you a new casket for Gram's sake should you feel that is appropriate."

"Do you cremate the body in the casket?"

"Only if the casket is made entirely of wood. Most caskets today are either metal or a combination of metal and wood. To be safe and effective, we generally transfer the body to a wood and cardboard box for the cremation."

"That makes sense. Thank you for explaining that. You have a nice manner about you."

"Thank you. Follow me and we will have a look at the preparation room."

Ethan followed her to a central hallway between the two family rooms toward the back of the house. At the very back of that space was a door to the outside. Before reaching that door there were two doors next to each other on the right and an elevator to the left.

"Elevator or stairs?" she asked.

"The stairs are fine."

She opened the first door and they descended the stairs. It was bright and spacious, not what he had imagined. When they reached the bottom, it opened into a spacious, almost sterile room. Straight ahead was a closed door. To the right, on the far wall was the head of the embalming table. The wall behind him was filled with upper and lower cabinets with glass doors. In between was a stainless countertop.

Behind the table to the left and right, were more cabinets, also with glass doors. Everything was bright, shiny, and unconcealed. There was no way to hide dirt and grime here. He was very impressed.

"This is where we do the work we don't talk about. Most people are just as happy not to visit this room."

"You know, I understand that," Ethan began. "But after seeing how perfectly clean you keep it and how bright and shiny everything is, I think I feel better knowing."

"Well thank you, but that makes you more of the exception than the rule."

"How long does it take, if you don't mind me asking."

"Not at all," she replied. It really depends on many factors including body size, the condition of the body and so forth. A typical embalming can take a couple hours. If there is going to be an open casket, it can take an addition hour or two to clean and dress the body, apply makeup and do the hair. If the person was in an accident for example, it could take several hours to several days to make them presentable."

"That is so interesting. How many funerals do you perform each year?"

"In an average year, about two hundred. With just two viewing rooms, we couldn't accommodate much more than that."

"And cremations?" he asked.

"Well, that is becoming very popular. Until a few years ago, we sent them out to a crematory, but we were sending so many and it took so long to get the cremains back that we applied for a license to add our own crematory. We currently perform about one hundred twenty per year."

"With the state of the environment, I imagine that getting a permit to do that in difficult," Ethan said.

"And you would be right, difficult, time consuming and costly. So far, it has been worth it."

"You spoke about inspections earlier, does some agency have to inspect the crematory as well?"

"Indeed they do. They schedule at least one each year but they can also perform unannounced inspections. In addition, the EPA and the Department of State require us to keep detailed records of number of burns, temperature and emissions. Paperwork makes up more than half of our effort."

"That's our government for you, they like to keep people employed," Ethan hypothesized.

"Very true. Would you like to see the crematory now?"

"Absolutely! I can tell you that I am very impressed so far and I think Gram will be very satisfied."

"That's wonderful. Follow me. They went back up the stairs and out the back door. There was a ramp in place of the stairs going down the three feet to ground level. They traversed the parking lot to a separate building. There was a heavy steel door that Lynette unlocked with a six digit code.

The inside was unremarkable. It wasn't as large as Ethan imagined. The entire space was twenty feet long and only twelve feet wide. The furnace was to the right with two feet of space around the entire circumference. The tray extended through the open gate of the furnace a good seven feet. To the left side was the control booth.

"As you can see, there really isn't much to it. We wheel the cart up next to the tray, drop the side and slide the box onto the tray. The side goes up and they tray goes in. The gate closes and we return to the booth and start the furnace. In an hour or so, the furnace turns off and we let it cool for a while.

When it is safe, we open the oven door and sweep the tray so that all of the small ashes drop through the tray to the plate below. We collect the ashes and put them in a container. The large bones will not turn to ash. The large, long bones like the femurs will be removed and pulverized in a grinder. These particles are then added to the ashes. The cremains are boxed, labeled, and returned as per the family's request. We complete the paperwork and clean the furnace."

"Amazing. I can't believe how clean that furnace is. You really do an amazing job here," Ethan said.

"It's more than a job, it's a service and an honor," Lynette corrected him.

"I can see that Lynette, Gram would be very happy with this. Do you keep the inspection reports in here?"

"No, let's go up to the office and I'll show them to you. We can also talk about next steps."

She opened the door for Ethan, turned off the lights and closed and locked the door. They went back to the house and up the front staircase to the second floor. The casket showroom was on the left and the office was straight ahead.

The house was beautifully kept and perfectly decorated. The office was large enough to comfortably accommodate six family members. Along one wall rested several locked file cabinets. Lynette knew right where to go. She unlocked the drawer and retrieved two files.

She sat down across from Ethan and handed him a report performed in the previous six months which was co-authorized by the NYS Health Department and the New York Department of State. It was for the funeral home services and the results reflected high scores across the board.

The next report she handed him was for the crematory. Again, the scores were all perfect. As Ethan scanned the document, he made note of the inspection date. He also looked at the section that listed the actual number of ignitions for the preceding year. The emissions were within allowable limits. This report was co-authorized by the New York Department of State and the Environmental Protection Agency.

"Wow," Ethan said, "I couldn't be more impressed. Let's talk cost. Not that it matters, Gram is loaded. Tell me how much and I will get a check for you."

Ethan looked at his watch.

"Oh boy, I'm sorry Lynette, this took a little longer than I expected. Could you prepare an estimate for me and I will drop by and pick it up next week? I really need to get going. By the way, include a new casket in your proposal. I think Gram would like that."

"Of course, Ethan. I'll have it ready by Monday. Could I just get a phone number for you?"

"Of course."

Ethan gave her a false number, thanked her again and said he would see himself out. When he got to the car, he dialed Greg's number and pulled out of the parking lot.

"Hi Kathy, it's Ethan, can you put through to Greg, please?"

"Hold on, Ethan."

"Ethan, what's happening?"

"Greg, I kicked ass! I mean Academy Award style. I was great!"

"When you get your arm back in your shoulder socket, maybe you can tell me what happened," Greg joked.

"Right, I met with Lynette and she showed me everything! It went exactly as planned. Here are the two takeaways from the meeting. First, the last inspection of the crematory was June 27th. The second is that the report also showed that the furnace was ignited two hundred times in the previous twelve months. Lynette told me they average one hundred twenty cremations.

"I have a theory. I have been thinking about why there has only been one body discovered in each area. What if a group is killing people and they have an arrangement with local funeral home to cremate the bodies? When the crematories are down for inspection, they need to dispose of a body another way."

"You got all of that by looking at one report?"

"I know it's a stretch but I think it's worth looking into. If we can get the EPA reports from crematories in the four other areas, we can easily dispel my theory. I mean why would the ignitions be off by forty percent?"

"I think it's worth a look. I'll make a call to someone at the EPA. What else did you find at the mortuary?"

"Inch for inch, I think it's cleaner than this hospital. Not that we're not exceptionally clean, but this place was spotless. From the embalming room to the furnace, every surface was clean enough to eat off of."

"Did you see any evidence of the other stuff?"

"You mean visitors? No. The place was perfectly quiet."

"Okay Ethan, good job. I have some news for you. Social Security is still making disability payments in Lilijac's name."

"What does that mean, Greg, is she still alive?"

"We have no way of knowing that for sure but we know where the payments are going. It appears that they are being electronically transferred to a bank account."

"Do we know where?" Ethan asked.

"Not yet. We need to subpoena the records. That could take a few days. But I will get right on it. I'll also make the call to the EPA and or Department of State today. Now, put your Oscar down on the seat, drive back here, and do some real work. Slacker!"

Greg rang Kathy's number.

"Kathy do we know anyone from the EPA or Department of State?"

"If you mean me, when you say we, we do not. But we know someone who does. What do we need?"

"I need inspection records for the past twelve months for all crematories within a thirty mile radius of Crystal City, Missouri; Quicksburg, Virginia; McMinnville, Tennessee and Custer, South Dakota. All we need are the dates of the inspections."

"I hope you're not planning to get blown up in any of these places," she joked.

"Really funny! Let me know, please."

Chapter 102

Custer, SD

Sheriff Til Sweeney left the diner and drove his cruiser to the office. He needed a few things before going to church. On the way, he dialed Charis' number.

"Andrews."

"Charis, it's Til Sweeney, how is your journey coming along?"

"Hi Sheriff, I think we have a solid lead here in Custer. I'm on my way over to the deceased victim's biological mother's house."

"The DNA came back?" Til asked.

"Yes, just a couple days ago. Sheriff Moran was waiting for me to go with him."

"Does that hit you as odd, Charis? If the roles were reversed, would you sit on valuable information in a murder case for two days?"

"I think he wanted to let me share in the excitement of the opportunity to break the case."

"Isn't this the guy that gave you all that grief on the phone?"

"One in the same, Sheriff, but we worked through it today. I guess we were just both having a bad day back then."

"Alright. Well, be careful. I was calling to tell you that I have a lead on my missing deputy. He frequently was seen at the diner with some young men who belonged to a church. I met up with those boys just a short time ago and they told me where the church was located. I'm on my way there now."

"That's great, Til, I hope it pans out. What's the name of the church?"

"They said it was the Church of the Redeemer but I haven't heard of it nor have I ever seen it. It's apparently stuck back in the woods."

"Til, would it be anywhere near a cave?"

"Yes, Shenandoah Caverns is just a couple miles from there, why?"

"My mind is just trying to put pieces together. Somehow, tourist mines keep getting pulled back in and from many angles. If you have time after visiting the church, would you mind checking out the cavern as well?"

"I would be happy to do that. Actually I think I'll do that first."

"Good luck, Til."

"Be safe, Charis. I hope you're right about that sheriff."

"I'll talk to you soon, Til."

Charis hung up. Lester was just a few car lengths ahead of her and they were heading further from civilization. The traffic was spotty but not nonexistent. There was always a car or two behind her, although very far back and every now and then she passes an oncoming car.

Her phone buzzed again. This time it was Greg Webster. She thought about letting go to voicemail. She would have more complete information for him after this visit. Maybe it was important. She picked up.

"Mr. Webster, I presume."

"Hello, Charis, how are things in South Dakota?"

"I am happy to report that all twelve people are good. The authorities here have been much more cooperative this time and I think we are actually making progress. I should be wrapped up and out of here before noon."

"Good for you! Do you have a minute, I wanted to update you on a couple things."

"I'm in the truck so you have as much time as it takes to get to my next destination."

"Which is where, exactly?"

"I don't know exactly, I'm following Sheriff Moran."

"I see. Did you say truck?"

"Yes, I did. I've rented two trucks in a row now. I could get used to this. My only complaint is climbing up in a skirt."

"Wait, did you say skirt? I have never seen you wear a skirt. You must like this guy!"

"I was out of clean clothes! And I hadn't even met him before laying out my outfit this morning."

"Alright, I believe you."

"Did you have something important to tell me, Greg or did you just call to discuss women's clothing?"

"I wanted to tell you that Ethan paid a visit to Mease Mortuary today. He met with Lynette under the guise of a dying grandmother. She took the bait and showed him reports and gave him a tour!"

"Did she also kill him then rape him?"

"I don't know about the rape part but he's still alive, wise ass. The crematorium was down for inspection the week before we found the body. Ethan thinks there may be a connection between furnace downtime and the bodies showing up in rivers. I am following that lead now.

He also said the report shows a discrepancy between the annual numbers Lynette shared and the number of recorded ignitions of the furnace."

"Maybe they fire it up now and again just to test it?" she asked.

"Once or twice perhaps, but eighty times?" he replied.

"That would mean there are a lot more bodies than the five we found in the river," Charis said.

"And that is just in New York! What if this was going on in every location? I am trying to obtain the inspection dates from the other four locations for comparison to when the bodies were found."

"I like the way Ethan thinks," Charis added.

"There is more. Ethan and I had another theory that involved money. We found out that disability payments from Social Security continue to be issued in the name of Lillian MacNamara. It's been going on for years. We are trying to subpoena the records of the bank to identify the recipient. I doubt it means that Lilijac is alive but it's a solid lead."

"I think she is alive, Greg! I think she is alive and she is in eastern Missouri."

"Why do you think that, Charis?"

"It's a long story and one that I thought had nothing to do with the murders, but now I think they're related. I'll explain later. Tomorrow, I will be in that area of Missouri and I will do some digging. Don't tell Ethan yet, I would hate to get his hopes up for nothing."

"I agree," Greg replied.

"Greg, Sheriff Moran is slowing down, I need to go."

"Good luck, Charis"

She disconnected and slowed down behind Lester. He was making a left hand turn into a driveway. It was a nice looking house, two story set up on a little incline. The driveway was at least two cars wide with one car already parked. He pulled behind the parked car and she pulled up next to him.

He came around to her side again, for another show no doubt. She turned the truck off, unbuckled, opened her door and slid out. The uneven driveway caused her to stumble in her heels. Lester quickly caught her and pulled her to her feet. He had his arms around her and she was holding on to his arm.

"That was clumsy of me," Charis stated, "Thanks for catching me."

"I'm glad you didn't fall. You may want to fix that though," he said pointing toward hips. Her skirt was almost up around her waist.

"Thank you." She said as she hurriedly put it back in place. *Never again will I wear a skirt to work!*

"Okay, I believe I'm ready now," she said.

"This woman's name is Gladys Bertram. I'll do the introductions and then you ask whatever questions you have."

"Right, let's roll."

There was a side door off the driveway. They walked between her car and Lester's to reach the patio. Charis did a quick evaluation of the premises. Sloping yard in the back, no close neighbors and lots of woods. *My kind of place,* she thought. She took out her phone quickly, checked for service and pinned her location. She put the phone back in her jacket pocket.

Les rang the doorbell. They waited thirty seconds and he rang again. The door opened just a crack.

"Gladys Bertram, I'm Sheriff Moran and this is Agent Andrews, we would like to speak with you for a few minutes."

"Can I see some identification?"

They both pulled out their credentials and held them to the screen door. She open the door to them.

"Come in and have a seat," she offered.

Charis did a quick eval of the woman. She was trim, probably early fifties, she was wearing a dress and what looked like a reddish, blonde wig. She was also wearing medium tinted glasses. She could still see her eyes but could not make out the color. She sat in the chair directly across from Charis.

"What can I do for you officers?"

"Mrs. Bertram, have you always lived around here?" Les opened.

"It's Miss Bertram and yes, I have lived my entire life here."

"So you have never been married?" Les followed.

"No sir. Can I get you folks something to drink?" she offered.

"No ma'am," Les answered.

"I'm fine, thank you," Charis replied.

"May I call you Gladys?" Les asked.

"Please do." she answered.

"Gladys, what do you do for a living?"

"I'm permanently disabled, I'm afraid, but I worked twenty odd years for the phone company."

Charis looked around the place and something wasn't adding up. It was a nice home, there was a really nice car in the driveway, she had no husband and she was collecting disability. The math wasn't working.

"Gladys, do you have any other sources of income?" Charis asked.

"None that I can talk about," she answered while crossing her legs slowly.

"Can you give us a hint at least?" Charis followed.

"Let's just say I have many friends."

"You mean friends that give you money?" Charis asked.

"They don't give me anything sweetheart, I earn it!" she said as if she was insulted by the question.

"Of course, I didn't mean to offend." Charis apologized.

"Why don't we get to the point here, officers. Unless you're here for unlawful reasons, which is fine with me, you must have another reason for visiting."

"That wasn't a cloaked proposition now was it?" Lester asked.

"Would you like it to be?" she answered.

Lester was starting to enjoy the charade. Charis detected a little excitement in his voice and some twitch in his body.

"Gladys, you may have read about a body that washed up a while back," Charis said, "we believe you may know something about that?"

"What? You listen to me, I could lay you upside down on a bed and lick you until you scream for mercy but I ain't no killer!" Gladys shouted.

"Gladys, you're walking a fine line here. Sheriff could take you downtown and ask the questions or you can stay focused and answer them here," Charis shouted back.

"The Sheriff can take me anywhere at any time. You can take me right now, right here in front of this young lady if you want," Gladys replied.

"May I use your restroom, Gladys," Les said as he stood up.

Charis could see the bulge in his trousers. He was turned on by this.

"You may. It's right down the hall." Gladys directed him. "Agent Andrews and I will continue talking while you're gone."

He didn't answer, he just disappeared down the hall.

"Do you ever let your hair down, Agent. I mean, do you know how to have fun, how to express yourself, sexually?"

Gladys opened her legs just a little.

"I don't think that is any of your business, Gladys. The young girl we found was your biological daughter. We have the DNA evidence to back that up. Do you want to tell me what happened?"

"I don't know anything about that, you must have the wrong person," she answered.

"Would you submit to a cheek swab so that we can verify your DNA?"

"I would submit to you swabbing my cheek with your tongue. Or any other place that you prefer. You see, agent, I am a helpless, harmless sexual addict. I don't force myself on anyone, I don't charge money and I don't inflict pain unless someone asks for it. I don't break any laws unless there is a law against being horny all the time. I am just insatiable!"

Charis had to think about that. She wanted nothing more than to bust this woman for something but all she had done was avoid answering the real question.

"You are being asked these questions as part of a homicide investigation. If you refuse to answer them here, we can arrest you for probable cause." Charis threatened.

"Fine," she said, "why don't you handcuff me and take me in," Gladys responded.

Chairs stood up unhooked the cuffs from under her jacket and approached her.

"Stand up, Gladys. You are under arrest for obstructing a federal investigation. Stand up and turn around."

She did as Charis asked. When she stood she also bent over the chair, pulled her dress up and placed her arms behind her. Charis placed the cuffs on her wrists and closed them. The woman was naked underneath the skirt and her cuffed hands rested on her bare ass. She was wearing thigh high stockings.

Charis was ready to stand her up when she felt a sharp prick in her neck. She reached under her jacket for her weapon but was stopped by a pair of strong hands. Her knees were starting to weaken and she couldn't get her tongue to form any words. She slouched over the back of Gladys.

"Now we're talking," Gladys said. "was the conversation getting too hot for you, Lester? Did you run and take matters into your own hands?"

"I went to get the needle ready and I was waiting for you to distract her. Why do you always think the worst of me, Doreen."

"Because you like it Lester, because it reminds you of your mother. Your poor mother who was just like me, a women who needed constant attention but couldn't get it from your father so she took it from you. You enjoyed being told what to do, how to please her. You enjoyed being punished. Now get this girl off of me and take her to the bed. Then take your clothes off and stick me like a good little boy. You can leave the cuffs on for now."

Lester picked up Charis and carried to the downstairs guest room.

"Why aren't you taking her upstairs?" Doreen blurted.

"Because she is our guest and she should be taken to the guest room," he answered authoritatively.

"Oh, growing some balls are we?" Doreen said.

"Shut up, Gladys!"

"Yes! Role play. I can be Gladys. How fun!"

She followed Lester into the guest room and watched as he laid her down.

"Pull up her skirt and unbutton her blouse, Lester."

"There's time for that, Gladys. First, I want to give you what you deserve. Bend over the bed, Gladys."

Doreen smiled and bent over the bed, her face resting on Charis' abdomen. Lester dropped his pants, raised Doreen's dress and entered her. As she started moaning and making demands, he uncapped the syringe. He place his left hand on her shoulder and began to thrust harder. He held the syringe at the ready in his right hand.

"Not yet, Lester, I'm not ready. Lester, do you hear me? Lester!"

"Fuck you, Doreen."

Lester stuck the needle into Doreen's neck as his body began to buckle with his climax.

Chapter 103

Quicksburg, VA

It took a while but Sheriff Sweeney found the church. The boys had their directions a bit wrong, perhaps by accident or perhaps intentionally. They seemed pretty worried they were going to be in trouble for talking to him.

There were no signs or markers indicating the church's location. He had no idea how they maintained a congregation in such a secluded place, but he suspected it wasn't within the law. He drove slowly past the tree-lined front with the iron fence. There were two openings in the fence about fifty yards from each other that he guessed were an entrance and exit of a circular driveway. The tall gates at each were closed and locked from the inside with an iron bar across the length of the gate, heavy duty chains and sturdy locks.

Not very welcoming. Definitely not Christian-like. He continued down the road for a good half mile until he reached the end of the fence. There was a dirt road that intersected, going left and right. He turned left and proceeded down the dirt road. In a mile, there was another dirt road that went left behind the property. There were tall, thick trees protecting the view of the inside.

About a half mile down, there was a single wide gate that was locked in the same fashion. He parked the car along the side and got out. He approached the gate and peered inside. Fifty yards inside the gate to his right was a five or six story silo that was not visible from the road due to the tall trees. He estimated the silo to be at least forty feet in diameter.

To the other side of the gate was a two story building. The few windows were tall and thin with dark glass. They reminded him of turrets. Straight ahead, a paved road led to an enormous building that must have been the church. It had a rounded wall that was at least four stories tall. Again, the windows were tall and narrow with black glass.

Where the rounded wall ended and the straight wall began on each side, he could see what appeared to be loading docks. He estimated the doors to be eight by eight feet and painted the same color as the brick walls so that they blended in. *Why would a church in the middle of nowhere need loading docks?* There were a lot of questions coming to mind. *How many people does it require to maintain this property? Who built it and when?*

Til continued to walk along the fence. When he was on the other side of the of the silo, he found a slight break in the trees. Up against the silo, there were what looked like several cars with protective covers. He could see that the rear license plate seemed to be partially exposed. He walked back to the cruiser and retrieved a pair of binoculars.

He returned to his place at the fence and had another look. The cover must have caught on the top corner of the plate guard, exposing some of the numbers. He could tell it was a Virginia plate and the first three letters looked like HTL and the first number was either a one or four. He could only see the lower quarter. He wrote the information down on his notepad and continued his walk.

He continued to walk on the far side of the silo. He heard a sound behind him and turned to look. There was no one there but the sound continued. He stopped walking and listened. It was a steady, mechanical sound. *Elevator! Why am I hearing an elevator out here?*

The noise seemed to be coming from the silo. The closer he got, the louder it became. He decided to go back to the car and wait it out. With his window down, he could just barely make out the noise. With the binoculars, he maintained a visual surveillance on the small amount of silo that was visible through the gate.

After five minutes, the sound ceased. From around the back of the silo, a car emerged and approached the gate. The mail driver walked to the gate and unlocked it. He removed the padlock and chain but the sturdy iron bar rose automatically. *Too heavy for an individual to lift.*

The car was a recent model Mercedes Benz. It was a black two door coupe with a Virginia plate. VCR 767. When the gate opened, he drove through and stopped. The driver retrieved the heavy chain, closed the gate and weaved it through the gate doors. He applied the lock, got back in the car and drove off in the opposite direction from where Til was sitting.

Now that he knew where the church was, he decided there was nothing else he could do there without breaking the law. He decided to follow the driver. *Stay way behind, this guy is not used to seeing traffic out here. One look in his rearview and I am made.*

Til made sure to let the guy turn a corner before moving. The car ahead made a left along the far side of the property. Til pulled out and slowly approached the corner. He waited for the driver to make his next move. He turned right. When he was out of sight, Til advanced. He continued this until they reached the main road. There was traffic flowing each way now so Til didn't worry about being spotted.

The Mercedes made a turn on Cavern Road. Til stayed back until he was out of sight. The elevation changed here so as soon as the guy crested the hill, Til made his way up. At the peak, Til stopped and observed the Mercedes pulling into the parking lot for Shenandoah Cavern. He rested there and watched as the man got out and walked to the store.

Til had been there several years ago. He wasn't a fan of caves but he was growing tired of not trying activities just because he didn't have a family. *This is perfect. I was planning to stop here anyway as Charis requested.*

Til knew he would stick out like a pig in a horserace dressed in his uniform but he couldn't change that now. He decided to leave his hat in the car. He walked slowly past the Mercedes, peering inside as he did. Nothing worth noting.

The doors to the store were open and just a few people were in line to get tickets. The man he was following was the first in line. He handed the clerk cash and she printed his ticket. He walked to the entrance without looking around. Til figured he would catch up to him inside so he waited his turn and bought his ticket.

He entered the first room of the cavern which consisted of a wall of informational materials and pictures of what he was about to experience. Ahead of him was the first walkway which took him down into the cave. He didn't see the man right away but as he followed the walkway which made circles as it declined, he found him well ahead on the path, across the gap of the cave.

Til picked up his pace as best he could but was hindered by the people in front of him. Each time the path widened, he attempted to make a pass. Periodically, he would lose the guy for a moment and then he would reappear.

Til had not prepared for the change in temperature inside the cavern. He was fully aware of the normal climate inside but he just didn't think ahead. With each turn of the walkway and each degree of declination, the temp dropped. He thought about Delilah being there beside him and that warmed him up.

They were coming to one of the large rooms where the passageway widened. While people stopped to view the Rainbow Lake Reflecting Pool, Til stepped right past them and continued down the path. He could still see the man at times as the path wound its way down. The man wasn't stopping to admire the views either.

Til had closed the gap until he had eyes on the man just twenty five yards ahead of him. They were coming up on another viewing area and the folks in front of him slowed down. That left the man he was after all alone at the front of the pack. Til watched as the man picked up his pace.

Til got as close as he could without drawing attention although the man never looked back. There was a blind bend up ahead that looked like it veered to the left. The man disappeared around the bend. When Til reached it, the man was no longer in sight.

Til knew he couldn't be that far ahead so he stopped and looked around. The lighting at this particular spot was much dimmer than most of the path to this point. There was nobody behind him and no one in front. He turned in a circle and looked for hiding places. He couldn't see anything obvious. He took out his phone and turned on the flashlight. Again he made a circle. Off to his right, beyond the retaining ropes, he could see another passageway.

He took a gamble and crossed the rope. After a few feet, the passage narrowed and became darker. The path was just wide enough that he could place one foot in front of the other. He kept his light on but pointed it straight down so that someone behind or ahead of would not be tipped off.

He could tell he was still descending but not steeply enough that he thought he might lose his footing. The path began to widen a little and eventually, he came to a junction. The path split in a narrow Y. He had to choose left or right and he picked left. He continued forward and down for several more minutes but didn't encounter the man. *Maybe he just stayed on the main walkway with the others?*

Til continued forward for what seemed like a long time. The path continued to get wider until at once, he was facing a door. It was made of steel and just slightly smaller than a standard door. There was nowhere else to go. The path ended at the door. No left or right, just through the door.

He placed his left ear to the door. He could hear a voice on the other side. It was just one voice. *Talking on the phone? They had to be several hundred feet underground, would a phone work down here?* Til looked at his phone. No reception. He listened again and the man was still talking. He couldn't make out the words but he could tell it was a man's voice.

He heard a noise and the handle on the door turned. He quickly moved his body to the hinged side of the door and pressed up against the rock. The door opened and the man walked out. He couldn't see if it was the same man. Til had his flashlight pressed hard against his shirt and the only light was a deep blue backlighting from inside the door. The door closed quickly and the person began walking back the way he came.

Til tried to twist the handle but it was locked. He walked quickly to catch up with the guy. When he was two steps behind him, Til whispered, "stop where you are."

Chapter 104

McMInnville, TN

Omega Owen received the call from Alpha Mark early in the morning. He gave very specific instructions and Owen put the plan in place immediately. He called brother Martin Ballard to inform him about the impromptu luncheon taking place at the church. He was to be there by 11:45.

Ballard accepted the invitation without hesitation. He had been invited to several such occasions previously and was totally satisfied with meal and the entertainment. As always, he was reminded to drive his personal vehicle and park in the back. Someone would greet him at the back entry.

Omega Owen then organized the other resources required to complete the task. He was proud to be placed in charge in Alpha Mark's absence. It didn't happen often, usually when Mark had a home office visit planned or when he went on vacation.

For Owen, it gave him the opportunity to partake of entertainment whenever he desired rather than waiting for the Alpha to sanction it.

Mark had only been gone for a little more than a day but already Owen had made good use of the time.

He started the previous morning with a visit from Lucinda. She had been at the church for a few years already and had adjusted easily. She was already accustomed to providing sexual gratification from her years on the streets of New York City.

Her pimp liked to beat her up now and again just for fun. He also liked to keep her hooked on heroin so that she wouldn't wander. They always came home when they needed a fix. One of the church's human resource specialists sought her out, rescued her and took her to Jordanville where she was cleaned up and cleaned out.

After a six month adjustment, she was sent to McMInnville to join the morale services team. She was given the job that she was best suited to perform. This time, she was protected, well cared for and respected for the work she performed. In exchange for wages, she received housing, healthcare, any foods that she desired and the family that she never had.

Lucinda was one of Owen's favorites. She enjoyed flirting and teasing and he allowed it. Some of the brethren just wanted it down and dirty and over as quickly as possible. Not Owen, he enjoyed the foreplay and he enjoyed taking care of the girls first.

His evening treat was Susanne who was in her fifties. She was full bodied and a lot of fun. She enjoyed reading and crossword puzzles when she wasn't working. She shared a similar past as Lucinda but at the hand of her husband. When she couldn't take it anymore, she stabbed him in his sleep. A friend had told her about the church's rehab program and she sought out the Crystal City location which was close to her home outside of St. Louis.

She was shipped to Custer for training and was happy there from day one. She has been a favorite of the younger men in the flock and was near the top of Owen's list as well. He liked talking to Susanne the best. She was mature and knowledgeable and truly enjoyed her new life as a Redeemed.

Owen knew he would be relieved of his charge soon but in a few months, it would happen again. Maybe for a day or if he was lucky, it could be a week while Mark sunned himself on the coast of Spain.

It was time to get things ready, his guest would be here soon.

Chapter 105

Custer, SD

"Move and I will blow your brains all over your girlfriend. Drop the syringe on the bed and put your arms behind your back. Slowly."

Lester dropped the syringe and took one step back. He pulled one arm back and then turned abruptly and took a swing at the man behind him. His punch fell short and he felt the immense pain of something hard hitting him under the chin. He fell back on top of Doreen who was still asleep.

Lester was out cold. He was cuffed and laid face down on the bed. The man picked Charis up off the bed and carried her to the sofa in the living room. He then went back to the bedroom turned Doreen and Lester so they were facing back to back and handcuffed them together.

He went into the bathroom and found the vile of Diazepam. He pulled out a syringe of Flumazenil and tapped the air out of it. He gave a little squirt and then proceeded to the living room.

He placed a tourniquet around Charis' wrist and tapped the vein in the back of her hand until it plumped up. He injected the dose and removed the tourniquet. He sat down across from her and waited. Thirty seconds later, she was starting to open her eyes. One minute after that, she was waking up.

She looked at him and closed her eyes again. He went to her and sat on the edge of the sofa and held her hand.

"Charis, it's okay to wake up, you're safe now."

She blinked her eyes a few times. She was fighting to hold them open.

"It's okay, Charis, you need to wake up now."

She looked at the ceiling with a vague memory of where she was.

"Where am I?" she asked.

"You're in hell, just a day later than you thought."

"Trey, is that you?"

"Yes Charis, it's me. You've had a rough morning."

"I don't remember it all. I do remember coming to the door and I remember that obnoxious bitch but how did I get on the sofa?"

"They knocked you out, Charis. They gave you a shot of Diazepam."

"But I was putting the cuffs on Gladys Bertram so who…"

"It was Lester Moran, Charis. He's the one that knocked you out. Bertram is really Doreen Hillabrandt."

"Oh, shit! How embarrassing," she said.

"Hey, we all get fooled once in a while, don't worry about it," Trey tried to console her.

"I was just starting to like him," she replied.

"Yeah, that I can't explain," Trey said, "That was just dumb."

"Thanks, Pal," she said.

"Where are they?" she asked.

"In the bedroom. You were there too when I came in. It's a good thing you were asleep, you missed those two trying to make a puppy?"

Trying to make a puppy? What the heck is he talking about? Oh, got it now. Yuck!

"Are they dead?" she asked.

"No, they should be waking up soon. After he dosed you, he dosed her. Then I dosed him. I'm feeling a little left out."

Trey explained the whole bedroom scenario to her.

"And why are you even here, Trey?"

"I came here because someone needed your back. It's no more than you would do for me. I couldn't get your messages out of my mind. I had a bad feeling about this trip from the beginning. I decided to come out a day early and check out those addresses you listed."

"How did you know they were bringing me here?"

"I didn't, the tracker I put on your truck helped me with that."

"And what if you didn't get here in time?" she asked.

"I knew exactly when to move. When I was in here yesterday, I installed a new audio-visual system for them."

"You bugged the house?"

"Yes, ma'am," Trey said proudly.

"Did you get a warrant for that? "she asked.

"Do you care?" he answered.

"Not really, no. Nice work. I am forever indebted to you," Charis said.

"Oh no, don't go playing that card. You are my friend and colleague and I like you! You don't owe me anything but your friendship," Trey replied emphatically.

"Forever," she replied.

"Alright, can you get up?"

Trey helped her into a sitting position and opened a bottle of water he had brought in earlier.

"Drink a little, it will help get that stuff out of your system."

Charis took a big swallow of the water.

"I'm okay." She stood with his assistance.

"Listen, it's not going to be pretty in there. He's a bit bloody and uh, messy down below. And she, she is just plain trashy."

"I'm ready," she assured him. "Lead the way."

"Hey," Trey said, "before I forget, here is your gun."

They walked to the bedroom. Doreen and Lester were back to back on the bed. Lester was awake but Doreen was still sleeping.

"Hey, Lester," she said, "I'm sorry it didn't work out between us. I just prefer to be awake when I have sex."

"Who is he?" Lester asked.

"Do you remember me telling you on the phone that I was your worst nightmare?" Charis asked, "I was wrong, he is your worst nightmare. Meet Detective Trey Lawrence of the New York State Police."

"You're a little out of jurisdiction, wouldn't you say, Detective?"

"No, I would say you're an asshole and you're lucky I didn't put a bullet through your head."

"You know this won't stick. If I were you, I would get these cuffs off of us and get out of here before someone comes looking for you," Moran said.

"Who might that be, Moran? Your wife perhaps? I have pictures of you "sticking" your police friend here. How do you think that's going to go over at home? Maybe your police friends will come, but they would have to drag your sorry asses to jail."

"It's your word against ours. Who do you think our departments are going to believe?" Moran said.

Trey pulled out his phone.

"Let's give a listen, Lester. You tell me," Trey answered.

He pressed the play button and turned up the volume. Lester listened to himself and Doreen on the tape planning their escapade in clear detail.

"How will they know that's us? Pretty weak if you ask me."

Trey pulled up video footage from the concealed cameras. And held the phone up to Lester's face.

"Let's see," Trey said, "here is a nice shot of the two of you saying the same thing on camera. Oh, and here is some nice footage of you jabbing Agent Andrews in the neck. This is my favorite, here is where you give "Gladys" a little pickle tickle while you stab her in the neck with a sleep agent! I'm no expert, oh wait a minute, I am an expert and it looks pretty convincing to me."

"Do you have a warrant for the surveillance?" Moran said sarcastically.

"That seems to be a popular question today. The answer is right here!"

Trey pulled out a warrant signed by a district court judge on order of the FBI.

"Now this looks pretty official to me, how about you Agent Andrews?"

Charis looked at the order with Paul's name on it and signed by a Judge Armand Spenser fixed with the seal of the Custer County, SD court.

"Wow, that looks really official to me," Charis replied.

"Play your next card, Lester, I'm ready." Trey said.

"I would like to sit up!" Lester insisted.

"I'm sure you would but the two of you are cuffed together so until she wakes up, you're going to stay where you are. We are going to have a little talk, Lester."

"I want a lawyer!" he proclaimed.

"And you will get one as soon as the FBI gets you back to their regional office. They should be here shortly. Tell me about this van that's coming here for a pickup," Trey said.

"I don't know anything about that," Lester said.

Doreen started to move. A few twitches at first then she started thrashing once she realized she was restrained. She was facing away from them so Charis went to the other side of the bed.

"Hey Doreen, or would you rather be called Gladys? How is it going?" Charis asked.

"Untie me!" she demanded.

"We will in just a minute. Can I get you some tissues or a mop maybe? You look pretty messy down there."

"Andrews," Doreen said, "when I get my hands on you I'm going to.."

"You're going to what, Doreen, lick me to death? I know what your little scheme was. Gladys is the truthful side of Doreen, right? A little role play so you can say exactly what you're thinking. I don't suppose you get to talk like that around the precinct," Charis stated.

"Where is Lester?" she asked.

"He's right behind you," Charis said, "he's keeping you from moving."

"Lester!" she yelled, "get up and let me move."

"Shut up, Doreen!"

"Children," Trey said, "you were playing so nicely before, now calm down and play nice and I will separate the cuffs."

They both piped down and laid still. Trey reached behind Lester's back and looked at the cuffs. He needed to unlock one cuff and it wasn't going to be Lester's.

He switched places with Charis and took his key out.

"I'm going to unlock one of your cuffs and then I'm going to close right back up again. If you so much as move a muscle, I will put you right back to sleep. Tell me you understand," Trey said.

"I understand," she answered.

Trey unlocked one cuff, pulled the open end out of Lester's cuff and then closed it again. They were separated.

"You can get up, one at a time. You first, Doreen. Stand up."

"How can I sit up with my hands behind my back?" she asked.

"You looked really athletic before with your hands behind your back, I'm sure you can manage," Trey said.

"Did you watch the whole thing, Trey?" Charis asked.

"Just the end, I missed the first four seconds," he answered.

"I knew it, Lester, you were probably a premature baby too," Doreen said.

Shut up, Doreen!" he replied.

Doreen was sitting. "Charis, would you escort Doreen to the living room, please?" Trey asked.

Doreen stood and Charis grabbed her by the arm. When they cleared the room, Trey helped Lester sit up.

"Let's go Lester," Trey said.

"You don't know who your screwing with, Lawrence. You have no idea who my friends are."

"We are going to talk about that, Lester. Let's go."

They were all seated in the living room. Charis did not sit across from Doreen. She was next to her and Trey was sitting across from her with Lester next to him.

"Alright, let's have a sharing session, shall we?" Trey said, "I'll begin. In thirty minutes, a small army of federal officers is going to be parked in your neighbor's driveways. In forty five minutes, your friend in the black van is going to pull into your driveway. I need you to tell me who he is, why he is coming here and where he is coming from."

"I don't know what you're talking about," Doreen said.

"This question is for Lester, Doreen, but thank you for jumping right in."

"It's all yours, Les."

"I don't know either," He said.

"Let me review what we already know. While you were sleeping, I took the liberty of going through your email and text messages which I have got to believe you were supposed to be erasing. Anyway, I know the van is coming soon. Tell me about it."

Lester didn't say a word. He had a defeated look about him.

"Lester, answer this nice man," Doreen said as she crossed her legs slowly while looking at Trey. Charis saw this and snickered a little.

"Lester, the FBI has a copy of your email and text files. They have had it for almost an hour. How long do you think it will take them to decipher your plan?"

"I want my lawyer." he said again.

"I told you, that's coming soon. I can make a guess if you would like to play that game. Let me take a whack at it. You two lured Agent Andrews here so that you could have your way with her before you either killed her or delivered her to someone else. How am I doing so far?"

"How would you know that?" Doreen said.

"Oh, I forgot, you were sleeping for this part. You see Doreen, I have been watching you and listening to you for a while now. I've already played some of the audio and video for Lester. Anyway, I know what your plan was. Here is something you don't know. Wait till you hear this, Charis. Our victim from the river was pregnant."

"So what," Doreen said.

"With Lester's baby!" Trey added. Now before we start pointing fingers and making denials, let me say that Dr. Short has verified the results of the DNA. Now you have both been in this game long enough to know that DNA is indisputable these days."

"Lester, what did you do?" Doreen moaned.

"What did you expect, Doreen, you threaten to fuck everyone on the police force if I don't come by here to satisfy you every day and you treat me like crap. So I screwed a young girl from the church. I've screwed more girls than you can imagine, Doreen and I have been doing it for years," Lester confessed.

"What church, Lester? What kind of church allows that?" Doreen asked.

"The kind that you were both about to become a part of, isn't that right, Lester? You knew you were the father and that your days on the outside were numbered. Doreen here was too great of a risk to you and the church so she was going to be delivered to them.

That van is coming, Lester and it was supposed to pick up Doreen and Agent Andrews. In return, the church was going to shelter you. That's why you gave the tranquilizer to Doreen as well."

"You did that, Lester? You did that to me while you were sticking me like you did your mother, you pathetic little shit! I should have killed you myself."

"You should have treated me better, Doreen, I deserved better," he whispered.

"Tell me about the church, Lester," Trey asked, "we're going to find out one way or the other."

"I can tell you this," Lester said softly, "we are all dead now."

"Not if you tell me the truth, Lester, you will do some time in jail but you will be alive," Trey continued.

"That's not how it works, detective, they're in the prisons too. Members who mess up have no place to hide. I'm dead either way, today, two months from now, it doesn't matter."

"Where is the church, Lester?"

"It's everywhere. I was almost on the inside. I was this close and you messed it up, Andrews. You and all your friends, they are all dead too. You are no match for the power of the redeemers."

"All you had to do was talk to me nicely on the phone and I would have never even come down here," Charis said. "One dead girl, who cares? is what you said to me. I care, Lester. Trey cares and every good law enforcement who ever believed the oath they were taking, cares. The two of you are just bad apples."

"I hope you like apples, Andrews, you're going to be meeting a lot of them," Moran said.

The black van turned into the driveway. The driver waited. Trey knew the drill from reading Lester's email. Trey dialed a number and said one word, "now."

"This is going to get exciting. I'm sorry that you two fell on the wrong side of the law but I will never be sorry for busting you. And if you had succeeded today, I would have hunted you down for the rest of your lives. Consider yourselves lucky.

"Doreen, I enjoy sex as much as the next person but you are just plain trashy. You should be thanking me too, I hear they like women like you in prison. You will be a very satiated women."

They could hear the cars speeding down the road. The noise grew louder until they heard the tires screeching outside the house. Charis looked out the window and saw four unmarked cars blocking the driveway. The driver tried to run but he didn't get far.

Charis stepped out to greet her colleagues.

Chapter 106

Quicksburg, VA

Til and the man he stopped were in a narrow part of the walkway. Til shined his light in the man's face. It was obvious that he was frightened.

"Who are you?" the man asked.

"I'm Sheriff Sweeney, who are you?"

"Benjamin Kane," he replied. "Why are you here? What did I do wrong?"

The man was getting emotional.

"I followed you here Benjamin. Can you show me some identification?"

"Do you have a warrant?" the man asked.

"Do you watch a lot of television, Ben? I don't need a warrant to request ID, do you have it or not?" Til asked him.

"Not on me, I must have left it at home.."

"I see, so you were driving without a license. That gets you a ticket in Virginia, Ben. Tell me what you were doing in that room back there."

"I'm an IT specialist and I was checking the network routers."

"You're a computer guy. Who do you work for, Ben?"

"I work for Shenandoah Caverns. I take care of their internet connection and website," he replied.

"I'm no expert, Ben, but a thousand feet underground seems like an unusual place for a communications room. I noticed that I don't get a cell signal down here, how would you get internet?"

"It's all digital cable from the outside," he replied.

"Now Ben, I don't pretend to know things that I don't but I have been walking this planet a little longer than you and I can't imaging running a digital cable thousands of feet to power a website and a ticket router when it can be placed right inside the front door. Show me your phone, Ben."

"I don't have too," he cried. I don't have to, I can't show you!"

"Whoa, settle down, Ben. No one is going to hurt you. You can show it to me, I'm your friend, Ben. I want to help you."

Ben took out his phone and reluctantly handed it to Til. It was locked so Til shined the flashlight on Ben's face and then held the camera up until it recognized his face. The home screen lit up. Til clicked on the settings button and selected Wi-Fi.

The default network name popped up, VCOR-SC15. Til took a minute to think about that.

"Ben, I followed you here from the church. I'm guessing VCOR stands for Valley Church of Redemption and the SC is for Shenandoah Caverns. The 15 probably indicates either the fifteenth server or the fifteenth location. That's a lot of horsepower for one website and a ticket counter."

Ben looked like he just soiled himself. His face was red as a beet and his big round head looked like it would explode.

"Take me to the room, Ben."

"I can't!" he exclaimed. "They have cameras in there."

"The church has cameras in there, Ben?"

"Yes."

He was actually crying now. The tears were running down his face and he was struggling to wipe them away fast enough.

"I will take care of you, Ben, they can't hurt you. You never have to go back there again."

"You don't understand, I have no place else to go. I have no home, no family and no money. I could never survive on the outside."

"You live at the church?" Til asked.

"Yes. I always have. I don't remember ever being anywhere else."

"Where did you learn computer technology?" Til asked.

"The taught me there. They trained me there. I want to go back but if you walk in that room, I can never return. They will redeem me."

"Alright, Ben, here is what we are going to do. You are going to give me the key, your shirt and your glasses, then you are going to wait right outside the door while I just take a peek. When we are done, you get to go back to the church and act as if nothing has happened. Do we have a deal?"

Ben didn't answer, he just took off his shirt and handed it to Til along with the key and his glasses. Til slipped the shirt on over his and put the glasses on. He could barely see with them on.

"Ben, come with me and wait outside the door. I won't be but a minute."

Til led the way back to the door and Ben positioned himself next to it. Til unlocked the door and peered inside. Without entering, he could estimate that the room was at least forty feet long and thirty feet wide. There were rows of stainless steel racks that held bank upon bank of servers.

The rack closest to him was stacked ten high and twelve wide. A quick calculation told him there were at least three hundred servers in the room.

He took one picture with his phone from outside the door, looking into the room. He closed the door, handed the shirt, glasses and key back to ben.

"Ben, why all the horsepower? You could connect a medium size city with that hardware."

"We do," he said proudly, "we can host ten thousand users from this location alone."

"There are more locations?" Til asked.

"Oh yes, several."

"One more question before I let you go, Ben. How many other people live at the church?"

"That's hard to say because people come and go all the time," he replied.

"If you had to guess, would you say twenty, thirty maybe," Til nudged him.

"Oh no, I would guess four to five."

"You can't keep track of four or five people?" Til asked.

"I'm sorry, I meant to say four of five hundred."

"Four or five hundred, you say?" Til said with disbelief.

"That's right. So you see, it really is a small city," Ben replied with excitement.

"And where is your room in the church, Ben?"

"I sleep on level G7 but I work On G4. The cafeteria is on G2 and entertainment is always on level 2 or 3."

"You mean G2 or G3?" Til asked to clarify.

"No I mean plain 2 or 3. Level five is at the top and G8 is at the bottom."

"That's a big place!" Til added.

"It certainly is. And it's beautiful too. It's much prettier than here and much brighter too."

"Ben, I'm going to let you go now. You won't be in trouble so just go back and go about your life as usual. And Ben, don't say a word about this, okay?"

"I won't Sheriff. I like you. I think you are a good man."

"Thank you, Ben, I like you too."

Chapter 107

McMInnville, TN

Martin Ballard came in the back and parked near the rear entrance. He drove his own car as instructed. He was a few minutes early and took his time walking to the door. He never paid much attention to the grounds of the property but today for some reason, he took the time to look around. He was impressed.

He rang the doorbell and almost immediately, it was opened. He was greeted by Raphael who attended the door quite often.

"Brother Martin, welcome home. I trust you're having a good day."

"Hello Raphael, I am having a good day and I am really looking forward to this luncheon."

"Wonderful," Raphael replied. "Omega Owen will be ready for you momentarily. May I get you anything while you wait?"

"I would love a scotch and soda if it isn't too much trouble," Martin replied.

"No trouble at all, brother, I will be right back."

Raphael went to the nearest service closet and prepared the drink. It was a heavy, sturdy rocks glass to which he added the scotch, soda, and a special flavoring. Once thoroughly stirred, he added plenty of ice.

"Here you are brother, I hope it is to your liking."

"Thanks, it looks great."

"I think Omega Owen is ready for you. I will take you to him. Follow me."

Martin followed Raphael up the circular staircase to the second floor. They turned toward the back of the church, down a short hallway and then made a left turn. At the end of the corridor, they turned right and walked straight ahead. There were double doors that reminded Martin of a swanky hotel suite entrance.

When they arrived, Raphael knocked and then opened the door. It was indeed a suite. Not very large but nicely furnished and decorated. There was a sitting room to the right, a restroom straight ahead and to the left appeared to be the bedroom. The door was closed.

"Brother Martin, please make yourself comfortable in the sitting room and I will let Omega Owen know you are here."

Martin didn't sit, instead he walked toward the tall narrow windows at the back of the room. He could look out over the expansive back yard with the tall silo toward the rear. His car was parked somewhere off to the right, out of view.

He heard a door open behind him and turned to see Owen entering the sitting area.

"I glad you could join me, Martin, Please have a seat."

Martin moved away from the windows and sat in a chair facing the Omega.

"I'm always happy to be here, Omega, I do love this place," Martin responded.

"We all do, there is a lot to love here. We do good work and we play hard as a reward for our efforts. I hope you don't mind, I have delayed lunch for twenty minutes so that I could show you around."

"I don't mind, Omega Owen but I have seen most of it, I think."

"Have you ever been below grade, Martin?"

"Below grade, sir?" Martin was confused.

"Yes where the real work takes place. Where redemption in all of its glorious forms happens. The heart of the church," Owen replied.

"Then I have not been below grade, sir."

"Excellent. Let's have a walk then shall we?"

Owen escorted Martin to the door. The moved left down the corridor until they came to an elevator. The door opened and the men stepped in. Owen selected G8 from the elevator panel. There were twelve options, Level 5 at the top and G8 at the bottom.

"Let's start at the bottom and work our way up. The bottom floor houses our medical facilities including a dental facility, laboratory, imaging, a clinic and infirmary."

"You have all of that right here in this building?" Martin asked with astonishment.

"That's just the beginning, Martin. Would you be surprised to know that almost five hundred people work and live her?"

"I'm not sure I would believe you, Omega, I don't see how."

The elevator stopped and the men exited. As they began to walk, Owen explained.

"There is ten thousand square feet of space on this floor alone. Multiply that by thirteen and you have two hundred and sixty square feet per person. That's a room thirteen by twenty feet for every person here. It may not sound like it but it is. You will see as we roam around."

"Omega Owen, is there a restroom I could use?"

"Of course, Martin, are you feeling alright?"

"I'm sure I will be once I use the restroom," he replied.

"There's one right down the hall."

Martin stopped for a moment and doubled over in pain. He felt feverish and dizzy.

"Oh you don't look good, Martin, we better hurry. It's just a short way now."

Martin tried to pick up his pace before he had an accident.

"Right in here, Martin. Have a seat and I will get some help."

Martin saw the toilet straight ahead and dropped his pants as he was moving toward it. He sat quickly but nothing happened. He was in terrific pain. A man came in and buckled him to his seat. Martin was very dizzy now and his vision was blurring. He could tell that the room he was in was large and had a shower and drain in the middle of it. No walls and no curtains around the shower.

"Just relax, Martin, help is on the way. By the way, Martin, Alpha Mark was not happy with the way you handled Agent Andrews. Because of your mishandling, trouble will be cast upon us. Nothing more than a nuisance really, but the Alphas don't like trouble.

You see, we are able to enjoy our lives and help others only as a result of our jobs. When a job is well done, we are rewarded but when a task is dismissed or performed poorly, there needs to be accountability. We cannot be accountable to those we serve without first being accountable to the church."

Martin could hear Owen's voice but he couldn't respond. His entire body felt like it was on fire and ready to combust.

"Let me put it more simple terms, Martin, you fucked up and now you will be redeemed. This is not our most favored level of redemption, but it is a necessary one and it is the final one. Martin Ballard, the brotherhood of redeemers sends you to you final rest."

Martins body was lifeless. The aide in the room transferred Martin to a wheelchair that had a large mesh nylon screen for a seat and a back. He wheeled the body into the center of the room and turned on the overhead shower. He left the room but would return in twenty minutes, By then, the waste and blood that would pour out of every orifice would be washed away.

Outside the restroom, Owen called for the black van.

Chapter 108

High Falls, NY

Kathy knocked on Greg's door.

"Come in."

"Hi Greg, I have the inspection information for you," she said.

"Already, that is amazing! How did you do that so fast?"

"I called Bill Dillon," she replied.

"Why Bill Dillon?" he said.

"Because Bill was involved closely with the EPA when he was our plant operations manager. They inspected our incinerator every year."

"Of course, that was very ingenious of you, Kathy."

"Thank you, Bill deserves all the credit though."

"Well, I think there is enough to go around. Let's see what we have."

Greg opened the folder which listed only one crematory near where each of the bodies was discovered.

"That makes it easier. There is only one inspection site in the five geographic locations. Let's compare dates."

Greg jotted down the dates each body was found and next to it, he wrote down the dates of the inspections.

He put his pen down and sat back in his chair.

"Are you okay, Greg?" Kathy asked.

"Not really. I think Ethan is right. The inspection dates coincide with the week prior to when the bodies were discovered."

"What does that mean, Greg?"

"We won't know for sure until we compare the number of ignitions with the number of cremations the crematories claim. If they claim fewer than the number of ignitions that are automatically tracked by the exhaust monitor, then it probably means that more people have died than just the ones found in the rivers."

"I think I followed some of that but are you saying the funeral homes are performing cremations on murder victims?" Kathy asked.

"It would be a nice sideline financially. Once it's done you can no longer test for DNA so the body is gone and without the body, how do you prove a crime has been committed? Ingenious really," Greg said.

"Hey, you just used that same word to describe Bill and me. Can you choose another one for them please?"

"How about dastardly or diabolical?" Greg replied.

"I like diabolical," Kathy answered.

"Diabolical it is! Kathy, I have one more favor to ask. It's actually one favor with four parts."

"You want me to call the other crematories, don't you?"

"You see, ingenious!" he answered. "Be cool about it though, we don't want to raise any red flags."

"I figured as much. I will be as cool as I can possibly be," she said.

"Can you have Ethan call me as well?"

"Sure, although I think you can dial from your phone too."

"It's so much more fun for me to ask you to do it," he joked.

She walked out and closed the door. Back at her desk, she dialed Ethan.

He was looking over the satellite images again trying to figure out a connection between the five locations. He zoomed out even further than the thirty miles that they used to locate the caverns. His phone rang.

"Physical Therapy, Ethan speaking."

"Hi Ethan, it's Kathy. Mr. Webster would like you to call him."

"Why didn't he just dial my number? He does it all the time."

"I guess he was in the mood to delegate. It happens," she said.

"Hey Kathy, why would you choose to live near a cave?"

"I wouldn't," she replied.

"I mean hypothetically. Why would people choose to live near caves?"

"I would guess that they either don't know they live near one or they're strange."

"That was a big help, Kathy, thanks!"

"I'm on a roll today, ingenious in fact."

She hung up. Ethan stared at the satellite maps for another minute. In the vicinity of each cavern there was a large parcel of land that was almost square and probably a mile wide in each direction. On each property was some similarly shaped buildings.

The buildings where all facing different directions which made it more difficult to notice. He centered the satellites view over the center of the building and zoomed in. They were almost identical.

The main building had rounded walls in the front and back. There was a large round structure toward the back of the property and thick trees surrounded the perimeter. *Rounded walls, why does that sound familiar? I have been somewhere recently with rounded walls. Holy shit!*

Ethan unplugged his laptop and ran to Greg's office.

"Kathy, I need to go in."

He didn't even think about stopping for permission. He opened the door and approached Greg's desk. Greg picked up the phone.

"What's that, Kathy, Ethan is here to see me? Send him right in."

"I get what you did just there, I'm sorry. This couldn't wait. I think the pieces are coming together. I was checking the satellite images again when I realized that near every cavern there is a large piece of property with the same size and shaped building. Look at this!"

He set his laptop down on Greg's desk and pointed at the images.

"Do these buildings look familiar to you?" he asked.

"Oh my, Jordanville." Greg replied.

"The church, that's the common denominator. No wonder they are so secretive. But why?" Greg asked.

"Maybe we will find out Sunday," Ethan responded.

"Yes, maybe we will. Hey, I have news too. I think you may be right about the crematories. There is one and only one crematory in each location that a body was found. And, they were down for inspection the week prior to each body discovered."

"Wow, that was just a guess," Ethan said. "Do the numbers add up?"

"That we don't know yet. Kathy is trying to call each one and get their estimated annual numbers. We have the automated exhaust numbers for each location."

"We need to talk to Charis," Ethan said.

Chapter 109

Custer, SD; High Falls, NY; Quantico, VA; Quicksburg, VA

Charis was on the phone with Paul at headquarters providing an update on the arrests at the house outside of Custer. She had an incoming call from Greg and asked Paul to hold. At the same time she had another incoming call from Sheriff Sweeney.

"Greg, hold on, my phone is blowing up. Hi Sheriff Sweeney, I have three other calls, can you hold?"

"In one sentence, Greg, tell me what's going on."

"We have a couple big discoveries, I mean huge!" Greg exclaimed."

"Hold the line, Greg. Sheriff, in one sentence, tell me what's happening," Charis repeated.

"Charis, I made what I think is an important discovery here,'" Til said.

"Stay on the line Sheriff, I'm going to create a conference call with three other parties."

Charis felt like an old-time telephone operator pushing and pulling cables into little holes on a console.

"Greg, I have Sheriff Tilman Sweeney on the line with us and I'm going to connect Paul from the FBI to the call. Stay on the line," Charis explained.

"Paul, I'm back and I have others who need to be part of this conversation. Here we go." Charis pressed a few buttons on her phone, connected all the callers and placed the phone on speaker. "Hi everyone, let me do the introductions before we get started."

Trey Lawrence is here with me in Custer, Sheriff Tilman Sweeney is on the line from Quicksburg, Paul Jenner from FBI HQ in Quantico, and Greg Webster and Ethan Baylor in High Falls, NY. No need to say hi to everyone. Greg and Ethan, tell us what you have," Charis requested.

"Charis, we have received information that correlates with our suspicions. Ethan discovered that in High Falls, the EPA number of ignitions at the crematory far outnumber the owner estimates. Based on that, we looked for similarities in the four other locations. All of the crematories near the locations of the five bodies found were down for inspection seven to ten days before the bodies appeared. We hypothesize that the only reason those bodies made it to the river is because their favored choice of disposal was not available."

"Mr. Webster, this is Paul. If what you're saying is true, we are looking at many more deaths than we know about."

"That's our suspicion, Paul. We also have satellite information we would like to share with you. Ethan has been studying these images and found that each body was discovered near a cave or cavern. That may or may not tie into the Thallium and calcium carbonate found in the bodies. Upon further review, Ethan also discovered five similar properties with nearly identical buildings very near those caves.

The outline of the main buildings resemble what we saw when we visited the church in Jordanville."

"May I jump in here, Charis?"

"Of course, Sheriff," she answered.

"I'm Til Sweeney in Quicksburg. I have had a deputy missing for a couple days. The last we knew, he was going to attend a dinner at a church. I tracked the church down finally but it wasn't easy. I've lived here my whole life and never knew it existed.

The place is locked up tight but while I was looking around the grounds, a car came out the back gate. I followed it to the parking lot of the Shenandoah Caverns, a popular tourist attraction here. I followed the man inside, watched as he bought a ticket, and then followed him into the cavern.

To make a long and unbelievable story shorter, I watched him jump the rope line after we were about a thousand feet down and he disappeared down a dark tunnel. I caught up with him just as he was about to enter a hidden room.

When he came out, I followed him a few feet and then stopped him. I made him open the door for me again and what I found, floored me. The room was a good twelve hundred square feet and housed enough computer servers to furnish a small city."

"Did this guy explain what they were used for?" Trey asked.

"He sure didn't want to but he spilled eventually. I wouldn't use the term man for this guy. He was probably in his mid to late twenties and obviously bright enough to maintain hundreds of computers but he was otherwise just a child. He seemed very simple minded and extremely frightened.

Anyway, he said they belong to the church where he has lived since birth or shortly thereafter. When I asked if other people lived there as well he answered four to five hundred."

"The church in Jordanville was huge," Ethan said, "but I don't see how it would hold five hundred people."

"I agree," replied Til, there is more to the church than meets the eye in more ways than one. This young man told me the building has thirteen stories."

"We saw just four or maybe five levels in Jordanville," Greg added.

"So did I," Til responded, "the other eight are underground."

"That sounds impossible," Charis said.

"But it would sure explain the calcium carbonate in the lungs," Greg replied. "Imagine living underground in what I assume is inside a cave for ten or twenty years, even with good ventilation, that stuff has got to creep in."

"Let me add to that what we found here in Custer," Charis said. "We just apprehended a police chief and sheriff for obstructing a federal investigation. They were also personally involved with each other and it turns out the man is part of a church which among other things, offers sexual entertainment to its preferred members."

"So the church is the common link," Paul stated. "We need to find out everything we can about this church."

"Paul," Charis said, "the FBI already has some information that my father had researched. It's called the Valley Church of Redemption. He could only trace the name back to a few monikers including VCOR and VCR LLC. He was only able to find small things doing web searches. Nothing about the company showed up."

"I think I can add to that, Charis, we know that someone has been collecting disability payments in Lilijac's name for years. We are waiting for court approval to obtain bank account information," Greg said.

"Let me take that from here, Greg," Paul said, "send me what you have and we will get to the bottom of it."

"I'll do that as soon as we are done here, Paul." Greg replied.

"What are the next steps," Trey asked.

"I think we need to stop our individual efforts and come up with a plan to take all five churches together," Charis said. "Paul, that is going to take a lot of manpower and coordination, but it needs to happen soon. In the meantime, Paul, what do we have in place for protection?"

"We already have your people covered in New York. Keep Trey with you for now and I am going to add a few people to watch after Sheriff Sweeney and the New York folks who are not staying at The Haven. Some of them have already been in place, for instance, the Chalmers' farm and Greg's wife and girls. Sheriff Sweeney, don't worry about it, you won't even know they are there."

"I'm not the kind who worries too much but I appreciate your concern, Paul."

"Alright everyone, thanks for your participation, I think we are getting close," Charis said. "So, keep your eyes and ears open but don't be too aggressive until we have a plan in place. I will still be going to Crystal City tomorrow just as a smokescreen if nothing else. I don't want them to know that we are on to them."

"Charis, what about our plans for Sunday?" Greg asked.

"Keep the plan in place for now, Greg. It may be valuable to have you on the inside. Let's see what happens in the next twenty four hours."

"Thanks everyone, we'll talk soon."

Charis ended the call.

"I guess you're stuck with me for another day or two," Trey said.

"There are worse people to be stuck with," Charis responded.

"You could have spent a couple days with Lester and Doreen," he stated.

"Don't remind me," she said.

Chapter 110

Crystal City, MO

Supreme Leader Leland Hadwell called the Alphas together once more. It was a rare afternoon meeting and disrupted the entertainment that most were taking advantage of.

Alpha Timothy began the meeting.

"Brethren, we are sorry that your private time was cut short but current events predominate."

He took his seat and Leland stood to address the small group.

"Alphas, we have some worrisome news coming out of Custer. One of our vans has not returned from the operation. It was due back almost two hours ago. None of our people on the ground have eyes on it at this time. In addition, Brother Lester has not been reachable since this morning.

We don't have the answers or explanations yet but we need to talk about tomorrow. It would be too coincidental that our people disappear the day that the FBI comes to town. While our people in Custer review camera footage and audio recordings, let's go over our plan for Crystal City. Timothy, if you would please."

"Thank you, Supreme Leader. Detective Laroy Climm will be meeting with Agent Andrews tomorrow at 9am. As usual, she will ask to go to the river where the body was found. She will also want to speak with the ME. Crimm has been instructed to take Andrews into custody using any means available.

If for some reason he us unable to do that, we will have a team waiting for her at the ME's office. Either way, our van will be close by, ready to transport her to the disposal location."

"Yes, unfortunately, I have chosen to forego the opportunity to enjoy Agent Andrews in lieu of removing her quickly," the leader spoke. Now, if we could hear from Alpha Sam."

"Supreme Leader, Alphas, steps have already been taken to reduce our risk in Virginia. Deputy Sheriff Alan Swart in Quicksburg has been redeemed. Sheriff Sweeney was off the radar today but we have a plan in place for him. With any luck, that will happen this evening.

Agent Myron Hawkins, who as our leader mentioned, is in the hospital. We have identified a parishioner willing to help us out. She will take care of the issue while he is in bed and then she will be picked up after work. Everything will be clean and tidy, as we like it."

Mr. Andrews, back in Dale City is in our sights again. Not that we will gain anything but it ties up another loose end. Our other target in Virginia is Charis' boss, Paul Jenner. We are still working on this one."

"Alpha Isaac, you're next," Hadwell said.

"There are several targets in New York. The first is Det. Trey Lawrence. He has been away but as soon as he is back, we will try to subdue him. Next is Greg Webster and his family. Greg is a hospital administrator who developed celebrity status as a sleuth when a killer was on the loose at his hospital.

After that, he helped solve another case involving college bombings and several murders. This is when he first met Agent Andrews. It is because of Myron's sloppy work that Andrews got Webster involved. He thought he could scare her off with a few personal threats.

Webster, his wife, and his son are all seemingly involved. His two daughters don't seem to have anything to do with it but we are going to recruit them to the church. Perhaps his wife as well. The family is spread out right now so it will require three separate missions. We have plans in place for all three which will take place tomorrow.

Webster also has an employee who has been snooping around. He even paid a visit to our funeral director member who didn't realize until afterward that he was not who he claimed to be. That should be an easy task."

"Alright then," exclaimed Hadwell. Custer is still an open question but McMinnville has been resolved. We will reconvene when we have more information from Custer. Thank you all."

Chapter 111

Custer, SD

Charis and Trey were still at the crime scene. Hillabrandt and Moran were taken away in separate cars. The black van was towed to an FBI location but the driver was still being interrogated at the house. The case had warranted elevation to a terrorist activity.

"Trey, I think we should return the rental cars and get on a flight to Barbados. When this is resolved, we will come back," Charis suggested.

"My vote is we finish the case and then go to Barbados, that way we don't have to feel guilty about bailing out."

"You're a good man, Mr. Lawrence. Maybe not the smartest, but good."

"What do you mean, not the smartest?" Trey replied.

"If you were really smart, you would accept the Barbados offer before you get killed. I would feel awful if you died because of me."

"Charis, if you promise you will go with me after this is over, I will promise to stay alive," he said.

Charis put out her hand. "I promise," she replied.

"It's settled then," he said while shaking her hand. "Now, let's talk about our plan to stay alive."

"How about we talk about that on the plane," Charis offered, "I need to make another call and then we should get out of here."

"I'll wait outside," Trey said.

Charis dialed her father's number.

"Hi Dad, did I get you at a good time?"

"Every time is good for you to call, Charis. How are you?"

"I'm fine, just finishing up a case here in Custer and then I'll be on my way to Crystal City, Missouri. After that, I'll be back home."

"Well I will be happy to see you, pumpkin. This has been one heck of a week for you! How is the case coming?"

"It has been a long week for all of us, Dad. You had some excitement too!" Charis replied.

"That was fun, it got my blood pumping!" He said.

"I'm glad to hear you say that, Dad. How would you like a little more?"

"Oh boy, that doesn't sound good, Charis."

"I think it is going to be fine, Dad but I need your help and I want you to be prepared again. We have evidence now that the Valley Church of Redemption may be at the bottom of all this. They are dangerous, Dad and I think we are all targets.

Paul has someone keeping an eye on you as we speak. He would like your help drawing out some players if you're willing. It's okay to say no, Dad, no one would fault you. I feel ridiculous even asking you to do this. I wouldn't if I didn't have every confidence that Paul can protect you."

"I'm willing and ready, Charis. Don't you worry about me. What can I do?"

"I would like you to go on a date." Charis said.

"That does sound dangerous, will I need protection?" he replied.

"I would bring your gun, if that's what you mean!"

"Of course that's what I mean, what did you think I meant?" he said.

"That's what I thought you meant too, Dad."

"Yes, bring your protection. The woman you're going to have dinner with is a recently retired agent. She is probably a few years younger than you and very attractive."

"Is she buying or am I? he asked jokingly.

"Funny, Dad, the agency will pay for the meal." Actually, you may not even have a chance to eat depending on how quickly it all goes down. There is a chance they won't take the bait at all."

"Well, we will hope for the best. Her name is Angela, Dad and she will pick you up at 6pm tomorrow. We usually plan these things later in the evening but we know you older, I mean experienced people like to eat earlier."

"Will she come up or should I go down to the lobby?"

"Wait in your room, Dad. I want her to escort you to the car. There be agents there as well."

"Where will be going for dinner, Charis?"

"I don't know yet, Paul is working on the details. He will let us know tomorrow."

"It sounds like fun, honey, I will be looking forward to it," Rennie said.

"Okay, Dad, thanks. Try to stay home until then, you don't want to make the agents work too hard. I love you lots!

"I love you too, sweetheart. Be careful!"

Charis hung up and went out to meet Trey.

"Let's return these vehicles and get on that plane," she commanded.

"Aye, Aye Captain," Trey said in a pirate's dialect, "might there be any bootie on the flying ship, miss?"

"Are you looking to join the mile high club?" she asked.

"What? No, I was talking about rum! I'm ready for a drink," he explained.

"Oh, so sorry, I misunderstood. It's been a while since I spoke pirate," she said.

"I accept your apology, thank you."

"You're welcome."

"Just out of curiosity," Trey continued, "was the other thing a possibility?"

"If you wanted that on an airplane, you should be taking Gladys!"

"I thought about it, but she's not available."

Charis' phone rang.

"Hi Paul, I just talked to Dad, he is on board with the plan."

"Charis, Myron Hawkins is dead."

Chapter 112

Quicksville, VA

Til stopped at the office to run the partial plate number from the church. He had already stopped at the diner to confirm dinner plans with Delilah. His connection to the DMV was painfully slow and the results were taking forever.

The plate number for the black Mercedes coupe came up first. It was registered to Samuel Jones, age fifty two, 5' 11" blue eyes 170 pounds but the address was a post office box. On his other computer, he checked the police file for Samuel Jones but came up empty.

The DVM computer finally spit out the data for the partial plate. There were nineteen possibilities. He did a quick overview and found just three that had local addresses. There were two older women and a forty five year old man.

He fed the name of the gentleman into the police database and waited for the search to complete. Randall Lowhie was reported missing four years earlier. He was a dentist who had previously been arrested for sexually assaulting a female patient while she was in the dental chair. He was arrested but disappeared while awaiting trial.

Til surmised he was either working at the church as a dentist or dead at the church leader's hand. He wondered how many other vehicles were on the property. He decided to take one more ride around the church property before going for dinner.

There wasn't any sign of life at the church. Five hundred people living there and not a soul outside. He couldn't comprehend how Ben found life so enjoyable there. *Is it possible he was making the story up?*

Til walked the around the perimeter on the side he hadn't seen yet. Toward the back corner he found a place where the trees and shrubs thinned just a little. He squeezed between two huge juniper bushes and walked up close to the fence. He was looking at the side of the enormous silo. There was movement behind it. A delivery truck was coming through the back gate.

He had a clear view of the side of the truck from his vantage point. It appeared to be about twenty four feet long with a refrigerated box. The truck approached the back of the church until it found a place to turn around, then it backed up to one of the two loading docks.

He couldn't see what was happening inside the dock. It was only there for about five minutes and then it pulled away again. Til ran back to his vehicle so that he follow the truck. He sat in his car until the truck cleared the gate. The side of the box had images of fresh produce.

He tailed the truck until it was close to the main road and then turned on his emergency lights. The driver either didn't notice or refused to stop. Till added the siren to the lights. The truck's taillights came on as it nudged to the side of the road.

Til parked the cruiser ten yards behind the trucks, centered to the left taillight. He typed the tag number into his computer and a few seconds later had the results. It was registered to a company called COR Produce whose address was listed as St. Louis, Missouri.

Til climbed out of the cruiser and approached the driver's side door. It was a man in his sixties and his window was rolled down.

"Can I help you officer?" the man said.

"I need you to step out of the truck and please bring your license and registration," Til said.

The man opened the door and stepped down to the pavement. He held out his license and registration. The registration information matched what he saw on the computer. He read the license information aloud.

"Abel Adams, Age 62, home address 722 Parkside South, St. Louis, Missouri. Is that all correct?" Til asked.

"Yes, sir," he replied.

"Stay where you are for a minute."

Til walked back to the cruiser and pulled up a map of the St. Louis area and typed in the address. *Your search returned "0" results.*

He exited the car and walked back to the driver.

"Would you like to try that address again?" Til asked him.

"I'm not sure what you mean, officer. That is my address."

"Mr. Adams, that address doesn't exist so why don't you tell me where you really live?"

The man was silent. Til asked him again but still no response.

"Mr. Adams, if you don't answer me, I will have no choice but to arrest you. My guess sir, is that you are housed by your employer, perhaps the Valley Church of Redemption?"

"Mr. Adams, I need you to open the back of the truck."

"I can't do that," he replied.

"Why not?"

"I don't have the key, I never carry the key. I just pull up and someone else loads or unloads and locks it back up again."

"So you don't ever know what you're carrying?"

"No, sir."

"Do you carry any paperwork for your haul?"

"No, sir, I'm just told where and when to go."

"You pick up at a distributor in St. Louis?"

"Yes."

"And do you always have the same route?"

"It varies, sometimes I go to New York or South Dakota. Sometimes it's Tennessee. There are times when I hit the road and stop at several places."

"I see. Where are you headed right now, Mr. Adams?"

"Back to St. Louis."

"Stay here for a few minutes, I will be right back."

Til returned to the car and called Charis.

"Hello Sheriff Sweeney, how are you?"

"Good afternoon, Agent Andrews. I would like your opinion if you have time."

"I'm on airplane so I don't think I'll be leaving for a while."

"I'll make it quick. I just pulled over a truck driver who I followed from the church here. His credentials are not legit and I believe he works for the church in St. Louis. He doesn't carry a key for the cargo area and he claims he doesn't know what he carries, ever.

"How would you feel about sending a man or two back with him? Til asked.

"I like it, I can request a couple field guys who may be close by. Can you hold him for a while?"

"I believe I can. I'll take him back to my office and hold him there until your men arrive. Would you like me to forcibly open the box?"

"Not until my guys get there, that will give me time to get a warrant. It's better to play it safe," Charis replied.

"Ten-four," Til said.

"I'll call you when I have the details, Til. Thanks."

Til directed the driver to follow him and then got back in the cruiser. He dialed Delilah's number.

"Hey, D, it's Til. I'm afraid there has been a change of plans for this evening.

Chapter 113

In the air over Nebraska

"I can't believe they got to Myron Hawkins inside the hospital," Charis said," "with a guard at the door no less."

"Was Paul able to get any information out of him?" Trey asked.

"No, I think Myron knew he had reached the end of his rope one way or the other. There wasn't any point in giving up information."

"So it was a nurse that got to him?" Trey asked.

"Yes, right at the end of her shift. She walked by the agent at the door, went into the room and gave him a bolus of something through his IV line and walked back out. Myron wasn't hooked up to any monitors so no one was aware until the change of shift which was two hours later. The officer looked in on him but believed he was just sleeping."

"Does the hospital know who the nurse was?" Trey asked.

"They are checking their records but my guess is she wasn't scheduled to be there at all. She is most likely a church member who works in another department or maybe not at that hospital at all," Charis replied.

"What was that call you had a few minutes ago?" Trey inquired.

"That was Sheriff Sweeney in Quicksburg. Now there is a cop with his head on straight. Not only that, but he is also a really nice man. Anyway, he followed a truck leaving the church and pulled him over a short time later. He had no manifest and no key for the back. On top of that, his license had a phony address.

Til asked if he should hold him so that we can send some agents to follow him to the distribution site in St. Louis. I thought that was a good idea."

"Wouldn't that alert them to trouble?" Trey questioned.

"Well, the driver would cause more suspicion by not showing up, I guess. We wouldn't need to expose him right away, we could just hang back and watch the location until we have a plan in place," Charis explained.

"I agree, that sounds like a good move," Trey said. "Can you believe that a church can yield that kind of power over its member, even to the point of holding them hostage?"

"History tells us it's been done many times before. Not churches necessarily but all sorts of organizations. They prey on the people who are most vulnerable, the ones that even a horrendous situation looks good compared to what they have already endured," Charis replied.

"Then I guess it's time to stop them," Trey said.

Charis' phone rang again. It was Paul Jenner.

"Hi, Paul."

"Agent Andrews, how is the flight?"

"So far, so good, "she replied.

"I have received some information about the corporation and the bank account that Lillian MacNamara's disability payments have been deposited to. It looks like the money is funneled to a shell corporation set up by the church way back in the beginning. The LLC was originally filed in Wyoming.

My guess is that they have multiple banks in multiple states that receive deposits under various account names, perhaps several in each state. That's going to take a while to expose but at least we know that one case is trackable. I have no doubt that others will follow."

"That's good news, Paul, it seems that we are beginning to put the pieces together. By the way, I have put in a request for a few agents to follow a truck from Quicksburg to St. Louis."

"Yes, I already received that request. The agents are on their way and should arrive within a few hours. You can pass that along to Sheriff Sweeney and give him my thanks."

"I will, Paul. I will talk to you tomorrow."

"Be careful out there," Paul said.

"Trooper Lawrence has my back."

"So do we," Paul replied, then hung up.

Chapter 114

High Falls, NY

The Webster clan including family and friends had just finished dinner at The Haven. Jack, Priscilla and Laddie had left a half hour earlier so that they could tend to the cows before retiring.

They had all worked out a plan for Sunday morning. Greg and Mary with their sons, Jack and Ethan along with their grandparents, Richard and Marilyn would be attending.

One of the sons would be permanently and severely disabled. Ethan, with his recent self-awarded Oscar was given the role of the disabled child. The plan was loosely scripted to allow for improvisation based on the circumstances they would encounter.

Once work was completed, the younger members headed off to the pool and the adults went to the bar.

Jack and Priscilla arrived home followed by an FBI agent, a noticeable but distant length behind them. Jack pulled the car up close to the barn and let Priscilla and Laddie out. He then proceeded to the house.

The barn lights were on and Laddie ran toward the back to find her water dish. Priscilla went up and down the aisles filling troughs with hay and water. The nighttime air was dense but there was a steady breeze that provided comfort. The big fans at either end of the barn provided circulation.

Through the side windows of the barn, Priscilla could see lights coming on in the house. First the kitchen, then the living room and finally, the upstairs bedroom. She enjoyed Jack's company and he was a good worker. He learned and adjusted quickly as if he had been raised on a farm himself.

She also liked him personally. She didn't think she could ever have enough trust to develop feelings for another man after the fiasco with Ben. She had just one date with the guy and that was inside a hardware store but her feelings for him were real and she believed he felt the same way about her.

When the ordeal was over and she realized Ben was her brother who was kidnapped as a baby, she understood that she was better off that nothing ever happened. The reality of losing a possible lover and a brother at the same time was overwhelming.

Having Veronica and Destiny around brought a degree of joy back into the family, especially for Dad. Jack was the one who got her to open up again. He was kind and sensitive just like his father, Greg. He had a great sense of humor which was just a little more constrained than Greg's.

She was finishing a row at the back of the barn when she heard a low growling coming from Laddie a few rows over. She stopped moving and listened. This had happened before when Laddie cornered a skunk in the barn. That didn't turn out so good for Laddie. It was two weeks of daily baths before he smelled good again.

"Laddie, come here boy." The dog came to her obediently but his eyes were wide and his tail was between his legs. "What is it, boy?"

Laddie left her and ran back to the far corner of the barn. Priscilla walked to the end of the aisle and saw the dog down on all fours sniffing under the office door. Priscilla had bad memories of that office. That was where her dad took a shot at Ben through the back window while she laid on the floor.

"Laddie, come here boy!" The dog didn't move and began growling again. Priscilla reach for her phone in her back pocket. It wasn't there and she remembered taking it out before she sat down in the car. There used to be a phone in the barn but since everyone started carrying cell phones, her dad had it disconnected.

She decided to go out the front of the barn and walk toward the house. She could get her phone out of the car and then go in to get Jack. She knew the Agent was out there somewhere but she couldn't see his car in the dark. She grabbed a small baseball bat that was in the corner by the front door and turned the corner of the barn. The house was only a hundred feet from where she stood and the car was parked right by the side door.

She left Laddie where he was. If there was someone in that office, she wanted Laddie to keep him there.

She made her move toward the house, not running but walking quickly. She looked up at the bedroom window and could see Jack's silhouette on the drapes. Her heart stopped beating for a second as she realized he was not alone. She crept quietly toward the car and gently opened the door. Her phone was on the passenger side dashboard. She picked it up and dialed a number then silenced her speaker.

She opened the door to the house and tiptoed to where she knew Jack kept the loaded rifle. She picked it up and set the bat down. She made sure the safety was off and went to the foot of the stairs.

In the barn, Laddie heard the back door of the office open. He stood up and dashed to the front of the barn and around the side toward the house. He could sense someone walking toward the side door. He approached quietly in a squat like a lion would approach its prey.

When the man got near the door, Laddie sprang from his back feet and flew toward him, catching him off guard and knocking him to the ground. Laddie was on his neck in a flash and pinned him to the ground. The man couldn't even let out a scream. His gun landed several yards away and was no use to him. Each time he tried to wiggle, Laddie increased the pressure on his neck.

Priscilla started to slowly climb the stairs. The old house had its share of squeaky joints and Priscilla knew where each one was. She stepped quietly until her eyes were at the level of the second floor. She looked right toward the front bedroom, the one that Jack had occupied.

The door was partially open and she could hear the other man giving Jack directions. She could not make either of them out visually.

"Get on the floor and put your hands behind your back," she could hear him say quietly. Jack didn't speak. There was a sudden noise that sounded like it was coming from outside the front of the house. The intruder must have heard it as well and moved quickly toward the window putting him in Priscilla's view.

He raised his gun to the window just as the glass exploded inward. He went down and Priscilla raced into the room pointing the rifle ahead of her. The man was not moving and Jack was face down covered with shards of glass.

She picked up the pistol where the man had dropped it, then moved to Jack.

"Are you alright, Jack?" she said anxiously.

"I'm okay," he said and tried to raise up.

"Wait Jack, your back it covered with glass."

She swept the glass off his back with her hands. She could hear someone coming up the stairs, she stood and aimed the rifle. It was the FBI agent.

"Is everyone alright?" he asked.

"Everyone but that guy," she said pointing at the floor to her right.

He went over and checked his pulse. It was very faint and erratic.

"An ambulance is on the way," he said. "Why don't you two go downstairs and wait. Oh, by the way, there is another guy out on the lawn. He is handcuffed now and being watched by Laddie."

Priscilla and Jack raced down the stairs and out the side door. Priscilla still held the rifle in her hands. On the ground just outside the door lay a man with his shoes pointing straight up at the evening sky. They could not see his face or upper chest because Laddie was on top of him with her teeth against his neck. The man's hands were cuffed in front of him.

"Laddie, off!" Priscilla said.

Laddie was reluctant to move. Jack approached gently and said,

"Good boy, Laddie, you can let go now."

The dog looked at Jack and released his grip. The man just laid there. He looked exhausted and very frightened. Jack sat the man up against the side of the steps.

"What's your name?' Jack asked.

"It doesn't matter," the man said defeatedly.

"You're from the church, right?" Jack continued but the man didn't answer.

They could all hear the sirens off in the distance. The man tried to stand up and Laddie knocked him back down and sat right in front of him.

"Good boy!" Priscilla said.

Agent Broderick was coming out the door. He looked at the man sitting down on the ground and then at Laddie.

"That's one hell of a watchdog you have there," he stated, "without him this may have gone differently."

"And without you as well, Agent Broderick," Priscilla replied.

"It was your open phone line that tipped me off and allowed me to have a sense of what was happening. That was a very smart move. Jack, where was the other guy hiding?"

"He was behind the bedroom door. I never saw him until it was too late."

"Priscilla how did you know Jack was in trouble?" the agent asked.

"From inside the barn, I saw the bedroom light come on. Inside the barn, Laddie was acting strangely. She was lying on her belly sniffing under the office door and growling. I became uncomfortable and decided to go get my phone out of the car. When I was walking toward the house, I saw two shadows in the bedroom window."

"You must have seen the shadows too, agent," Jack said.

"Yes, that's when I created the noise. I figure the one in charge would look out the window. The guy's hair gave him away. It was much longer than yours. In a hostage situation, as soon as you have a shot, you take it," the agent explained.

Two ambulances, a sheriff's car and a state police car were turning in the driveway.

"Why don't you kids finish up in the barn and I'll talk to the police. They will want your stories too but this should buy you a little time."

Jack, Priscilla and Laddie walked to the barn. Laddie turned and sat facing out. His job wasn't finished.

Chapter 115

Quicksburg, VA

Delilah arrived at the office about ten minutes after Til and his guest. She brought with her fried chicken, sweet corn, okra and fresh biscuits. She also brought a tablecloth, silverware and sweet tea.

She covered the small office table with the tablecloth and prepared three place settings. When the table was set and the food was laid out, Til escorted his guest to the table.

"Delilah, this is Abel Adams from St. Louis. This is Delilah and you can call me Til."

"I hope you're hungry, Mr. Adams, we're happy that you can join us," D said.

"It's nice of you to offer and I sure appreciate it. It has been a while since I've had a real homecooked meal."

"Well you are in luck, Abel, Delilah is one of the best cooks I know," Til said. "Please help yourself," he said passing a plate of fried chicken to him.

"I am sorry to be causing you this inconvenience, Abel, I hope you know that. My interest is with your employer, not you."

"I understand, Sheriff, I just hope we can be on the road soon or they will think I've done something wrong. They don't give us drivers a very wide berth. If we are more than two hours late for a delivery or pickup, they get pretty upset. That is unless there is a good reason like bad weather or a breakdown."

"I think you will be on the road in less than an hour but if need be, we can come up with a pretty good alibi for you," Til promised.

"Mr. Adams, do you have any family?" Del asked.

"No ma'am, I had a wife a number of years ago but I was a long haul driver and she didn't like the lonely nights. That's when I took to drinking and my life started to unravel. My company had received a few complaints about my driving but turned a blind eye because licensed long haul drivers were scarce at the time. Then, one night outside of Albany, I fell asleep and crossed the center line. I was so deep in the whisky that I didn't remember anything about it. When I came to, I was in a hospital bed. I didn't know where and I didn't care really, my life and career were over as far as I was concerned.

I had some pretty deep cuts and some bruises but nothing was broken. I received wonderful care there and had improved to the point of walking myself around but I was never allowed to go outside the unit."

"Were there other patients in the hospital at the time?" Del asked.

"I never saw any. I was in a large but private room. I was able to watch TV some but there weren't any news channels or anything local. I never even saw a commercial. There were a lot of reruns from the sixties and church programs.

When I was well enough for release, I had a visit from a man named Alpha Isaac. He was a good man, very kind and had a pleasant way about him. He told me that I had been redeemed and that I had a new family. One that didn't care about my past and one that would never leave me.

He said all my needs would be taken care of forever. He said I could have a job driving for the church and that I wouldn't need to worry about licensing and tests anymore. He said as soon as I was clean of the booze, they would put me back on the road."

"What did you do in the six months you were there?" Til asked.

"I exercised and I ate healthy and I attended meetings with other alcoholics. I was given a new name and had one on one sessions with a nice woman who made me forget about my old name and my old self. I knew it was a brainwashing tactic but I didn't fight it, why should I? There was no life for me on the outside and I had everything I would ever need where I was. I was an easy convert."

"It sounds like they took away your very freedom, Abel," Til said. "You lost your freedom to choose what you wanted out of life."

"Til, we throw that word freedom around a lot in this country but it's not for everyone. There are plenty of people whose lives were chosen for them right out of the birth canal. People don't chose to be poor and less intelligent. I don't know anyone who chose to have an angry side or become an outlaw. People play the hand they were dealt for the most part and they become who society has made them. Sure, some people just make bad choices but that is probably part of the genetic code as well. Nature or nurture, we are never free to make that choice. Some of us just don't fit in and the church provides a place for that."

"How do they do that?" Del asked.

"First, they give you some space to heal from whatever affliction you have. Next, they surround you with people who have shared similar backgrounds. Then they take care of all your needs from healthcare to dental work, clothing, personal care and they even supply food items that you request. All they ask in return is to give them an honest day's work and to follow a few simple rules."

"What about friends and lovers?" Del asked.

"I have plenty of likeminded friends. We have down time and we have activities. We have a morale services team that provides anything we need from a companion for dinner to an overnight guest. I state my preference in women and one is supplied. How is that for freedom?"

"It doesn't seem very natural to me," Del said.

"I feels like the most natural thing in the world to me," he replied.

"Aren't you worried that the women are there against their will?" Til asked.

"No sir, I would never be with someone against their will. These women came from a place that they totally enjoy what they are doing. They were selected for their job based on experience and their natural libido. No one is forced to do a job that offends them. Maybe that's why it all works so well."

"Are their families there?" Del asked.

"We are all one family now. Everyone there had already lost their families for one reason or another. That's part of the selection criteria for being chosen to join the church family," Abel replied.

Til's phone rang.

"Sheriff Sweeney."

"Yes, we will be ready," he said into the phone.

"Your escorts will be here in thirty minutes, Abel," Til said.

"If you would like, Mr. Adams, I can pack the rest of this food up for you to take with you," Del offered.

"That's very kind of you ma'am but I don't want any evidence that I've been helped along the way. Too much interaction with outsiders is discouraged," he replied.

Til could see headlights approaching from the driveway. It looked like tow vehicles. As they came closer, he could see that one of them was a black van.

"Del, I need you to go to the basement. There is a phone down there and I need you to dial 911 and tell them we need backup. Do not come out until I see it's clear, okay?"

She could tell by the look in his eyes what was happening and she followed his orders, disappearing into the basement. Til told Able to get down in the corner behind a desk and then opened the gun cabinet and pulled out two automatic rifles that held sixteen rounds each. He shoved an extra clip into the back of his pants.

He slipped on a vest and snuck out the back door, turning the lights out on the way. He watched around the corner of the building as two men approached the main entrance. They were carrying guns. He picked up a rock and threw it at the car.

It landed with a thud on the hood and the men turned to look. Til fired one shot and hit one of the men in the back of the leg. The other man turned and fired in his direction. He took cover behind the wall. Til ran around the building in the other direction coming up on the other gunman from behind.

"Put it down and get on the ground!' Til said smoothly.

The gunman didn't move.

"Last chance," Til said. "I'd rather not shoot you but I will."

The gunman turned quickly and Til caught him in the left shoulder. The gunman got off one round but it went up in the air. He was still holding the rifle in his right hand and Til put another bullet in his right shoulder. The man dropped the gun and fell to the ground, Til took his rifle and went back to check the other gunman.

The man Til shot in the leg was gone. There was a trail of blood that led back toward the cars. The black van started to back away. Til raised his weapon and unloaded three quick shots, The first two hit each of the front tires and the third went straight through the radiator.

The man in the passenger seat got out and walked toward Til who was thirty yards away, between the van and the office door. The man was limping. It was the one he hit earlier. Til laid flat on the ground, out of the light from the headlamps. The man stumbled toward him.

"Put it down!" Til yelled.

The man fired a round and kept coming. Til kneecapped his good leg and the guy stood still for a moment and raised his rifle once more, aiming at Til. Before he could squeeze the trigger. Til put a round in the right side of his chest, near the shoulder. The man went down.

The black van was still trying to make it down the driveway. Til let him go. Before the van reached the main road, two state police cars blocked the exit and a Sheriff from an adjoining county pulled in behind them.

Til could hear other sirens coming. He went to check the last gunman he shot. He was bleeding badly from all three wounds but he was still alive. The other guy wasn't in much better shape. Til opened the door to the office and turned on the floodlights canvasing the parking area and lawn in artificial daylight.

A lieutenant that Til knew from the state police precinct in Harrison-burg walked up to greet him.

"Is everyone alright here, Til?"

"I wouldn't say everyone, there are two down and they're bleeding pretty badly. I need to check on people inside, I'll be right back."

Til ran inside and called for Able on his way to the basement.

"I'm okay, Sheriff," he heard Able say while he passed.

He ran down the stairs and found Delilah crouching behind some boxes.

"It's over D, come on out."

She ran to him and threw her arms around him, sobbing.

"I was afraid I would never see you again, Til" she cried.

"It's all over, D, it's all over now." He held her tight for as long as they both needed.

Chapter 116

July 11, 2016

Festus/Crystal City, MO

Charis and Trey met for breakfast at the hotel restaurant. The night before, after they rented new vehicles, drove to Festus, and checked in at the hotel, they had dinner together.

Trey insisted that they rent two vehicles so that he could keep a tail on her as she went about her day. Charis went with a truck once again. She was hooked. Trey picked a sedan in a color no one would look at twice. He liked to blend in, especially when he was involved in a stakeout.

They didn't make a late night of it because they were both exhausted.

They believed they would both be on flights home in just a few hours if things went as scheduled. They had talked about calling off the day's meetings and waiting for a joint plan to formulate but decided that canceling at the last minute would raise some flags.

In just over an hour, she would be meeting Det. Laroy Climm at the police station in Festus but before that, she and Trey would be attending a conference call with the other team members. They had a cordial discussion over breakfast and then returned to Charis' room for the call.

At 8:15 her phone rang. She answered and placed it on speaker. She was joined by Paul, Greg and his crew, Til Sweeney and for the first time, Montgomery County, New York Sheriff Judd Bentley and NYS police Lt. Cliff Alvord.

"Good morning," Paul welcomed everyone and made the introductions. "I am going to share updates from yesterday's events and then we are going to talk about our plans for tomorrow. First, let me say that we have brought in Sheriff Bentley and Lt. Alvord to lead the Jordanville portion of the plan. They were instrumental in getting the ball rolling in this case and it's a pleasure to have them with us.

So much has happened in the last twenty four hours that it is difficult to wrap one's head around it. There were major events in High Falls, Custer and Quicksburg and all involving apparent attacks on our people by members of the church. I am relieved to say that none of our people were seriously injured. I am also proud to say that there are many heroes among you. I have no doubt that when our work is finished here, this case will be a prime example of the power of collaboration between law enforcement and the community."

Paul went on to describe the events that happened in various locations the previous day and how they all fit together. He then moved on to the events that needed to take place that day in preparation for Sunday.

"All of Sunday's events will take place at 12:30 pm eastern time. That should be when the service in the east is finishing and the ones to the west are beginning. Our goal is to identify as many church goers as possible because we know tracking them down individually will be difficult.

The priority for today is to locate the communications room for each church. We believe that they follow a common blueprint for each location right down to the tiniest detail so we will be looking at the closest public cave in relationship to each church.

We are assigning someone from each location to lead a team to find the communications room in each cave. You will use an invisible spray paint that glows only under black light. Once you find the entrance to the room, work your way back placing a small, six inch spray every twenty feet at one foot off the ground.

A team of FBI agents will use your trail to locate the room quickly. Our experts will gain entrance to the room and disconnect the feed to the church and more importantly each other. We can't risk one warning another of our presence. Precision timing is critical for the best outcome.

I will be sending an email in the next few minutes assigning leadership roles and the caverns that you are assigned to. I need everyone to check in by 5:00 pm with confirmation that the room has been found and the path marked. Are there any questions?"

"Hearing none, I will initiate the next call at 1700 hours. Be safe out there."

Paul ended the conference call and called Charis privately.

"Hi Paul," Charis answered.

"Charis, there are three agents on the ground in your immediate area. The transponder that Trey placed on your vehicle will be monitored by all of them in addition to Trey. Trey and the others will maintain contact with each other.

Don't spend any more time than necessary with these people, Charis. We have all the information we need, your job today is as a smoke screen only."

"I understand," Charis replied. "Paul, is the dinner with my dad still on?"

"Yes, and for the same reason. My guess is no one will take the bait and your father will just enjoy a nice evening out."

"Okay," she replied. "It sounded like a close one in High Falls last night."

"It was closer than it should have been. We should have had another agent watching the house while the kids were at The Haven. That one is on me," Paul said.

"You can't think of everything, Paul, and sometimes everything is not enough. It all worked out," Charis replied.

"Well, we are not taking any chances today. Priscilla, Jack and Laddie will be joining the others at The Haven. We have some of our people coming in to take care of the farm."

"We have farm people?" Charis asked with disbelief.

"We have everything, Charis. You would be amazed."

"Trey and I will check in at 1700. Have a fun day, Paul!"

"Fun? I don't think so."

Charis had twenty minutes to get to the police station.

Chapter 117

Quicksburg, VA

Til awoke to the smell of bacon cooking. It took him a moment to realize he wasn't in his own bed. It was coming back to him now. He sat up and let his body settle before trying to stand.

He slipped his pants on and ran his fingers through his hair to try and tame it. Then he walked out to the kitchen. Delilah was working at the stove with her back to him. She was wearing a short nightgown that looked good on her. She had great legs.

"Good morning," he said from across the room, not wanting to startle her.

She put the spatula down and walked briskly over to meet him. She wrapped her arms around his neck and gave him a big kiss.

"Great morning!" she said. "Breakfast will be ready in just a minute." She went to coffee maker and poured him a cup. She fixed it just the way he ordered at the diner and brought it to him.

"Have a seat and I will fix you a plate," she directed.

"It smells great, D. I'm sorry about all the activity last night. The last thing I wanted to do was put you in harm's way."

"I know that Til, you were doing your job. You do it very well by the way!"

"We're still talking about my job, right?" he joked.

"You do that very well too and neither of those is a surprise," she said happily. "I was very proud of you last night and never worried about my own safety. I was petrified for yours though."

Til heard his phone ringing from in the bedroom and ran to get it.

"Sheriff Sweeney."

"Sheriff, it's Paul Jenner, do you have a minute?"

Til slipped on his shirt while he talked to Paul. It was over in less than a minute and Til walked back to the kitchen.

"Sorry about that, D, it was Paul at the FBI. He wants to have a conference call in about twenty minutes. Would it be alright if I did that from here?"

"Of course, Til, mi casa es su casa. Anything you need is fine with me," Del said.

Delilah set a plate in front of Til and one for herself. She sat down next to him and grabbed his hand.

"Thank you for last night Tilman, I had a lovely time."

"Which part?" he asked.

"All of it!" she exclaimed. "You know Til, I believe that life is a series of ups and downs most of which we don't have any control over. I think the secret to a happy life is keeping the downs as close to the ups as possible. Last night reminded me of that. I know you have a dangerous job at times and I know that we won't always agree on everything but I also know I can trust you to work through the rough spots with me. That's all I need, someone to work through things together. And the love making wasn't bad either."

"Wasn't bad?" Til asked.

"It was great, Til. Just as I imagined it would be for all these years. Now eat your breakfast before it gets cold."

Til enjoyed the breakfast of scrambled eggs, country sausage, bacon, toast and grits, but he enjoyed the easy conversation even more. When they were finished, Til helped clear the table and prepared for the conference call.

When the call ended, he went looking for Delilah. He entered the bathroom quietly and removed his clothes.

"Mind if I join you?" he asked.

"I would be disappointed if you didn't," she replied.

"D, I need to ask you something."

He sounded serious so she turned to face him. She pushed her wet hair back away from her face and he placed his hands on her shoulders.

"D, we have known each other a long time. By the way, you look really nice when you're wet. Anyway, If it's not asking too much, would you.. *she was waiting for it!* Would you go to the Shenandoah Caverns with me today?"

He had this boyish grin on his face like he had just pulled off the world's best prank.

She just stared at him for a minute. She grinned back.

"Tilman Sweeney, that is the nicest offer I have had in a long time. Is anyone going to be shooting at us?" she asked.

"I can't guarantee that, Del," he answered.

"I think it's worth the risk. Hand me the soap, Sheriff."

Chapter 118

The Haven, Outside of High Falls, NY

Everyone had been moved to The Haven as a safety measure after the attack on the Chalmers' farm. They had gathered around the huge dining room table to attend the conference call with the FBI.

The plan for the church visit had been altered by Paul Jenner. It was no longer going to be a family affair. Paul had narrowed the group down to just Greg and Ethan. Paul wanted to know how the church recruited the people on disability. He thought having the entire family there would draw suspicion. A widowed father with a disabled son might be a more palatable target for the organizers.

Greg figured he would borrow a wheelchair from the hospital and

Ethan could pull together a neck brace and some other paraphernalia that would add to the authenticity. The story would be that Ethan developed viral meningitis at age 18 in his first year of college. He had been permanently disabled for nearly ten years now.

Ethan had worked with numerous patients with similar conditions over the years and felt comfortable with the role. Mary felt differently.

"Greg, after what happened last night you are willing to put yourself and Ethan at risk again tomorrow? Why can't the FBI do it?"

"It's because of last night that I am more compelled than ever to do this. They are threatening our freedom as well as their captives' freedom. How do we turn our backs on that, Mary?"

"I'm not saying we turn our backs, I'm suggesting that maybe the FBI is better equipped to handle it," Mary added.

"The FBI will be storming the place before the service is over, how much trouble can we get ourselves into in that short period of time? We should show up fifteen minutes early, find out what we can, sit through the service and observe the calvary coming in."

"Mary, you were willing to be a part of it until just a few minutes ago, What changed?"

"I don't know, maybe me not being there makes me feel helpless," she replied.

Greg held her hand.

"I understand, but this is the least dangerous option of all. Ethan and I can be very agile when we need to be," Greg said.

"I believe Ethan can get out of the way, but I'm not sure about you. You're track record isn't great and you may not have a rug to curl up in."

Mary was grinning beneath the tears.

"I promise I won't get blown up again," he said.

"Oh why do I bother? You are you and nobody can change that. And I don't want to change that. I love who you are."

"I think this will help. If it makes you feel any better, you can come to the cavern with us today," Greg said excitedly.

"Let's see," Mary said, "I can stay here with a pool, a bar, great food and protection or, I can walk inside a cold, damp cave. That's really a toss-up," she joked.

"It looks like it's me and you again, Ethan," Greg said. "How about you, Jack? Would you and Priscilla like to go?"

"I would like to. How about you, Priscilla?" Jack asked.

"I think if I have one day this year away from the farm, I would prefer to use it at this lovely spa," she answered.

"That's a smart girl, Jack," Mary said.

"Okay then, it looks like it's just us guys," Greg concluded.

"You guys are all about man caves, right? You will feel right at home," Mary quipped.

Chapter 119

Festus/Crystal City

Charis pulled up to the police station which looked vacant at this hour on a Saturday. Trey had attached the GPS locator to the chassis of her rental as soon as they picked it up. He was able to test it on the drive from the airport to the hotel.

She backed the truck into a vacant space right up front with a sign that read thirty minute parking. She didn't plan on being there more than fifteen. Trey parked across the street where he could maintain a good visual. The only thing different about today's surveillance was that Charis was wearing a wire.

She entered the building and was greeted by the officer at the desk. He directed her to have a seat while he contacted Climm. She did as she was told and looked around. The precinct appeared clean and orderly. There was no one else in the waiting area.

After a few minutes, *Just to keep me waiting. He'll show me who's boss in his neck of the woods,* a tall, rugged looking man appeared in the waiting area.

"Agent Andrews, I'm Laroy Climm."

She stood to greet him and they shook hands. *Wimpy handshake for a big guy.*

"Would you like to talk here for a few minutes or head right over to the river?" he asked.

"I think we should get moving. We can talk when we get there," Charis replied.

"Or," Climm interjected, "You can ride with me and we can talk on the way."

"You know, that's a nice offer but I think I will follow you in my own vehicle. That way, I can just make a quick escape when we're finished," Charis replied.

Slim chance of that, Andrews. There will be no quick escapes today. "That's fine with me," Climm said. "Where are you parked?"

"Right out front," Charis responded, "The grey pickup."

"I'll pull around and stop in front of you. It's about a twelve minute ride to the spot."

Climm walked away as she watched. His service weapon was under his jacket but she could also tell by the way his right pantleg laid that he had a backup in a calf strap.

Charis walked to the exit. Once outside, she whispered to Trey.

"On the move. One in the rack and one on the right leg."

Trey could hear her loud and clear. Climm came around from the parking lot behind the building and came to a stop in front of her. She started the truck and waved indicating she was ready.

She pulled in behind Climm, heading east. She watched in the rear-view as Trey pulled in at a comfortable distance behind. East Main Street in Festus turned into Bailey Road just beyond the overpass of Rt. 67. They turned right heading south on Virgin Street and followed it to the end.

Climm made a left turn off Virgin onto a gravel road which gave way to a dirt road after a half mile. Just before the river, there was a wide area that was covered with gravel. *Lover's Lane right off Virgin Street.*

Climm pulled to a stop allowing space for Charis to park her truck. She didn't see Trey but she knew he was back there. He needed to keep out of sight of Climm. Charis noticed a smaller, dirt trail about twenty yards south of the gravel road. She guessed is was put there by dirt bikes or four-wheelers.

Climm got out the car carrying two coffee cups. He waited for her to get out and come to him. *You wouldn't have done that if I was wearing the skirt, I bet.* Charis climbed out of the truck and walked toward him.

"I brought an extra coffee for you Agent," Climm offered.

"That's very kind of you, Detective," she said taking it from him. "I think I'll rest on the hood here so it stays warm. I just finished one on the way over and if I drank any more right now, I would have to run off and find a rest room. I will enjoy it later though, I promise."

"Sure, no problem," Crimm said.

"Well, the spot is a good thirty yards past the end of the gravel but there is some long, wet grass between here and there."

"I understand, Charis said, "This is close enough. I just wanted to put the pieces together in my mind. Were you ever able to locate a place of entry?"

"No, it could have come from anywhere. The old Miss is a crazy river, very unpredictable. In fact, if I were to drop a body in the river right here, you could end up in Cape Girardeau or even Memphis. With a heavy rain you might even make it to New Orleans," Climm projected.

"You mean "it," right?" she questioned.

"I beg your pardon," Climm said.

"You used the word you, meaning me, but you are referring to just any body, correct?" Charis explained.

"Are you asking if it was a Freudian slip?" Climm inquired.

"I was just looking for grammatical clarity, detective. Words are important, especially when a murder has happened."

Climm's face turned red and he stared down at his feet, his butt resting against the side of his car.

"You know, you Yankees think you're so smart. Always poking fun at us dumb southerners. Especially you, Andrews, chewing me out on the phone, thinking you can move into my territory and take over. You have a lot of nerve. What gives the FBI the right to pull trump on me?"

"Listen, Climm, I wasn't attempting to be rude or to upset you.

Words are important and it doesn't matter if you are in New York or the land of Dixie. The reason I was upset on the phone is because I had been dealing with law enforcement in several states where serious crimes were committed and I wasn't getting any cooperation.

As for who gives me the right to investigate a crime in your area, I guess that would be the federal government and I don't think you're a dumb southerner because of the way you speak, I think you are just stupid when you say "Who cares" when a body washes ashore. We are all hired to do a job and I was asking you to do yours."

Climm stayed quiet but he was still fuming. Charis was watching for a sign that he was thinking about his gun. Finally, he spoke.

"Are you ready to pay a visit to the ME?"

Charis thought about that for a bit. She didn't see the value and she didn't want to elevate the awkwardness of this situation.

"I think we can be done for today, detective. I don't believe there is any value in talking with the pathologist. I think we know what is going on now. It's the same in every example we have looked at."

"So what do you think is going on?" Climm asked.

"I believe there is an organization out there that is holding people captive, cashing their disability checks and using them as slave labor. I think the regular members reap rewards in the form of services provided by the prisoners of this organization. I also believe that a fair number of the membership consists of law enforcement officers and other professionals who have fallen from grace and who are recruited by this organization that preys on the vulnerable," Charis said emphatically and with conviction.

"That's an interesting story, Andrews. What evidence do you have to back that up?" he asked.

"We have enough to make your head spin, detective," she answered.

"And you think that I'm involved in this organization, Agent Andrews?"

"I'm not saying you are, but I think you could be."

Charis moved to the front of the vehicles and Climm followed her. She had her back to him and he had drawn his gun.

"You think you're so smart, don't you?"

Charis turned to see his gun pointing at her.

"Climm, you don't have to do this. Put the gun down," she said.

"You're the one that is going to put their gun down, Andrews. Right now, on the ground," he demanded.

"You're smarter than this, Climm, you must know you can't get away with this."

"You would be amazed to find out how much we get away with, Charis. It's a good life, you could have joined us," he said.

"And how would that work, me being a woman and all?"

"The same as it does for the men, sort of. I mean men rule the roost, that's just the natural way, but women have roles too. They would probably give you a job in surveillance and they may expect you to entertain now and again but you would be reserved for the overseers and Alphas, I would imagine."

"Who are the Alphas?" she asked.

"They are the leaders of each congregation."

"You mean each location?"

"That's right, each location. The Alphas answer to the Supreme Leader."

"And who would that be, Laroy?"

"Why would I tell you?" Climm asked, "talking about that could get me redeemed."

"Isn't that a good thing?" Charis asked.

"There are all levels of redemption, Charis, but the ultimate redemption is final. That is reserved for members who break the rules or go outside of the church. "

"What did the person who washed up in your river do wrong?"

"I'm not sure but the body washing up like that is a mistake," he said.

"I guess that will lead to more bodies, right?" she asked.

"It could, I mean, that sounds like a pretty big mistake to me. It's hard to say what will be forgiven and what will be punished," he claimed.

"That doesn't sound like a system that would suit me, I think I'll pass," Charis stated.

"It's not like we have a choice now, Charis, we're a little too far down that road to turn back now."

"There are always choices, Laroy. You can choose to put that gun down, for example."

"And go to jail?" he said, "no thanks."

"Think about it. What have you really done wrong up to this point?" Charis asked. "Sure you knew about it but you probably haven't broken any laws yourself. I can't lie, this little fiasco might get you removed from your job but it sure beats going to prison forever."

"And how would that happen? By the time they find you, all your friends will be gone and the church will go on forever," Climm speculated.

"That's not how this story ends, detective. You won't be leaving this spot a free man and the church has been uncovered. It's time to call it a day," she advised.

"That's a lot of big talk for a little girl who gave her weapon away," he said.

"I didn't give it away, you took it away, at gunpoint I might add. Ask yourself this question, Laroy. Would any girl in her right mind come out here alone with you?" she asked.

"I don't see anyone standing along with you," he answered.

"Just because you don't see them, that doesn't mean they're not here. Trust me, Laroy, before a single bullet leaves your pistol, you will be lying face down in a pool of your own blood."

"Wow, the nerve of you, is there no end to your confidence?" he asked.

"Who would you like to hear from first, Laroy, how about your chief? That's right, we even invited Chief Canlon to witness this absurd display of injustice."

There were fifteen feet between Charis and Climm.

"Laroy Climm, this is Chief Canlon, put your gun down Laroy, it's over."

Laroy looked over his right shoulder and could see Conlon standing there. He took one step toward Charis and three FBI agents in camouflage stood up from the tall grass, guns pointed at Climm. He quickly looked behind him between the vehicles and was staring down the barrel of Trey's service revolver.

"It's time, Laroy, put the gun down."

He didn't move. Charis raised her voice.

"Climm, I am going to count to three and these nice officers are going to open fire. One! Two!"

Charis was preparing herself to take a bullet on the next count. She opened he mouth to yell three but before she did, Climm dropped his weapon. Charis moved quickly and pulled a second revolver out of her back holster. She held her aim on Climm while the other officers charged him. He was on the ground and cuffed within seconds, removing his ankle weapon.

They stood up and she walked toward him. Climm looked directly in her eyes.

"You did the only sensible thing, Climm. You made the right choice. I have questions for you. Do you really think I am stupid enough to come out here alone or were you secretly hoping that this charade would end? And two, what did you put in the coffee? Never mind, it doesn't matter."

Chapter 120

Quicksburg, VA

Til stood just where he had a day earlier, in line at the caverns. He wasn't wearing his uniform this time. He purchased two tickets and went to meet up with Delilah who was reading the informational materials posted on the wall near the entrance.

"There are a lot of people here. I had no idea it was this popular," Del said.

"It's much busier than it was yesterday," Til observed, "but it will still pale in comparison to tomorrow."

"Will anyone let them know ahead of time?" Del asked.

"I don't think so, D, I think they are counting on the element of surprise."

"There will be some disappointed children here," she stated.

"Maybe not, it will just be a different kind of excitement," Til offered.

"You're an optimist, I like that about you Til."

The line ahead of them moved and they made it past the ticket taker.

"Do we need to hurry right to the spot?" Del asked.

"No, we can take our time, we don't want to raise suspicion anyway. We can enjoy the experience."

Til checked his pocket for the small bottle of spray. He palmed it in his hand so that no one could see it. Every fifteen or twenty feet, he sprayed a little on the rock about a foot above the floor. He felt like a dog marking his territory.

Delilah was fascinated with the rock formations and all the colored lighting that projected on the walls and ceiling. She was as excited as a schoolgirl on prom night and it tickled him. The crowd moved slowly and they took their time reading all the small informational signs that accompanied each feature.

The air got cooler as they descended but they were prepared. It seemed strange putting on a heavy sweater in the middle of summer and if it hadn't been for his trip there the day before, they would both be freezing.

"I didn't have a coat or sweater yesterday when I was here," Til stated.

"You must have been cold," Del replied.

"I was, but then I thought about being close to you and it warmed me," Til confessed.

"Well Tilman, that is the sweetest thing anyone has ever said to me."

"Really?" he asked, "I can do much better than that."

"I look forward to finding that out," Del responded.

It was a good forty minutes before they neared the passage that led to the secret room. They waited for the rest of their group to pass and then Til stepped over the rope and felt his way along the corridor to the room. He didn't want to use his flashlight and alert someone to his presence.

As he sprayed along the way, he could see the material luminesce in the dark. He found the door and sprayed a spot on the walls on each side. Then he sprayed the words: *In Here* on the door.

He made his way back down the tunnel but when he neared the end, there was another group approaching. Fortunately, there wasn't a lot to look at right there and they passed quickly. When they were around the bend he stepped over the rope and followed the crowd.

He didn't see Del right away but he assumed she was with the group ahead of them. He followed the crowd until they came to a wide spot in the cave. It looked like a stage but instead of musicians and instruments, it was limestone formations washed in a multitude of colors from the hidden lights. They admired it for several minutes, until the group began to move.

Del just stood there, mesmerized by the scene. Til reached into his pocket and then turned Delilah to face him.

"Delilah, I have known you as long as I can remember, and in my soul, I have loved you even longer.

Til got down in one knee.

"I know this is only our second date but I know that I am ready for this. I hope you are too. Delilah, would you be my wife, my partner and my best friend forever?"

Til held out a diamond ring that was not new and not perfectly clear but it sparkled in that magic lighting in every color of the rainbow.

Delilah kneeled down with him.

"Tilman, when you are down, I will bend to meet you and when you are at your highest, I will climb to join you. Yes, I will marry you!"

They hugged on their knees and then stood and hugged again not knowing that the next group had been watching, until they heard the applause.

Chapter 121

Crystal City, MO

The Supreme Leader and the Alphas had gathered again. This time, there was a little more desperation in the tone of the address.

"Brothers, I stand before you laden with sadness and fear. The creation that my father made a reality is at risk of being destroyed. Along with it will go the home that we provide for thousands of the world's castaways.

We need a solution and we need it quickly. The efforts we have made to stabilize the situation through fear and retaliation have failed repeatedly and have provided the other side with a deeper look into our operation.

Utilizing members from the outside has been a mistake. We need to secure our fortresses and arm our own people with the resources to protect our way of life. I would imagine that the other side is planning to move quickly. We have no way of knowing when or where but we need to act soon.

I want each of you to follow the directions written on the sheets in front of you. You will need to rely on your Omegas to carry out the tasks in your absence. You will do so via a direct video link to them. I want them to see your faces, the faces they trust, as they listen to your message.

We may reach a point where preserving our legacy will outweigh our own survival. Our belief in and our dedication to redemption will be carried out to the last degree if necessary. We shall prepare for that moment by planning the ultimate party.

Your dietary staff will be furnished with everything they need in quantities that will guarantee the desired results. We have been entrusted with their care which includes the responsibility that they never return to the unthinkable existence that waits on the outside.

The surface people have demonstrated repeatedly that they cannot adequately care for the less fortunate. Homelessness continues to grow, a blind eye is turned to the military veteran, substance abusers are switched from reliance on one drug to another because no one has the fortitude nor patience to help them through the cleansing process. Children of abuse and neglect will continue to abound without our intervention. Women of the night will be mistreated and the weak will be misguided.

We must ensure their peaceful passage should we lose our stand. It will be hard but the faithful will understand and abide. Have your people plan for the best day of their lives. If we prevail, it will be a celebration of our continuation and if we fail, it will be a celebration of our history.

Dietary will prepare food and drink of two varieties. One regular and one made of special flour and water. Only the Omegas will know which is which.

Please read through the materials regarding the defense of our great properties should we be attacked. We will meet again later in the day, after you have had your video conferences with the Omegas.

Chapter 122

Howes Cave, NY

Greg parked the car at the furthest point from the entry. Jack and Ethan looked at each other and just shook their heads.

"Don't forget your jackets," Greg advised. I know it's getting hot out here already but when you step off the elevator, it's going to be a very cool fifty-two degrees."

They all grabbed their coats and walked up hill to the beautiful Tudor style mansion that serves as the entry in addition to the gift shop and restaurant. Greg stood in line to purchase three tickets while the boys looked around the gift shop. He returned with the ticket and brochures.

"Jack, you were here when you were maybe seven or eight, do you remember?" Greg asked.

"I remember being here but not much of the real experience below," Jack replied.

"Have you even been before?" he asked Ethan.

"Not that I remember," he replied.

"Well this is going to be fun!" Greg said.

They proceeded down a short hallway to the elevator. When it was their turn, they climbed aboard and the attendant took them down.

"You are about to visit one of the most unique places on the planet," the attendant began, "a place that has existed for over six million years. The walking tour is a mile and a quarter long and takes roughly ninety minutes. There is a boat ride that will carry you a quarter mile as well.

The temperature is a constant fifty-two degrees and when the elevator door opens, you will be fifteen stories underground. Please stay on the walkways at all times. If you need assistance, look for one of the attendants along the path. Thank you and enjoy your journey."

The elevator reached its destination and the door opened. They immediately felt a rush of cooler air coming in. They stepped out to a landing area that was fairly large and well lit. The path began to the left and Greg led the way.

"Keep an eye out for a passageway that may lead to the secret room," he said. "When we find it, I will cross the barrier while you remain on the trail. I will then retrace my steps and mark the location and the path leading up to it. I will meet you in the restaurant afterwards."

The boys nodded their agreement and they all continued on. The line moved at a slow pace and there were several points of interest along the way. When they reached the entry for the boat ride, the boys veered off to the line for the boat and Greg continued along the path.

The crowd ahead of Greg thinned out as most of the people in the group opted for the boats. He was about twenty minutes into the tour when he saw what appeared to be a small, vertical opening. He looked around for security and guests but he was alone. He quickly stepped over the rope and pressed himself between the narrow opening in the wall.

He could feel the moisture against his clothing as the limestone closed in around him. He had a flashback to being wrapped in the carpet in Syracuse and it forced him to pause. He felt slightly claustrophobic and took a few deep breaths to calm himself down. He reached out his lead hand and could feel the opening on the other side widen.

He squeezed the rest of his body through to find himself in a comfortable space. He could only see a few feet in from of him so he took his phone from his pocket and held it inside his thin jacket before activating the flashlight. From inside the jacket, the light gave a soft glow directly ahead of him. He could make out the path three or four feet in advance.

The tunnel was only three feet wide and cleared the top of his head by just a few inches. There were several curves along the way but no adjoining tunnels. That gave him some relief knowing he would be able to find his way back. He did notice that the air in the small tunnel was not circulating well and that made him more conscious of his breathing.

After a few more minutes, the path widened again and the air felt fresher. There was a small door straight ahead. Greg turned off the light and could see a razor thin line of blue light leaking from underneath. He put his ear to the door and could hear the sound of air being circulated by fans.

He turned the light back on and removed the spray from his pocket. He sprayed the rock on both sides of the door and on the door itself sprayed the words *It's Over.*

Greg took a picture of the door with his phone. He was blinded by the intensity of the flash and had to wait for a minute in the dark before he felt comfortable retreating. He sprayed his way back to the opening and listened until he didn't hear any talking before he birthed himself back through the wall.

He stepped over the rope unnoticed and continued along the path. Forty minutes later, he met Jack and Ethan in the restaurant. They were seated in a table when he approached.

"I found it!" he exclaimed excitedly.

The boys just stared at him.

"What?" Greg asked.

"Look at your coat and slacks, Dad," Jack said.

Greg checked himself out. He had damp, greyish-white residue all over his jacket and pants.

"Did you fall out of the boat?" Ethan joked.

"Funny," Greg replied, "no, but I did do a little squeezing between the rocks. So what looks good on the menu?"

Chapter 123

Crystal City, MO

By the time Climm was hauled away and all the paperwork was done, it was mid-afternoon. Charis and Trey went back to the hotel to shower and have lunch before going to the cave. They were sitting at an outside table at a café near the hotel.

"I'm sorry you don't get to go home today as planned, Charis. I would be happy to stay and pick up the pieces if you need to leave," Trey offered.

"That's very kind of you, Trey but I would like to be here for the conclusion tomorrow."

"If there is a conclusion tomorrow, Trey said, "I don't see how this can all come down in one day, do you?"

"I think each location can be permeated in one day but the relocations of all the people may take a long time. I can't imagine how that is going to happen. I suppose social services will lead the way in placement but they all need to be screened first. There are probably open arrest warrants for many of those people and many more arrests will come as a result of the raids."

"Hopefully, the folks at the FBI have thought this through," Trey added.

"So, what do you know about caves, Trey?"

"I know that Batman lived in one and it was pretty cool," he replied.

"Do you have any useful knowledge of caves?" Charis asked again.

"I know the country and the world for that matter, is full of them. I once read that somewhere in the world there is a cave that's over six thousand feet deep. That's like almost center of the earth deep!" he said.

"I'm a bit skeptical of caves, always have been. I would read about miners being trapped and kids falling into hidden wells and I would dwell on it for days. I don't know what the term is for the fear of being trapped, but I know that I have it, Charis said.

"I think it's called ohfuckaphobia," Trey said.

Charis laughed hysterically and he joined her.

"Sorry, I think this mission is getting to me," Trey explained.

"I think that sounds about right," Charis replied, "no apology necessary."

"You know, we could ask someone else in law enforcement to look at the cave. There is no reason, we need to do it," Trey commented.

"You're right, we could pass it off but that's just not my nature. Besides, it's an opportunity to address a phobia and get over it. Having you with me will make it that much easier."

"Whoa," Trey said, "you think I'm going down there? Those things freak me out!" he said jokingly.

"We will work through our fears together," she said.

"Alright, let's finish up here and get going," Trey said, "before I lose my nerve."

They finished their lunch and headed off toward the caverns called Crystal Underground. It was in the same general vicinity where Climm tried to take Charis down. Just on the other side of Plattin creek, a road veered left off of River Hills Rd.

"Hey Trey, didn't Ethan say the church was around here somewhere too?"

Trey looked at his phone and she was right.

"Yes, it must be farther up River Hills Rd. According to the map, River Hills dead ends a few miles past here."

They made their way to the entrance, paid the fee and fell in behind several other amateur spelunkers. They hadn't been on the path more than two minutes when they felt the cool rush coming from inside. Neither had planned for the cool temperatures nor packed appropriately. Trey had a long sleeve shirt at least.

Charis stopped frequently to view things along the way. Trey thought it was more about the fear of going deeper. He removed his long sleeve shirt and placed it over Charis' shoulders.

"I think you need this more than I do," he said.

She turned to look at him and he was wearing a warm, knit Henley tee shirt so she didn't feel quite as bad.

"Thank you, Trey, just let me know if you need it back.

"I will," he promised. "Hey what do you think of that?" he said, pointing to a dark crevasse in the wall.

"I don't know, it doesn't look very wide," she replied.

"I'll go have a look while you keep a lookout," he said as he walked away.

Trey stood in front of the opening until everyone passed by. When it was clear, he stepped over the chain retainer and angled his body between the rocks. Once inside, the passage opened up. He felt his way along for about fifteen feet before he lost all light. He pulled a small penlight from his pocket and turned it on.

The path continued forward at a downward slope. When he reached the end, he could hear water running to his left and there was a door to the right. He turned off the light momentarily until his eyes adjusted to the diffuse light coming from the opening where he heard the water.

Beneath the door, he could see a pale thin fragment of light. The door was locked. He pulled out his jackknife and tried to pick at the lock. It was too secure. He moved to the left to follow the sound of water. He reached a wooden rail that kept him from falling into the river below.

There were people in Kayaks in the river. He made his way back to Charis, spraying the invisible paint as he moved. He paused at the opening and looked out at Charis. She gave the all clear sign and he emerged from the small opening.

"That didn't take long," she said.

"It wasn't a very long walk but it's back there," he said.

"You found it? That's great! We can get out of here now," She said excitedly.

"Not quite yet," he replied. "We need to see what's around the corner."

He led the way and she followed. As they turned the corner, they were looking at an indoor beach with kayaks for visitors to paddle around in. The river flowed away from them and he needed to see where the overlook he stood on came out.

"Are you ready for a boat ride?" he asked.

"Should I be?" she responded.

"Yes, it won't take long. Come on, it will be fun. We can take the two person one and I'll do all the paddling."

She followed him down the path where an attendant was helping people in and out. They put on the cold damp vests and sat in the plastic canoes. Trey was in the back and began to paddle. After just twenty yards, he could see the loft over his right shoulder.

"The door is just down the hallway from that overlook," he explained. "Let's see what lies up ahead."

He continued to paddle and Charis realized she was having fun.

She wasn't afraid any longer, now she was interested. They only went a hundred yards before they reached a barrier and had to return.

"That was a tease," she exclaimed.

"Maybe there is something even more fun up ahead," Trey said.

They stepped ashore and followed the path. Before long, they were standing at the loading dock to another water feature. This time, it was a twenty passenger boat. There was one bench seat left open and they climbed aboard.

Trey sat on the outside and Charis slid in next to him. She put her arm through his.

"Do you mind?" she asked.

"Not at all," he responded. "Your hands are cold, let me have them."

She opened the hand that was through his arm and reached out the other one to him. He placed one hand on each of hers and held them tightly. He was warm in spite of the coolness of the cave. It felt nice, not just the warmth, but the security as well.

"Trey, I was really impressed with the way you handled that whole situation yesterday. You were so cool about everything. You subdued two potential killers and didn't break a sweat. You amaze me."

"It may not have showed, but I was nervous. Not so much about taking them down, but about what their intent was. I could have lost you and I was not about to let that happen. I know I made some jokes about it but the depravity of Moran and Hillabrandt was appalling."

"What would have happened if you hadn't shown up?" she asked.

"I don't want to think about it," he replied.

"Why did you show up, Trey?'

He paused for a long moments, looking at her hands in his. He squeezed a little tighter.

"Because I knew no one had your back. When you were telling me and texting me your schedule. I became worried. At that point, you still didn't know who could be trusted. I called Paul to ask if I could cover you discreetly and he agreed without an argument.

So, I flew out a day ahead of you and followed you. I didn't want you to know I was there. If everything went smoothly, you would have never been the wiser. I used the time to plant the listening devices and look around. That's when I surmised what the plan was. I found the sleep agent in the bathroom which made it easy to find the antidote.

I hated the thought of them drugging you but it seemed like the best alternative at the time. It turned out to be the right decision."

"You felt obligated to keep me safe?" she asked.

"Not obligated, Charis. I felt driven to protect you," he replied.

"Driven by a sense of responsibility or camaraderie? she asked.

"A little of both, I guess but secondarily."

"And the primary reason? she prodded.

"My heart told me I needed to do it. Charis, the first time we met, I knew something was different about you, and it made me feel different too. Whenever we were in the same room or same neighborhood for that matter, I could sense the closeness, and not just the proximity, but the pride and happiness. I feel good being around you.

When I took that shot that ended the Korben episode, I was protecting you. I know there was more at stake than that but you were my primary concern. I don't want you to think that I am a stalker or something, I just want to be friends. That's not entirely true either, I would wish to be more than friends but I could still be happy just being your friend."

"We are friends, Trey, and I have always held a special place in my heart for you too. I have always been afraid of relationships because I didn't think I would ever find someone who could understand my schedule and my line of work. I know you would be able to understand. I would love to explore a relationship with you, Trey."

"That makes me very happy, Charis. No hurry, no pressure, just getting to know each other would be wonderful," he said.

She leaned into him and enjoyed the rest of the ride.

Chapter 124

Hilton Head Island, SC

Dean was looking for someone online who could help him publish his first book. He was perusing the same website where he found Audra. There were several listings of people claiming expertise in that arena.

He was drilling in and out of listings, looking at credentials, reviews and prices when a chat box popped up.

"Sorry to bother you Dean, something has changed here. I think they're gearing up for something important. The supervisors who are always around must have been called away to do something else. That is how I was able to log in to the computer. Everyone seems nervous. I would have liked to have met you, Dean."

Dean called Charis Andrews but she didn't answer. He left a voice message to call him back.

Chapter 125

Crystal City, MO

Charis and Trey exited the cave to find the late afternoon sun lowering in the sky and making it difficult for them to see. They stopped walking until their eyes adjusted to the bright light.

Charis felt her phone come alive with messages she must have missed while being underground. They stepped back into the shade of the entrance and she checked her messages.

There was a long one from Paul laying out a plan for the next day. She would save that for the hotel. The next was from Dean Madris, he was just asking for a call back but she could hear the tension in his voice. The last text from her dad saying he was ready for his big date.

She texted back asking him to relax and have a good time but to also be aware of what was going on around him. She thought about it and erased the last part, he didn't need the added pressure.

She dialed Dean's number.

"Dean, Charis Andrews, sorry I missed your call."

"Thanks for calling Charis. I received a note from Audra. She is concerned about some new events. She said the supervisors who are always around have gone off to do something else and she believes something big is about to happen. Any luck down there?"

"We are getting closer, Dean. We are hoping to have this all over by the first of the week," she replied.

"Are they aware that you're getting close?" he asked.

"We have made several arrests on the outside so I'm guessing they have a hunch."

"Then maybe they are preparing for you?" Dean said. "Do they have the means to defend themselves?"

"We don't know much about what is going on inside, Dean, I suppose they may have," Charis replied.

"Charis, if the cause of death in the discovered bodies was poisoning, what would stop them from using that to contain the evidence?"

"Are you suggesting a Jonestown scenario?" she asked.

"I'm not suggesting anything, I'm just asking questions."

"My God, Dean, you may be right. I have to go Dean, but I will let you know what's happening. Thanks for the info."

"Trey, we need to find the church. I'll explain on the way."

She didn't need to explain because the first the thing she did when they got in the car was call Paul. Before Paul could say hello, Charis was giving him an earful.

"We may be looking at a mass poisoning if we move too quickly, Paul."

Chapter 126

Dale City, VA

Rennie opened the door to find a stunningly beautiful woman standing on the other side.

"You must be Angela, I'm Rennie, would you like to come in?" he offered.

"It's nice to meet you, Rennie, and thank you for the invitation but the driver is waiting and we should probably be on our way. Another time perhaps?"

"Of course, I would like that," he said as he grabbed his keys and locked the door.

They rode the elevator down to the lobby in complete silence. Rennie knew it was her mission and he was just along as the decoy, so he let her set the pace.

There were three men sitting around the lobby trying to be inconspicuous but they weren't fooling Rennie and he doubted they were fooling anyone else. Angela put her arm through Rennie's and they walked outside. The car was parked straight ahead. The driver opened the door and Rennie watched as Angela climbed in gracefully.

She slid across the seat to make room for him to follow. The driver closed the door and walked around to the driver's seat. Rennie looked out the window and watched the men inside exit the building.

The driver waited for the men to get into the car behind them before pulling away. Angela began to speak.

"I heard what happened in your apartment. I'm sorry," she said, "it seems you know how to take care of yourself."

"Thank you, I had a good teacher," he replied.

"If you are referring to your daughter, you had the best teacher. You raised an amazing woman, Rennie."

"Most of that was her mother's doing, not mine but thank you."

"I wouldn't be so modest. From what I have heard, you were a great father and a valuable role model for her. Now, let's talk about what we may expect tonight."

She explained the operation to him quickly and thoroughly but not treating him like a novice. Rennie found himself looking out the corner of his eye at his date. He was disappointed it wasn't a real one.

Chapter 127

The Haven/Near High Falls, NY

The family was gathered around the dinner table at The Haven. They were discussing the visit to the cavern from which Greg, Jack and Ethan had just returned.

"We need to have eyes inside the church," Greg said.

"We will have eyes inside tomorrow, Greg, our eyes," Ethan returned.

"I mean deep inside, not just the sanctuary but underground," Greg said.

"Maybe they will give us a tour," Ethan replied.

"Perhaps," Greg said, "but that seems pretty risky for an organization that relies on secrecy to survive. There must be another way."

"They must have security cameras inside," Jack said, "maybe we can hijack them. We take over the data feed of their own security system."

"How do you propose we do that Jack?" Greg asked.

"Well, we know where the servers are stored, we just need to get in there and find the ones that control the surveillance cameras," Jack stated.

"According to Sheriff Sweeney in Quicksburg, who is the only person who has seen the inside, there are several hundred servers. How would we find the ones that control video?" Greg asked.

"That, I don't know, but I'll bet the FBI has people who would. They need to gain access to the rooms anyway, right? I mean, that is why we went through the trouble of finding the secret room."

"You're right, Jack, let me give Charis a call. If they can get their people in there tonight, they might have time to figure it out," Greg said.

Greg dialed the number for Charis and she answered on the first ring.

"Hi Greg, what's up?"

"Hello Charis, we found the room in the cavern and marked it. We also have an idea that may give us a huge edge."

"I'm all for that, what do you have?

Greg spelled it out for her and she agreed.

"Let me get ahold of Paul. I will get back to you later."

Trey had driven River Hills Road to the end. There was a long, wide driveway that led to the church. It was just as others described it. While she called Paul, Trey drove the perimeter just to check it out. Paul liked the idea and ended the call so that he could put it in action.

Trey pulled back up in the front of the church and parked. They exited the car and walked up to the fence which was backed by a growth of tall, thick trees and shrubs. What they were able to make out beneath the fully leafed hood of the trees looked nice.

The lawn was beautifully mowed and the landscaping looked

professionally done. There were flowers and ornamental grasses that edged the walkways as far as they could see. Through the front gates, they could see the red brick and stone of the building. It was huge.

The front walls were rounded just as the satellite images had indicated. At least four stories above ground, there were tall but slender windows that appeared darkened. The front door was made of wood that looked large, thick and impenetrable.

"They are able to raise a bunch of money somehow," Trey said, "This place can't be cheap to maintain."

"I would say it wasn't cheap to build but the maintenance is probably done by the inmates," Charis argued.

"Inmates or parishioners?" Trey asked.

"I think it's safe to say that people who are kept against their will and are not free to even go outside when they want, are prisoners. I think the parishioners are the ones who show up on Sunday and then go back home," she stated.

"You're right, I stand corrected," Trey said. "I didn't see any power lines coming off the streets around the building. They are either underground or this place is off the grid. I would guess some of both. Some power probably comes in from the cavern along with the internet and computer lines.

They probably use heat pumps for heating and cooling and that probably doesn't require much. All that lies beneath only needs to be heated and only about ten degrees. I'll bet I spend more on energy on my two bedroom apartment in a month than this place does."

"Let's drive around back again, Trey."

They walked to the car and then drove to the back gate.

"You can see the loading docks at the back of the building from here. And what do you suppose this huge silo is for? Have you ever seen one that large?" Charis asked.

'Never," Trey said, "and it's on land with no apparent farming going on. It must have other purposes. You know what I don't see? Vehicles. How do these Elders get around?"

"Maybe they don't ever leave the grounds," Charis said, "Maybe they have everything they need right here."

"Hey, listen," Trey said, "do you here that?"

They were silent as Charis strained to hear what Trey was talking about. She did hear it but couldn't place the sound.

"That's coming from the silo. It sounds like air being vented. Of course!" he said. "They would have to exchange a lot of air to sustain life down there and they do it through this huge ventilation shaft. I would love to have a look in there."

"And how do you propose to do that?" Charis asked.

"The easiest way would be up and over," he replied.

"Trey, the braces holding the fence together are at least six feet apart, you won't have any foothold."

"I think if I straddle three posts, I can shimmy my way to the top. Then I just drop down on the other side."

"And what if they have cameras on us right now?" Charis asked him.

"If they have a camera on us they would have been out here a long time ago," he replied.

"I would feel better if we had some backup but if you think you're up to it, go ahead," she acquiesced.

Trey placed his feet three rungs apart on the bottom weld and hoisted himself up as if he were climbing two separate ropes. We he reached the spiked top, he gently lifted himself over and once he was clear, he dropped to the ground.

"That couldn't have felt good," Charis said through the gate.

"I've had softer landings but what's done is done."

Trey walked quickly toward the silo. Charis walked the outside of the fence parallel to him. When he reached it, Trey disappeared behind it. It took him several minutes to circumnavigate it. When he had finished, he went over to the fence where Charis was standing.

"Did you find anything?" she asked.

"Well, the sound is definitely coming from inside the silo. Also, there is a door on the front facing surface that is large enough to drive a Mack truck through."

"Is the door locked?" she asked.

"It looks like more of a panel than a door. It doesn't appear to have hinges or a handle. I think it must turn on the outside of the lower section of wall to expose an opening. There is a paved driveway that leads away from the panel. It's unique for sure."

"Alright, Trey, come on back over now," Charis pleaded.

"Let me have one more look and then I will jump back over," he said.

He ran back toward the silo and disappeared around the front once more. He was gone for a good ten minutes this time. When he came back, he had an astonished look on his face.

"What's wrong?" Charis asked.

"I was able to move the panel a few inches. In the center of that silo is a gaping hole with a light emanating from somewhere way below," Trey said.

"That must be the air shaft," Charis suggested.

"Yes, but I think it may be more than that. I think it's an elevator shaft."

"Like a people elevator?" she asked.

"It could be, but it's also big enough that cars and trucks would fit in it. I think I know where they park their cars."

"Trey, if you had more help, could you move that door enough to get through it?"

"I think so, it's really heavy and hard to move but I think it could work."

"Then I think we have found our way in," Charis stated, "I'm guessing the setup is the same at every location. I need to call Paul."

Chapter 128

Dale City, VA

Rennie had driven by Chip in Dale several times but had never had the occasion to stop in. In contrast to the silly name, the atmosphere was elegant and modern. A lovely young girl escorted them to their table and took their drink order.

"Have you ever been here?" he asked Angela.

"No, I'm afraid I haven't been to many restaurants in this area. In fact, I haven't been to many restaurants, period," she replied.

"Your schedule wouldn't permit it?" Rennie quizzed.

"I guess the real answer lies a step deeper than that. My schedule was not conducive to romance. I was married a couple years out of training but it only lasted a brief time. A new romance requires time and attention and I couldn't give it either," Angela stated, "and without a partner, dinner out seemed like a waste of time and money."

"I'm sorry, but I do understand. I see a similar fate for Charis if she continues down the path she is on. There is nothing wrong about choosing a career over romance, I guess, I just feel that loving your work and loving another person intimately are very different things."

"It is a monumental sacrifice that becomes more noticeable the older I get. I don't think I could have changed things at the time, but looking back, I would have changed it all," Angela offered.

"Hindsight and all of that, right?" Rennie said, "The clock continues to move even when we don't have time to notice."

The waitress was back with their drinks. She had ordered a cosmopolitan and he, an old fashioned.

"I think our drink order gave away our ages," Angela joked. "Tell me about you, Rennie."

"Not much to tell really, I was married for nearly forty years to a wonderful woman who died suddenly six years ago. I also had a career that I paid too much attention to. I taught history at the university level for most of that time but it was different then.

Today, you might have a caseload of two courses plus a weekly lecture. Back then, I carried five classes in addition to lectures, field trips and individual counseling. I would be at work by seven in the morning and get back home by six at night."

"But you managed to keep a marriage together and raise a child."

"That had much more to do with my wife than me. But it was different then, men worked and women, for the most part, were content being housewives. It was expected of the husbands to work hard and be the breadwinners."

"Yes, you're right and I was in the minority because I wanted the career. Even if my husband wanted to stay home and raise a family, it would have been nearly impossible to do. Can you imagine how other men would react to that?"

"He wouldn't have been invited to join the bowling league," Rennie said. "I think women and men sharing the workforce makes sense. I just wish we hadn't bought into the two income lifestyle. All it brought us was higher prices and greater unemployment. The government should have rewarded single worker families."

"I think you're exactly right, Rennie. Let's have a toast to sexual equality with common sense!"

They raised their glasses, touched them together and sipped their drinks.

The waitress returned and took their dinner orders. The room was filling up but there was no sign of nefarious activity. They continued their conversation which they both found to be effortless. After a few minutes, Rennie felt a little dizzy. Angela noticed the difference right away.

"Rennie, are you alright?" she asked.

"I guess I'm not used to drinking the hard stuff. I usually have a beer or two a week with the guys but never liquor. I think if I slow down, I'll be okay."

"Your color doesn't look good, Rennie. Let me feel your wrist."

He held out his wrist for her. Her touch felt cool and comforting, but he wasn't okay.

Angela signaled the other agents in the room and took a small vial from her purse. The agents were at the table in a matter of seconds.

"Rennie, you need to drink this, now."

She was out of her seat and placed the vial to his mouth.

"Hurry, Rennie, swallow this and take a sip of water."

He did as he was told. She dialed 911 and requested an ambulance.

"Close the place down and find the waitress and bartender. Everyone else stays inside," she ordered the agents. "Rennie, talk to me."

"This stuff tastes awful, what is it?"

"It's Prussian Blue, Rennie, the antidote for Thallium. You are going to be okay. The ambulance will be here shortly and we will get you to the hospital for observation."

"You knew they would try to poison us?" He asked.

"No, but they have a history of using poison and I wanted to be prepared," she replied.

"I'm glad you were. Thank you."

Rennie closed his eyes. He was too tired to speak but he could hear what was going on around him. There was a lot of commotion and yelling by the agents. He heard the sirens coming from a distance but growing louder.

The paramedics checked his vitals, strapped him onto a stretcher and wheeled him off. He could hear Angela's voice.

"I'm riding with him and I need one other agent to ride with us. Let's move!"

Once they were all in the ambulance and it was moving, Angela called Charis.

"Andrews," she answered.

"Charis, it's Angela, there has been an attack on your father but he is going to be alright. We are on our way to the hospital right now."

Charis could hear the siren almost overpowering Angela's voice.

"Was he shot, Angela?"

"No, it looks like they poisoned his drink."

"With what?" Charis asked.

"My guess is Thallium but I gave him the antidote. He should be fine in a few hours. I will call you every twenty minutes until we know he is on the mend. Don't leave your phone."

Trey was back on the outside of the fence.

"What is it, Charis?" he asked.

"They tried to poison my father."

Trey pulled her close to him and she buried her head in his chest.

"Thallium?" he asked.

"Yes," she replied through her tears. "They gave him the antidote at the scene and Angela assured me he is going to be alright."

"Then I'm sure Angela is right. He will be okay."

He held her more tightly.

"What is the antidote?" he asked.

"Prussian Blue. Activated charcoal will also work but more slowly."

"That's good to know," Trey responded. "I'm sure you're sad and holding yourself responsible, but don't, your father wanted to do this."

"I'm sad but I'm even more pissed! I want to get these guys more than ever. They can screw with me but attack my family and suffer my wrath!"

"I'm glad we are on the same side. Charis. Let's go back to the hotel. We can do more good there than here, right now."

She knew Trey was right and she was glad he was with her.

Chapter 129

Crystal City, MO

"Our person on the inside got away," Alpha Samuel said, "he left as soon as he mixed the drink. Rennie Andrews should be redeemed within the next twenty four hours."

"Well, maybe we actually did one thing right," Supreme Leader Leland Hadwell said sarcastically. What about the other locations? Do we have updates?"

"We know that Laroy Climm failed his mission here is Crystal City. He has been taken to a federal lockup in St. Louis. Agent Andrews is still out there somewhere," Alpha Timothy said.

"What about the truck driver in Quicksburg?" Hadwell asked.

"He returned to the distribution center in St. Louis," Alpha Samuel said, "but the others in the raid at the Sheriff's complex were injured and detained."

"Can we get to them?" Hadwell asked"

"We're trying, sir. We know where they are but they are heavily guarded. We are trying to find someone on the inside," Samuel replied.

"We need to tie up these loose ends. Speaking of the Sheriff, do we have another plan in place? One that has a chance of working this time?" Hadwell was pissed.

"Yes," Samuel said. "That should be over soon."

"Are the party plans in place?" Alpha asked.

All the Alphas responded in turn.

"I hope you're ready. This cannot fail even if it's our last act. We will meet first thing in the morning."

Hadwell walked away and went to his suite. He was preparing for the end. He thought of his father who had started it all in Utah so many years ago. They never saw eye to eye on the scope of the ministry. His father wanted to care for the less fortunate but didn't have a means to do it. Leland knew that the collection plate and the use of volunteers would never cover the costs. It would take government help but the separation of church and state was an issue so Leland had found a way to receive federal money in exchange for fudging the records of the disabled.

The end result was better than anything Washington could ever come up with. Those bastards would first have to find a way to put thirty percent in their own pockets and then get support across the aisle which would never happen.

He found a way to care for the people, employ the people and offer rest for those who would never survive in the best laid plans. It required more than his father had and certainly more than elected officials had the guts for. History would show that he was a hero, a friend to all the people.

He worked too hard to die along with the rest of his followers. If they had done their jobs effectively, he wouldn't be in this situation. They deserved to stay behind and reap their just rewards. He was just going to disappear. He had stockpiled enough money to live a good life forever in some tropical place that didn't extradite criminals.

He would finalize the arrangements soon. He didn't want to give anyone advance notice of his departure. He would need to make one stop on the way out of the country. He was taking the girl who exposed the operation with him. The one who can draw. She might come in handy down the road and if nothing else, she could still provide him with his nightly entertainment.

Chapter 130

Quicksburg, VA

Til and Del were on their way home when Til's phone rang.

"Sheriff Sweeney."

"Sheriff, this is Myrna Swart, Alan's mom. I just wanted to tell you that Alan has come back home and he would like to see you."

"Well, Mrs. Swart, that is excellent news. Where has he been?"

"I'll let him give you all the details when you come by Sheriff. Are you able to come by tonight?"

"I suppose I can be there in an hour if that's alright," Til offered.

"I think that would be fine, Sheriff." She hung up.

"That's the craziest thing," Til said, "Alan came back home and wants to meet with me tonight."

"What's the urgency, Til, couldn't Alan just stop by the office to-morrow?"

"I suppose he could but he wants to meet tonight. Maybe he has some information about his disappearance that can't wait," Til said.

"It still seems a bit strange to me but you know more about these things than I do. I was just hoping we could do a little celebrating tonight, just getting engaged and all," Del said, pouting just a bit.

"I know D and I promise I won't be long. I'll drop you off at home and I'll be back within thirty minutes."

"Til, we will be driving right past his road, why don't you stop on the way and I'll just wait in the car for you," she suggested.

"Sure, that will work. That's a good idea, Del."

They drove to the Swart place. It wasn't much to look at but with the sun setting, it appeared nicer than it was. There was just one car in the driveway but it didn't look like Alan's. *Probably his mom's. Maybe he left his somewhere.*

Til pulled the car within twenty yards of the house.

"I'll only be ten minutes, D. I'll just get the quick story and follow up in the morning. I'm going to keep the car running for the AC, and I want you to lock the doors behind me. If you need to use the radio, just push that button right there and dispatch will pick up."

"I'll be fine, Tilman, don't worry about me," she said.

Til exited the vehicle and locked the door before closing it. He walked up on the porch and knocked on the door. No one answered. He knocked again and opened the door a crack.

"Mrs. Swart, it's Sheriff Sweeney. May I come in?"

"I'm in the kitchen, Sheriff," she answered.

Til moved slowly toward the back of the house. When he reached the kitchen door he stopped and looked inside. Mrs. Swart was tied to the kitchen table. The long phone cord from the wall mounted land line was tied around her neck and taped to her ear.

"We're alone here Sheriff, the man left after we hung up."

"Is that your Chevy in the driveway?"

"Yes," she replied.

Til walked toward the woman and she yelled.

"Be careful Sheriff, there is a bomb under the table and if I move my foot, it is going to go off. Now, if I were you, I would turn around and go after that man."

"Not before I get you out of here," he replied. "I'm going to have a look under the table, please don't move anything."

"I'm trying not to Sheriff but my legs get jumpy sometimes and I can't hold them still for too long."

"I understand, Myrna, I'll find a way to get you out of there, I promise."

"He's dead, Sheriff. My Alan, he's dead."

"The man told you that, Myrna?"

"Not at first, but on his way out he said so."

Til lifted and moved one of the kitchen chairs. He got down on his knees and took a look. There was a box on the floor with a smaller box on top of it. Myrna's foot rested on a button on the small box.

It looked like a pressure switch that once depressed, triggered the bomb. Once the pressure was released, the bomb would explode. It worked the same way as a field mine. Til was familiar with them from his time in the Army.

"Myrna, do you have a roll of duct tape?"

"It should be in the back entryway, in a cabinet. Upper left I think."

Til went to the cabinet and pulled out the roll of tape. He ripped a piece about four feet long and set the roll on the floor. He laid on the floor with the piece of tape ready.

"Myrna, I am going to tape your foot to the switch so that it won't explode if you move. Whatever I do down here, you keep your weight on that button, okay?"

"I'll try Sheriff," she replied.

"I know you will, Myrna. Just relax everything except your foot."

Til took the middle of the strip of tape and push it down on Myrna's foot and down the sides of the box.

"Myrna, I am going to lift the box a little. I need you to push against the button while I do it. On the count of three, push hard."

Til counted to three and she pushed as he raised the box a few inches off the floor. He quickly wrapped the tape around the box and back over the top of her foot until he ran out of tape.

"Myrna, you can stop pushing now."

She did and her foot was secured tightly to the button.

"Myrna, I am going out to my car and call the bomb experts. They will send someone but it may take a while. What can I do to make you more comfortable?"

"Can you get me to the bathroom? I really need to pee."

"I'm afraid we can't move you. I could place a couple towels under you so that you can go right where you are sitting."

"That beats nothing, I guess. In the bathroom over there. Under the sink."

Til retrieved the towels and returned.

"Place your hands on the side of the seat and raise your bottom," he directed.

She did and he slid the towels underneath.

"That feels better on my back too," she exclaimed.

"That's great. Okay, I'm going out to make that call."

Trey left the kitchen and headed toward the front door. When he reached the car, Delilah unlocked the doors.

"How is Alan?" She asked.

"He's dead, and his mother is tied to a kitchen chair with her foot on a bomb."

Til grabbed the radio and called dispatch. He explained the situation and gave them the address.

"I'm sorry, D but I need to go back in there."

"I know you do, Til."

She reached out to him.

"Please be careful. Come back to me."

"I will," he said.

He leaned over to give her a kiss.

"I love you Delilah."

"I love you too, Tilman."

Til got out of the car and stepped quickly to the porch. When he reached the door, the house exploded.

Chapter 131

Quantico, VA

Paul had gathered the members together for a conference call. It was 8 pm on the east coast and 7 pm central.

"It sounds like we have almost everyone on the line. Rennie Andrews and Til Sweeney are also with us. Unfortunately, they are both seeking emergency medical services at this time. They will be communicating through their partner from each location. Angela in Dale City, are you there?"

"Hi Paul, Rennie and I are here," Angela said.

"How is Rennie doing, Angela," Paul asked.

"He is tired and a little nauseated but otherwise fine. He should be discharged within the next few hours. He will be spending the night at my house where I can keep an eye on him and reduce the risk of another attack."

"Glad to hear that, Angela. That was quick thinking on your part," Paul stated. "In fact, everyone attending the raids tomorrow will be pre-dosed with Prussian Blue just in case. That means all of you folks too. Packages and instructions are on their way to you tonight."

"Delilah Morgan is with Sheriff Tilman Sweeney in Harrisonburg, Virginia. Delilah, welcome and what can you tell us?" Paul asked.

"Hello Paul, HI everyone, Til has received cuts and bruises mostly and should recover nicely. He too should be discharged tonight," Del replied.

"Can you tell us quickly what happened tonight?"

"Til was called to the Sweet home by Myrna Swart, the mother of his missing deputy. I waited in the car as instructed while Til went into the home. He found Myrna tied to a chair with her foot on a bomb switch. Til taped her foot to the box so that she wouldn't move it and came back to the car to call for assistance. He was going back in when the bomb exploded."

"Were you injured, Delilah?"

"No, I was safe in the car which did take some damage from debris. Til was blown off the porch onto the ground. They did a thorough exam and some x-rays. He doesn't have any broken bones, just the cuts from the glass from the front door."

"Thank you, Delilah. I have arranged for two agents to escort you home and guard the house tonight. I will send details to your email. Thank you for your service and bravery."

"Here is the plan everyone. At 8:30 tonight eastern time, agents with warrants will enter the caverns in the five locations. One call will be made to the emergency contact at each site to respond to a problem at the cave. They won't be told anything else and they will be forced to stay for the duration of the mission.

They will find and enter the computer room quickly thanks to all of you and isolate the servers that control the surveillance video. They will redirect that information to our servers that will be housed in surveillance vehicles outside each location.

Once we control the data, one set of teams will enter the churches through the front door while another set will break through the back gate and enter through the silos which we believe will take us to the underground facilities.

We have no idea what we will find there or how long it will take to assume control of the facilities. If we can isolate the power for just the lighting, we will disrupt it to give us an advantage. If we are not able to separate the power, we will have to go in with the lights on. We cannot risk shutting down the air exchangers.

We are coordinating raids at several other locations simultaneously. All five funeral homes and the distribution facility in St. Louis will be breached as well. You are all part of one the largest FBI led missions in history. There will be more than five hundred federal, state and local law enforcement personnel involved. And none of this would have been possible without a few concerned citizens leading the way.

I hope you can all get some rest tonight while we put this plan into action. Tomorrow morning, you will all be called into service. Communication will take place via coordinated emails to all of you. We will receive all of your feedback and redistribute it accordingly. Thank you all."

Chapter 132

July 12, 2016
Hello-Goodbye
Quicksburg, VA

Del woke up before Til and looked out her bedroom window. The agents' cars were still parked in the driveway and the agents were leaning against them. She threw on her robe and went to the kitchen.

She had coffee brewing and breakfast ready in fifteen minutes. She felt arms surrounding her waist and turned quickly.

"It's just me D, stay still for a moment."

She rested her hands on his arms and let him hold her from behind. His head was resting on her shoulder and he was kissing her neck. She could feel his tears on her skin. She knew he would feel responsible for not being able to rescue Myrna.

"You did everything possible to save her, Til. Her passing is not on you. She knows that and so will everyone else."

"It not just that, D, I am overwhelmed by the gift of you. After all these years of patiently waiting for the right time, I realize how close I came to losing everything. I am not willing to wait any longer. Let's set a date."

He loosened his grip so she could turn around. They both had tears in their eyes and she greeted him with a long but gentle kiss being careful not to hurt him.

"I am ready when you are, Tilman, we can set the date today of you wish."

"I would like that, D."

"Sit down and let me pour you some coffee. I made some breakfast for the men outside as well. I'll take that out to them quickly and we can enjoy breakfast together. I'll be right back."

She kissed the top of his head, picked up a tray with two plates full of food and coffee and went out the front door.

"That's very thoughtful of you ma'am but we really need to stay focused," one of the agents said.

"Then stay focused one at a time," she replied, "but at my house we play by my rules. Please enjoy your breakfast."

She set the tray down on the hood of one of the cars and returned to the house.

"How about a week from today?" Til asked?"

"That sounds perfect, Til. What would you like as far as a service goes?"

She brought him a plate and refilled his coffee. She also set a plate down next to his and slid her chair closer.

"Why not right at the diner?" he replied. "We can do it mid-morning when all the regulars are there. We can surprise them all, and I will pay for all the food. That can be our reception."

"You know, any other woman would be disappointed in your idea, but I think it's perfect. Should I wear my uniform?" she joked.

"Honey you can wear anything you want as long as it includes a little heel," he replied.

"It's all about the heels, I get it. Maybe I'll wear just heels and nothing else!"

"Maybe after the guest have left and the diner is closed," he answered.

"Would that be the honeymoon?" she asked.

"It could be the start of it but it won't be the end. D, I am going to resign my post as Sheriff."

"Why Til, you love your job. What would you do all day?"

"I was counting up all the hours we have missed by not being together and I know we can't get them back, but I don't want to miss any more. I wouldn't expect you to quit your job, D, but I want to make myself available whenever you are."

"One of us should probably work, don't you think?" she said.

"D, I have been working a lot of years and haven't had anything or anyone to spend money on. I have invested wisely and if you don't want to, you never have to work another day of your life."

"I guess for you, having a dangerous job, that makes sense and it would give me peace of mind. I wouldn't consider my job dangerous, would you?" she asked.

"Hey, you might slip on a banana peel, or spill hot coffee on yourself. You never know," he replied.

"What if we make some decisions now and some later?" Del recommended. "We can agree that you will retire, if that's what you want, and I will take a nice long break from the diner. At the end of that time, we can talk about me going back to work, if the diner still has a place for me."

"That sounds fine, D, and if they don't have a place for you, we will buy the diner if that would make you happy."

"You are all I need to make me happy, Tilman Sweeney."

She leaned in and gave him a kiss on the cheek.

"By the way, D, I thought I would still go to the church today. It will be my last official duty and I need to see it through."

"I didn't expect anything less from you Til. Promise you will be careful."

"I promise."

Crystal City, MO

Charis opened her eyes slowly. As the ceiling began to come into focus she realized her head was resting on Trey's shoulder. She peaked under the covers to make sure she hadn't awakened from a good dream.

"Is everything still there?" Trey asked.

"You're awake," Charis said.

"For about an hour now. I didn't want to disturb you," he responded.

"You could have moved me if you needed to."

"You were just fine there. Better than fine really, I could stay like this all day. That is if could take one pee break," he said.

She moved her head off his shoulder.

"Pee away, my friend."

Trey rose out of bed and walked to the bathroom as Charis watched. She liked the view. His skin was the color of creamed coffee and she could tell he worked out often. His muscles were toned and tight.

She looked under the covers once more. She was not as toned or tight but she was happy with what she saw. She felt refreshed yet excited. She finally had the passion she was looking for and with a man she could build a relationship with.

Trey returned from the bathroom and Charis approved of the frontal view as well. He climbed back in and snuggled up to her. Facing each other, he spoke first.

"Thank you for last night. I haven't felt that comfortable with anyone in a long time, actually, ever."

"I feel the same way, Trey, thank you."

"So, what's on your agenda today?" he asked.

"Gee, I don't know, do you feel up to taking down a few hundred criminals?" she joked.

"I would rather stay here and start my own brand of trouble," he replied.

"So would I but we have come this far, I think we should see it through, don't you?" she replied.

"If you want to be pragmatic about it, sure," he said. "How much time do we have?"

"Enough," Charis said as she climbed on top of him.

Hilton Head Island, SC

Dean and Shelly had just finished their morning walk on the beach. Shelly was making toast and Dean checked his computer. There was an email from Audra.

Dean quickly opened it. There was a file attached and he moved it to his software to open. There were twenty layers of digital paintings. He could see that layer five was text. He enlarged the image.

"Dean, things have become really strange here. I was invited to attend a church service this morning which hasn't ever happened. We were also told that there was going to be a big party tonight for all the residents. That has never happened either. I have a feeling it is all a ruse and that something bad is happening.

This file is my parting gift to you. All the images for a second story are here and all you need to do is write it. If you don't mind, make it about a girl who had found it all even though it lasted just a few moments. Make it a happy ending, one with two heroes.

The first hero would be you. You are the friend who reaches out to strangers in need and never deserts them. The second hero would be the love interest who never forgets and never stops searching for his lost love. As with all happy love stories, he comes to her rescue just in time.

It will be a best seller for sure, and Dean, you deserve it. I wish you peace and happiness. And most of all, everlasting love.

Friends forever,

Audra

He knew he shouldn't do it, that it was adding risk but he could let this young woman leave without her knowing how much she meant to him.

Dearest Audra,

You faith in love and your perseverance for life is both inspirational and heartwarming. My life will forever be changed for the better for having met you. I promise that I will continue my search for you and I will find and bring justice to those responsible.

I will fight with my last ounce of energy to prevent other young girls from going through what you have experienced. I also vow to find your Ethan and let him know how much you loved him and how much you miss him. You will be together again, if not on this earth, then in heaven.

Hold on to your strength and fight for you safety. Thank you for the drawings. I promise I will make the book happen and everyone will know your name. I am confident that we will meet one day soon.

All my love, gratitude and admiration,

Dean.

Dale City, VA

Rennie awoke to the sound of gentle music playing and the smell of some earthy scent that was exotic. He thought he had died and gone to heaven and heaven was in the Caribbean Sea.

He was in a nice room or at least the ceiling was nice. He raised his head a little so he could look around. The room was light but not bright. The windows to his left had the drapes drawn which blocked the harsh rays of the sun from entering the room.

He looked to the right and found Angela sitting in a chair next to the bed. She was covered in a blanket which assured him she had slept there all night. She was just opening her eyes.

"Good morning, Angela."

"Good morning, Rennie, I'm so sorry, I must have dozed off. How are feeling?"

"Don't apologize, it looks as though I have been responsible for you losing a night's sleep. I should be the one to apologize. I'm very sorry," Rennie said.

"Don't be silly, you were doing the agency a favor and it worked against you, you poor man. I should have sampled your drink first," Angela responded.

"Then you would be dead because I would not have known about the antidote. You saved my life last night and I am forever in your debt."

"I'm just sorry it happened," she replied, "I was really enjoying your company," she said while yawning.

"Angela, would you come lie down next to me? It's such a big bed and I promise I will behave. You need some sleep and I could use a little more myself. What harm could come of it?"

Angela thought for a moment and then joined him. She was dressed in a pretty robe and climbed in wearing it. Rennie moved over to accommodate her. He hadn't even thought about what he was wearing. He felt beneath the covers and discovered he still had his underwear on.

"I don't remember coming in last night. It was nice of you to bring me here."

"I wasn't going to let you go home alone and I wasn't going to risk any more harm to you. I knew I could protect you here, she replied."

"It's a lovely room, I thought I had died and gone to heaven. The music and that scent is very relaxing."

"The scent is cedarwood and wintergreen and the music is alternative something or other. I really don't understand music anymore," she admitted.

"I know what you mean, and that frightens me. I sound like my parents."

"Did you ever think you would be at this stage of your life so soon?" she asked.

"Are you kidding, I thought I would be young forever, that if I kept moving, time wouldn't catch me," Rennie replied.

"Are you afraid?" she asked.

"Of getting old, or death?" he replied.

"Of getting old. Death is death, we won't know the difference, but aging alone scares me and saddens me." Angela stated.

"I have a few old cronies that I see regularly but it's not the same as a life partner. I think the thing I miss the most about my wife is having someone to love and care for. It gave me a sense of purpose," he explained.

"You have Charis, does that help?"

"Of course it does, but she is so self-reliant that I don't really feel needed any longer. That's life, they grow up and they still love you but they don't need you. I'm sure there are plenty of people that don't need to be needed and I guess I don't need it either, but I really like it."

"I've always felt that the only place I was needed was at work. Do you know how sad that sounds? It's my own doing but it makes me sad to think that no one has ever needed me."

Angela was tearing up. Rennie reached out and touched her hand.

"Think of all the people like me who needed you to be there for them. You have been vitally necessary to hundreds of people," he offered.

"But none who remember my name or send me a birthday greeting. I want to know what it's like to be loved, Rennie, not parental love or a friend's love but passionate, 'you are my person' love. The love that says someone is waiting for me at home, someone will care for me and let me care for them. I want someone who will hold my hand when I am afraid and who will let me hold theirs when they feel threatened, weak or vulnerable."

"Angela, do you believe in love at first sight?" he asked.

"I always thought that anything at first sight was probably lust. Maybe I never knew the difference. Now that my eyesight isn't what it used to be, perhaps I should try again," she replied.

"I believe that you can tell a lot about a person the first time you meet them. The way they make eye contact, the ease of conversation, their sense of humor. I knew the minute you stood in my doorway that I was going to like you. You met my eyes, you smiled genuinely and you took my arm when we walked. I knew you would be kind and sincere even through that tough exterior that your career has demanded.

I also knew that you were incredibly beautiful and my eyes are just fine. If you are open to it, I would like to try a real first date. I would like to get to know you and for you to know me. Perhaps we were brought together for that very reason. I know that when Charis asked me to do this, I didn't hesitate. I'm usually more contemplative than that but something told me to just jump in."

"I felt that way too, Rennie, I didn't need to do this, I'm retired. I'm not even sure why they came to me but I jumped at the chance. You may be right, maybe it's destiny and perhaps it's just coincidence but either way, it feels right now. How many more chances will we have, Rennie? I don't want to waste this one. Let's give it a shot. I accept your offer!"

Rennie reach around Angela's back and pulled her closer.

"Do you mind if we start right now, Angela?"

"I would like that," she responded.

Rennie moved toward her and kissed her tenderly. They looked into each other's eyes for a short time, then she kissed him back with passion.

Jordanville, NY

Greg and Ethan had breakfast with the family, enjoyed a relaxing swim with everyone and said their goodbyes. They wanted to arrive at the church twenty minutes ahead of time to make sure they could follow the rest of the congregation in.

They got off to an early start and took their time driving along Rt. 167. It was a beautiful, sunny morning and the reflection of the sun off the leaves made the valley look like it was laced with thousands of mirrors.

"Let's go over the plan once more," Greg advised. "We follow the others, park where they do and speak very little. I lift you out of the car and place you in the wheelchair. I cover your lap and legs in a blanket. You will already have the neck brace and the ankle straps on when I get you out of the car."

"I appear to be non-responsive," Ethan continued, "if someone asks and we hope they do, you tell them I contracted bacterial meningitis ten years ago and have been like this since. Your wife passed a few years ago and you are at the end of your rope. You love me but can no longer provide the physical care than I need. You have searched but can't find a suitable facility."

"if someone does reach out to us, I say we had heard about them from a friend of a friend. If they ask for a name, I say Alfred MacNamara. We stay for the service and follow the crowd afterward. If they separate us, I will come find you after the service. Alright, here we go."

Greg turned left on Hicks Rd. He remembered he needed to turn left again before picking up Hicks Rd. a second time just up ahead. He did so and could see a few cars in front of him.

"It looks like we are right on time," Greg said, "do you have the vials?"

"Yes," Ethan replied.

They approached the gate where they stood just a few days ago. The doors of the gate were opened wide and there was an attendant stopping every car on the driver's side. Greg approached slowly and opened the window.

"Good morning, brother," the man said. "you don't look familiar, is this your first time?"

The man looked past Greg to Ethan who had his head cocked toward Greg at an awkward angle.

"Yes, sir. That's my son, George Jr. I am George senior and I was told I might be able to find help here. Either way, we would enjoy attending your service if that's alright."

"Brother George, park over on the right side there and you'll see a ramp to a side entrance. Someone will greet you on the inside."

"Thank you, sir."

Greg drove to the right side as instructed. He found a parking space near the ramp and turned off the car.

"George?" Ethan questioned. "We didn't talk about changing our identities."

"Spur of the moment," Greg replied as he pulled out a pair of dark sunglasses and put them on.

"That doesn't look spur of the moment, Greg. You had this planned. You look like you have had recent cataract surgery."

"That because these are cataract glasses. I want them to think I am older than I look."

"I think you achieve that without the glasses," Ethan said.

"You know, I'm kind of hoping they do take you away, smart ass! Alright, let's have a drink."

Ethan pulled out two small vials of the Prussian Blue and uncapped them. He held one out for Greg.

"You first," Ethan said.

"Oh no, we do this together. Get ready with the chaser."

Ethan uncapped two bottles of water and rested them between his legs. Greg held up his vial.

"A toast, to an upstanding young man whom I would be proud to call my son. And, to the successful completion of our mission."

"And to a man whom I would be proud to call my grandfather! Just kidding. To a friend and mentor, and to a father figure to whom I owe so much."

They tapped their small brown vials, raised them to their lips and drank. They looked at each other with disgusted stare.

"Your lips are purple, Greg."

"So are yours, knucklehead, that's what the water is for."

They drank a large amount of water, swishing it around before swallowing.

"Is it gone," Ethan asked.

"Almost," Greg acknowledged. How about mine?"

"All clear," Ethan told him.

"That tastes like crap," Ethan exclaimed.

"Worse than crap," Greg replied, "but better than death."

"Amen to that!" Ethan said.

"Are you ready?" Greg asked Ethan.

"Let's rock and roll," Ethan exclaimed.

Greg got out, took the wheelchair from the back seat and rolled it around to the passenger side. He opened the door and reached in to get a hold of Ethan.

"You're a lot heavier than I expected," Greg said.

"Maybe you're a lot weaker than you expected," Ethan joked.

"Maybe I'll just drop you on the pavement," Greg replied.

"I will stiffen my body to make it easier," Ethan offered.

"How is that going to help? You still weigh the same."

"Yes, but a stiff object of equal weight is easier to move than a flaccid one. Have you ever lifted a dead body?" Ethan asked.

"Yes but only in a casket with five other guys," Greg replied.

"Alright, I'm going to stiffen up and then you try to lift me again," Ethan advised.

Greg lifted him easily this time and placed him in the chair.

"Is that true of all things stiff and flaccid? Greg asked.

"I know where you're going with this, Greg, forget about it. Do you think you can push me up the ramp Rambo, or should I push with my foot like a kid on a skateboard?"

"Keep that up and I'll let you roll down the ramp backwards," Greg replied.

They made it to the door and as promised, there was an attendant there to greet them. She held the door for them.

"Good morning brethren, welcome to the Valley Church of Redemption. I understand this is your first time joining us. My name Is Beth and I will be your hostess. What brings you here if I may ask?"

"My name is George and this is George junior. I was told by a friend of a friend that the church offers special care to the infirmed. I have cared for Junior here since his mother passed away four years ago. I am becoming physically unable to do it alone."

"I understand, we have many similar requests and with God's grace, we have been able to offer help to thousands of people from all walks of life. There is a screening process of course and I would be happy to introduce you to one of our intake counselors immediately following the service."

"That would be wonderful. Is there somewhere special we should sit?" Greg asked.

"It's open seating but you can see that we are filling up quickly. I would suggest the end of an aisle, perhaps that one right back there. I know it's a bit far from the front but we have a special guest today so in that respect, you have chosen a perfect day to join us."

"That row will be just fine, thank you. Oh, and you will find us after the service?" Greg asked again.

"You can count on it George. Just remain in the chapel and I will find you," Beth assured him.

Greg pushed Ethan toward their assigned seat.

"Look at this place, Ethan, it is huge!" Greg said.

"It's beautiful too," Ethan whispered, "I think I'll be very happy here, Dad."

"I hope so because you are not riding home with me. I am not lifting your fat ass into the car," Greg joked.

"Not with those wimpy arms, you're not," Ethan returned.

Greg sat in the pew with Ethan parked next to him in the wide aisle. Greg looked around the room while Ethan held his award winning pose. The sanctuary was nearly the length and width of a football field. He guessed it would seat close to eight hundred people if every seat was taken and it looked like today could be the day.

There was plenty of legroom between the pews and at least twelve feet between the end of the pew and the wall. The altar was at the front with huge doors on either side. It was elevated so that even the people in the back had a good view. There was one pulpit to the left side as Greg faced the altar.

There was background music playing quietly but not from an organ or piano. It was pre-recorded instrumental songs. People were mingling but the volume was very suppressed for the number of people present. They were beginning to take their seats quickly now. The music stopped and a louder song began to play. The people stood to sing along.

He was trying to follow the lyrics but it was fast paced and he was missing much of it. *All hail the redeemer for the gift that he instills in us. Blah Blah the power of redemption lives in us all and we use this gift to lead people on their paths to Blah Blah Blah. We straighten the crooked path and lead them to redemption for all are worthy of their own level of redemption. Not the same for each but right and fair for all. All hail, All Hail, All hail the gift of redemption.*

The people applauded and then sat. A man of about fifty years crossed in front of the altar and made his way to the pulpit. He climbed the three steps to the top and opened a book. Audra was positioned in the front row.

"Brethren and sisters in redemption I welcome you to our Sunday service. I am Alpha Isaac and I am happy to be with you here today. I have some special announcements for you. Most importantly, as you may have heard, we have a special guest with us for today's service.

Our Supreme Leader Leland Hadwell will be providing the message this morning." The church thundered with applause followed by a chant of *Hail the Supreme Leader, Hail the Supreme Leader, Hail the Supreme Leader.*

Alpha calmed the group down a notch then continued on with his announcements.

"I flew in with Leader Hadwell just this morning from our church in eastern Missouri where we held an Alpha's leadership meeting. I am happy to tell you that our church is healthy and that we will be able to continue caring for our flock well into the future."

"That leads me to the next announcement. This afternoon at 3:00 pm, we will be having a celebration in the event center. For those who may not have been there before, it is located on the fourth floor, above the sanctuary. A light meal will be served followed by desserts, beverages and entertainment. I strongly recommend that you all attend."

"That may be preempted by a visit from the FBI," Greg whispered so that only Ethan could hear."

"Without further delay, please welcome home, our Supreme Leader, Leland Hadwell!"

Everyone stood, including Greg and applauded feverishly. Greg leaned toward Ethan.

"I hope this guy never runs for President," he said.

"I think he'll be running soon, but not for public office," Ethan whispered back.

The applause lasted several minutes. Greg thought he might see women throwing their underwear at the stage as if it was Elvis or the Beatles up there. Hadwell finally raised his hands to quiet the crowd down. When they were seated, he changed places with Isaac in the pulpit.

"I am joyful at your presence and delighted with your welcoming. It has been a long time since I have received that level of warmth. Thank you.

Nearly fifty years ago, I left my Mormon upbringing and Utah, destined to create a new church that was based on helping others and rewarding those that do. I had a vision of a church built not on repentance and the fear of retribution but on freedom from guilt and the promise of redemption.

We are all sinners in God's eye but we need not be to each other. If you believe that we are all here as a result of a creator who set us up for failure by placing Adam and Eve in the garden with temptation that no one could deny and you carry the guilt of that event throughout your entire life, I am sorry for you.

I choose to believe that God is in each of us and that it is by our works that we receive redemption. Different than what we were taught, I know. To think that children are born with disease because we as parents have done something wrong is off the mark. To believe that the only way we can be redeemed is through divine intervention lessens us as humans and individuals.

How many people do you know whose primary goal in this life is to move on to the next? Living for the second coming which has been promised for over two millennia? People that believe that only through the son of God can we be cleansed enough to be worthy of an afterlife?

Many things that we have learned from scripture are valuable tools for living life but are we to believe that the earth was created just a few thousand years ago when we have learned through science, through the intelligence God has given us that the earth has been here for four and a half billion years?

If God created the heaven and the earth just six thousand years ago, how were dinosaurs able to roam around on it for sixty-five million years before He created man? It doesn't add up and if we take it as absolute truth, it can harm us.

I witnessed a story being told by a man in a church I attended long ago. It was a believers church and its members were by and large born again. The church was undergoing a renovation which this man was helping with. The project involved opening up the second floor above the sanctuary to make room for a nursery.

This man brought his young child with him one day while he worked on the project. The child made her way up the stairs to the opening and fell through to the floor below. The child was not mortally wounded and so the people began to praise God for saving this child from harm. Yes, be thankful for a safe landing but did this father become blind to common sense through his blind faith? The God I believe in would have reached down and slapped him for doing something so stupid.

The spirit inside of me is screaming that we are intelligent beings and asking a remote God to not only watch over every breath we take but to be the absolute control over every breath is an insult to ourselves and to whatever or whoever we think God is.

I was reading about a man who has been hit by lightning seven times. The odds against that are incalculable yet it has happened. He was struck seven times and lived to tell about it each and every time. I also read a similar story about a young man who plugged a household utensil into a faulty outlet and died as a result of the small amount of electricity coursing through his body.

Some will argue that it's the Amps that will kill you. I'm sure most of you had heard that before. Let's follow that for a second. A bolt of lightning contains three hundred million Volts and thirty thousand Amps. Typical household current is 120 Volts and fifteen Amps.

Was God favoring the old man and hit him seven times just to prove a point while at the same time letting a young man perish for touching a household circuit? Most believers will say only God knows why he does the things he does. Others will say God doesn't cause bad things to happen but he can turn bad things into miracles. He doesn't cause bad things to happen yet He created a world and the first thing He threw at his new creatures was temptation essentially telling us that your life on this earth should be hard and I am going to make it so by throwing in a few added extras like plague and pestilence.

You have the freedom, we each have the freedom to believe what we want to believe. I choose to believe that we have more power to control the outcomes of our lives than we give ourselves credit for. People can look at birth defects and illness as payback for some sin in their lives or they can realize that bad things happen because we are human and sometimes our bodies fail and sometimes things just don't go right in the womb.

When things do happen that we can't control, we have two choices. Wait for God to intervene or help each other through it. Help by sharing the load, help by giving shelter, help by becoming doctors and scientists and creating drugs and devices that treat our ailments. We can help by first understanding that we are not all created alike, that we each have different talents, that none of us can truly define right from wrong.

Not all things are black and white, in fact, most of the time, if we really want to admit it, we live in the grey area between the two. It is not only possible but quite inevitable that we can sometimes cross the line on the wrong side. Not because it's wrong in our own minds but because we don't get to draw the lines. The majority draws the lines. In a democracy, the majority draws the lines by electing representatives who share our belief of where the lines should be drawn.

So we live in a world where the majority rules. Not so bad really until you think that the minority can still make up just under half of the population. I guess that's why intelligent people invented paper, pens and telephones so that we can make our feelings known. Unfortunately, it's the green paper, the one we call currency that really draws the lines.

That is why we are here. We know how to care for each other and we do so by circumventing the normal channels. If you have a child who is an addict, bring him or her to us and we will make him whole again. Do you know someone who is living on the street and just needs a second chance? Bring them to us and they will be redeemed to their full potential. Do you have a sick child that you cannot care for yourself or that you cannot afford the treatment to help them? Bring them to us and let us help them.

I am not going to lie to you. A few folks that we take in are not savable. For whatever reason, they are just incurable but while they are here, they will be treated with respect and they will live their lives to their full intent. We do lose some earlier than we wish but the greater good is always achieved.

My friends, you have been a part of history. You are a part of an experiment in trying things that make a difference in people's lives. You should take pride in that. Some of the things we tolerate or even encourage would not stand before the current laws. But we do them privately and no one participates against their will.

One of those things is polyamory. The law forbids polygamy or the act of taking more than one spouse at time but it cannot tell you how many people you can love. Only we know what our capacity to love is. Is it wrong for someone to give love and attention to someone who may otherwise go unloved just because they also love someone else?

Who is hurt by genuine love if all parties involved consent? We don't condone a husband cheating on a wife or vice versa but if a couple can strengthen their own relationship by bringing someone else in, who loses?

That's just one example of something that cannot be governed by a black and white law nor should it try to be. I believe that grownups need more control over their lives and their choices. Don't judge your neighbor for doing it and he won't judge you for choosing not to do it.

Brothers and sisters, it is my hope that this ministry will continue long after we are gone and that we will continue to grow. It is your belief, your confidence and your discretion that will make it so.

I hope you all attend and enjoy the gathering this afternoon. Have a wonderful day. All Hail the Redeemer!

Greg was speechless. There wasn't one thing the man said that he could disagree with. Knowing that the man also considered murder brought him back to reality.

"How are you doing, Ethan?" Greg said leaning over to him.

"I'm never going to be able to move my neck again," he whispered.

"Hey, at least it was relatively short. We still have almost an hour before our guys break down the doors."

"Great," Ethan said, "do you think anyone will notice if I move my head to the other side?"

"Let me move it for you. That will seem more realistic," Greg answered.

Greg left the pew and bend down over Ethan.

"Well, what did you think of that?" Beth said standing behind Greg.

"That was amazing! Greg answered. Would you excuse me for just a moment? I need to reposition Junior's head."

"Of course, take your time. When you are ready, I will escort you to the back to meet the counselor," Beth added.

Greg moved Ethan's head slowly and carefully. He even moved it up and down a few times.

"I'm sure that's better now," Greg said, "we are ready to move on."

Greg pushed Ethan ahead of him almost bumping into Beth's bottom. Ethan was pressing his feet as if trying to stop a bicycle.

Approaching the front of the church, Greg could see numerous people gathered around Hadwell. Most of the others had gone through one of the doors on each side of the altar. When they passed the front row, Ethan's head caught a glimpse of a young woman sitting alone with her head down.

Greg kept moving in stride with Beth. They were now through the right side door and emptied into a large reception room. There were several long tables set up with refreshments.

"Would you like coffee or tea to take with you, George?" Beth offered.

"Coffee would be great," he replied.

"Shall I fix it for you?" Beth offered.

"No, but if you don't mind staying with Junior for a moment, I will fix it myself."

"I would be happy too," she replied.

Greg disappeared and Beth came around to the front of the wheelchair.

"Hi Junior, I hope you enjoyed the service. Leader Hadwell is really a remarkable speaker, wouldn't you agree?"

Ethen kept staring straight ahead.

"You are such a handsome you man. What a shame."

She looked around for Greg who was way down the line shoving a donut in his mouth. Ethan saw this too. *Wait until I get out of this chair buddy. You had better have another one stuck in your pocket for me.*

"Junior, have you ever made it with an older woman? If you end up staying here, I promise to visit you. I think we could have some fun. I'll bet you were a real crotch rocket in your day!"

Ethan was having a hard time restraining his laughter. *I hope she goes after Greg too.*

Greg returned and Beth stood up straight to greet him.

"He seems like a fine young man, George, I would love to spend some time with him," Beth said.

"I think I saw a cannoli back there, I could go back," Greg joked, looking at Ethan.

Ethan's eyes squinted in anger.

"I think we should get you to see Mrs. Dawson, George, I can bring you the cannoli if you like," Beth offered.

"That's nice of you but I guess I should stop while I'm only a donut in the hole."

"Right this way then."

Beth led Greg and Ethan further back in the building to an elevator. From top to bottom the floor indicators were 5,4,3,2,1,G1,G2,G3,G4,G5,G6,G7,G8. *Five floors above ground and eight below.*

She selected level 2 and the elevator rose smoothly. When the door opened, Beth held the door to allow Greg to push the chair forward. They turned to the right and proceeded down a corridor just a short way before entering an office on the right side.

The hallway and office were finished in beautiful oak with deep red carpeting. The waiting room in the office was decorated nicely with several pictures hanging on the walls. The images represented outdoor scenes including oceans, mountains, and national parks.

There was an inner door that was closed.

"If you would like to have a seat George, Mrs. Dawson will be with you momentarily," Beth said and left the room.

"You're doing great Ethan. Do you need to turn your head again?"

"I've turned my head ten times already and you haven't even noticed. You were busy having coffee and donuts!" Ethan raised his voice.

"Shh.." Greg said, you're not supposed to be talking."

They waited quietly until the door opened. When it did, a beautiful middle-aged woman entered the waiting area.

"Good morning, I'm Kate Dawson, and you must be George and Junior. It's a pleasure to meet you."

"Thank you, we are happy to meet you as well," Greg replied.

"George, it's probably best that you begin by telling me what you would like to achieve here today," she opened.

"Very well," he replied. My son came down with bacterial meningitis ten years ago. My wife and I were able to care for him at home with little outside assistance. When she passed four years ago, I had to bring in outside help. I'm afraid that I can no longer keep up with the physical requirements of his care and his disability payments don't cover the cost of basic care."

"I'm sorry for your loss, George. I think we can help you. We can provide excellent care for Junior and at the same time help you get your life back. There are some sacrifices to be made on your part.

We will accept Junior into our program for life. You won't need to look for a new option every time the wind blows in a different direction. We have certified physical and occupational therapists on board 24/7. Our dietician will design a meal plan customized to Junior's specific needs.

We have loving caregivers who specialize in mainstreaming members classified as handicapped although we prefer the term physically challenged.

He will have a private room within a unit housing individuals with similar needs. All of our staff live here on the premises so they are always available.

He will have regular access to a movie theater, gymnasium and swimming pool. We have a few dogs and cats around to keep the residents company and we have regular social gatherings. I would say that life on the inside here, is more than anyone offers on the outside."

"That sounds wonderful!" George replied. "Will I be able to visit him?"

"George, we have found that it is better for everyone in these situations to move on in different directions. After the first few weeks, every client here adapts to his or her new family. A constant routine provides the best chance for him or her to develop a rich sense of belonging. Familial visits tend to diminish the progress we have gained.

The excitement, then hurt, of loved ones coming and going leaves the client with the feeling of abandonment and resentment. It can take weeks or months for him or her to get over the episode. Trust me when I tell you both the parents and the loved ones they leave in our care do much better without visitation. Junior will enjoy a new, always available family and you will resume a normal life.

"Wow, that's going to be difficult," George said.

"Yes, it is, for a while," Kate replied as she moved toward Greg.

She put her hand on his shoulder.

"You will learn to accept the fact that you did the best possible thing for your son and the church will also help you move on."

"How will you do that?" George asked.

"We understand the various needs that parents in your situation have to live a full life. We offer social gatherings for the family members that keep them busy and provide moral support. You will be gaining a new family as well, George, one that anticipates and fulfills your every need."

She was standing very close now with hand both hands on his shoulders. She locked eyes with him briefly and then walked back to lean against her desk.

"How do we start the process?" George asked.

We begin by completing some paperwork. We will be transferring his disability payments to this facility to offset the cost of his care. The good news for you is that we return two hundred dollars of that money to you every month. All we ask is that you attend one social event per month. We feed you, provide a community gathering and offer entertainment while paying you two hundred.

"Wow, that sounds too good to be true," George said. "Would we be able to take a quick tour first?"

"Of course, George. Let me take you to the unit that Junior would be joining."

Kate opened the office and outer door for the men and then led them back to the elevator.

When they were all in, she selected level G2. The doors closed and they were on their way. Greg looked at his watch. It was 11:15.

"Someplace you need to be, George?" Kate asked.

"Just a habit I guess. I am yours all day," he replied.

The door opened at level G2. The corridor was wide and bright with pastel colored walls and cream colored ceilings. There was calming music playing quietly in the background. They passed a few staff in the hallway and they all seemed genuinely happy. They were dressed professionally even though few people from the outside would ever see them.

Kate stayed a few steps ahead of the men and proudly displayed her well-kept and well-formed body. They reached an intersection and turned left. There was a central nurses station where two young women and a young man monitored closed circuit televisions and medical devices.

They walked around the station and entered a clients room. The man in the room looked to be about thirty five years old and was missing his right arm.

"This is James," Kate said, "He has been with us for over three years now. He suffered a battle injury and found himself unable to re-adjust to normal life. Since joining our family, James has become somewhat of a spiritual leader for his unit and had also written and published two books on his battlefield experiences."

"It's a pleasure to meet you James," George said.

"The pleasure is all mine sir. Who is this young man?" James said as he approached Ethan.

"This is George Junior," Kate said.

"Well hey, Junior, I hope you will be joining the family. I'm sure we can find you a more comfortable ride than that. Something that supports your head and allows you to look ahead. Do you like movies? We have a theater here that kicks butt. We really have a good life here, Junior. We really are one big family.

"Sir, don't you worry about him. He is going to love it here and you will have peace of mind knowing that he is getting the best care available."

"Thank you, James," George said, "that means a lot."

They left the room and stood in the corridor.

"Kate, I don't need to see any more. "We're ready," George said.

"That's wonderful. George. Shall we go back upstairs?"

"Yes but would we be able to stop by the sanctuary once more? I want to have a private moment with Junior and he seemed to enjoy that space."

"Of course, George. I'll take you back there and you can have all the time you need."

They followed their path back to the elevator and then to the sanctuary. People were still mingling and Leader Hadwell was just breaking away from the last few worshipers.

Ethan saw the young lady in the first pew again. She was looking straight ahead this time. He grabbed Greg's hand suddenly.

"Stop," he said.

Ethan sat up straight in his seat. He couldn't break his stare. There was a difference, she was older and softer. She no longer had the fire of adventure in her eyes, it was replaced by acceptance and defeat.

Greg was speaking but Ethan couldn't make out the words. He pulled the blanket off his lap and stood up. She was still fifty feet away from him and she was just staring at the altar.

He moved slowly, afraid of frightening her. When he reached her, he knelt in front of her, interrupting her stare. He didn't say anything, he just looked in her eyes. A smile began to appear and then tears formed in her eyes.

"I've been waiting for you, Ethan."

She stood and they wrapped their arms around each other, tears pouring from their eyes and their chests heaving with so much emotion that they couldn't speak. They could barely breathe.

Greg watched in amazement as the two clung to each other. He too was moved to bitter sweet emotion. On the other side of the altar, Greg perceived rapid movement. Before his eyes had time to adjust, Ethan and Lilijac hit the floor. He began to move toward them but then found himself looking at the ceiling. He felt like he was pinned to the floor by a car. He could hear Ethan trying to yell but it was stifled.

Greg twisted and turned trying to break free from the weight above him. After what seemed like several minutes, The pressure lessened and he was able to move. Two large men helped him to his feet and set him down in the front pew. He tried to stand but was pushed back down.

Ethan was now screaming.

"Bring her back! Lilijac! Bring her back to me. Lilli!"

Two other men plunked him down next to Greg in the pew.

"Ethan it will be alright, we know she is alive now and we know where she is. In a few minutes, all hell is going to break loose and we can go look for her."

"I need to find her now, Greg, I can't wait another minute."

"Ethan, these goons are not going to let us go. We need to wait the calvary."

Greg looked around. Hadwell was gone and so was Lilijac. Most of the other people had moved to the reception room. Even if they could get away, they had no idea where Lilijac was taken and it would take forever for the two of them to find her. To move now would spoil the surprise.

"Ethan, our best chance to find her is after the help arrives. You saw the elevator, there are thirteen stories in this place, it would take us all day to locate her. I have an idea though. Try to be patient. When our guys come knocking at that front door, follow me.

"So, what happened to us now?" Greg asked one of the goons.

He didn't answer. He asked the guy on the other side and he was talking either.

"Here is how I see it," Greg started, "There are many, many people who know we are here right now and they're not going to wait too long to come looking for us. If I were you, I would set us free, help us find our friend and we will get out your hair. What do you say?"

At that moment, Kate returned to get them. She stopped in her tracks when she saw Ethan sitting up. She walked over to them.

"What is going on here?" she asked.

"This place is better than you said, only been here an hour and my son is cured. That will be worth every penny of his social security that you will pilfer from the government. You can help us out and we'll make sure we put in a good word for you or, when the feds come a knocking, they're going to be a locking you up for a good half century. If I had to guess, I would say that would make you about a hundred and two when you're eligible for parole."

"We have ways to deal with infidels like you, George, and it isn't pretty. We do great work here and you're trying to ruin that!" she exclaimed.

"I think you are doing tremendous work here most of the time. The problem is that you're doing it illegally and when it stops working your way, your solution is to redeem a few trouble makers," Greg said.

"The good of the whole outweighs the rights of the few," she countered, "society can't accept that but we do. We are willing to sacrifice ourselves for the greater good."

"That sounds good until it comes down to you. You just gave an outsider a tour of your inner sanctum, that must be punishable. Are you going to drink the poison willingly or wait until they come for you?"

Her eyes froze with a sudden fear.

"I have done nothing wrong and I will not be punished. I am a valuable member of this family and they will not forsake me," she bragged.

"Yeah, okay. Well here is a tip, I would stay away from the fruit punch at the party this afternoon," Greg offered.

"Really George, and what do you think will happen this afternoon?"

"First of all, my name is Greg and this is Ethan. Secondly, anyone who partakes of any food or beverage at that party is going to die. This is not a celebration Kate, this is a farewell party. This is Jonestown, you read about that, right?"

"You are out of your mind mister. If that were true, why would you voluntarily come here today?" she asked.

"That's a good question, wouldn't you say Ethan?"

"That's a very good question, Greg, what are we doing here today?"

"Well, in retrospect, I would say we weren't thinking straight. But then again, how many people get to witness the largest single raid in the history of law enforcement?"

"Well, there's that," Ethan replied.

"Listen, Kate, I like you and I wasn't born yesterday. In fact you may actually have heard of me. The hospital killings in High Falls or maybe the university killings in New York, Vermont and Pennsylvania last year. Do they ring any bells?"

"I've heard of them. What do you have to do with those?" she asked.

"I spoiled them. Actually, my friends, family and I spoiled them. You could say we are major party poopers. Isn't that right, Ethan?"

"Major, definitely major," he concurred.

"I can help you, Kate but we have to move now. Any minute now, that front door is going to disappear, anyone who moves will be shot or apprehended and the underground is going to have a spectacular infestation problem. You help me now and I swear I will help you later."

"What do you need?" she asked.

"We need to be released from this room, then we need to use your office for a few minutes. We also need to find Lillian MacNamara, she was in this front row for the service."

She approached one of the men who were guarding the boys and said something quietly to him. She came back and paused in front of Greg and Ethan.

"Let's go," she said.

Greg and Ethan rose and followed her out the back of the sanctuary and through the reception room. Greg and Ethan grabbed a hand full of cookies on their way through. When they reached the elevator, Greg pushed the stop button.

"What are you doing?" Kate asked nervously.

"We're not going to your office. What floor is the communication room on?"

"You can't get in there, That room is guarded," she responded."

"It won't be for long," Greg replied, "which floor?"

"G7," she said.

Greg released the stop button and pressed G7. The elevator was fast and quiet. When they reached their destination, the door opened.

"Not quite as fancy as the client units, I see. Not bad though, it just has more of a utility feel. Where is the Com room?"

"Left, then right, then straight ahead," Kate offered.

"What's between here and there?" Ethan asked.

"Electrical room mostly. The power enters the complex on G7."

"Are the rooms locked?" Ethan asked.

"I'm not sure," Kate replied, "I hardly ever come down here."

"Do you have a master set of keys?" Greg asked.

"No, I don't have any keys. Not even to my own office," she replied.

"How do you get in the building?" Greg asked.

"The utilidor," she replied."

"What's the utilidor?" Ethan asked.

"For lack of a better explanation, it's the highway we use to get in and out," she stated.

"And it's seven floors beneath the surface?" Greg said with amazement.

"Eight actually, but most of us live here so there are very few opportunities to leave."

"How do you get back up to the surface?" Ethan asked.

"There is an elevator at the other end of the utilidor, you drive the vehicle on and up it goes. When it arrives at the surface, a door opens and you are at the gate. Form the outside, it looks like a giant silo," Kate explained.

They were off the elevator just standing in the corridor. Greg looked around and saw a stairwell. He opened the door stepped partway in.

"In here," he said.

They followed him in. Greg checked his watch.

"Can I send a text from in here?" he asked.

"Yes, if you have the password," Kate answered.

"What's the password?" Greg asked.

"I've got it Greg," Ethan said.

"Already? How did.."

"It's Redeemed. Capital R." Ethan said.

Greg connected to the network using the password and created a text.

"Paul, we are on the inside. The silo leads to a utilidor on the eighth floor below ground level. There are no stops in between. Be careful. We are going to access the Com room as soon as you breach the perimeter."

"Thanks, Greg. T-2 minutes. Good luck!

"Password for the network is Redeemed."

"Of course it is," Paul replied. Thanks.

Greg, Kate and Ethan were sitting under the stairs out of site.

"Get ready to move. One minute left. Let the troops clear the stairwell, then we go. Ethan you take charge of the Com room. I'll provide lookout. Kate you stay close to me, okay?"

"Yes," she said. "I'm scared."

"I know. We will be alright. The lights are going to go out. Has that happened before, Kate?"

"Yes, we test the emergency system quarterly. There will be low level backup lighting, she answered.

"You have been a great help, Kate. Thank you."

Chapter 132A

Quantico, VA

Paul and his team had occupied the large situation room at headquarters. It was a spacious configuration with two dozen giant display panels consuming the two story front wall. In the middle of the room sat curved rows of smaller consoles one behind the other. A dozen men and women filled the seats in front of the consoles. To the rear of the room was theater seating with a booth for the commander and twenty seats for observers.

There was a large digital clock on the wall that was counting down from forty five seconds.

"Give me a final check in with all locations," Paul spoke into his headset.

"Loc one ready to go."

"Loc two ready to go."

"Loc three ready to go.

"Loc four ready to go.

"Loc five ready to go.

"On my command," Paul said.

Paul hadn't slept more than an hour in the past two days. His adrenaline was tiding so high that no one would know. The caverns all received a visit a 7: 00 pm the evening before. The people on call for the caves were picked up at their homes and delivered to the caverns to open up. Those people were detained until the raid began. His people followed the markings laid out for them and located the server rooms easily.

Lock experts led the way and gained access to the rooms. Each location contained nearly three hundred servers except for Crystal City, that room had double that number, and appeared to be the host for all the others. At the back of room they found electrical panels that provided power for the servers.

Paul was now staring at the results of that work. By seven am, he was able to see the data from every camera in every church. All of the feeds were being recorded for further review and for litigation purposes.

"All units, on my mark. Three, two, one, go!"

Paul watched and listened as gates were opened, fences were climbed and door were broken down. He could isolate the sound and images from each location and rotated through them with a click of a remote.

Periodically, one of the controllers in the room would provide an update of any issues. It was early but things were going as planned.

Crystal City, MO

Charis was posted outside the front door of the church. Her role was to engage in any resistance and then find the person in charge. Trey was with the unit approaching from the rear.

Paul gave the order and both teams entered the property. Charis and twenty other agents and officers entered the unlocked doors of the sanctuary. The room was clear but they could hear voices coming from beyond the altar.

Trey was helping several other people slide the giant door away from the opening of the silo. Once they had moved the door about four feet they stopped pushing and entered. They stood around the huge opening in the floor and waited for the power to go out.

Charis and her group approached the rear of the sanctuary and spilt into two teams, one took the left door and one the right. The paused until the light went out and then made their move.

The entered the room quickly from both sides. The emergency backup light had kicked on.

"FBI, everyone down on the floor."

There were two big men at the back of the room who came toward them. They looked like they reaching into their jackets.

"Show me your hands and stop moving!" Charis shouted, her weapon trained on their chests.

They put their hands up. Two officers approached from the side and subdued them. They were placed in cuffs and seated in chairs. The other hundred or so people were asked to face the wall. One by one, they were frisked and then seated around the perimeter of the room.

"Who is charge here," Charis asked one of the men. He wasn't talking. She went to one of the women in the group and asked the same question.

"That would be Alpha Timothy," she answered softly.

"Where would I find him?" Charis asked.

"His chamber is on the third floor, toward the back," she replied.

"Where are the stairs?"

"Right through there," the woman said and pointed to the exit at the back of the room.

Charis left the room in that direction. Outside the room was a foyer with a staircase that was off to her right. She climbed the stairs carefully, looking in both directions as she moved. She cleared the second floor and rounded the corner and proceeded up the next set of steps.

The lights went out and Trey and ten other men with ropes attached to them rappelled down the eight levels of the shaft until they reached the bottom. When they landed they turned toward the opening and could see car lights coming in their direction.

They waved their arms and shined their lights straight at the car. It didn't appear to be slowing down. The offices pulled their revolvers and pointed at the drivers' side windshield.

It was still several hundred feet away but if it didn't slow down soon, they would send a warning shot into the radiator.

It began to slow and then jackknifed across the road. Several men jumped out on the far side of the vehicle and fired shots at the officers. The men didn't have any cover and retreated into the floor of the silo.

The offices at the top of the silo heard the shots and lowered three wheeled safety shields down to the men. Trey and two of the others got behind the shields and began walking toward the car. Trey was on the left wing while the other two came up the center and right side.

"You have one chance to surrender," Trey yelled. "There are a hundred armed officers behind us, put your weapons down and come out with your hands on your heads." There was no response. The three shields inched forward. They were closing the gap.

Quantico, VA

Paul was watching the action taking place in Crystal City. He had already received reports that Custer and McMinnville gave up without a fight. He texted Charis who he could see was on the third floor now and approaching a double door that looked like a hotel suite entrance.

She tried the handle but it was locked. She raised her weapon and fired one shot through the lockset. The door opened a few inches under its own weight. She stepped in carefully and looked around. There was an open room to the right, a bathroom straight ahead and a closed door to her left.

She scouted out the open room and found nothing. She opened the door to the left and entered a bedroom. On the other side of the bed was another door, probably an ensuite bathroom. She moved around the bed and approached the door which was open. The room was empty.

The only room left was the one on the other side of the sitting room. The door was closed. She approached quietly. She tried the handle. It opened. She swung the door open and found a man lying on the bed. He was unconscious. He had a weak, irregular pulse and it looked and smelled like he had soiled the bed.

There were several TV monitors mounted on the wall across from the bed.

They were closed circuit cameras from several areas of the building. One caught her attention right away. She could see three FBI moveable shields approaching a car from the far side. The camera showed four men with automatic rifles squatting behind the car.

She knew where they were and had to find a way to come in from behind. She ran back down the stairs and toward the sanctuary. She found another elevator near the front of the building and pushed the button. Nothing happened. The power was out. She looked around for an exit to a staircase and found it.

Charis raced down eight flights of stairs and didn't come across anyone in the stairwell. She opened the door carefully at the bottom and stepped out onto a two lane highway. She could just barely make out the car parked across the road a couple hundred yards away.

The road resembled a real highway except it was made from black tile rather than asphalt. Even the white dividing line was tile. Along both sides of the road were walkways with a knee wall separating them from the road. She ducked down and ran briskly toward the vehicle.

When she was ten yards away Trey spotted her. He was on her side of the road behind one of the shields. She held up her hand with four fingers extended. Trey passed that on to the other cops. She waited for Trey's next move.

"We have you surrounded. This is your final chance to come out. We won't hurt you if you surrender right now. You have five seconds to make up your minds."

Charis was in a crouch position behind the knee wall just five yards behind the car. She took aim in that direction.

"Five, four, three, two, One."

Charis fired off one round that ricocheted off of the side of the car. All of the men got flat on the ground but didn't surrender.

"That was your last warning. There is still time to redeem yourselves. We don't want to shoot you, but we will."

As Trey was dictating terms of surrender, the other two shields were moving forward, They were even with the opposite side of the car and easily had a shot at two of the men.

Charis fired off another round that hit and broke one of the widows and sprayed glass on top of the men. As she did that, Trey and the other two officers walked around the front and back bumpers and trained their rifles at the men. They were three feet away.

"Put the guns down and stay where you are. It's over," Trey shouted.

The other men rushed the car from the safety of the silo. They had the men cuffed in seconds. Charis jumped the wall and ran toward Trey.

"Let's go see what else we can find," she said.

Trey and Charis ran back down the road toward the stairwell.

Quicksburg, VA

Til Sweeney had dressed in slacks and a fine western shirt and headed off to church. He arrived early to be sure he was there before they locked the doors. A few people greeted him, asking if he was new and where he was from.

He said he had lost his wife and didn't know where to turn. Within ten minutes he was surrounded by women ages twenty five to sixty. They were all very sorry for his loss and offered everything they could to help him recover.

Til thanked them and explained that he needed just a little time but he would keep them all in mind. He took a seat at the end of a pew in the next to last row. He gazed around at the place while he waited for the service to begin.

It was beautiful. Hand crafted wood beams that arched three stories above where he was sitting. It was extremely spacious with plush padding on the seats, natural light penetrating the tall, darkened windows above.

There was a lot of activity now in front of the altar. A man with a white robe climbed the steps of the pulpit. Everyone stood as a song began. Til had spent time in church when he was younger but had never heard this song. It wasn't a traditional hymn and he was having trouble making out the words. It had something to do with redemption. At the end, the people chanted "All Hail the Redeemer."

They clapped and then sat down. The man in the pulpit welcomed everyone and talked candidly about the church. The work they do, what they believe and even how they necessarily walk outside the lines of the law sometimes. It was all about the greater good.

Before he finished he made a few announcements. He told the

congregation how he had flown in this morning from Crystal City, Missouri where the leaders of the church were meeting. The news was good, the church was meeting its goals and there would be a celebration at 3:00 pm that afternoon. People were strongly encouraged to attend.

When he finished, Til walked up toward the altar. When a clearing opened in the crowd, he approached the pastor.

"I wanted to introduce myself, I am Til Sweeney and I liked your message, Samuel."

"Thank you, Til, is this your first time here?" Samuel asked.

"To be truthful, it is not. I was out here having a look around the property a couple days back. You have some really pretty grounds here."

"Thank you, Til, it's nice of you to say so. How did you find out about us if you don't mind me asking?"

"No, I don't mind at all. There were a couple people who let me in on it. The first was a nice truck driver from St. Louis that I stopped on the road. He had a lot of nice things to say. Then that same evening, I met a couple more of your followers. They didn't have much to say at all."

"I'm afraid I'm not following you, Til."

"Let me see if I can clear it up for you, Sam. You see the other two men were sent to kill me and the driver. Unfortunately for them, the failed. Now I'm sure you would like the opportunity to come down real hard on them but I doubt you will have the chance."

Sam looked like he saw a ghost and started inching away from Til.

"Now hold on there, Samuel, I'm not finished talking yet," Til continued. "You see, my young deputy disappeared after coming here for dinner one night. Now he could appear simple at times but he had a good heart. It was bad enough that you "redeemed" him, but then you had the nerve to tie his mother to a bomb. You see, Sam, I can handle being shot at but when you come after people I care about, well that just gets my dander up."

"I don't know what you're implying mister, but I think this conversation is over," Samuel said nervously.

"You're right, Sam, I'm done talking."

Til pulled his weapon so fast Samuel didn't see it coming.

"I'm going to count to three and when I'm done, I'm going to put a hole the size of a basketball through your skull. If I were you, by the time I reach one, I would be lying face down on that carpet. You are being redeemed, Sam."

Samuel dropped to his knees and then face down. The parishioners just stood and watched.

"Y'all get back now, Til said, Go have your coffee and mingle while you can."

Til lifted Samuel up and sat him on the altar, facing the front door. He looked at his watch.

"Sam, I want you to have a ringside seat to watch your world come to an end. You see, In exactly one minute, thirty FBI, State of Virginia and Harrison County police are going to walk through your front door. Another thirty are going to enter the silo and take your control center."

A woman approached and asked to give Sam a drink.

"Of course he can have a drink but you drink that one first and then go get him one without the poison." She started to walk away.

"No, right here, you drink that glass of liquid right in front of me," Til commanded.

The woman ran away.

"I didn't think so. By the way Sam, your little celebration scheduled for later has been postponed."

Right then, the front doors opened wide and dozens of officers barged in.

"Police, you are all under arrest. Stay where you are."

All but five or six ran toward the reception room while the others rounded up the members left in the chapel and made them all take a seat.

"It's too bad, Sam, I'm inclined to think you did some good work here. Bending the law is one thing but playing God is another. Under no circumstances do you have the right to determine who lives and who dies."

"That's ironic," Sam replied. Isn't that what you do?"

"Not at all," Til replied. The outlaws make that decision themselves.

I don't choose to kill anyone, but I will defend myself and others. You chose to tie Myrna Swart to that bomb. That's on you."

Quantico, VA

Paul had just watched Sheriff Sweeney arrest Alpha Samuel. That was preceded by Charis and Trey capturing the resistors in the tunnel. The raids in McMInnville and Custer were quelled easily and without incident. He was now watching the last scene unfold.

Greg, Ethan and Kate hid beneath the stairs until the footsteps stopped.

"Alright, time to move," Greg said.

They left the stairwell and headed down the corridor toward the communications room. Their goal was to find Hadwell and Alpha Isaac. There was a small glass window in the top portion of the door. As far they could see, there was only one person left in the room.

"Kate, you're going in first to distract the guy. I'm sure you know how to do that. We will follow right behind and help subdue him."

Greg nodded at Ethan and he turned the handle. Kate walked in and went directly to the young man. Within thirty seconds, she was swapping tongues with the kid.

"She's good at her job," Greg said.

He and Ethan entered without the kid even knowing they were there. With one on each side, Greg tapped Kate on the shoulder. She didn't stop. He tapped harder.

"Oh come on, Kate, you can finish that later," Greg stated.

Ethan pulled a long wire from a shelf near the monitors and they tied the kids hands behind his back.

"I'm Ethan, I'm your replacement for the next little while."

The kid didn't say a word. Ethan and Greg studied the screens. They didn't see Isaac or Hadwell.

"What's your name son?" Greg asked the kid.

"Julius," he replied.

"Julius," Ethan said, I want to see the sleeping quarters for Isaac and Hadwell. How do I change the camera selections?"

"You won't find Alpha Isaac or the Supreme Leader on camera, especially in their rooms. Cameras aren't allowed in there," Julius answered.

"Where else would they hang out?" Greg asked.

"It doesn't matter where they are, they are never on camera. They know the placement and the range of each cameras. There are designated blind spots that only we and the leaders are aware of," Julius explained.

"Okay then, I want to back up the tape to the moment the service ended and I want to see the sanctuary, the reception room and all of the outdoor video from the time the service ended until after the police entered," Ethan said.

"I can tell you how to do it in ten minutes or I can do it myself in thirty seconds. Which would you prefer," he asked.

"Untie him, Greg, we don't have ten minutes," Ethan said.

"Alright, but if you twitch the wrong way, I'm taking you down!" Greg threatened.

"Kate maybe but not you, Greg," Ethan joked.

Greg untied him and Julius sat at the controls. In just under thirty seconds, they were watching three views of the sanctuary and six views of the exterior.

"Hey, Greg said, if you have all these angles of the outside, how did you not know we were coming?"

"I knew you were coming. Heck, I watched you two walk around the fence several days ago. I chose to keep quiet," Julius admitted.

"Why?" Greg asked.

"Because somewhere out there, I have a friend and I want to see him again. I have been waiting for two years for you to show up. What kept you?" he replied.

Greg looked at Ethan who just shrugged his shoulders.

"Hey, we just got involved in this a week ago. I would say going from zero to breaking this case, in five states mind you, is pretty good! I think you need to cut us some slack," was Greg's response.

"Stop the feed!" Ethan said. "Back up this camera fifteen seconds."

Julius did and hit play.

"Right there, freeze it,"

"Look, Hadwell and Lilijac are walking to that car. How did they get out there without running into the police?" Ethan asked.

"There is a side door just off the back of the altar, when you two stirred the pot, Hadwell got nervous and split. He must have parked his car on the side," Julius explained."

"But how did they avoid the police?"

Julius switched cameras and they all watched the car drive down a path away from the church.

"Zoom in on the plate," Ethan said.

Julius did and Ethan typed the number into his phone.

"Where does that path go?" Greg asked.

"I don't know," Julius said, "my world ends where the camera ends."

"That side of the building faces west," Greg said. "That would take them toward route 167. Didn't Isaac say this morning that he and Hadwell just flew in? That means there is an airport or airfield somewhere nearby."

Greg pulled out his phone and texted Paul.

"Hadwell escaped with Lilijac and is headed for a local airport or airstrip. Need help."

"If there is something around here, the FBI will know about it," Greg said.

Within a minute he had a response.

"Satellite images showed a small craft landing at Sky Ranch off route 167 just south of the Mohawk south of High Falls. The other close by field would be Hickory Acres off route 163 southwest of Canajoharie. Images don't show anything new there. I am sending a team to each. They will be there within the hour."

Greg read the response aloud.

"An hour is too long," Ethan said, "they will be long gone by then."

"I have an idea," Greg said. "In the meantime, let's get going. Kate and Julius, we thank you.

Chapter 133

Crystal City, Mo

Trey and Charis were standing at the bedside of Alpha Timothy.

"This is what our victims went through before they were tossed in the river," Charis said.

"Not to mention the countless others who were cremated," Trey added.

They left Timothy to the other agents and began exploring the unknown facets of the building. They wanted to find where most of the people were housed. They checked the remaining above ground floors and found several interesting rooms but not any residents.

They then started with G7 and worked their way back up. In addition to the communications room, they discovered the medical unit which included six regular hospital rooms, a three bed ICU, a nursing station with full monitoring capabilities, an operating room suite and a pharmacy that would embarrass any national chain store.

They also found the dental suite, physical and occupational rehab departments and several prep rooms. There was a small morgue and several restrooms. One was particularly large that featured a toilet with straps and a shower system that was central to the room and totally open.

"Delousing?" Charis asked.

"I haven't thought about it that way but a similar purpose I guess. That scares the shit out me, Charis!"

"I know, me too. Let's have a chat with one of the nurses," she said.

There were three people at the nurses station watching the monitors. There were two patients in regular rooms and one in ICU.

"Hello ladies, I'm Special Agent Charis Andrews with the FBI and this is Trey Lawrence, a detective with the New York State Police. Do you mind if we ask you a few questions?

"May we ask you a question first?" one of them asked.

"Please do," Charis responded.

"What is happening right now?" she followed.

"This facility and four others just like it have been occupied by law enforcement officials. They have all been under investigation involving murders in five different states," Charis replied.

"Murders? Of our residents?" another asked.

"Yes," Trey said," would you know anything about that?"

They all shook their heads no.

"We are here to care for our people, not to harm them. Every resident here is family to us."

"What happens in that big bathroom down the hall?"

"That is off limits for us. We were told it's used for some housekeeping function, we have never been in there," one of them answered.

"Have you seen anyone go in there," Charis asked.

"Yes, I have," the quiet one asked.

"Who did you see?" Trey followed.

"It was man I didn't recognize. I don't think he lives here. At least once I saw Alpha Timothy with him," she answered.

"Do you know what the man does in there?"

They looked at each other and shook their heads again.

"Some housekeeping function, we presume," they answered.

"Do you mind if I ask one of you a personal question?" Charis said.

"I'll answer," the quiet one said.

"Thank you. What brought you here?"

"I lost my parents when I was seven, they were at the home of some friends while I was at a cousins house. She and I were the same age so our parents took turns babysitting. On the way home, there were hit by a drunk driver. They perished instantly.

I was sent to live with my grandmother who was estranged from my mother at the time. It was apparent that she didn't really want me there and she wasn't very nice to me. I didn't blame her really, her life was turned upside down just like mine was.

I endured as long as I could. When I was sixteen, I ran away from home. I wandered for a while then ended up on the outskirts of St. Louis, doing anything I could to survive. I learned that if I was friendly with older men, they would give me money.

Then I met Timothy. He was a very gentle man and he made me feel worthy and wanted. He asked if I would like to live with a family that cares for each other in a place where no one would find me. I wouldn't have to worry about money and they would give me a career.

I had always wanted to be a nurse. As a young child, it was because my mom was a nurse. After her death, I just wanted to be there to help people. When I came here, my life changed. I had no worries and my brothers and sisters made me feel welcome.

I finished my high school education here and then completed the nursing program. I knew that I wouldn't see the outside again but I didn't want to anyway. There was hurt out there and peace in here.

I met my husband here and we raise our child here in a safe and wholesome environment. I have absolutely no complaints," she finished.

"So they allow you to marry and have children? Charis asked.

"Not only allow it but encourage it. They know that people will age, become ill, and eventually die. It is our way of keeping the church going. Bringing forth a new generation," she said.

"Your babies are born here as well?" Trey asked.

"Yes, we have a delivery room and a small nursery. We have an obstetrician on call and a resident nurse practitioner/midwife."

"We also have our own teachers," another spoke up, "our school is more akin to how the Amish teach than public or parochial schools. By the time our children are seven or eight, they are introduced to career sampling. Once they show a particular interest, they begin learning that trade in addition to the basics."

"It all sounds wonderful, ladies, thank you for your cooperation, "Charis said.

"What will become of us now?" one asked.

"I honestly don't know," Charis replied, "but I'm sure there are several government agencies working on a plan. For now, we just take it one day at a time. In any event, you will be cared for until it all resolves. By the way, try not to eat anything prepared by the kitchen today. If you can, eat something pre-packaged for the next day or two."

Chapter 134

Jordanville, NY

"Audra, you look lovely today. Did you enjoy the service?" Hadwell asked.

She was crying and didn't answer. All she could think about was Ethan.

"I asked you a question young lady and I expect an answer. I have cared for you for years and I deserve some respect," he said angrily.

"The service was fine," she answered.

They were driving on nothing more than a path through the woods and she was feeling queasy.

"I'm not sure you know the seriousness of what just transpired. You may or may not be aware that you are the nexus for all of our trouble."

"I really don't know much of anything. I have been kept pretty much in the dark regarding the world outside of my space at the residence," she replied.

"Do I detect a tone of ungratefulness? Do you know where you would be right now if it weren't for me and the church?"

"Yes, I do," she said solemnly. "I would be with Ethan. I would have been with him all along."

"And what about the care and the therapy we provided? Do you believe you would have had that same level of treatment on the outside?"

"I am grateful for the care and the rehab and I can't say whether or not I would have done as well outside of the church but I do know that I would have traded it all to remain with Ethan," she professed.

They finally reached a paved road. It was just shortly after noon and the sun was straight up in the sky. She had no idea what direction they were traveling.

"It won't be long now, Audra. Have you ever flown in a private jet, my dear?"

"Not that I can remember. Where are we going?" she asked.

"Far away, love, to a place where we can enjoy the long days of summer all year long. Where no one will find us and we can whittle away the hours sipping fruity drinks and making love."

Her heart sunk in her chest. She would not do that, She would rather die than partake in anything that would bring him pleasure. She needed to find a way out of this. She could make a run for it the next time the car stopped. Her legs were not great still but she could muster enough energy to outrun the old man.

"Perhaps we should consummate our relationship before we take off. You can give me a taste of what I have to look forward to," he said as he placed his right hand on her thigh.

She pushed it away. He laughed and put it back. She pushed it away again and he raised his hand and slapped her face with the back of his hand. She grabbed her stinging flesh and started to sob.

"I don't think you are grasping the concept here, missy. I call the shots and you do as I say. Without that basic understanding, you are in for a painful, miserable ride. Do I make myself clear?"

She sobbed more and he placed his hand back on her thigh. She didn't fight it this time. If there was one thing had learned over anything else in the last ten years, it was patience.

She ignored him and let her mind wander. She thought of Ethan and of Dean, her writer friend. She played out his story in her head, the one with the happy ending. He had pulled her skirt up above her knee and was stroking her bare skin. She wanted to throw up.

She continued to think positive thoughts. She listened for the sound of the waterfall that she and Ethan hid behind, the one that protected them from the sounds of the world around them. She could feel the cool mist on her warm skin. How could she have forgotten him for so long?

Everything came flooding back to her the moment she saw him. Was her body protecting her from the pain of losing him? Perhaps it was a blessing. If she had to think about him every moment she was gone, she would have gone mad. She opened her eyes to see where they were going. She was determined to pay attention and find a way out of this. They were climbing and descending one hill after another. There was a road sign, RT. 167N. They were headed north. She knew the route number but couldn't place it.

His hand was roaming freely now but she kept her mind focused on the surroundings. At the peak of a hill, she could see a gold dome off to her right. She had been this way before. *The Russian church!*

She could get help there. He needed to stop the car, but for what? She opened her legs a little and let him reach further up. She unbuttoned the top two closures at her neckline.

"Now you're coming around," he said excitedly.

"Pull over!" she said,

"What, why?" he replied.

"I can't wait. I need you to take me now, right here. Pull off the side of the road. I'll lean against the car and you can take me. Please, I need it now."

He slowed the car, looking for a side road. He found one and pulled over.

She opened another button, exposing the top of her bra. He came to a stop and reach for her breast.

"Not yet, outside," she said. Come around to my side while I get ready."

Lilijac opened the door and got out. She bent over as if inviting him to come. He opened his door and walked around the front of the car. She was still bent over as he approached, she could hear him unzip his pants. He was next to her now, reaching for her. She turned and helped him pull down his pants.

He reached into his underpants and she came around hard with a rock she had picked up. She connected with his left temple and he went down hard. She ran around to the driver's side and sat in the seat. The keys were gone. She looked on around and realized he must still have the keys with him.

She got out and rushed around the front of the car again. She stepped over him to check his pockets which were tangled around his ankles. She begin feeling for the keys.

Suddenly, his arm reached out and grabbed both of her ankles. One quick pull and she went down like a sack of apples. She was lying on her back not knowing what hit her. In a moment he was on top of her, the blood from his head wound dripping in her face and on her dress.

She couldn't move under his weight but was helpless. He placed both of his hands around her neck and squeezed. She tried kicking him with her knees put he had them pinned. She beat him about the back with her hands and arms but she was running out of strength. She could feel herself drifting away. *I'm sorry, Ethan, I tried.*

Chapter 135

Quantico, VA
Paul was sending a text to all parties.

All locations are secure and under our control. The Department of Health and Human Services is rounding up teams to handle the logistics but it's Sunday and it may take some time. Please stay where you are until further notice. It could be a long day. We will need to keep everyone there until we have statements from all the visitors.

Food and beverages are being delivered from the outside for all of you and the residents. Do not consume any food or beverage products that are currently onsite. I commend all of you for a job well done, or should I say begun. We are setting up a video conference call for 7:00 pm at all locations. The lights and elevators should all be working now.

"I want to thank all of you in this room and all of those at the sites for your hard work and dedication. This is a long way from being over. Stay tuned."

Paul looked at his watch and then turned to the wall of monitors.

There were five main screens carrying live footage from the five funeral homes. The video stream was coming from one agent at each location whose only job was to video the action.

Paul watched as four agents at each location enter the facilities and rounded up the staff and owners. They were all home on this beautiful

Sunday afternoon. Agents with subpoenas delivered them while the others confiscated any and all evidence.

The video coming from High Falls was particularly interesting. The camera agent walked through the door of the morgue to find three naked adults fondling each other and a naked corpse.

"There is something you don't see every day!" Paul exclaimed.

Chapter 136

Jordanville, NY

Greg and Ethan raced to the car and took the same path out through the woods. When they reached the main road, they turned north on 167. Ethan drove so that Greg could make a call.

"Hello, Bill, this is Greg Webster."

"Hi, Greg, what emergency do you have now?"

"Now Bill, do I only call you when there is an emergency?"

"Yes," Bill answered.

"I called you to invite you to the fourth of July party, Didn't I?"

"No, that was Mary."

"Alright, you got me. I need you to go to Sky Ranch airfield off 167. That's pretty close to you, right?" Greg asked.

"No more than ten minutes," Bill replied.

"That's what I thought. Can you do it.?"

"Sure I can, Greg, what's going on?"

"I need you to stop an airplane from taking off," Greg explained.

"Do you want me to lasso it around the tail and skid down the runway?"

"Is that asking too much? Should I call Richard Ingraham?"

"I'll do it!, Boy, you know just the right thing to say, don't you?"

"We have known each other a long time, Bill."

"Maybe too long. Alright, I'll figure something out. We shouldn't be far behind you, maybe fifteen to twenty minutes. The FBI should be there a little after that," Greg said.

"What did you get yourself into this time?" Greg.

"It's a long story but one I would love to share with you when it's over."

"I'll see you in a bit, Greg."

"Thanks, Bill."

"Bill Dillon is going to stop a plane from taking off?" Ethan asked in amazement.

"Yes, I don't know how but he's very resourceful," Greg answered.

"Maybe we can catch the guy before he gets there," Ethan stated.

"Not the way you're driving, the gas pedal is on the right."

Ethan picked up the pace. What if we don't make it in time, Greg? They had a significant head start."

"We will cross that bridge when we get there. Let's try to stay positive," Greg advised.

"I can't believe Lilijac was this close to home for all these years. I should have looked sooner."

"You did look sooner. How could you have known that she was living underground all this time? No one could have figured that out," Greg said. "It's pretty amazing when you think about it. A small, self-contained town all underground. Why can't normal people come up with great ideas like that?"

"What do you think will happens to it?"

"You mean the complex?"

"Yes, do you think the government will just tear them apart?" Ethan asked.

"I hope not," Greg said, "I think they should study it and learn from it. Besides, where are all these people going to go? They have viable homes and jobs. They would all be on the street for a while if they can't find a way to keep them running."

"I agree with you, if you remove the power driven evil from the equation, it's a pretty workable operation. I don't know about the hooker thing though, I don't see that continuing."

"I don't either, Ethan, but then again ten years ago, I didn't think you would be able to buy pot in a dispensary. Things change."

"Hey," Greg said, looking at his phone, "Paul sent a video clip."

Greg pressed play and watched the scene from Mease Mortuary.

"Holy crap!" Greg exclaimed, "here's a video of the raid on Mease Mortuary. Our friends Maury and Lynette are doing a naked dance with a couple customers, one dead and one alive."

"Oh boy!" Ethan replied, "and that all started with my award winning performance."

"No, it all started with my viewing of the videos from fifteen years ago. I should be getting the award," Greg argued, "the gas is still on the right, Lightfoot."

Chapter 137

Crystal City, MO

The police had relocated all of the residents to the sanctuary. The only ones left behind were a few nurses and a few attendants to watch the children. Charis was chosen as the spokesperson for the police. She took her place in the pulpit.

"Hello everyone, my name is Charis Andrews and I am with the Federal Bureau of Investigation. At 11:30 am eastern time, federal, state and local law enforcement officers in five states performed search and seizure procedures on Valley Church of Redemption facilities.

The searches are part of several murder investigations that began last week. We have taken statements from many of you and will continue to talk to the rest of you throughout the day. The vast majority of you have done nothing wrong and will not be subject to arrest.

I want to thank you all for your peaceful cooperation thus far. From what I have seen and heard, you have made remarkable strides in turning your lives around during your stay here.

I can't pretend to know what will happen over the next several days. This a complex situation that will take time to sort out. I can tell you that you will be cared for with all due respect. We have not come here to upend your lives but to protect them. We are here to help.

I am asking that all of you refrain from eating and drinking anything from the kitchen and cafeteria until we can confirm it is safe to do so.

Food from outside sources will be arriving soon and we will all share in that. I am certain that for the next few days at least, life will go on as usual for most of you.

Let me ask you all a question. You can answer by a show of hands. How many of you have been outside in the past week?"

There were five or six hands in the air.

"Keep your hands raised. How many have been out in the past month?"

Another five hands joined the first.

"You may put your hands down. By a show of hands, how many have not been outside since you have been here?"

All but twenty to thirty hands were raised. Charis felt herself getting emotional. She took a moment to calm herself down before speaking.

"Please put your hands down. We are going to try an exercise. The gates of the property have been closed for your safety. Not to keep you in, but to keep others out. In a moment, we are going to open the doors and we are all going to go out and enjoy the sunshine and fresh air.

For those of you with children, the attendants will be bringing them up to join you. Are there any of you afraid to go outdoors?"

More hands went up than Charis could have imagined.

"You do not have to go out, no one is going to force you. You may stay here in the sanctuary if you wish until you feel comfortable. The doors will remain open and you are free to go in and out as you wish. All we ask is that you stay on this level. If for some reason you need to return to another level, come to one of us and we will escort you. Again this is for your safety.

Charis nodded her head and the two officers at the back of the church opened the doors.

"You may walk orderly to the exits. Feel free to move anywhere inside the fenced area. Your skin may be sensitive to the sun so if you feel like you're getting too warm either seek shade or come back in for a while. The doors will remain open until dinner time. Enjoy!"

Charis watched as some people walked quickly and others approached slowly, not sure what to expect. Some sat still not knowing what to do. They were approached by officers offering to help them with the adjustment.

Trey came to the front of the altar. "You look good up there! Sound good too," he said. "Have you ever thought about a career in the ministry?"

"Are you kidding? I'm surprised the roof didn't cave in. I don't think I'm pure enough."

"You're pure of heart, you care about people, you want to help people. I think you're one of the purest people I know, Charis. I am proud to be your friend."

"Thank you, Trey. Can you imagine not seeing the sunshine for years? To not feel the warmth of the sun on your face?"

"I can't imagine that but I have a whole new awareness that some people can. It isn't right. Speaking of sunshine, when do we leave for Jamaica?"

"Are you really going to hold me to that?" she asked.

"Oh yes," he replied, "a deal is a deal."

"Just as soon as we know our job is done here. When we know everyone is safe."

"That works for me," Trey said, "I get the window seat!"

"Then so do I," she responded.

"In a different row?" Trey asked.

"Nope!"

"That works for me too," he said.

He held out his hand as she descended the steps on the lectern.

"Join me for a walk outside?" he asked.

"I would love to."

Chapter 138

Sky Ranch Airport south of High Falls, NY
Bill Dillon arrived before the pilot and other guests got there. With a small tool bag in hand, he walked toward the small jet. It seemed out

of place among the two seater pleasure aircraft that were sparsely spaced around the field.

He checked the cockpit door and found it opened. He climbed the three small steps and entered the plane. He closed the door behind him. He removed a screwdriver from his bag and loosened the throttle handle all the way. For good measure, he adjusted the altimeter from eleven hundred feet above sea level to thirteen thousand feet. *That should keep them on the ground.*

He thought about leaving the aircraft when he saw a car approaching. He went to the back of the plane and squatted down behind the last seat.

Greg and Ethan pulled up next to Bill's car and walked toward the plane. They saw another car pulling in and ran quickly to the door of the aircraft. They were surprised to find it unlocked. The quickly boarded and closed the door behind them.

Bill could hear Greg and Ethan talking so he stood up.

"What are you guys doing?" Bill asked.

"We're looking for Lilijac," Ethan said.

"They're not here yet," Bill told them.

"Well someone is, they pulled in shortly after we did," Greg said.

"Okay," Bill said, "Greg you go in the bathroom and Ethan you go in the cockpit. Quickly!"

They did as they were told. Bill resumed his place behind the last seat.

The outside door opened and the stairs descended. Bill heard one set of footsteps. *The Pilot.*

When Bill heard the door beginning to close, he stood up.

"Hold it right there, Captain Kangaroo, Sit down and put your hands up."

The man did as he was directed. Greg came out of the bathroom and Ethan opened the cockpit door.

"Where did you get a gun, Bill?"

"I've always had a gun, never used it but I've always had it," he replied, "Here is what happens now. Skipper, you're going into the cockpit as usual and Ethan is going in the right seat. Greg you're going back in the bathroom.

Now skippy, when your boss boards the plane and takes his seat, we are going to get the girl off the plane. When we are clear, you and your passenger can take off. Do we have a deal or should I shoot you now?"

"We have a deal," he said.

"Good. Now tell me where you are going. I need stops and final destination."

The pilot and Ethan entered the cockpit and closed the door. Greg went in the bathroom at the rear of the plane and Bill took his place in the last seat. It was just a few seconds before he saw headlights dancing across the wall of the interior.

He heard two doors close. The main cabin door opened and the steps went down. Bill crouched down. He could hear a man ordering someone to get on the plane.

"Get up those steps now or I'm going to give to you again. I don't like playing games and you're already walking on thin ice. Do as I say."

Someone was coming up the stairs slowly.

"Sit in the first seat you come to. We can get comfortable after we take off," the man ordered.

Bill watched in the reflection of the opposite window as the young lady sat down. She looked weak and fragile.

Bill heard more footsteps coming up the stairs. The door closed and the man picked up the phone.

"Curtis, I'm ready."

He hung the phone back in the cradle and took the seat across the aisle from the girl.

"Buckle your seatbelt sweetheart, you don't want to get hurt," the man told her.

Bill waited until they were both buckled in before he made his move.

He tiptoed up the center aisle careful to not cause any motion. He stood behind the man and put his pistol to his head.

"The slightest move and I will shoot," Bill said. "Keep your hands where I can see them. Greg, Ethan."

Greg exited the bathroom and made his way to the front of the aircraft. The cockpit door opened and Ethan stepped out. He immediately went to Lilijac. He got on his knees and held her. She wouldn't look at him. He raised her head.

"Lilijac, it's me, Ethan."

Her head raised up and Ethan could see the bruising on her neck.

"Oh my God, he said. Did he do this to you?"

She didn't answer. He stood and moved to stand in front of Hadwell.

"Why?" he shouted.

Hadwell didn't answer.

"I'll ask again, Hadwell, why did you do this."

"She wouldn't obey my commands, I had no choice."

"You had no choice?"

Ethan lunged at Hadwell but Bill and Greg held him back.

"It won't help, Ethan. "Be with Lilijac, she needs you now. Take her to the car," Greg suggested.

"Greg, you follow right behind him. I'm going to have a chat with Mr. Hadwell here and then I'll follow in just a minute. Go on now," Bill Said.

Ethan went down the steps and helped Lilijac out of the plane. Greg followed close behind. Greg went to get the car while Ethan held her close to him.

"I'm so sorry, Lil, I should have been there sooner. I'm so sorry."

"It's not your fault, Ethan, I tried to get away and I failed. I hit him in the head with a rock and he retaliated. My mistake."

"You are innocent, Lil, that man is a monster. All you did was try to protect yourself. You did what you had to do and I'm proud of you. We're going to get you to a hospital."

"No, not again, that last time you took me to a hospital, I didn't see you for ten years. I won't do that again, I can't!"

She was crying. Ethan helped her get in the car. He pulled the seatbelt across her chest and lap and latched it. He touched her face with his hand and stared into her eyes.

"We're going to my hospital, Lil, no one can hurt you there and no one will send you away ever again. I promise you. I will not leave your side."

Ethan went around to the other rear door and sat next to her. Greg got in the driver's seat.

"Let's just make sure Bill gets off the plane and then we will go," Greg stated.

Bill stood with his back to the exit, just a few feet away from Hadwell. He still had the gun pointed at him.

"I know a few things about God and religion," Bill said. "You don't represent either. Any man who can physically abuse a woman is not a man at all in my book. I think you're a coward who found a little bit of power and it went to your head."

"You don't know anything about me Bill, I have a lot of power and I earned it by helping people. My name will be remembered for being not God's servant but God himself. I am more of a God than he has ever proven to be. People who believe in Him blindly are weak. Even our government is weak. They can't get out of their own way long enough to make any real difference. I am the kind of government this world needs. A doer, a thinker and a visionary. I see what needs to be done and I act on it. I am able to make decisions that serve the greater good."

"Well, I believe in God and His son, Jesus Christ and I would say I've done okay. As for our government, I think you learned your lesson today. A week ago, you were all powerful and this afternoon, you are broken. I don't confess to hold any real power Hadwell and I've know you all of five minutes but in that short amount of time, I totally kicked your ass.

"Now you think about that as you fly off to some country that doesn't care that you're a killer. But you are going to spend the rest of your life looking over your shoulder. You can't hide from God, Hadwell.

Now I'm going to keep my promise and let you go. I'm not going to hit you or spit on you although God knows I want to. That's the human way, but my God sees it differently. I'll leave it up to Him. You take it easy now and remember how this eighty year old nothing of a man brought you to your knees. While you're there, you may want to say a prayer.'

Bill knocked twice on the cabin door and walked off the plane. He paused on the steps long enough to push the button for the cabin door to close.

Bill walked to Greg's car and got in the passenger side.

"Aren't you taking your own car?" Greg asked.

"Oh I thought we would just sit a minute and watch them take off," Bill replied.

They could hear the engines rev just enough to make the plane move forward. When he reached the end of the runway, the pilot turned and prepared for takeoff.

There were flashing lights and sirens coming up the driveway to the airfield.

Hadwell was looking out the window.

Too late you weak bastards! Adios.

The pilot pushed hard on the throttle and the handle came off in his hand. The plane lurched forward down the runway but couldn't gain enough speed to lift. Curtis tried to pull back on the throttle with his bare hands but the metal was sharp and cut his hand. He hit the kill switch on the engines and pumped the breaks but without reverse thrust he couldn't stop.

The plane slowed but Curtis was running out of runway. The plane hit the tall grass which thrust both Curtis and Hadwell forward violently. Curtis made out alright but Hadwell's seat broke loose and he smashed against the bulkhead.

The plane came to rest in the tall weeds and was immediately surrounded by police cars.

Greg's phone rang.

"Hey Paul, how are things going?"

"All good here. Hey, I was just watching our men arrive at the airstrip on video, You wouldn't happen to be there, would you?"

"As a matter of fact, we're just leaving, Paul. We were able to get Lilijac off the plane before takeoff. Hadwell roughed her up a bit so we need to get her to the hospital."

"I'm sorry to hear that Greg, I won't keep you long. What happened to the airplane.?"

"I can honestly say that I don't have the slightest idea, Paul."

"How do always manage to be in the right place at the right time?"

"I have good friends that always answer when I call."

"We'll talk tomorrow, Greg. My best wishes to Lilijac."

"Thank you, Paul."

"What did you do, Bill?" Greg asked.

"Not a thing, Hadwell and I just had a chat."

"I mean with the plane, Bill," Greg said.

"The Lord works in mysterious ways, Greg, that's all I can say."

"Amen to that, Bill," Greg said.

"Thank you, Bill," Ethan said from the backseat.

"You take good care of that young lady, Ethan."

"Bill," Lilijac said, "we will take care of each other. Thank you."

Bill winked and left the vehicle.

Chapter 139

July 15, 2016

Dear Kathy,

Please let the board know that I will be out of the office for a while. John Shand is available to handle any urgent situation. It's been another life changing week and Mary and I decided to get away to talk and think things through.

It's only been a few days since the siege ended and there are some important decisions to make. I am happy to report that all of our people came out of it whole although there were some extra exciting moments for some.

By the way, Trey Lawrence will be stopping by later today to pick up the computer that is in my desk. Make sure he leaves a receipt. This will be in the papers soon so I can give you a heads up. Our friends at Mease Mortuary are going to face some difficult times not only for their involvement with the church but because Maury Slater was involved in some nefarious activities when he worked at the hospital all those years ago. Keep this one under your hat until the story makes the press.

You already know that Ethan has scheduled some time off. It's a long story but he has rediscovered the love of his life. I'm sure he will fill you in upon his return. For now, I wouldn't bother him unless it's absolutely necessary.

Our friend, Bill Dillon came through again. He prevented the escape of the man who will come to be known as the ringleader of the church behind all this chaos and he did it with his bare hands on ten minutes notice. Please send him some flowers and put them on my account.

Charis Andrews was amazing as usual, risking her own life several times in one week. She has also found a love interest. When Trey stops in, you may want to congratulate him. He's a lucky man.

You will no doubt find the story about the church upsetting in numerous ways but I want to tell you that much good will also come from it. Leland Hadwell aka Grady Braxton was a brilliant man but a bit of a narcissist and I guess a misogynist. That doesn't dismiss the fact that most of what he was doing helped people.

There are more than twenty-five hundred people across five states whose lives were changed for the better by the church's involvement. Now, the government faces the dilemma of what to do with these folks.

This next part stays between you and me until I say so. I trust your discretion and I value your opinion so I am letting you in. The department of Health and Human Services has asked if I would assist them at least temporarily, with managing the facilities.

It's a big ask and a lot of responsibility. It's also a great opportunity to directly help a large number of people. It would be a ton of work and it would involve a good deal of travel. I told them I would need a few days to respond.

If I agree to take the job, I would have to resign from the hospital. That is not something I take lightly. It would also mean that I would need to recruit the necessary resources to help me. How would you feel about becoming a federal employee?

I don't need an answer today. Tomorrow would be fine. Here is where I would usually follow that statement with "just kidding" but this time I'm not. Kathy, I need someone who knows me and someone I can trust, not to mention someone who has the skills and the tact to pull it off.

I would also want Ethan to manage the physical medicine component of the program. I think he would be perfect and I think Lilijac could fill a role as a resident liaison. I haven't spoken to them yet but I will be when we're done here.

Charis and Trey are also on my list. I think they would be awesome in establishing safety and security measures for all the facilities. I'm not sure where the list ends but I want to surround myself with good people, my people.

Please think it over, Kathy. Our office would still be local, probably Jordanville so you wouldn't need to relocate. You would have a nice office as well. Did I mention a federal pension?

I had better go now, lots to talk to Mary about. Let me hear back from you ASAP please. Thanks for listening,

Greg

Greg closed his tablet and turned to Mary.

"I'm finished for now honey, are you ready for lunch?"

"I am getting hungry, do you think they would deliver to the pool?"

"If they won't, I'll go get it and bring it back down."

Greg looked around.

"I still can't believe that this place is just minutes from home."

"I know dear," Mary said, "you've said that a hundred times in the last year."

Chapter 140

Epilogue
Two years later..
July 4, 2018
Jordanville, NY

"If you would all please have your seats." Greg Webster announced from the pulpit of The Federal House of Hope Chapel.

"Thank you. It is with a great sense of pride and joy that I welcome you all here today. Yes, it is Independence Day, a time to celebrate our great nation but it is also a day to celebrate a different kind of independence and to celebrate the joining of two friends in matrimony.

This gathering is being broadcast to our four sister facilities in Quicksburg Virginia; McMinnville, Tennessee, Custer, South Dakota and Crystal City, Missouri. Thanks to all of you for joining us as well.

The week of July 4th two years ago changed all of our lives forever. We were brought together by a great idea that got out of control. One that bent some rules of law and totally obliterated others. But the underlying desire to help each other was still there.

We were given an opportunity to redesign a flawed system and make it whole, without shutting it down and without displacing one individual. At times we are too quick to condemn and tear down things that need improvement.

Not this time. Our officials in Washington, in unison with state and local leaders had the good sense to look for the good and repair what wasn't working. We have retained ninety percent of our workforce and our residency rate is a nearly constant ninety-nine percent.

Every six months on average, we turn around thirty percent of our residents. These are our friends who by receiving the care, compassion and education they needed, are ready to go out and embrace the world with skill and enthusiasm.

Not everyone makes it the first time. It is often difficult to readjust, especially for those who were here for most of their lives. They do not fail, they just need to be held a little longer. Still our recidivism rate is just under two percent.

So yes, we celebrate our success and we praise the men and women who risked their lives to make it so, many of whom are in this room today. People who were strangers one day and family the next. I would like to mention just a few.

The gentleman who led the investigation and the operation from Quantico, Virginia, Special Agent Paul Jenner. Next, dear friends and investigators extraordinaire, Detective Trey Lawrence and Special Agent Charis Andrews Lawrence.

Retired Detective Dean Madris from Hilton Head Island, South Carolina who couldn't let retirement get in the way of answering a call for help. He found Audra on a website while he was exploring illustrators for his first book. Thank God he had done that or none of us would be here.

Dean and Audra, who we also know as Lilijac, have co-authored and illustrated several best selling books. I'm sure most of you familiar with 'The Girl That Had it All' the best selling children's book two years and running.

From Quicksburg, Virginia, Retired Sheriff Tilman Sweeney and his wife Delilah who despite being outnumbered, and pinned down in a shootout took down the resistance.

Bill Dillon has been a friend and a hero of mine for almost twenty years. On that Sunday afternoon two years ago, he responded to my call for help. With nothing more than a screwdriver, his quick thinking and five minutes notice, he brought the nightmare to a close.

I would also like to introduce Rennie and Angela Andrews from Dale City, Virginia. Rennie is a historian who helped us identify the church and Angela is a retired FBI agent who together went on a blind date at the request of the FBI. During that week, Rennie was attacked in his home which he successfully defended, and he was poisoned which he survived, thanks to Angela. That's some first date. Who says retirement is boring?

There were many others involved including most members of my family. They all did a wonderful job, sometimes behind the scenes and sometimes creating a scene.

Then there are these two. One of them, the residents here will remember as one of their own. She is now in charge of resident services here and also teaches graphic arts. The other is a young man who never gave up searching for a lost love.

Music started playing. A young man in a tuxedo came from behind the altar and stood in the center facing the main doors. Greg left the pulpit to assume his place next to the young man. A Reverend came around the other side of the altar and stood on the other side.

Pachelbel's Canon began to play and the large rear doors of the church were opened. The bridesmaids came down the left aisle and Jack, the single groomsman down the right. He arrived first and stood next to Greg.

Jillian was first, followed by Jocelyn and Maria. Veronica and Priscilla were next. Down the center aisle, all by herself was three year old Destiny carrying a basket and dispensing red and white rose petals. When she reached the front, she stood by Jack. The music stopped and they were all facing the back of the church.

The sunlight breaking through the door was blinding. Ethan could barely make out the silhouette standing in the door. She looked angelic. The room of seven hundred plus stood and faced the open doors.

The wedding march began and Lilijac stepped slowly forward with her arm threaded through the arm of Dean Madris. She didn't wear a veil. She felt as though she had lived behind a veil her entire adult life. She was free now and she was walking toward the love of her life. She had waited twelve years for this and the last hundred feet felt like the longest.

She wanted to look at the pretty petals and all the peoples' faces but all she could do was stare at Ethan. When she reached the front, she handed her flowers to Priscilla.

She turned to face Ethan who was both smiling and crying.

"Dearly beloved, we are gathered here to witness and celebrate the union of Ethan Baylor and Lillian Jacqueline MacNamara. Who gives this woman to this man?"

"No one does. I come freely and of my own will," Lilijac stated.

"Very well. If there are any opposed to this union, please keep it to yourself. Lilijac and Ethan have written their own vows."

The Reverend moved aside.

"Lilijac, I want you to be by my side forevermore. Whether I am leading or following, or we are walking hand in hand, there is no place I won't go for you. I will care for you, graciously accept your care and I will love you until my dying breath. To take your hand in marriage would make me the happiest man on earth."

"Ethan, I want to be by your side forever. I will follow where you lead and I will lead when appropriate. There is no place I will not go if you hold my hand. I will care for you and graciously accept your care and I will love you until my dying breath. Marrying you will make me the happiest woman on earth."

They faced the people and said in unison,

"Together, we promise to love all of you. We will be here for you and always do our best to protect you."

"Do you have the rings?" the reverend asked. Jack handed them to him.

"Lillian and Ethan, you have come here today to promise yourselves to each other forever. Do you, Lilijac take Ethan to be your husband, lover and friend for now and forever?"

"I do," she replied.

"And Ethan, do you take Lilijac to be your wife, lover and friend for now and forever?"

"I do," he replied.

"Then by the great honor vested in me by both of you and the state of New York, I welcome you as husband and wife.

What love has brought together let no man separate. You may kiss each other.

Thousands of friends and family, new and old, across five states, rejoiced.

About the Author

Gerard Michael resides in the Mohawk River Valley region of upstate, New York with his best friend and partner, Marilyn. In addition to writing, Gerard is a musician, gardener, saponier, paintographer, and of course, father and grandfather.

His work can be found on Amazon, Ingram Spark, Pinterest and Etsy. Or, you can visit your local bookstore. You can also visit him at www.gerardmichaelmcallister.com.

Other works by this author...

Deadly Ethics: Death May Not Be the End

Buried Ethics: Digging Up Bones

Twisted Ethics: How Thin the Line

Children's Collection

A Tale of Two Fishermen by Michael McAllister

Why Do We Have to Move? by Michael McAllister and Marilyn Keenan